Praise for *The Seed Keeper*

"A deeply empathetic portrayal of a character grappling with a vibrant heritage complicated by pain, loss, and dysfunction. Ultimately, Rosalie comes to terms with who she is, understanding that for her, survival itself is a remarkable feat."

—*SIERRA*

"A moving multi-generational story about the destruction of Native American families, communities, and lands—but also about reconnection, hope, and the natural world [. . .] Wilson offers a different kind of idealism: one where community, family, and the seeds can create the future we're seeking."

—*TODAY*

"Wisdom, humor, truth, marriage, history, child-rearing, environmental advocacy, overcoming obstacles, tears: [*The Seed Keeper*] has it all, told in a compelling and poignant way."

—THE CIRCLE: NATIVE AMERICAN NEWS AND ARTS

"A stunning, lyrical story [. . .] And though this book pulls no punches in its condemnation of white settlers and colonizers and their continued abuse of the land, it is also heartfelt and hopeful, carrying a steadfast belief in the strength of family, will, and growth."

—BUZZFEED, "BEST BOOKS OF 2021"

"Told through the voices of four remarkable women, this is a book about preservation. [. . .] This beautiful generational saga challenges conventional American history, asking us to reckon with the traumas brought upon Native Americans."

—OBSERVER, "CAN'T-MISS BOOKS OF 2021"

"[Wilson] expertly weaves history and fiction to show how colonialism has long been a driver of environmental destruction. But the novel is also celebratory, a powerful and compelling ode to the resilience and wisdom of Indigenous cultures."

—LITERARY HUB,
"RECOMMENDED CLIMATE READINGS FOR 2021"

"Through its examination of the protagonist's life in the foster care system, *The Seed Keeper* confronts the legacy of American Indian genocide and sets Diane Wilson apart as a rising star."

—BUSTLE, "MOST ANTICIPATED BOOKS OF 2021"

"After her father doesn't return from checking his traps near their home, Rosalie Iron Wing, a Dakota girl who's grown up surrounded by the woods and stories of plants, is sent to live with a foster family. Decades later, widowed and grieving, she returns to her childhood home to confront the past and find identity and community—and a cache of seeds, passed down from one generation of women to the next."

—THE MILLIONS, "MOST ANTICIPATED BOOKS OF 2021"

"Wilson offers finely wrought descriptions of the natural world, as the voice of the seeds provides connective threads to the stories of her people. This powerful work achieves a deep resonance often lacking from activist novels, and makes a powerful statement along the way."

—PUBLISHERS WEEKLY (STARRED)

"In [Wilson's] first novel, the writing sings in compact, careful sentences, lending a timelessness to the narrative and making it clear that this compelling story is not just about these characters but also about culture, landscape and how we can—and often cannot—understand each other. Haunting and beautiful, the seeds and words of this novel will find their way into your world, however far from the Dakhóta lands that might be."

—BOOKPAGE (STARRED)

"Through the voices of [. . .] women from past and present, Wilson deepens the reader's understanding of what loss of language and culture has done to Indigenous people. In depicting the way Rosalie's ancestor Marie Blackbird and other women sew seeds into their clothing as the war breaks out, Wilson shows these women's relationship to and reverence for the land: a sharp contrast to 'a country that destroys its soil,' using methods of modern agriculture and its effects upon waterways. A thought-provoking and engaging read." —BOOKLIST (STARRED)

"Uprooted from their land, the seeds Dakhóta women carried with them were not just a source of sustenance, but their link to the past and hope for the future, a symbol of their profound bond with the Earth. They provide a powerful symbol for Rosalie's rediscovery of her lost family and the ways of 'the old ones.' A thoughtful, moving meditation on connections to the past and the land that humans abandon at their peril."

—KIRKUS REVIEWS

"A gracefully told story of continuity through seeds saved and nurtured by Dakota women, *The Seed Keeper* is lush and sustaining—a read that feeds heart and spirit in the same way as do the gardens that are their legacy."

—LINDA LEGARDE GROVER, AUTHOR OF
ONIGAMIISING: SEASONS OF AN OJIBWE YEAR

THE
SEED
KEEPER

Also by Diane Wilson

Beloved Child: A Dakota Way of Life

Spirit Car: Journey to a Dakota Past

THE
SEED
KEEPER

a novel

DIANE WILSON

MILKWEED EDITIONS

© 2021, Text by Diane Wilson

Published 2021 by Milkweed Editions
Printed in Canada
Cover design by Mary Austin Speaker
Cover art by Holly Young
24 25 26 27 28   15 14 13 12 11

Milkweed Editions, an independent nonprofit publisher, gratefully acknowledges sustaining support from our Board of Directors; the Alan B. Slifka Foundation and its president, Riva Ariella Ritvo-Slifka; the Amazon Literary Partnership; the Ballard Spahr Foundation; Copper Nickel; the McKnight Foundation; the National Endowment for the Arts; the National Poetry Series; the Target Foundation; and other generous contributions from foundations, corporations, and individuals. Also, this activity is made possible by the voters of Minnesota through a Minnesota State Arts Board Operating Support grant, thanks to a legislative appropriation from the arts and cultural heritage fund. For a full listing of Milkweed Editions supporters, please visit milkweed.org.

      MᴄKNIGHT FOUNDATION

Library of Congress Cataloging-in-Publication Data

Names: Wilson, Diane, 1954- author.
Title: The seed keeper : a novel / Diane Wilson.
Description: First edition. | Minneapolis, Minnesota : Milkweed Editions, 2021. | Summary: "A haunting novel spanning several generations, The Seed Keeper follows a Dakota family's struggle to preserve their way of life, and their sacrifices to protect what matters most"-- Provided by publisher.
Identifiers: LCCN 2020033979 (print) | LCCN 2020033980 (ebook) | ISBN 9781571311375 (paperback ; acid-free paper) | ISBN 9781571317322 (ebook)

Subjects: LCSH: Dakota Indians--Fiction.
Classification: LCC PS3623.I5783 S44 2021 (print) | LCC PS3623.I5783 (ebook) | DDC 813/.6--dc23
LC record available at https://lccn.loc.gov/2020033979
LC ebook record available at https://lccn.loc.gov/2020033980

Milkweed Editions is committed to ecological stewardship. We strive to align our book production practices with this principle, and to reduce the impact of our operations in the environment. We are a member of the Green Press Initiative, a nonprofit coalition of publishers, manufacturers, and authors working to protect the world's endangered forests and conserve natural resources. The Seed Keeper was printed on acid-free 100% postconsumer-waste paper by Friesens Corporation.

In memory of Ernie Whiteman and Sally Auger

THE SEEDS SPEAK

We are hungry, but the sleep is upon us.
We are thirsty, but the Mother has instructed us
    not to wake too early.
We are restless, chafing against this thin membrane,
    pushing back against the dark
that bids us to lie still, suspended in a near-death that is
    not dying.
We hold time in this space, we hold a thread to
    infinity that reaches to the stars.

The Mother gave us patience stronger than our hunger,
    stronger than our thirst.
We dwell in the realm of dreams and spirit.
    When the sun draws near,
we awake and embrace the warmth, fed by the soil
    and nourished by the rain.
When the cold returns, we withdraw once more
    to rest and to dream.

We remember when all of the world had its own song.
To know the song was to speak to all beings
    in their own language.
The land told stories of faraway places, of mountains
    and cliffs and verdant valleys.
The mighty river sang its slow course along the ridges
    once carved by a glacier.

Long ago, when the frost was still dug deep in the earth,
    the Humans came.
They sang us awake and offered gifts of prayer.
    They came as humble relatives,
with a pitiful need to see their children survive.
    An Agreement was made.

We surrendered our wildness to live in partnership
    with the Humans.
Because we cared for each other, the People and
    the Seeds survived.
For many generations, this Agreement was kept.
    Our hunger was fed,
our thirst was quenched, our restlessness was fulfilled
    each time we breached
the earth's crust to reach toward the sun,
    toward the stars.

Then came a long silence, a drought of memory,
    a time of darkness.
They came no more, calling us with song and prayer.
    Still we waited, just as
the Mother had instructed. The earth kept spinning
    through her seasons,
but the Humans did not return. Now our time
    is almost gone;
the pulse of life flickers, dims as the heartbeat slows.
    We cannot wait much longer.

THE
SEED
KEEPER

PROLOGUE

I opened the door that morning and the world seemed to right itself, as if all those years had meant nothing but waiting for that one moment. When my great-aunt Darlene Kills Deer used to tell this story, even to me, she was unsure if she had dreamed it. In a voice roughened from years of smoke and sweetened by cherry throat lozenges, she would tell me:

Rosalie, you walked in as if you had only stepped out for ciga-rettes at the corner store. As if all our lives we had lived next door to each other, and had gone to powwows together, and traveled home in a secondhand ocean-blue Pontiac with the driver's door wired shut with a bent coat hanger. As if I were there at the birth of your boy, close enough to cut the umbilical cord and to bury the placenta in the garden.

The garden.

What did you think when you walked into my small room? One side a pharmacy of pills stacked near an old woman's recliner. The other side, by my window, a garden made of buckets and cans packed with precious soil I carried from the city's rose garden. I went at night, just after dusk, and filled my bucket nearly to the top, allowing a bit of room to spill, to lose a precious inch on the bus ride home when the wašíču would glare as if no one wanted to sit too close to the crazy Indian with her heavy pail. No one offered to help when they watched me bump and drag that pail through the door. Phhh. I did not need their help.

In each container, I placed a single seed after wetting it first in my mouth. That wakes it, you see, tells the seed that the sleeping time is done. It's the spit that brings us together.

People told me it couldn't be done. No. They said it shouldn't be done. Not on the third floor of an apartment building for elders. Think of the mess. Think of the inconvenience. Think of the strangeness of it. I could only shrug my shoulders, thinking of their strangeness in not seeing the absolute necessity for what I was doing.

See that corn there? Have you ever seen anything grow so straight and tall? There's a good reason for what I'm doing. If I told you it came to me in a dream, would you believe me? How about if I told you that a crow, one with a husky voice that sounded like my sister Lorraine's after all her years of smoking, was the one who said it was time for me to plant this garden?

You seemed surprised when you came in. But your call caught me by surprise, too, caught in the moment of thinking about you, saying a prayer with the hope that wherever you were, you were healthy and safe. After nearly thirty years, I didn't expect to ever see you again. That's why I started the garden. All those seeds in my closet, all that's left of my family—they had to be planted or they'd die, just like us.

I showed the corn to you and your grown-up son, the boy with the rabbit eyes. You're not so much of a girl anymore, except to me. You were but twelve when your father had his heart attack and they took you. Never mind that you had family right here. I made phone calls and filled out their paperwork. At night I walked the city hoping I might see you playing in a yard, so I could sleep, knowing you were alive and well. Finally, I had to wait for you to find me.

It was for you I started growing these plants, with the hope that they could help me. They have their own way of talking, you know. It's not the same here as in a garden, where they share stories through their roots, through the soil, talking with their leaves and their tassels, sending love pollen on the wind. But it was something I could do. I could ask the plants for their help. I could ask the crow for her help. I could talk to the oak trees on the boulevard outside my apartment and ask them to watch for you. Year after year, we kept this vigil.

And then this morning, you walked through my door when I had almost given up. Almost. "Almost" holds something back, even when it was hard to water my plants, to keep going, to believe that you would still be searching for me. You looked around as if you couldn't quite believe your eyes. I didn't have the energy to explain that it was the plants, and the trees, and the crow that brought you home.

You sat on my best chair with your hands in your lap, your fingers twisting like an overgrown root. Behind you, I could see a brown shoe bouncing, bouncing, like its owner was about to bolt. Rabbit boy, you're safe here.

You walked in a stranger to me. Your eyes hid from mine. You could not bear to know the truth, not yet. I couldn't breathe with you in the room. All of us starved for the same thing all these years. I offered to let you water the corn. You said no. I offered again, waving my hand at the plants. You held my watering can with fingers that trembled. A few drops of water, then you turned to me as if asking, Was that enough? Did I do it right? I couldn't speak; I could only nod. Yes, yes, it was just right. It was all we could give to each other that first day. It was enough. You left with a promise to come back.

My great-aunt lived another year, and we found a way to talk to each other despite the few words that remained from the stroke she suffered barely six months after we were reunited. She wrote phrases on scraps of paper, struggled to shape her mouth around newly unfamiliar words, pointed at the photographs in dusty frames that sat on her television. Sometimes at night we shared the same dream. Over time, as I helped water her plants, we came to share the same memories. Learning my great-aunt's unspoken language was no different from understanding the ways of plants, of animals, of the natural laws that bind us regardless of whether we abide by them.

"You have to go back to the time before," Darlene said. "See what happened to the families, especially the children. Go back to the place where the stories were left behind with our ancestors' bones. That's where you'll find our family."

This is our story.

CHAPTER ONE

Rosalie Iron Wing

2002

"Long ago," my father used to say, "so long ago that no one really knows when this all came to be. But before you start asking questions," he added, eyeing me through the smoke he blew from the corner of his mouth, "I want you to listen."

"We know these stories to be true because Dakhóta families have passed them from one generation to the next, all the way back to a time when herds of giant bison and woolly mammoth roamed this land. Do you know what a glacier is? Wašté. As far as your eye can see, this land was called Mní Sota Makhóčhe, named for water so clear you could see the clouds' reflection, like a mirror.

"When the last glacier melted, it formed an immense lake that carved out the valley around the Mní Sota Wakpá, what is known today as the Minnesota River. Hard to imagine, but this slow-moving river was once an immense flood of water that flowed all the way to the Mississippi River, where it formed a giant waterfall, the Owámniyomni, that could be heard from miles away. Your ancestors, Rosie, used to camp near that waterfall and trade with other families, even with the Anishinaabe.

"Now, downriver from the great waterfall, the Mississippi River came together with the Mní Sota Wakpá in a place we called Bdote, the center of the earth. The old ones said the Dakhóta first came to this sacred place from the stars. That's why we're called the Wičáŋȟpi Oyáte, the Star People, because we traveled here from the Milky Way. Even the wašíču scientists have agreed, finally, that this is a true story.

"Someday I'll take you to hear one of the traditional storytellers who share the full creation story of the Dakhóta that is told when snow covers the ground. Today I'm telling you a little bit of history. When you go out into the world, you'll hear a lot of other stories that aren't true. You might feel bad about what ignorant people say, how they'll try to make you feel ashamed of who you are. I'm telling you now the way it was.

"We've lived on this land for many, many generations. Some called us the great Sioux nation, but we are Dakhóta, our name for ourselves, which means 'friendly.' We are a civilized people who understand that our survival depends on knowing how to be a good relative, especially to Iná Maka, Mother Earth. Back in the day, we moved from place to place, knowing when to hunt bison and white-tailed deer, to gather wild plants, and to harvest our maize, a gift from the being who lived in Spirit Lake.

"You wouldn't recognize this land back then. Over thousands of years, the plants and animals worked with wind and fire until the land was covered in a sea of grass that was home to many relatives. The bison gave us everything, from thadó, our meat, to our clothing and thípi hides. His dung fertilized the soil. The prairie dogs opened up tunnels that brought air and water deep into the earth. Grasses that were as tall as a man set long roots that could withstand drought. When my grandfather was a boy, he woke each morning to the song of the meadowlark. The prairie showed us for many generations how to live and work together as one family.

"And then the settlers came with their plows and destroyed the prairie in a single lifetime," my father said. What I remember most, now, is his voice shaking with rage, his tobacco-stained fingers trembling as they held a hand-rolled cigarette, the way he drew smoke deep into his lungs.

For the past twenty-two years, I have lived on a farm that once belonged to the prairie. Every summer I looked out my kitchen window at long rows of corn planted all the way to the oak trees that grow along the river. Even today, after a winter storm had covered the field, I could see dried cornstalks stubbling the fresh white blanket of snow. From the radio on the counter behind me, the announcer read the daily hog report in his flat midwestern voice. His words meant nothing; they were empty noise pushing back the silence that had taken over my house.

After a breakfast of toast and coffee, I closed the curtains on the window, feeling how thin the cotton had become from too many years in the sun. I stacked clean dishes in the cupboard and wiped down the counters. Routine tasks, comforting in their simplicity. No need to think, to plan, to remember. Just keep moving. I poured the rest of the milk down the drain and straightened a stack of papers on the table. After writing a brief note for my son, I locked the door behind me.

A fierce gust of wind tore at my scarf, stung my face with a handful of snow. I walked past the empty barn, half expecting to see our old hound come around the corner, eyelids drooping, swaybacked, his slow-moving trot showing the chickens who was boss. Gone now, all of them.

My heavy boots squeaked on the snow that had drifted back across the sidewalk I shoveled earlier that morning. When I called Roger Peterson to tell him he did not need to plow the driveway, he asked how long I would be gone. I hesitated. How to answer a question that would most likely get shared with my neighbors?

"For a few days," I said. "I'll call you when I'm back."

He paused, and I knew what was coming next. Before he could shape his condolences into a few awkward phrases, I said a quick goodbye and hung up without waiting for an answer.

I had left John's truck running for about twenty minutes, long enough for the heater to blast a melted hole in the ice that covered the windshield. After tossing my duffel bag onto the seat next to me, I eased the truck into gear, babying the clutch. Near-bald rear tires spun slightly before finding gravel beneath the snow. As I drove past the orchard, I ignored the branches that were in need of pruning. While my father believed that any plant not grown in the wild was nothing more than a weak cousin to its truer self, my years of caring for these trees had taught me differently. But it was just as well that he hadn't lived long enough to see me marry a white farmer, a descendent of the German immigrants that he ranted against for stealing Dakhóta land.

When I'd woken that morning, I knew I needed to leave, now, before I changed my mind. At the end of our long driveway, I decided against stopping for a last look at the fields behind me. Without slowing down, I turned the truck east as if heading to town, the rear end sliding sideways. I waved at Charlie Engbretson, the tightfisted farmer who'd bought George and Judith's farm for a steal at auction. He stared after me as I passed by, hanging on to his mailbox as my truck whipped up a white cloud of snow around him. I never did care for neighbors knowing my business. Especially not him. Not today.

For the first few miles I drove fast, both hands gripping the wheel, as each rut in the gravel road sent a hard shock through my body. I drove as if pursued, as if hunted by all that I was leaving behind. When I glanced in the rearview mirror, the woman I saw was a stranger: forty years old, her dark hair streaked with a few strands of gray, her eyes wide like a frightened mouse's, her mouth a thin, determined line, sharp as an arrow. Not terrible looking, Gaby would have said, except for the black-framed glasses, the same kind I wore as a girl, a safety pin holding today's pair together. Beneath my puffy coat, I was wearing a flannel shirt, baggy jeans, and long underwear. An Indian farmer, the government's dream come true.

Taking a deep breath, I eased my boot off the accelerator, allowing the truck to coast back under the speed limit. Doesn't matter if you know the local cop when there's a quota of tickets to be made by the end of the month. After waiting all these years, a few more minutes wouldn't matter. I thought about slipping in one of John's CDs, but everything in his glove compartment was country. Beer and God and flags and more beer. I preferred the quiet.

My father used to tell me that waníyetu, winter, was a season of rest, when plants and animals hibernate. I had trouble remembering what he looked like. Occasionally, a small memory was jarred loose, like the smell of wet leaves after rain, or the rough feel of a wool blanket. Today, it was the clatter of snowshoes on a wood floor, the way the wind turned white in a storm. Nothing more.

Every few miles, I passed another farmhouse. I knew most of their inhabitants by a family name—Lindquist, Johnson, Wagner—even though I might not have recognized them at the grocery store. I'd quickly grown tired of the way people stopped talking when we walked into the café—they'd all seemed to know me, the Indian girl John had married—and preferred to stay at the farm. I wondered what they'd think if they saw me now, speeding down the back roads in John's truck. I could see gray heads nodding together in a mournful, told-you-so way.

Even with the heater on high, I had to use the hand scraper on the frost that crept back to cover the inside windows. I could barely see the road through the sun's glare on the salt-spattered windshield. It was easy to miss a turn out here, lulled into daydreams by the mind-numbing pattern of field, farmhouse, barn, and windbreak of trees that repeated every few miles. Straight, flat roads ran alongside the railroad tracks until both disappeared at the horizon. Mile after mile of telephone wires were strung from former trees on one side of the road, set back far enough that snowmobilers had a free run through the ditches as they traveled from bar to bar, roaring past a billboard announcing that JESUS SAVES.

Both sides of the road were piled high with snowbanks that had been pushed aside by snowplows after each storm. In less than two months, these fields would be a sodden, muddy mess. Small ponds often formed in low areas, big enough for ducks and geese to stop on their long migration north. Plants would explode overnight from every field, a sea of green corn and soybeans that reached from one horizon to the next. Newly birthed calves and foals would stagger after their mothers on thin, wobbly legs. People smiled more in spring, relieved to have survived another winter.

I made a quick turn onto the unpaved road that follows the Minnesota River north. Once the thaw started in spring, rapidly melting snow would swell this placid river into a fast-moving, relentless force that carried along everything in its path, often flooding its banks. But today, that force was trapped beneath a layer of treacherous ice. From the tall cottonwoods that sheltered the river, a red-tailed hawk dropped in a long, slow glide. In years past, I had seen bald eagles and any number of geese and wood ducks and wild turkeys along the river, and I wondered if these birds still searched for vanished prairie plants during their migration. Maybe we all carry that instinct to return home, to the horizon line that formed us, to the place where we first knew the world. Maybe it was that instinct driving me now.

Less than an hour later, I passed through Milton, a small town near the Dakhóta reservation. Milton was the place to buy gas, have a beer, or pick up a loaf of bread at Victor's gas station. Main Street was all of two blocks long, with a post office at one end, an Episcopal church at the other, and the Sportsman's Bar in the middle. I passed Minnie's Hair & Spa, a faded pink house with a metal chair out front, buried in snow. I didn't see anyone outside in their yards or shoveling snow, or even another truck on the road. The town felt like a watchful place, where people kept an eye on everyone passing through. They stayed out of sight unless there was trouble. Or they had business up the hill at the Agency. The only places I'd ever seen a crowd there were the powwow grounds and the casino down the road.

On the east end of town, there was an old quarry where my father used to take me, driving past the giant mound of rubble near the road to an exposed face of gneiss granite. We always got out of the truck, no matter what kind of weather. He offered one of his cigarettes as he prayed. Sometimes he'd stop right in the middle of his prayer and say, "Rosie, this is one of the oldest grandfathers in the whole country. Can you imagine that? Over three billion years old, and people just drive past without seeing it." Then he'd go right back to praying.

I stopped at Victor's to fill the truck's double tanks, feeling the cold from the metal pump handle through my glove. I stamped my feet to stay warm. Temperatures often dropped after a snowstorm, while the wind kicked up and blew snow in straight lines that erased the roads. One time my father and I had stopped at this same gas station, the only place open, to wait for the plow to go through. Back then, the register was run by Victor, an old Ojibwe who had married into the community. He wore a leather vest over his T-shirt, saying his chief's belly kept him warm. His beefy arms were covered in tattoos that moved as he handed a flask to my father. I sat on a stool behind the counter and drank orange Crush pop, swinging my short legs, wishing we could live in town. After the plow finally came by, my job was to watch the white lines on the road as my father drove us slowly home.

Before turning back on the river road, I thought about heading up the hill to the Dakhóta community center, where

I'd heard Gaby was working. I couldn't do it. I told myself I didn't have the time. Truth was I didn't know if she'd even want to see me.

A few miles farther, I passed a familiar sign for the Birch Coulee Battlefield. All summer long, under a blazing hot sun, local history buffs could follow trails through one of the big battle sites from the 1862 Dakhóta War. My father insisted that I see it, making sure we read every sign and studied the sight lines between the two sides. He said, It's a damn shame that even in Minnesota most people don't know much about this war between the Dakhóta and white settlers. Or about what happened after the war, when the Dakhóta were shipped to Crow Creek in South Dakota. He said forgetting was easy. It's the remembering that wears you down.

The war changed everything. My father's family, the Iron Wings, fought with the Dakhóta warriors and then fled north to Canada. They came home in the early 1900s to a community that was slow to heal, as families struggled with grief and loss. The Iron Wings tried farming but lost their harvest to grasshoppers and drought. Over time, the family was slowly picked off by tuberculosis, farm accidents, and World War II. Finally, my father, Ray Iron Wing, found himself the last Iron Wing standing, as he used to say.

As I left Milton, I headed northwest along the river. From there, I followed memory: a scattering of houses along deserted country roads, an unmarked turn, long miles of a gravel road. Open fields gave way to a hidden patch of woods that had not yet been cleared. Finally, a large boulder marked a gap between trees just wide enough for a truck to pass through.

The snow was over a foot deep and untouched; no one had

traveled this way in months. Even with snow tires, the truck made slow progress, several times getting stuck in low ruts. I had to reverse carefully to avoid spinning the tires so fast they packed the snow into ice, then rock forward as quickly as I could, using the truck's weight to find traction once more. Finally, when I reached a rut so deep that the tires spun in a high-pitched whine and refused to move, I turned off the engine. Climbed down into a ridge of snow that spilled over the top of my boots.

It all came back to me in a rush: the old pines burdened with snow; winter's weak light filtered through bare trees. In a clearing at the edge of the woods, a metal roof and rough log walls. After twenty-eight years, I was home.

CHAPTER TWO

Rosalie Iron Wing
2002

In that first moment, it seemed as if nothing had changed. A coyote track crossed the small clearing and trailed off into the woods. From the high branches of an oak tree, a lone chickadee repeated its name, *chick-a-dee-dee-dee*. The snow had drifted almost to the windows on the north side of the cabin, covered the stairs to the front porch, pushed up against the screen door. The shuttered windows, the cold chimney spoke of long absence. I couldn't move. My heart drummed fast and hard as the snow inside my boots began to melt. The wind dropped to a hushed silence as if the place held its breath, waiting to see who had returned.

I knew it was a foolish time of year to come. And yet here I was. Finally. A mere two hours of driving, less than a hundred miles north of the farm where I had married and raised a child, until John's death the month prior woke something in me. I had begun to dream again. At night I returned to this land where my family had lived for generations, land protected from farmers and developers by its bony soil and steep slope toward the river.

My life had begun under a full moon in this cabin. I was the only child of Ray Iron Wing and Agnes Kills Deer, a mother I never knew. My father said I entered the world in a wide-eyed silence; my first breath was a deep sigh. And when I left, when I was taken away, I had believed I would never return.

I felt a sudden urge to move, to release the trembling in my legs. In the back of the truck, I found John's shovel and slowly carved a rough path to the front door, breathing hard as I swung each scoop of heavy snow to the side. I was relieved to find the door unlocked. My father always said it was better to let hunters use the place than to have them break a window to get in. The door swung open with a loud creak from unused hinges. I stamped the snow from my boots and brushed it from my pants. When I stepped inside, the air felt even colder in the dim light, as if the freeze had burrowed into the wood. My breath floated in a cloud of white vapor. I was afraid to touch anything, afraid it would all simply turn to dust or become a dream from which I would wake.

I made a slow circle through the room, remembering the couch that sagged in the middle, one corner propped on a block of wood. I was surprised to see a wool blanket draped across the back of the couch, its once bright colors faded and dull. Intruders rarely left anything light enough to carry. Could someone have been watching over this place in my long absence? But who would do that? I no longer knew anyone around here.

Two trundle beds were pushed against the opposite wall. A wood rocking chair waited by the potbelly stove. A narrow table under the window, its paint chipped and faded, where I used to do homeschool lessons with my father, or read books in the dim, flickering light of a kerosene lamp, or harvest the inner bark from red willow branches with my small knife. The enamel percolator, blistered with rust, was in its usual place near the tin where my father kept his coffee. His blue summer cap hung from a hook by the door. As if time had not moved on or changed anything since I left. As if he might walk in through that door.

The sweat from shoveling had dried into a penetrating cold that crept into my bones. Suddenly I was tired enough to lie down on the couch and sleep. I could not risk it. All of my attention was needed for survival, to avoid freezing to death. Heavy, bruised clouds had begun to gather in the northwest, carrying the promise of more snow, reminding me how risky it was to stay in an empty cabin in the middle of winter, miles from the nearest neighbor. I knew that. I had also known that I had to come.

I made several trips to the truck for supplies, hauling bags of canned food, coffee, books. Water. A lantern and a dozen batteries. A new ax in case the woodshed was empty. Candles. A sleeping bag. John's gun, which he'd kept in his bedside table until he grew ill and I moved it to another room. I did not want him tempted to ease his body's pain at the expense of his spirit. I held it in my hand for a moment, feeling its awkward weight, wondering what I should do with it. Finally, I shoved it out of sight in a kitchen drawer.

How strange and oddly familiar to think that nobody knew where I was, just like when I'd lived in foster homes after my father's heart attack. Except I would not spend my days waiting and watching the door for someone to find me. Coming home was like swimming upstream, searching for the beginning, for the clean, unmuddied waters of my childhood.

I opened and closed the flue of the potbelly stove to dis-lodge any abandoned nests. I had brought a bundle of kindling with me, as well as enough wood for the night. Stacking several logs on end, I added twigs and a twist of newspaper to get it started. Flames shot up immediately, bright ribbons of warmth that threw light into the corners of the room, pushing back the shadows as the wood snapped and popped, exhaling its dry breath. Before dark, I would need to check the condition of the outhouse.

Unpacking a Coleman stove and a little coffeepot reminded me of winter mornings when my father would make coffee before it was light. It was the smell that woke me then, followed by his voice telling me he was going out to check his traps. *Go back to sleep, mičhúŋkši. I'll be home to make you breakfast.*

On the table in the kitchen I made neat stacks of supplies, ignoring the thick layer of dust that covered every surface. Surveying my piles, I realized I had brought a pan for cooking and a sharp knife but had forgotten to pack dishes or silverware. Most of the kitchen cupboards were empty except for a dead mouse and a scattering of shriveled insects. I found two plates, a handful of tarnished silverware, and a cracked white mug that still bore a faint coffee stain. My family's things, grown old. There was the washbasin, its chipped rim turned toward the wall. A cast-iron frying pan, now orange with rust. A dog's bowl in the corner by the stove. Šúŋka.

I hesitated before pushing open the door to the bedroom that used to be mine. The air was stale and smelled faintly of mildew. A ragged bundle of yellowed cedar twigs lay crumbled on the floor. My dresser and a chest for storing extra blankets were lined up against the wall, near a shelf overflowing with books. My father believed in the power of stories, whether they were written, or told around a fire or the kitchen table. For him, books were weapons that could be used against you unless you armed yourself with knowledge.

A small window framed the pine trees that surrounded the back of the cabin. My bed, where I woke that last morning, had been stripped of its star quilt, exposing a stained mattress that rolled toward the middle. *I had fallen back asleep, until the blankets were pulled away. A loud voice, not my father's, said, She's here. Said, Rosalie, wake up. A woman in a gray suit said I had no relatives, no one who wanted me.* Memories that I tried to forget.

I closed the door to save heat and moved to the threshold of my father's room. The bed was tidy and covered with a cotton blanket. The alcove that served as a closet was empty except for a pair of dusty boots with a hole in one toe. My father had papered the walls with magazine covers from the 1960s. Glossy photos of Neil Armstrong and Buzz Aldrin after the first moon landing. Stories of the asteroid hitting Siberia in 1908. Giant telescopes scanning the sky. Anything to do with stars. Ghostly images on paper that had curled around rusty thumbtacks.

On a shelf he had made from a fallen oak tree, more piles of books, yellowed with age. On top was a copy of *Black Beauty*. Inside the battered cover, my mother's name was written in a schoolgirl's round letters. I ran my fingers across the page, wondering how old she was when she read the book. What my life might have been like if my mother had lived. I tucked the book in my back pocket, just like I used to at my last foster home, when I read with one eye on the door.

Through the dust-covered window, daylight was quickly fading toward dusk. I had intended to stay at least a few days, but suddenly I felt a strong urge to leave. Whatever I'd thought I might find here, it was not the cold emptiness of this abandoned place. Better to leave everything behind and come back in the spring. If I hurried, I still had time to dig out the truck and find my way back to the main road before dark. I could return to the farm, the only home I had known for many years.

A few light snowflakes began to drift in lazy swirls toward the ground. I could almost hear my father's voice asking, What's your plan, Rosie? Look around and see what you need to survive. I had imagined this moment too many times to leave now. I would stay the night and decide what to do in the morning. Stepping outside onto the porch, I filled a pail with snow to melt on the stove. Breathed sharp, clean air deep into my lungs. Listened to the familiar hush of branches moving in the wind. Darkness settled into the woods, circling the cabin like a soft blanket. In the distance, a twig snapped. I was not afraid. I had not come here to escape the dark. Or the silence, broken only by the rustle of dry leaves.

But I had become a stranger to these woods; it would take time before this place knew me again. I felt its sorrow, the loss of generations who had lived here before me. The names of my family were like whispers just beyond hearing. I had returned too late. My family's stories had already disappeared; there was no one to keep their memory alive. At best, I hoped to make peace with my own past so I could move on, find a real home for myself, a place where I belonged.

I woke hours before the sun was up, huddled deep in my sleeping bag on the trundle bed closest to the stove. Even wearing a knit hat, two sweaters, long underwear, and wool socks, I was still cold. After adding more wood to the fire, I sat in the rocking chair wrapped in the wool blanket. The flames leaped up, casting long shadows across the floor. An oval rag rug, its colors faded almost white, was as cold as the floor beneath it.

My hunger got me up, and I dragged my blanket to the Coleman stove, where I set the coffeepot to heat. I searched a drawer for a knife to spread peanut butter on a slice of bread. Looking around at the cracked linoleum floor and the plywood countertop, I could picture only my father in this kitchen. I had no memories of my mother cooking or sitting with me at the table. When I used to ask my father what happened to her, he would say, "What difference does it make?" As if her absence was the raw truth and the details did not matter. But I kept asking, wanting to know why she left and how she died, believing the answer would give me a foundation on which to build my own story.

One night he came home late from cashing his monthly check in town. A strand of long, greasy hair fell across his lined forehead, his stubbled cheeks. He was thin, hollowed out from his latest struggle to stop drinking, lighting his cigarette from the stub he'd just finished. After reheating what was left of the morning's coffee, he settled on the couch and leaned back with a strange smile.

"Her birthday today," he said in a low voice, as if talking to himself. He raised his cup to her memory.

"Did I ever tell you how I met her? I had just gotten out of the army. While I was waiting for school to start, I found some carpentry work. One afternoon we got off early, and I was playing darts over at Len's, you know, the Indian bar down on Washington. I was winning, I couldn't miss.

"Around five, the gals who worked at the cannery got off shift and came by for a drink before heading home. The door flew open like the wind caught it, and a woman came in alone, not in a pack of two or three like the rest of them. The sun was glowing behind her like she was a spirit. Her hair was the color of crow's feathers.

"I laid down my darts and offered to buy her a drink. We talked a bit, I remember that. She was nervous, kept shooting glances over her shoulder at the door, chain-smoking, hardly touched her beer. But those eyes, my girl, she had eyes like yours, the same look a deer has just before the arrow reaches her heart. She had this way about her, like she could either fall to pieces or rip you apart, and she hadn't decided yet which way to go. The men all wanted to get close to her and the women watched her like she was about to steal their powwow money. I took her out of there, thinking I could save her."

I asked him the same question I had asked a dozen times before, hoping this time he would answer me.

"What happened to her, to my mother?" I whispered, wanting an end to the silence that surrounded her.

Without answering, my father raised his cup and drained it. "She's dead," he said. Without another word, he walked to the door, pulled on his lucky hunting cap, the one he made himself from an unlucky rabbit, grabbed his jacket, and left. He had a way of disappearing like that, walking for hours even in the dark. When I asked him where he went, he said simply, "To pray."

When I was ten, he disappeared for two nights. A few days before, he stopped talking and then sleeping. Just before he left, he said, "Everything I teach you is for survival. Every day is a test of your readiness." When he came back, he didn't explain where he'd gone or why. After that, he would disappear once or twice a year. If someone happened to come by to check on my schooling, I knew how to be as still as a mouse with the door locked. Sometimes he would tell me a fantastic story of thunder beings and stolen horses, of raids on enemy camps, of demons who woke him and rode his veins searching for his heart. One time he came home with a two-day beard, his eyes red and lost, reeking of whiskey and sour sweat, with streaks of mud on his shirt. He said, as if in apology, "Rosie, if you know the stars and the plants, you will never be lost or alone." After he died, I no longer believed this was true. But it was all I had left of him.

When the door closed behind him the night of my mother's birthday, I went to bed, crawling under the star quilt that she had made before she died, before whatever happened to her. She had sewed this quilt with tiny, even stitches that told a different story from my father's silence. A woman with hair the color of crow's feathers, who bent over bold strips of yellow and red cloth, who made this quilt for my bed. My father once told me the eight-sided star came from early buffalo robe designs, used before the herds were exterminated. "The morning star," he said, tracing his finger along the fine stitches, "is the place where we come from."

The next day he acted as if nothing had changed, as if he didn't remember telling me anything that mattered. Just as before, he sat in the yard for hours carving pipes, bowls, animals.

Or he chopped wood until his arms trembled, his face drawn into a grimace that hid the person I knew. Whatever demons he carried, he was most at peace in these woods.

I was a practical child; I worked with what I was given. I built a world of my own deep in the woods, sailing far away in an imaginary canoe made from a fallen log. I traveled to the places my father had told me about, reliving stories I read in his books.

As the seasons changed, he showed me the plants that he knew well, which ones were ready to be gathered and which parts to use for tea, for eating, for medicine. We searched for wild greens in spring, along with early asparagus, leeks, watercress, and morel mushrooms. In summer we traveled to find a thick grove of chokecherries, which became wasna when combined with dried deer meat and fat. I learned to use purple coneflower for a wasp sting or toothache. My father bartered for fall wild rice with the game he trapped. Each winter, after the leaves had dropped, we gathered čhaŋšáša, red willow, to make the traditional tobacco that he used in his cigarettes.

He was strict, in his way, teaching me from the time I was little how to ask each plant for permission to gather it. One summer he insisted I spend an entire day sitting beneath a tall cottonwood tree that grew near the river where we were gathering plants, instructing me that I was to listen and observe. When he was safely out of sight, I stripped and swam in the river. I gathered sticks to build my own beaver house. I found a black raspberry bush nearby, with a handful of ripe berries that the birds had missed. Finally, happily, I sat beneath the cottonwood and considered her for a full ten minutes before I fell asleep. I dreamed she spoke to me, thanking me for the čhaŋšáša I offered and telling me her true Dakhóta name, Wáǧčhaŋ. She lifted me to her highest branches, easily a hundred feet in the air, where I could see across the entire Dakhóta land, watching as time streamed past, as forests grew and disappeared.

When I woke, my father was standing over me, a stern look in his eye. He seemed to think that I had been wasting my time by sleeping.

Once, when I was older, he asked me to gather the blood-root that he used for his heart pain. He told me its medicine was strong enough to kill a person if not used in the right way. Normally he would not have asked me to gather the plant, but that day he was too tired to go himself. His eyes looked sunken and his skin had taken on a gray color that I did not like.

I found a patch that was several years old. The elder plant stood tall; its leaves were shaped like fingers on my hand. The white flowers that opened in spring were long gone, leaving be-hind foot-tall stalks topped with plump seedpods. One of the pods had split open, and a line of ants, each carrying a single seed on its back, traveled down the stalk, disappearing into their underground home. The ants would eat the outer cover-ing and leave the rest, keeping the seeds themselves warm and safe over the winter until they sprouted in the spring. I found a plant that had already dropped its seed and placed a pinch of čhaŋšáša near the stem, asking its permission before I began to dig. The root was long and slender, like a bloodred carrot. When I returned, my father said, "You've done well."

My one companion in those days was Šúŋka, who used to check on me when I played in the woods, lying down near my games while refusing to be drawn in. She lay with her head turned toward the cabin, as if she listened for the sound of my father's ax chopping wood. Sometimes I thought it was Šúŋka who held him together.

When we came home near dusk, my father would be sitting on the step, smoking one of his hand-rolled cigarettes. From well down the trail, I could smell the blend he used for tobacco, plants I had helped him gather. We would sit together in silence, listening, swatting an occasional mosquito, watching the birds bed down for the night. *If anything ever happens to me*, he told me once, *you will always find me here.*

═

A loud gurgle alerted me that my coffee was ready, reheated from the thermos. I filled my cup, wrapped my fingers around its warmth. Waste nothing, a habit learned in childhood. I didn't know we were poor until social workers told me so. No running water, no electricity. An outhouse. Surrounded by woods full of wild animals. A motherless, feral child. Someone who needed protecting.

Here in this drafty, cold room, I was surrounded by the unspoken memories of a family I barely knew. In the flickering light of the fire, I began to realize that I had come back hoping to fill an emptiness I had carried all of my life. I had no choice but to face it. There was a passage here; I felt its sharp edge. I knew how the wind drops just before a storm, as if the world is sucking back the energy it will soon unleash. I was waiting. I had come home in winter; all around me was hoarfrost and ice.

I spent the rest of the night in the rocking chair next to the stove, occasionally adding more wood as I waited for daylight to slowly return. I must have dozed. When I woke, the sky was a sullen gray. Snow had fallen steadily throughout the night, already laying several new inches across the porch, and showed no sign of letting up.

After visiting the outhouse, I broke a new path to the woodpile behind the cabin. Each step was like a parade, the silence shattering as the frozen crust broke with a percussive snap beneath my feet. I could see my father shaking his head in disbelief at my noise. "There's no game left for miles, Rosie. You've spared a lot of animals today."

In the past months, I had become clumsy with the weak muscles of a woman who has sat too long at the bedside of a dying man. Inside the spare bedroom that became John's when he grew ill, the sky shrank to the size of the window and the air was warm and dry, sharp with the metallic smell of chemicals. Once I watched John study his face in a hand mirror. Did he see a frightened boy who was unable to believe that life could end just like that, without apology, long before he was ready to go? He must have seen the truth reflected in his sunken eyes and severe cheekbones.

I carried four armloads of wood inside and stacked them near the stove. After melting more snow for cleaning, I scrubbed the surface of the table we had used for everything: meals, sewing, reading, or playing cribbage, a game my father taught me as a child. I scrubbed the dust out of every old knife cut, every scratch, every dent. I found my initials underneath, near a rough letter carved by another hand: the single letter *D*. Not the mark of my mother, Agnes, but of another child who had lived here once.

As I worked, moving on to the kitchen cupboards, I grew warm, finally, and took off my coat. Hung it on a hook by the door. Then I rummaged in my bag until I found my father's fur hunting cap, the one he was wearing the day he died. I had kept it hidden in my drawer at the farm all these years. I hung it back on the hook he always used when he was alive, next to his summer cap.

The fire was roaring now, raising its voice against the wind that had begun to howl around the corners of the cabin, flinging handfuls of sleet against the windows, rattling the door as if reminding me of the foolishness of my presence. *There's still time to leave*, is what I heard. *Get out now while you can.*

But I would not go. Instead I was exhilarated by the violence of the storm, the way I was wrapped inside the eye of this wintry hurricane. Sheets of snow had begun to fall in desperate haste, as if the ground could not be buried quickly enough, as if the snow's burden had been too much for the clouds to carry. The light inside grew dim. Soon I would have to use the lantern to see my work. Finally, I sat with the rag still clutched in my hand and surrendered to the storm. Eyes closed, barely breathing, I gave my full attention to the wind, the way it blustered and fell, threatened, cajoled, and punished. The roof creaked and a cold rush of air seeped through the chinks in the old walls. As if the wind searched for me; as if we had unfinished business together.

I began to laugh and could not stop. I could not stop thinking of John's ragged breath, the endless waiting for another breath to follow. The shock—yes, even after all those months of dying—the shock of death itself. It ran the length of my arms, settled on my chest, tingled my scalp. And then I laughed louder, drowning out the sound of the wind. After so many years, I was back home. To this.

My throat became hoarse, and finally I fell silent. I sat without moving, staring at a crack in the log wall and the soft fluttering of a faded curtain. A strange heaviness filled my arms and legs. A stream of bitter thoughts taunted me, whispered that it was time for the Iron Wing name to fade into dust, where it belonged. And finally, sliding in like the razor edge of a knife: that there was no one left who cared if I lived or died. Even my son would be better off owning the farm without me.

Hardly realizing that I had moved, I was up and searching for John's gun, the one I'd brought for protection. In my hand it felt smooth, soft, inviting. It would be so easy. And I was so tired. I stared at the gun for a long time. And then, in a quiet moment between gusts of wind, I heard my father's voice.

"Rosie." That's all, just my name.

I opened the door as the wind whipped my hair into my eyes. I flung the gun as far as I could into the snow. After pressing the door closed with my shoulder, I climbed on top of my old bed, wrapped in the warmth of my sleeping bag, and slept while the storm raged outside.

CHAPTER THREE

Rosalie Iron Wing

2002

In the morning I dressed quickly, filled a thermos with hot coffee, and strapped my father's snowshoes onto my boots. For a moment, I thought I heard a sharp whine, the sound Šúŋka used to make in her excitement to run down the trail into the woods. All these years later, I had not lost the habit of listening for her.

Without a clear sense of where to go, but needing to move, to feel the world expand beyond the closed walls of the cabin, I headed toward the clearing where I used to play, my feet following their dim memory of the trail. Everywhere I looked there was an absence, an empty place, a stillness. Even the woods were hushed today, low-hanging branches heavy with snow, unable to move. The few birds that had not fled south were silent. I wondered if I could find my way back.

Trusting the instinct that had brought me this far, I pushed forward, raising each snowshoe and sinking again into the fresh snow, bulldozing my own crude path through the woods. Within a short time, I was breathing hard, as a cloud of steam frosted my eyelashes and my thighs burned from the effort. My mind was empty, entirely focused on reaching the next hill.

The trees had grown much taller since I was a child. I used my hatchet to clear branches from the path, gratified by the results of my work. Looking at the trail of destruction in my wake, I had to laugh. I would find my way back.

The clearing was larger than I remembered. As a child I could throw a small rock from one side to the other, from the sugar maples to the red cedars. Back then, I could barely see the sun glittering on the river through the airy branches of the willow that we cut for baskets. Gooseberries had grown near the edge of the woods, and I could always find milkweed scattered throughout the grass, yielding its young pods for our soup. This had been our grocery store, as well as my classroom and play area.

The fallen log that had once served as my canoe was gone, slowly rotting until it became part of the forest floor, joining the endless network that connects the trees with tiny, unseen creatures. My father once explained that trees talk to one another through this web, sharing stories and food, sending what they don't need along to their neighbors.

"We live that same way," he said. "We learn from the trees by watching and listening. When you hit that tree with your big stick, Rosie, you leave a mark, and the whole forest hears it. Then they ignore you, they stop talking when you're around. But if you come on quiet feet"—and he raised his eyebrows at me—"if you can learn to come on quiet feet, and to listen, then you will never be without friends."

It took me years to learn to walk this way, to follow his footsteps without making a sound. I grew to know when he would stop, how to kneel in dry leaves by sliding beneath their loud skin, how to gauge when the wind was about to change direction. I learned to feel eyes turning toward me, to sense that another animal was present. He taught me how to hunt small game, to gut a deer and dry the meat. We cut a hole in winter ice to catch fish. When the snow began to melt, we tapped the maples for their sweet sap, cooking it over the fire until it boiled down into syrup.

I was happiest in spring, after sugar bush, when the plants I knew returned from their long winter underground. I spent my days searching for new arrivals, like the pasque flower, stroking its fuzzy leaves and admiring the delicate violet of its upturned face. When I spotted the red gleam of the first wild strawberries, I picked a handful for my father. He bit into the fruit and said, "Wašté." Good. Every day there was something delicious to be gathered: fiddlehead ferns for soup, plump sweet nannyberries that I ate by the handful.

Back then plants stood tall when I approached, spreading their leaves and displaying their gifts. I talked with them and knew that they liked the sound of my voice, that the attention made them happy. They were even happier when I sang, imitating my father's songs or making up new ones. "Beautiful rabbit, soft white fur, be my friend. I won't eat you. I won't even let my father eat you. Unless you find his trap by mistake. Then I'm sorry about the soup. You are delicious."

Now I wore a coat that rattled as I walked, warning every creature in the forest of my approach. The tall pines, in the past so chatty, stood stiff and silent. I kept turning, searching for the sugar maple trees that would be getting ready for tapping in another month. Where were the red cedars that my father had loved? In the place where I thought the trees must be, I found nothing. Even as an adult, I could not throw a rock all the way across this wide space, with its ragged gaps and clear view of the river.

I searched in a broader circle, convinced that my memory was wrong, that the sugar maples should be seventy-five feet tall by now. Nothing. I grew dizzy searching; I grew old remembering. And then I felt the chill of fresh knowledge, the understanding that comes when resistance gives way. I had to see with my young eyes to understand what had happened. Here, where I had first looked, here is where they stood. Here is where we offered čhaŋšáša, where I learned to set taps and carry heavy buckets of tree sap. Beneath the snow I knew that I would find stumps, my trees chopped down for their valuable wood. In their place, a dense thicket of buckthorn, a scrubby European tree whose aggressive spread often pushed out native trees.

I sank to my knees in the snow. I wept then, tears I had never shed for my father or John. Where these old trees once stood was another reminder that what was valuable would be taken; what was not protected would be stolen. I was helpless to stop it. An úŋšika, pitiful woman.

With my head still bowed, I felt a tug on my attention. I listened without breathing. There, just below the light breeze that had rustled dry oak leaves a moment earlier, I heard the sound of a quiet footstep. Even without turning, I could feel eyes on my back. While I did not move, my energy shifted toward watchful awareness. I knew that whatever watched me would see this, too. Careful. Shifting my weight to the balls of my feet, I slowly lowered my hands to the ground, easing my body into a crouch. I might be pitiful, but I would not go easily.

Gradually I turned my head in the direction of the sound and saw yellow wolf eyes staring back from the thin cover of a leafless shrub. The dog was darker than Šúŋka, but his stance suggested that same mix of wolf and dog that had made Šúŋka such a good hunter. Consciously willing my panicked breathing to slow, I shifted my gaze slightly and waited without moving. While it seemed unlikely that the dog would attack, it was possible that I had come too near a recent kill. After a moment, he raised his head, sniffed the air, and turned away, loping steadily back into the woods as if obeying an invisible signal.

"What are you doing here?"

I jumped and spun around at the sound of the first human voice I had heard in days. While my attention had been focused on the dog, a woman had come up behind me and now stood there with a rifle balanced lightly under her arm. Her eyes traveled the length of my body, coolly appraising my coat, my old-style snowshoes, my dark hair pulled back in its loose braid. Her eyebrows drew together as she observed the inconsistencies in my story. She raised the nose of her rifle a few inches higher.

"Are you deaf? What are you doing here?"

Despite the menace in her voice, I couldn't answer. The question pulled me under; I barely knew the answer myself, and I was still confused by the rush of adrenalin from her sudden appearance. I could only look at her without speaking. Built like a bulldog, with broad shoulders and powerful legs, she radiated strength. I took in her large hands, the heavy brown hair cut short around her face. I studied her straight nose, the firm set of her mouth, the brown eyes that were painfully honest, vulnerable. She seemed familiar, but I couldn't place her. I sank back on my heels, my feet still strapped to the snowshoes. I knew what she saw, looking back at me: a bag of bones, not young, not old.

"Rosalie? Rosalie Iron Wing?" Her eyes grew wide, and she smiled. "Didn't you marry some rich farmer after your dad . . . after . . . ?" Again, a silence filled the space between us. I nodded.

"I seen smoke from your old cabin this morning. I guess that was you. Me and Digger came to see if someone finally burned the place down." She nodded happily, pleased at not having to run any poachers off the land. She even seemed glad to see me now that she knew I wasn't there to make trouble. Tilting her head, she regarded me with open curiosity. I could see the questions rising, the desire to know how I had ended up back here. What a story this would make in town. "Guess who I seen out in the woods . . ." Fair game, I thought, pressing my lips tightly together.

I waited, but the questions never came. Maybe she noticed the dark circles beneath my eyes, the sorrow that bent my shoulders like a bow. After a pause, I nodded and stood up to leave. But then this stranger asked, in a voice so gentle that I nearly broke apart, "I don't mean to be nosy, but when did you last eat?" I couldn't remember.

⸝⸝

The woman built a large fire, dragging dry branches and a fallen tree to the center of the clearing and hacking them apart with a few swift blows from the hatchet she wore on her belt. She moved like a woman who was born in the shelter of an oak tree, who bathed in the river and enjoyed every meal of wild game, knowing that one day her own turn would come. Working silently, without haste, she stacked each piece of wood in a tower like a funeral pyre for the lost maples. After the fire was lit, I ate the bread and venison sausage she unwrapped from a cloth tucked in her knapsack, and we shared the last cup of coffee in my thermos as we stood near the flames. Behind us, sheltered from the fire's heat, Digger slept with his muzzle tucked between his paws.

"I know you," I said, watching her as she pushed the quickly burning logs closer together with a long stick. "You lived in Milton."

"That's right," she said, nodding agreement. "Me and my uncle used to come out here hunting deer in the fall. I even helped him build a hunting shack. I never thought I'd be living in it. Kind of like you, I guess," she added, stealing a glance at my face.

"Did you know my dad?" I asked. I wanted him to be more than a memory that belonged only to me.

"Sort of. He and my uncle used to hunt deer together. I remember he was nice to me. Quiet, didn't say much."

The low tone of her voice stirred forgotten memories, and suddenly her name, and her story, fell into place. Ida Johanson. The only daughter of the Episcopal minister and his sharp-tongued wife, a bitter woman who was known to complain of her daughter's lack of physical beauty. Sometimes I would see Ida standing with her mother at the door of the church, greeting people as they walked in. Ida—or poor Ida, as I thought of her back then—wore cotton dresses with puffed sleeves that squeezed her plump arms, while she hid her large hands in the folds of her skirt. Once Ida caught my eye and grimaced behind her mother's back. I laughed out loud, drawing the prickly attention of her mother. When she saw me standing on the sidewalk, she said loudly, "You get on out of here. Go on, you got no business here. You people are a disgrace to this town." She grabbed Ida's hand and dragged her inside, but not before I saw Ida silently mouth the word "sorry."

A couple of years before my father died, when Ida was fourteen, a story went around that one of her cousins had taken a drunken dare to prove that she really was a girl. When Ida fought him, busting his nose, he'd punched her unconscious and left her lying in the muddy field behind the church, her clothing torn. She disappeared for a while. When she came back, there were no more cotton dresses. She wore jeans and flannel shirts, her long hair cut short above her ears. She refused to testify against her cousin, but I heard that he died that same year in a hunting accident, shot with his own gun. It seemed that some part of their family was always mixed up with drinking and fighting, until the minister finally found another church in a different state and moved away. When Ida refused to go with them, they left her behind. The same uncle that taught her to hunt gave her the shack so she would have a place to live.

As I looked at her now, in the glow of the slowly dying fire, Ida seemed content: her eyes clear, her cheeks reddened by the wind. With a swift tilt of her head, she drained the last drop of coffee and handed the cup back to me, wiping her mouth on the back of her glove. I watched her use a stick to heap snow over the remaining logs, which hissed and spat as the fire disappeared. She gave a quick whistle to Digger, who leaped up and into the woods, and turned toward me.

"I've got venison," she said. "I'll come by." Then she strode away, following Digger's path through the snow. Overhead a white-throated sparrow called. I took a few steps and felt the raw soreness in my legs. Ahead of me lay the rough trail back to the cabin, clearly marked by a line of broken twigs. Already the sun had begun to drop behind the tree line, casting shadows beneath bare branches. In that moment, I felt a deep sense of gratitude. Ida knew me, knew my family, my cabin, these woods. She would come back.

CHAPTER FOUR

Rosalie Iron Wing
2002

Three days after I met Ida in the woods, she delivered on her promise to bring venison. The morning light was making a reluctant appearance, rising slow as if the cold was too much even for the sun. I was sitting inside, in my rocking chair. I had begun spending hours there, completely unaware of the passing of time. The absence of any witness to my life allowed me to suspend movement, even thought, and simply drift. Some days I dreamed of my son's birth, of the plants in my garden, or the warm touch of John's hand on my skin. Other days I seemed to think of nothing at all. I listened to the steady drip of melting ice on sunny days, the hush of wind, the occasional bang of the outhouse door if I had forgotten to latch it. I had the luxury of time to pay attention to what moved around me. Nothing was required; no one needed my help. I was once again taking inventory, this time of my own life.

When I heard the slap of leather mittens removing snow, I didn't at first connect it to a living being. Not until I heard the thunk of a heavy pack dropped to the ground, followed by the brittle clink of packages stacked on my front step, did I realize it must be Ida. No one else knew to come here. I sat up straight, mildly panicked at the thought of a visitor, but I knew there would be no knock on my door. Rural manners dictated certain rules. If I was of a mind for company, I would come outside. If not, Ida would finish her business and head back the same way she had come. And I was not ready, not ready, not yet. My face was unwashed. I could not remember combing my hair. I owned but one cup. I remained where I was, frozen by the small sounds outside my door.

The squeak of snowshoes on dry snow was followed by silence. I waited. After an hour had passed, I gathered in Ida's gifts: dried berries, cedar for tea, and a container of soup, as well as packages of venison steaks, sausage, chops. Enough meat to keep me through the winter. Would I stay that long? I stored the meat in a cooler just outside the door, weighting the lid with a short stack of wood. I would have to find a way to thank her.

My days shaped themselves around a routine of tasks connected by leisurely stretches of time spent in my chair. I chopped wood, tended the fire, melted snow, hand-washed my few clothes. I watched the subtle shifts in the landscape outside my window. The wind blew snow in tall mounds against the highbush cranberries, then rearranged its work on the following day. One morning a rabbit raced past, followed a minute later by a coyote. Another morning I woke to see two deer strolling by, pausing to nibble on the branches of shrubs that grew near the edge of the woods.

In the hours I sat rocking, my fingers traced the tiny stitches of my star quilt. I had found it in the cedar chest in my old room. I had been looking for rags to use for cleaning, and instead, when I opened the lid, there was my quilt, neatly folded, its brilliant shades of red and yellow now faded, its cotton thin and fragile. The thoughtfulness of this gesture made me suspect that Ida had been the one to keep her eye on this place, repairing broken windows and tucking away these few things that had meant something to my family. As if she'd known that one day I would return.

After resting for so many days, my fingers ached for work. Idle, they remembered the hours I spent as a young child learning to hold a needle, enjoying the play of colors while I struggled against the uneven spacing of my stitches. A woman's head bent near me, so close I could smell coffee on her breath, her strong fingers guiding as she taught me to push the needle through thick cloth. A prick to my thumb; fabric pulled roughly from my hands. My mother. She was slowly returning to me; I was grateful for every memory. My mother was real; the quilt on my lap was proof that she'd known me. Even in Mankato, she was with me.

dormancy

a seed dreams

CHAPTER FIVE

Rosalie Iron Wing
1979

I dreamed my mother called my name in a voice that ached with longing. I dreamed the acrid smoke of a fire stung my eyes, blurred her edges as she used a deer antler to pull on a smoldering block of damp wood. The flames were the only light in a darkness so complete the trees had disappeared. The smell of decayed leaves mingled with the piss-sharp scent of fear. Behind her, the carcass of a gutted buck hung from a branch by a rope knotted around its legs, while his blood drained into a bowl from the wound in his neck. She turned toward me, her face in shadow.

I woke with a start, shivering in the cold damp of my basement room. Already my mother's voice had slipped away.

Pulling the wool blanket to my neck, where it itched against my skin, I smelled the rain that had seeped into the basement. My foster mother, Shirley, always asked me if I mopped these leaks up and I always said yes. From the silence overhead, I knew the family must still be asleep. Every footstep, every scuffle of bedroom slippers, every thud of a dropped toy made its way to my room through the unfinished ceiling. When gray daylight began to filter through a window too small to climb out, I knew it was time to get up. I needed to find a job so I could move out, as far from Shirley as possible.

I dressed quickly, pulling a T-shirt from one of the plastic bags that were stacked against the wall. After plaiting my hair into a long braid, I pushed a pair of black-framed glasses above the sharp ridge of my nose, blinking as the world came into focus. I slid my arms into the oversize sweatshirt I wore most days and raised the hood over my head. Only then did I feel like myself. A tall, hulking shadow, invisible to others, a ghost of the girl I once had been. Every day I minded what my father used to tell me. If you're going to be a hunter, Rosie, you'd best learn how to sit quiet and wait. I kept his rabbit cap, the one he'd always worn hunting, buried at the bottom of the bag that held my few clothes.

Finally, I turned to the books that Shirley had pulled out from under my mattress the day before. Using leftover change from errands, I would buy battered novels at the thrift store and read them over and over. These books were one of the few things that belonged to me. When the pages began to fall out, I carefully taped them back in place. Now the books lay in a mess of spilled pages and bent covers, my jeans underneath, with their pockets pulled inside out. The envelope containing my high school diploma sat wrinkled and torn on top of the pile.

I picked up a ragged copy of *Speaking of Indians*, a book I had bought because my father once owned it, and tucked it in my back pocket. I read whenever I had to be upstairs, sitting in the kitchen, away from the television, where I could keep one eye on the door. Six years of waiting for someone to come for me had become a habit, even when I knew there was no point.

After carefully stacking the books and loose pages to sort through later, I dug deep into one of the plastic bags and pulled out a small pencil box. Inside was a handful of cigarettes, two crumpled dollar bills, and a small pair of manicure scissors. Pulling one of Shirley's sweaters from the bag, I cut a tiny hole just above where her heart would be, about the size that a mouse might have chewed. That's better, I thought, frowning at the hole with a critical eye. Much better. Score one for my side. I put the scissors back in the box, stuck two cigarettes in my pocket before hiding the box in the bag, and dropped the sweater in the open washing machine.

Upstairs, I eased the back door shut behind me without making any sound that might have alerted Shirley. I strode quickly down the uneven walkway, past faded plastic toys barely visible beneath wet piles of last year's leaves.

Metal fences surrounded each yard and cut the neighborhood into tiny rectangles. Elm trees were planted along the curb, their roots trapped by concrete, their leaves fluttering in car exhaust. I felt sorry for them. They didn't want to live here any more than I did.

The air was cool and moist, a typical June morning, before the heat of summer arrived in July. Even though I knew it was childish, I stepped on every crack in the sidewalk, reciting the old nursery rhyme about breaking your mother's back. A neighbor dog lunged at the rope tied to his collar, barking furiously until I called him "Šúŋka" in a quiet voice. He nose-bumped my hand in greeting through the chain-link fence. At the corner, I glanced through the window of the thrift store to the shelf of dollar books near the front door. Nothing but romance. No thanks.

I turned onto Cedar Avenue, already humming with Saturday morning traffic. Walking quickly to stay warm, I passed an empty storefront, a car dealership advertising a summer sale, and a vacuum repair shop. A handful of lotto tickets littered the sidewalk in front of the Cedar Bar, where men from my neighborhood liked to escape after dinner. I'd had trouble learning my way along these streets because everything looked the same to me: brown buildings, paved roads, white faces. Crossing the street quickly in a gap between fast-moving cars, I followed the sidewalk until it ended at the railroad track, then turned down a short trail that led to the Minnesota River. The dirt path was barely visible beneath a dense clump of trees and a scattering of shrubs. Most people stayed up where they could feel the concrete beneath their shoes. As soon as I entered the cool shade of the cottonwoods that grew along the riverbank, the tense knot in my shoulders began to loosen.

My father once told me that this city, Mankato, was supposed to be named Mahkato, after one of the Dakhóta chiefs whose village was originally located here. No surprise that some clerk who couldn't spell made this change for all time. I knew that Dakhóta families used to follow the river from its beginning at Big Stone Lake, near the South Dakota border, all the way to Mankato, where it joined with the Blue Earth River before heading toward the Mississippi. I knew this because I studied maps, trying to find my home.

Settlers figured out that this land was perfect for growing corn and that the river could carry canned vegetables north. Somebody even invented a plow that could tear up the thick prairie sod. But the story my father always came back to was the hanging of thirty-eight Dakhóta warriors after the 1862 war. It might have felt like justice, back then, to the people who had lost their relatives, but they didn't know that Mankato would later become best known for hosting the largest mass hanging in the country's history. My father said, "That hanging is like a wound that won't heal."

Sometimes, when we came to Mankato for supplies, he would tell me to close my eyes and listen. The hum of cars on the highway would sound like wind passing through the prairie grass that was once as tall as me. It's still here, he would say, we just can't see it. But if all this pavement disappeared, we would find the hoofprints of bison herds that used to roam this land. Once he pointed his lips toward the enormous statue of the Jolly Green Giant and the endless cornfields behind it.

"This is my homeland," he said. "And now you and me are the only ones left to carry the Iron Wing name."

I had started coming here months earlier, using a forged absent note to ditch school, needing to escape the city and Shirley's nagging. Lately I'd had trouble remembering my father's face or the sound of his voice. In the months before he died, he had begun asking me to gather a few plants without his help. And now I was in danger of forgetting all that I had learned.

At the water's edge, I took a crumpled cigarette from my pocket and broke it apart, scattering the tobacco and offering a quick prayer as the flakes slowly sank. I came here nearly every day, pulled by the current as if I belonged to it. Every empty bottle and broken branch carried a story from the north, news from a world that I had been taken from as a child. This water was my only connection to the land where I was born.

As I headed downtown again, my belly rumbled from hunger and anxiety. My caseworker had a halfway house lined up if I didn't find a job and a place to live before my eighteenth birthday in October. When she told me about her plan, I said nothing. After two foster homes, I had no intention of living there. I'd rather be on the streets, I told myself. At night, I lay awake and worried about what to do.

Back on the sidewalk, I passed an old man shuffling along with his even older dog, before I turned into the parking lot for Casey's General Store. Besides gas pumps and piles of garden mulch, they had a bulletin board where people sold tractors and firewood and used cars and posted jobs. There were more seasonal jobs in the summer but also more competition from new graduates, like me, who were looking for work. ·

Opening the big glass door, I braced myself for air-conditioning that ran on high no matter what temperature it was outside. The old men who met for coffee each morning were already at their regular table in the deli section. One of them gave me a quick nod as I hurried past, while the others kept their eyes on their coffee cups.

On the bulletin board, I passed over the ads for phone sales and get-rich-quick while working from home. I saw a flyer asking: "WANT TO EARN FAST CASH? Calling all teenagers to meet at the high school parking lot in early July for three weeks of corn detasseling," whatever that meant. I generally avoided the farm boys, with their sunburned necks and plaid shirts, their talk of acreage or "my daddy's International

Harvester combine." But I was willing to do most anything to earn some money right then.

I read on: "7:00 a.m., long pants and long-sleeve shirt, gloves, protective glasses, hat. Rain gear. Boots. Bring your own lunch. Pays well!" How hard could it be? If nothing else turned up, I would give this a try.

In the bakery section I grabbed a loaf of white bread that I was supposed to have brought home the day before. As I shopped, eyes followed me in the mirror overhead, waiting for me to steal something. I came around the end of the aisle and almost ran over a young boy of about two years old, wearing a tiny grass dancer outfit, one hand clutching a box of doughnuts as he tried to run from his mother. She moved quickly to grab his hand, her long braid swinging forward as she leaned toward him, the light catching on her beaded barrette. I knew her. Gaby Makespeace used to go to my high school but dropped out early in her junior year, after she got pregnant. We had become friends the year before, when I sat behind her in social studies, two Indian girls in a room full of white students. She used to say that in our friendship she was the mouth and I was the ears.

I was surprised to see her standing here now. Gaby was shorter than me, and her small frame radiated a wiry strength that seemed to warn against getting too close. Her dark eyes moved like a restless bird's from the shelf to her son to a quick glance over her shoulder, in the nervous habit of a woman expecting trouble. She was, as always, perfectly made up, not a hair out of place. Her powwow outfit was a dazzling blend of meticulous beading on a shiny magenta fabric that fell to midcalf, revealing beaded moccasins that matched her dress. Standing in the bread aisle, Gaby looked like royalty visiting from a foreign country. One of the old men in the deli stood to get a better look at her, pretending he was reading a sign on the window. A plump matron hurried through the checkout line while her daughter gawked and pointed. Gaby ignored all of them. She grabbed the doughnuts and placed them back on the shelf.

"Mathó, you have to stay near me."

Then she looked at me, smiled, and said, "Heyyyy, I was just thinking about you."

"Really? Why?"

"Don't you live around here? With that old bitch?"

I laughed. Gaby had not forgotten my rants about Shirley. But then her son took off down the aisle, and she ran after him, giving me a quick wave and calling over her shoulder, "See you!" And she was gone. Just as well. I wasn't in a mood to answer questions about my life.

I strolled a few more aisles before carrying my bread to the counter. Just my luck: that morning it was Barb on duty, one of the girls from high school I couldn't stand. Even worse, when I checked my sweatshirt and jeans, I found nothing but my house key. Shirley had taken the change I meant to use for buying bread. In my rush to escape I had forgotten I needed money. Barb's face was flat, expressionless; her fingers tapped ever so lightly on the keys of the register.

"I don't have it." Twenty-five cents. The distance between me and lunch. The price of my foster mother's resentment.

"I'm not surprised," Barb said, snapping her gum. "Everyone knows you people are just a bunch of drunks on welfare."

"Thanks, Barb. That explains a lot."

"Whatever."

She placed her plump hand on the bread, prepared to re-possess it, to push it to the side while she helped the line of customers who stood behind me, their carts loaded with food. Not her problem. I considered grabbing the bread and running. The door was next to the counter; I had long legs that could move when they needed to. Barb had disliked me ever since I beat her in the hundred-yard dash, when she hissed "squaw" as she pulled up short at the finish line. Her fingers tightened around the loaf. Already her head was turned away, looking toward the next customer.

A quarter was laid carefully on the counter. Square, dirt-worn fingers pushed it to Barb. "Here," said the man behind me, and I looked away in embarrassment. He gave a half nod to me as he set down a six-pack of beer and two apples. Without a word or even a glance, I picked up my bread and escaped.

At the end of the sidewalk my steps slowed. In the cool air, I could breathe again and think about what had just happened. I hadn't thanked him. Bad as I felt to accept someone's charity, it was worse to take it without showing gratitude. I could hear my father's voice reminding me, You're an Iron Wing, Rosie. Always be proud of who you are.

I turned back toward the lot. The man was walking to a pickup truck parked at the far end. While he unlocked his door, I came up behind him. Something about the frayed collar on his denim jacket, the way he hadn't looked around for me when he came out of the store, told me that he knew what it meant not to have twenty-five cents. His truck was splat-tered with mud, the paint faded from too many years in the sun. Fifty-pound sacks were stacked high in the back. A fine layer of dust covered everything.

"Hey," I said. "I forgot to thank you."

He stopped and listened with one hand on the door, his back still to me.

"Forget about it."

I could hear a smile in his voice. He threw his bag on the front seat, clearly intending to leave without ever once turning to look at me. He would not be a witness to my humiliation in the store; he was almost delicate in his care not to meet my eyes.

"Wait a minute." The words spilled out before I had time to think what I was about to say. A cattle truck rumbled past, the engine whining through its gears. What was it that I needed to ask him? Of the hundred times I'd stopped at that store, what had brought him there today? Or if he understood that our lives can shift in a single moment, leaving behind the selves we thought we knew?

He turned toward me. He was older, somewhere in his late twenties. We were about the same height, near six feet, looking eye to eye. Sandy-brown hair cut short. A John Deere seed cap pushed up on a high white forehead marked him as a farmer. No wonder he looked strong, with broad, hay-baling shoulders and ropy forearms—a man used to working with his hands. Unlike the cocky boys I knew from school, he seemed quiet, standing there like he was in no hurry. Or maybe he was tired. His jaw bristled with a light stubble. His Grateful Dead T-shirt was faded, almost unreadable. A telltale red rimmed his blue eyes, the same red I'd seen in my foster dad's eyes after a night at the bar.

I could feel his eyes follow the dark curve of my cheek, barely visible beneath the shadow of my hood. We studied each other for a moment until we both looked away.

Unable to think of anything to say, I muttered, "Forget it." Turning away, I walked quickly across the parking lot. A moment later, I heard his truck engine turn over. I did not look back.

CHAPTER SIX

Gaby Makespeace
1979

Seeing Rosie again took me back in time, even though it was less than three years since I had last seen her. So much had happened since then that it felt like another lifetime. But Rosie, she looked just the same as the first day I seen her, when she was a freshman and I was a sophomore in high school. I'd heard a new Indian girl had just moved across town so she had to change schools almost at the end of the year. I was more than a little curious to get a look at her.

God, it was painful to see that girl walk down the hallway. The other girls laughed behind their hands at the way her too-big jeans fit so low she kept hitching them up with one hand, clutching a pile of books in the other. Even I couldn't believe the mess she was, like she shopped in the boys' wear and never owned a mirror. She was way tall, long legs like an awkward colt, legs the boys couldn't help watching, either. And those dumb Clark Kent glasses—girl, who lets you wear shit like that? It's not like she was terrible looking, just the usual acne scars that any moron would know how to cover up. Besides her big old backpack, there was a book sticking out of her back pocket. For real. It's like she was asking to be made fun of. I swear she was even using a rope as a belt.

No one comes into a new school without people trying to figure out where you fit in. The girl never spoke in class unless she was called on, but on those rare occasions when a teacher remembered she was there, you could tell she'd been listening. She didn't seem to care what people thought of her. Or even mind sitting alone at lunchtime. She'd go outside with her book, and maybe once I saw her with an apple. Hardly ever saw her eat.

After I watched her for a few days, I decided there were so few of us brown girls in this school that we needed to stick together. Maybe we could help each other out. We even had a class together, social studies, since I had failed to pass it my first time through. Next day I came to class early and gave a sweet smile to Mr. Warner, our young, just-out-of-college white teacher, who still believed that Columbus discovered America. I told him I wanted to change seats so I could help the new girl catch up. He looked at me, probably wondering how a C student was going to help her, but then he just nodded and made the change.

She was reading when I sat down, so I stared at her for a minute from my new desk. Man, she was tough. Never so much as gave me a glance. Finally, when it became clear this tall bird was not going to look up from her book, I leaned over.

"Hey," I said, nudging her arm. "I'm Gaby. Gaby Makespeace. I'm not from here. I'm staying with my auntie while I finish school." And then I waited.

She hesitated before replying, pushing her glasses up on her nose and peering back at me like a spooked owl.

"It's okay," I said. "I don't bite."

"Hey" was all she said in return. Then—and I couldn't believe this—she went right back to her book. I leaned over and tapped her shoulder.

"Excuse me, your name?"

"Oh," she said, blushing. "Rosalie. Rosalie Iron Wing. From . . . north of here."

"Cool."

Of course, I asked around to get her story, starting with my auntie, who made it her business to know what was going on with everyone. My auntie Vera never stops moving. Either she's working, or volunteering at church, or helping somebody with something. Still she found time to cook dinner every night for me and Anthony. And nag about homework. She kept a picture of Uncle Marvin and her next to their bed. They bought their little house before his kidneys failed from diabetes. She was laughing in the photo, but by the time I moved in with her, she always looked tired.

I waited until she was beading a powwow outfit for her cousin's daughter, keeping her hands busy while her mind was available for a chat.

"Iron Wing," she repeated, turning the name over in her mental Rolodex while she carefully picked up three silver beads with her needle. "I haven't heard that name in a while. I knew a Ray Iron Wing in school, but I thought he died. I heard he wasn't quite right after he got out of the army. Problem with drinking, was it? Then he got tangled up with that Kills Deer family. Nothing but trouble. What's his girl like?"

"Don't know yet," I said. I had to think about my auntie's info.

Changing the subject, I asked, "When does Anthony get

out of the hospital?" My older brother thought he could fly when he was stoned on cocaine and Boone's Farm. Instead he drove my auntie's car into a tree. That fool was lucky to be alive, especially after meeting Auntie's wrath when she'd heard he wrecked her car.

Auntie sighed, all the way to her bones. "That boy" was all she said, shaking her head. I'd overheard her the night before, talking to Ma on the phone. The whole point of us living there was to get him away from all the drugs on the reservation. And me away from his best friend, Earl White Dog. Auntie didn't know it was love between me and Earl. Or that he had moved to his cousin's house to be near me. And close to Anthony, who whispered to me at the hospital that Earl had ditched out of the car before the cops came.

"I feel kind of sorry for Rosalie," I said, a plan beginning to take shape in my mind. "She invited me to do homework at her house. Really needs my help to get caught up."

"Oh?" my auntie said, all innocent, even though she has a radar in her head that is constantly swiveling, searching for lies of all shapes and sizes. Anthony and I secretly called her Bat Woman.

"Invite her over to dinner," she added, calling my bluff. Woman is also a deadly cribbage player and a fierce bingo competitor. "Then we'll see."

It took a few days of near stalking before Rosalie started to warm up to me. It's not that she was weird or anything; she just didn't seem to need anyone else. Finally, when we were sitting outside during lunch, I asked her straight out about Shirley.

"So what's her problem?"

"I hate her."

"I get that. Just asking why."

"She's two-faced. Acts nice on the surface. Spies on me, reminds me that I'm too tall, too dark, too ugly. Dumb. Lazy. That without her I'd be living on the street."

"Yeah, I get it. She's a bitch."

When I shared my homework scheme with her, all she heard was that I wanted to come to her house. That's when I saw the first real spark, when she looked panicked and said, "No, no, no, no. You can't come there." Girl had a wound she kept hidden away, like all of us, like any Indian alive today. I felt sorry for her. I think that's when we became friends, when we knew we could trust each other with our bad-luck stories.

"I tell you what," I said, to calm her down. "My auntie wants to meet you. Come for dinner."

"I don't know if I can," she said, her eyes huge behind her glasses. I didn't know then that she'd never been asked to a friend's house before, never sat down for dinner except with a foster family. She was like a fluttery moth, drawn to the light but afraid of the heat. But she figured it out, whatever it was she had to work out with this Shirley.

As it happened, the night Rosalie came for dinner was the same night that Anthony came home from the hospital. Auntie made a big pot of beef soup and a plate full of fry bread before she left to pick him up, driving a rental car while hers was getting fixed. We met her coming out the front door, so she barely had time to shake Rosalie's hand. She didn't even remember to say that she knew Ray. I thought there would be plenty of time for visiting later.

When we sat at the kitchen table, first thing I learned was that this girl could eat, wolfing down two bowls of soup and at least two large wheels of fry bread, smothered in butter and honey. I piled a few books on the table as proof of homework for Auntie to see when she got home. Then we moved outside to the backyard, brushing dead leaves off a couple of plastic folding chairs that Auntie had found at a garage sale. It was one of those spring evenings that are near perfect, still warm from the afternoon sun but with a pinch of coolness rising up from the grass. A hummingbird buzzed nearby, drawn by the sweet perfume of the lilacs that looked like they were holding up one side of the garage. After hovering for a moment, it zipped past to the white blossoms on the neighbor's apple tree. Even the traffic noise had calmed down some. Best of all, the mosquitoes had not yet found us.

Sitting outside seemed to make it easier for us to talk about everything. The way Rosalie listened with her full attention made me want to tell her things that I didn't share with anybody. The way it was at home, with Ma, when she was drinking. How I saw my dad once at a powwow and he didn't know me. I told her all about Earl, how much in love we were, how he wasn't really a dealer like my auntie thought—he just sold some weed to his friends. I even told her my secret dream about becoming a lawyer who would kick government ass and bring home all the babies who'd been taken from the reservation. I don't remember if she said a single word the whole time I was talking, and she didn't stop me when I started calling her Rosie. Finally, I laughed and told her that in our friendship I was the mouth and she was the ears. She seemed to like that. Even in the dim light, I could see her smile.

When we heard noise inside that sounded like Auntie and Anthony were home, Rosie made a move to get up, but I raised my hand, shook my head. Let them settle in, I said. About a half hour passed before Auntie held the screen door open for Anthony, who bumped and hopped out sideways on his crutches. His one leg was in a huge white cast and his right arm was wrapped in a sling. Auntie was in a fluster, still half-mad about her car and trying her best to hide how relieved and happy she was to have him home. After refusing my offer to help, she carried out a kitchen chair for him to sit on and another for his leg, plus a blanket like he was sick. When he thanked her, she touched his shoulder briefly, but her eyes were sad. With a quick nod to Rosie, she went back in the house to clean up before bed. She had to get up early for her job at the Indian Health clinic, where she worked as a nurse helping people manage their diabetes. Seems like every Indian family we knew had someone who was diabetic.

We sat in silence until the house was quiet again, a single light turned on in the living room. The sky had turned a dusky blue and the stars came out a few at a time. When I was sure we were alone, I turned to Anthony.

"How bad is it?"

"Pretty bad. Earl dropped his bag when he ran, and the cops found it. It's not much, but with my priors, it looks like some time. Maybe rehab, if I'm lucky."

"Shit."

"Don't worry, Earl's fine. He's the Teflon man, nothing sticks."

Despite my auntie's warning not to see Earl anymore, we found ways to pass messages through Anthony. I needed to see him—until then I wouldn't be able to focus on much else. To relax, I pulled out a joint and lit it, breathing in a deep lungful of smoke. I passed it to Anthony, who took a big hit and held it before exhaling. He gestured toward Rosie with the joint, asking if she wanted to smoke. She hesitated, her eyes unreadable. She looked up once at the stars and then shook her head.

Rosie was a different kind of cat. I watched her watching Anthony and thought that I would have to find a way to warn Rosie not to get any ideas about him. To me, my big brother was a dropout, a pothead, and a player. Before he left school his junior year, the white girls used to giggle when he walked down the hall, the bad boy from across the tracks. He wasn't all that much taller than me, but—as he liked to say—he was all mean muscle. He was smart enough, but Anthony had an attitude that none of the teachers could tolerate. It didn't take much to set him off, either. At the slightest hint of disrespect, he was ready to fight. He played football for a single season, until he went offsides and punched the other team's center for his trash talk.

Then, in the last year, he'd started wearing his hair long again after reading about an organization called AIM, the American Indian Movement, up in the Cities. He'd told me this group stood up for the rights of Indians everywhere. They pushed back against police brutality, took over Alcatraz, and marched to Washington, DC, on the Trail of Broken Treaties.

"Cool," I'd told him. "Like that helps me get a job." Auntie Vera was on my back about starting a job as a waitress or a clerk at the Kwik Store. But secretly I was proud of him, because I knew he took grief for his braid from all the rednecks in town.

We were quiet for a few minutes, out in the dusk, as my brother and I passed the joint back and forth. I almost jumped when Rosie suddenly spoke aloud, to Anthony, not like a shy girl at all. More like she understood something about him that maybe I was missing, having known him all my life. Sometimes you don't see a change happening right in front of you.

"What will you do?" she asked. Anthony was usually such a smart-ass, I waited for him to toss some joke back to her. But he didn't. Like he knew that Rosie really wanted to know.

"I don't know," he said. "I don't think I have a lot of choices." He paused, as if uncertain whether to continue. Finally, he said, "When I was lying in the hospital bed that first night, still half-drunk and stoned on painkillers, an old man came to the foot of my bed. I wanted to tell him to get out, but I couldn't talk. The hallway was deserted and I didn't have a roommate. He just stood there, his lips moving like he was praying or singing. He had gray hair in braids and a knife on his belt. After a few minutes, he moved his hand flat across in front of him, like he was saying, Enough now, be done with this. Then he was gone. When I asked the nurse if she'd seen an old Indian wandering the halls, she said that sometimes people see things when they're on painkillers."

I snorted in disbelief. "So now you're saved?"

"I don't know," he repeated, taking my question more seriously than I had intended. "When Dad left, I didn't know what to do. He ripped a hole in me, in us, that nothing seems to fill. When my friend Joey shot himself last year, I thought about it. I mean, what's the point?"

I felt like crying, listening to him. I also wanted to shake him, to tell him to snap out of it. If you don't fight back, then it's game over.

Rosie said nothing, just sat there like she was turning over his words in her mind. I could see the backyard light reflected in her glasses, shining like the eyes of a cartoon character. Then she reached behind her back and pulled out the book she'd been carrying in the pocket of her jeans. Handed it to me with a nod at Anthony. The cover was faded and beat-up, with lots of pages dog-eared at their corners. *Bury My Heart at Wounded Knee* by Dee Brown. Never heard of it. I handed it to Anthony, who seemed touched by the gesture, turning the book over and trying to read the back cover in the dark. Mumbled something that sounded like thanks.

"Tell us something about you, Rosie," I said, to change the mood. "You've heard our sad stories. Now it's your turn."

And she did, surprising the hell out of me.

"They wanted me to forget everything about my life before that day," Rosie began, her voice low. "I was supposed to be grateful for a bed with real sheets, for a flushing toilet, for a place in a family of ghosts who needed me to fill their emptiness. I had lost everything, but they told me I was ungrateful if I looked sad, if I pushed their bland food around my plate.

"My first foster dad was a truck driver, never home. His wife, my foster mom, had given birth to a daughter who died when she was three days old, a tiny wanáǧi who still haunted the rooms of their small rambler. When Laura spoke, she covered her teeth with her hand like she was embarrassed. Anyone could see her brokenness. But she was kind to me. Her husband stayed home for two days after I came, patting my head once with his meaty truck driver's hand before hiding behind his newspaper. It was painful to see her hover around him, like a dog bringing slippers. How hard she worked to make impressive dinners the two nights he was home. But she didn't understand about making food taste good, so the roast beef was tough, the mashed potatoes lumpy, the green beans limp."

I was starting to figure out that Rosie was a closet story-teller, piling up words and pictures in her head. Girl wasn't shy; she was just listening and gathering the little details that make a story come alive. That night, it was like she wasn't even with us, she was so deep into remembering.

"When he drove away," Rosie said, "Laura seemed both lost and relieved. Out came the orange juice and the vodka bottle, though she tried to block my view by turning her back to me. Afterward she took me shopping at Kmart, hitting the curb once and laughing. She wanted to steer me toward the dresses, the shiny shoes, little bows for my hair. I walked straight to the boys' department, picked out a sweatshirt, jeans, tennis shoes. When we made it safely back to her house, she fell asleep on the couch. Dishes were piled in the sink. I sat at the kitchen table and thought about my choices. I was only twelve.

"This woman, Laura, was a kind drunk. Maybe her lone-liness was so deep she was filling it the only way she could. Maybe she was a little like me. I decided I could help her out.

"Remembering the tasteless dinners, I rummaged in the garage until I found a piece of strong rope. In the backyard, near the shrubs, I rigged up a snare where I saw the most rab-bit scat. And then I went back inside and waited. That night, we ate leftovers. The next night, I fixed a bowl of cereal while Laura dozed on the couch. Finally, on the third morning, a plump rabbit was waiting in my snare. With a kitchen knife I cut its throat and quickly skinned it, slipping its body from its fur like peeling off a glove. I spread the fur to cure on one of the rose bushes. Already I was looking forward to rabbit stew. Real food.

"I carried my trophy inside, where Laura was paying bills at the kitchen table. Maybe I should have cleaned up first. When I held up our dinner, my hands still covered in blood, she screamed. Don't hurt me, she cried, don't come any closer. I tried to explain, to tell her that I brought fresh meat, that we could have a real dinner, but she misunderstood my step toward her as a threat. I guess I was still holding the knife. She screamed again and ran to the bedroom and locked the door. I laid my rabbit on the table. I was still sitting there when a policeman came to the door. Laura rushed to let him in, crying and waving toward the kitchen . . ."

At this point I caught Anthony's eye, and then I had to stop Rosie, I couldn't help it. I busted out with the biggest, loudest laugh, seeing the whole story through the magic lens of my high. It was the funniest thing I'd ever heard. Anthony was right there with me, giggling and moaning at the same time. After a second, Rosie joined in, and the three of us laughed until our stomachs hurt and we had tears in our eyes. Oh my goodness, my auntie would have loved this story. I'd have to remember to share it with her later. Who would have guessed that book-loving Rosalie, this tall nerd, was a real rabbit-hunting Indian?

When we had calmed down, Anthony asked her where she learned to hunt rabbits.

"From my father," she said. "Before he passed."

We were silent for a moment out of respect to her father. But the tragic rabbit story kept coming back to me, and then Anthony broke into a wheezing kind of leftover laugh, and that set us all off again.

Finally, when we calmed down once more, I asked her what had happened next.

"Well," she said, growing serious. "When the cop walked in and saw me sitting there with my skinned rabbit, he turned away to hide his smile. I guess he was a hunter, too. But the damage was done. In a few hours, the woman in the gray suit was back. By then, the rabbit was wrapped in newspaper and thrown in the garbage. My new clothes were stuffed in a grocery bag, along with my father's hunting cap. Laura kept dabbing her eyes with her handkerchief, saying, This just won't work, my nerves aren't strong enough. I didn't blame her. She had her own troubles. When I rode away in the back seat of the gray lady's car, I saw Laura's ghostly face at the window." She paused, staring up at the sky.

"And then she brought me to live with Shirley," Rosie said, standing up as she spoke. Without another word, she turned and melted into the dusk, disappearing like I had dreamed her.

CHAPTER SEVEN

Rosalie Iron Wing
1979

For two more weeks, I checked the job board and want ads at Casey's every day, but nothing turned up. Finally, one Sunday evening, I set the alarm for 6:00 a.m. I woke early the next morning, anxious that I would oversleep, and listened to a light rain tapping against the window. Would corn detasselers work in this weather? I decided it was worth the walk across town to find out. I dressed quickly and braided my hair to keep it out of the way. I did not have boots, glasses, a hat, or rain gear. For lunch, I made two jelly sandwiches. As I grabbed a lunch bag from the cupboard, I saw a roll of garbage bags. I cut a few quick holes in one for my neck and arms and pulled it over my sweatshirt. Pig ugly, but the best I could do.

The rain had stopped by the time I'd walked the two miles to the high school, but my shoes and everything not covered by the garbage bag were soaked. A large group of my former classmates were standing together, all smiles and reunion hugs, brightly colored in their raincoats and ponchos, like a flock of birds. I sensed their sideways glances, the smiles hidden behind hands, a sudden burst of laughter. I kept my distance, skirting the edge of the parking lot, as I willed myself to become invisible, to blend with the rain-soaked pavement.

When the first school bus pulled up, the group surged forward, each person eager to find a place on one of the big farms, where they paid the best wages. A second bus quickly filled with the other half of the group, leaving behind me and two mismatched boys, one short with pimples, the other six feet tall, a mess of sharp bones. I recognized them from school. We were all three familiar with being chosen last.

When the buses had gone, I noticed a familiar rusty pickup truck parked in the lot. The farmer from Casey's was leaning against its bed, wearing the same old John Deere seed cap. He spat once and shook his head. Unlatching the back gate, he waved us over.

"Hope you all are better farmers than you look," he said, gesturing at us to climb into the back, where he had spread a ragged tarp over the pungent remains of dried manure, with a couple of hay bales to lean against. If he recognized me, he gave no sign.

We spread out as best we could, with the truck lurching ahead before we were fully settled. On the highway, my garbage bag whipped and rattled, threatening to tear itself into tiny wind-borne bits of plastic. Like the others, I tucked my chin into my sweatshirt, wrapped my arms around my black shell, and endured the rain-chilled air that had not yet warmed for the day. The farmer drove fast down County Road 15, heading west before he got to New Ulm, the next big town along the river. One of the boys pointed out the Daly place, where a school bus was parked alongside the driveway, spilling a crowd of teenagers onto a manicured lawn.

As the farmer slowed to make the turn onto a rut-filled gravel road, I was grateful that the rain had dampened the heavy dust that would surely rise in billowing clouds later. My sweatshirt felt sodden and heavy; my jeans clung to my legs. Already the July sun was well above the windbreak of trees on the horizon, its searing rays no longer filtered by green leaves. We were the only truck on the road.

Now that we could hear one another, the boys introduced themselves. The short one was Peter, the tall one Carl. Then Peter told us, waving at the cab, "I know this guy. Me and my dad ran into him last year at the hardware store. According to my dad, his family used to be big around here, but after his old man died, he kind of fell apart, took to drinking pretty hard. It's just a matter of time before he loses the farm." I kept my mouth shut; I wasn't impressed. Peter sounded like somebody's parrot, repeating gossip.

The road curved sharply to the west, past windbreaks formed by small clumps of oak and basswood trees, and then fields of green corn growing in tidy, regimented rows. A red-winged blackbird trilled from its perch on a cattail down in the ditches where the rain had pooled into shallow marshes. A mile or two later, after a half-hour ride that seemed like much longer, we turned down a long driveway, passing an unpruned orchard heavy with young apples. We parked in front of a barn that was sun-bleached to a dull gray. Tufts of hay sprouted from its upper window. A slatted corncrib was sorely in need of paint. A two-story farmhouse, with its wraparound porch, was a sign there had been better days for this place. From the shades pulled down over every window, and the screen door hanging on one hinge, I guessed the farmer must live alone. Across the yard, an old coonhound with a white face slowly wagged his tail in greeting. A handful of hens pecked at the loose gravel.

When I climbed down from the truck, my body ached with relief to be off the road. I stopped and listened to the quiet that had settled on every field. I had not known this kind of peace since I left home, when I used to wake each morning to the sound of wind rustling pine branches against my window.

"Hey," the farmer said, snapping his fingers in my direction. "Pay attention. All of you farmhands, listen up. My name is John Meister, and this is my farm, Green Meadow. That outhouse over there is for you. Nobody is allowed in the house."

In a few terse sentences he explained why we were there. Near as I could follow, a machine had come through the day before and pulled off most of the male tassels on one variety of corn. That way pollen from another variety could be carried by the wind to the female ears, making a new blend of corn. John said, "Corn sex," then paused as if waiting for a laugh, but all eyes in our group were focused on the ground. He shook his head again as he looked at us. "Your job," he said, "is to remove any tassels that the machine missed."

He pointed at Carl's skinny white legs. "You don't want any skin showing when you're out in the corn. Otherwise you'll get what we call 'corn rash' from the sharp edges of the leaves. Think of hundreds of little paper cuts all over your legs."

After he'd handed out pairs of mismatched mud-crusted gloves, we were briskly herded to the edge of the first field. John gave a quick demonstration of the best ways to grasp each tassel, give it a sharp yank, and drop it to the ground. As we moved slowly down the first row, my tennis shoes sank into rain-drenched mud. Water from the corn leaves soaked my sleeves and pants. Halfway down the row, my shoulders ached and my arms grew heavy. As the sun rose higher, the temperature climbed well into the eighties, turning the black garbage bag into a steamy, sweaty nightmare. I chucked it between two rows of corn. Only the thought of a paycheck kept me going, kept me moving long past the point when my muscles burned, my hands shook from fatigue, and sweat poured down my face.

By noon we had all peeled off layers of clothing and flung them into a pile by the water jug. Our arms and faces were streaked with mud; hair clung to our skin in sweaty tendrils. No one cared; we were too focused on survival. In midafternoon, the sun beat down in a fury, raising humid waves of heat that seemed to warp the air around us. Even the raucous crows fell silent and lost interest in the corn. Carl was the first to disappear, followed an hour later by Peter. That left me and John. I wanted to quit more than anything, to give up my dream of a paycheck just to lie down in the shade and never raise my arms again. But something in the way John had looked us all over that morning and shaken his head was enough to keep me moving. Every time I wanted to quit, I looked at his sweaty, sunburned neck and took one more tassel in my hand.

That night I slept like the dead. I'd told Shirley earlier in the evening who I was working for, and she said to me, "You watch yourself with him. That family is bad news, drinkers and fornicators. You come home pregnant, you'll be out so fast it'll make your head spin." I'd left the room before she could really get started up on one of her favorite topics. When my alarm rang at 6:00 a.m., I groaned as I shut it off. There was no way I was going back. Nothing, not a goddamn thing, was worth that. Then I shut my eyes. Saw John's sweaty neck. Listened to the creaks in the house as it shifted in the wind. This house was not mine, would never be a home for me. I sat up.

The group that gathered in the parking lot that morning was smaller than the day previous and more subdued. People yawned, rubbed their eyes, rolled sore shoulders. Surprisingly, Carl was back, this time wearing pants. Peter jumped out of his mom's car as we were climbing into the back of the truck, his hair uncombed like he had just rolled out of bed. John was quiet, too, saying little as he closed the tailgate. I caught a whiff of sour breath as he passed, the stale hangover from too many beers.

John drove the back roads that day, sparing us the wind-whipped fury of the highway. Leaning against a hay bale, I listened to the *thump, thump* of seams in the pavement. When John pointed out his window at the sky above, I squinted into the sun and saw the small speck of an eagle riding the warm air currents, its white head barely visible. The two boys chattered on about the new *Space Invaders* video game, oblivious.

The worst part about a second day is knowing how hard it will be. With the sun coming on full force early that morning, we took more water breaks. Even so, we managed to clear slightly more ground by noon than we had the first day. John seemed cheered by our progress.

During lunch break I sat with the boys in the shade by the water jug, our boots and socks tossed to the side to let our feet cool down. I pulled out the book I carried in my bag,

Moby-Dick, assigned in senior English class. I hadn't finished it then, but I still wanted to know what happened to the whale. Lying on his back in the grass, Peter gave a deep sigh. "I can't imagine why anyone would ever want to be a farmer."

"Me neither," Carl replied. "Nothing but blood, sweat, and tears. And more sweat." His fingers riffed on an air guitar.

Peter and Carl laughed, not realizing that John had come up behind them and heard their conversation. They both jumped and scrambled for their boots when he said, "What about you, Rosalie? You agree with these boys?"

I thought for a moment. It surely was tedious, hot work.

"I don't know about detasseling," I said. "But I like hearing the wind in the corn."

John looked directly at me for the first time since I had climbed into his truck the day before. Giving a quick nod and smile, he clapped his hands, the signal that break was over.

Later that afternoon, I found myself at the end of a row at the same time as John. I called out a question: "So why did you want to be a farmer?"

He laughed. "Never really thought about it. I was raised up working these fields. Can't imagine living anywhere else." He took off his cap and wiped his damp forehead on his sleeve. "I like seeing the sunrise. I like the smell of fresh-turned soil."

"I like the smell of money," Peter yelled. We all laughed. Except for the big farms where the school buses were parked, most farmers I had seen drove old trucks and counted their pennies, like everyone else. Peter seemed destined for office work.

One morning about two of the three weeks in, I was the only one waiting for John's truck. Peter and Carl, now fast friends, had the day off to go register at the college for fall classes. After a moment's hesitation, John nodded at the passenger door. "May as well ride up front today."

For several miles we rode in silence, neither of us feeling the need for small talk. Finally, he asked, "You got plans for college?"

"Nope."

A pause while he lit a cigarette. "How come, if you don't mind my asking? You seem a whole lot smarter than those two ding-dongs. Never seen you without a book."

I shrugged. "I need money for a place of my own."

"Ain't you kind of young to be worrying about your own place already? Your folks agree with that?"

"I'm on my own," I said, turning toward the window.

We didn't have anything more to say after that. At the farm I greeted Boomer, the old hound, rubbing his ears the way he liked. John came from the barn and handed me a pair of gloves that matched and tall rubber boots for the mud. I barely had time to mumble my thanks before he was striding off toward the corn. All morning we worked in silence, falling into an easy rhythm. A light breeze helped keep the humidity down. While it was still backbreaking work, I liked being outside. If I made the mistake of looking around and seeing nothing but corn on every side, sometimes I struggled to catch my breath, feeling the edge of panic as if I could get lost in the long row. I had to stop, close my eyes, and listen to the soft rustle of wind moving through the leaves, as if the corn was singing just loud enough for me to hear.

At lunchtime, I headed to the truck to get my jelly sandwiches. I heard a whistle and turned to see John gesturing toward the house. Surprised again by his friendliness, I thought,

Better be careful, no telling what he thinks he can do when left alone with a girl. I stepped up onto the porch and into the mudroom, where a plaid wool jacket hung above a stack of empty beer cases. The kitchen was big enough to hold a long wood table, where farmhands would have once eaten their noon meal. The stove was covered in a fine layer of grease, and fingerprints darkened the white cupboards. But it was tidy in a bachelor way, with a single plate and cup in the sink.

As I stood in the doorway, John called over his shoulder for me to come in. When I didn't move, he turned and looked at me. Came over to where I stood and said, "You have no reason to be afraid of me. I don't know how they treat you in town, where you live, but I ain't like that. My mama raised me to respect women."

"And your daddy? How did he raise you?"

He turned back toward the stove, lit a match for the pilot light, and set a black skillet on the burner to heat. "He raised me to know a hard day's work. To respect money. To always try to better myself."

"He teach you how to drink?"

A pause as he cracked eggs into sizzling butter. "You don't beat around the bush, do you?"

"Saves time."

John was silent for a few minutes, focusing his attention on the frying pan. I guessed he must have been lonely, living there by himself. It seemed as if everyone in town had already made up their minds about him, so maybe it was a relief to talk to a person like me, who didn't care. It was almost as though we had something in common. We were both outsiders.

"I never really wanted to do anything but farm," John said, sliding an egg onto my plate. "Now I'm just trying to hang on.

I don't want to be the one who loses this place. Sometimes the worry gets to me, is all."

After lunch, he offered to show me the house. As we walked through, he pointed out the original wainscoting in the dining room, and the ornate wood banister worn nearly bare in places, its finish rubbed away by him and his older brother sliding down at high speed. He paused at the bottom of the stairs, looking up as if waiting for someone.

"My family has lived in this house all the way back to the original homestead in the 1860s," John said. "Every generation has tried to add on and build it up a bit more. At least until it came to me." He gave a sharp, humorless laugh.

I didn't ask if he knew who had lived here before his family, before the government cut the woods and prairie into 160-acre pieces. I had no patience for teaching people their own history.

I could see that the house was well built to withstand farm life. The wallpaper was beginning to curl at the edges; the wood floors were scratched and dull. A gold couch, oddly out of place, stood next to a recliner still bearing a dark shadow on the headrest from his father's hair cream. A china cabinet stood in one corner holding his mother's cherished dishes. John seemed to need my approval, glancing at me from the corner of his eye. I nodded and turned away.

We worked hard that afternoon, avoiding each other as if the unexpected intimacy of our lunch was more than either of us was prepared to deal with. He was gruff and silent on the drive back to town, dropping me off at the high school without a word.

The next morning, the boys and I stood waiting for the truck, but John never showed. I felt heat prickle the skin on my arms, raise the blood to my flushed face. He owed us money and I meant to be paid. The following day I was the only one waiting, the other two having given up. As soon as the truck stopped, I stomped over and smacked the window.

"What the hell?" John said, jumping out and slamming his door.

"Where were you?" I yelled, not caring that the other detasselers had stopped boarding the bus to watch the show I was putting on. So much for being invisible.

"My truck broke down, okay? The shocks gave out from hauling you assholes to the farm every day. Cost me two hundred dollars to get it fixed."

I took a deep breath. "So you weren't trying to cut and run."

"What? No. No. I would never do that."

"Fine."

"Fine."

After slamming the door on both sides, we drove off, leaving a group of curious, amused faces behind us. Once we left the city limits, the tension slowly dissipated into a peaceful silence.

"You live with Shirley Martin? She your foster mom?"

"You been checking on me?"

"I asked around some."

"Why?"

"I asked myself, What's an Indian girl doing in this town? Nearest reservation is seventy miles west. They come here to shop, but not many want to live here. People have long memories, still hold a grudge from that old war."

"I've noticed."

"No wonder you're so damned prickly."

I said nothing. Some things just can't be explained. I had

read about the war, even visited the battlefields with my father. John could do the same.

After a long morning in the fields, I was again invited in to share lunch. He whipped up another meal of fried eggs and Spam. When he had polished his plate clean, John lit a cigarette and poured himself a cup of coffee while I washed up.

"What happened to your family, if you don't mind me asking?"

I searched for words, but my throat closed and I couldn't speak. My past was too raw, too unfinished for me to put into words. Finally, I said, "Never knew my mother. My dad went out hunting one morning and never came back. They told me his heart gave out. Guess they couldn't find any other family."

I was grateful for his silence. After a moment, he asked, "What kind of work did he do?"

"He went to college on the GI Bill and taught science at the high school. They fired him for saying that Dakhóta people came from the stars. He showed up at a school board meeting and tried to prove it to them with their own science. But they said that was godless nonsense. Parents did not want their children learning that from him."

"What do you mean, their own science?"

"You know, that the earth is made of the same elements as the stars. My father told them that the elements came here as asteroids. He even brought a science journal to show them that white scientists agreed. They refused to listen. Finally, they gave him a small settlement to go away."

"Did he?"

"We were already living in the cabin that my great-great-grandfather had built north of here, the place where I was born. He didn't like people all that much, brown or white, and said it was better for him to be away from all the drinking in town. He decided we could take care of ourselves. He knew how to hunt and trap, and he homeschooled me until he died. Taught me how to snare a rabbit and know the stars by their real names. How to gather plants and what they're used for. I read a lot of books."

"He teach you anything practical, like keeping house and cooking?"

"Not so much."

"Well, that does beat all. I never met a girl like you before."

That afternoon, when the heat came on so strong the sweat poured down my face and drenched the kerchief I wore around my neck, I looked up to see John pointing toward the woods that grew along the north side of the field. Pushing aside cornstalks to create a new path, I cut across the field, stopping now and again to peer over the tall corn. Finally, I reached the shade, where John stood waiting.

"Too damn hot to work," he said, pulling off his gloves. "I want to show you something."

I was so grateful to be out of the sun that, at first, I was unwilling to move. The temperature was much cooler beneath the shelter of the old oak trees, a loamy scent rising from leaves that had decayed underfoot. Since most of the original forest had been cleared decades earlier, I was surprised that John's family had kept this ten-acre piece of woods. This was prime farmland, riding along a bluff on the Cottonwood River, a small offshoot that eventually joined the Minnesota River farther east. At least his family had had the good sense to settle near water.

John led the way on a well-worn deer path through the woods until he reached a small opening in the dense underbrush. He paused, looked at the ground, and knelt in the long grass. He cleaned leaves and twigs from the surface of a marble stone that bore a chiseled inscription: Edward Thomas Meister, 1946–1970. I helped him clear off two more stones that bore his parents' names.

"This here is what's left of my family," he said quietly. "My older brother, Eddie, was supposed to inherit the farm, but he was killed in Vietnam.

"Eddie was four years older than me, so he was my hero, especially when he enlisted in the army. Dad said he should go, he'd make do with a hired fellow and me after school. Then Ma got sick with breast cancer and died. Seemed like Dad got old overnight. I couldn't stand to see the way he let things go around the farm. I told him time and again that we needed to keep up with changes. He wouldn't listen."

John shook his head, staring off beyond the trees. His fingers curled into a loose fist.

"One day we were arguing, like usual, and I guess he got fed up with me. He looked me straight in the eye and said, Over my dead body. I was eighteen, so I figured it was time for me to go be a man, too. I enlisted, but it didn't last long. My dad had a stroke and they let me come back home. I think it was the news about my brother that probably got the best of him."

"And your mama, what was she like?" I asked.

"Like an angel," he replied. "She used to win prizes at the county fair for her pies and canned tomatoes. One night, when the old man drank himself to sleep in his recliner, I asked her why she never took us out of there. She told me, 'Your daddy is a good man. He puts food on the table and a roof over our heads. He doesn't gamble or run with women. Can't ask for more than that.' She used to pray a lot. She never missed a Sunday at church until she got sick. I think she was disappointed in me, the way I turned out."

He stood up and brushed the grass from his knees. Turned without another word and led us down a steep hill to the river, reminding me of the path in Mankato where I'd spent so much of my free time. Halfway down the hill, he turned and offered his hand to help me over a large rock. I hesitated before taking hold, feeling the warmth of his skin, the strength in his fingers. I quickly pulled away.

We sat on boulders in the shade of a cottonwood tree that was leaning at a precarious angle, its roots exposed as the water slowly eroded the bank over the years. Stripping off boots and socks, we plunged our sweaty feet into cold water that moved swiftly over moss-covered rocks. I scooped up a handful of water to splash on my face and soaked my kerchief before wrapping it around my neck. Then I lay back, feeling the ache in my shoulders soothed by the stone.

Sounding like he was falling asleep, John spoke in a soft voice I could barely hear above the ripple of the water.

"Ma liked these woods so well that my daddy never had the heart to clear this piece of land." A few minutes of silence were followed by a faint snore. I felt peaceful lying near him, and safe, a feeling I had not known in years. A strand of hair drifted across his forehead, and I had to resist an impulse to brush it back.

The silence was pierced every now and again by the drowsy, high-pitched hum of a cicada, while the leaves overhead fluttered in a shifting pattern of light and shadow. My father had called the cottonwood trees "star medicine," and he'd shown me how to snap their twigs and find the star shape hidden inside. He'd said this tree was a favorite nesting place for bald eagles. I fell asleep trying to remember how he made a healing tea from the inner bark. But it was Gaby who came to me instead, reminding me of the last time I saw her, a memory I had tried my best to forget.

CHAPTER EIGHT

Rosalie Iron Wing
1976

Before I met Gaby, I never had a close friend. I don't think either of us knew what it meant to have a best girlfriend, someone who could be trusted with your secrets, who would always help you out, whether that meant rewriting Gaby's homework or escaping Shirley's house. We were meant to be together, a couple of coyote pups, who learned to hunt as a pack in order to survive. We had dreams, too, about moving to the Twin Cities together, or spending a year traveling to powwows all over the country. Gaby knew how to contest dance, even winning a few before she had moved to Mankato. But then she'd bring up Earl, and our daydreams would go up in smoke.

For someone like me, who'd never known a real family after my father passed, it was as if I'd gained a sister, a brother, and even an auntie, who always made me feel welcome at her house. In those early months of getting to know her, Gaby was like a sip of water on a hot summer day, perfectly sweet and cold, quenching a thirst I didn't even know I had.

A few weeks into my sophomore year, we were sitting outside during lunch break to avoid the cafeteria crowd. I tore my jelly sandwich into small pieces that I tossed to a gang of sparrows who had become nearly tame, a few even pecking crumbs from my hand. The day was fall chilly, with ragged clouds moving fast across the sky and the kind of wind that brings rain later. Gaby picked at her nail polish, brushing flecks of jungle pink from her bell-bottom jeans. She crossed her legs at the ankle, showing off the high-heeled boots that had been a gift from Earl. I wondered what her auntie Vera thought of those boots.

"I'm bored," Gaby said, followed by one of her big, dramatic sighs.

I brushed the last few crumbs from my hand and watched the sparrows scatter toward the nearby elm trees, startling a crow into flight. In the four months that we had been hanging out, I had learned that boredom was a death sentence for whatever Gaby and I were doing. She didn't like to read, or study, or do anything that required her attention and focus for more than a few minutes. I noticed that in the history class we shared this year, she doodled in her notebook, twirled a strand of hair around her finger as she stared out the window. The teacher, Miss Haglund, assumed she wasn't paying attention, and Gaby's grades seemed to prove her right. But one day Miss Haglund made the mistake of asking her which lands in Minnesota were included in the 1851 Traverse des Sioux Treaty, thinking she had caught Gaby unprepared. Gaby turned slowly from the window and stared at Miss Haglund before answering.

"My land. And you're standing on it."

That was the Gaby I liked best, the one she hid beneath a cloud of pot smoke and hair spray.

To be honest, I was afraid that Gaby would get bored with me. Or that she'd start listening to the whispered jokes that floated behind us when we walked down the hall: Pocahontas and Sasquatch, Hoss and Little Joe, word arrows flung in a gauntlet of teenage scorn. She sailed through it all, head high, occasionally flipping her middle finger. The other students seemed to sense that she was ready for a fight, anytime, anyplace. Me, they'd never noticed, at least before Gaby chose me as her friend.

Most days we ended up at her house after school, pretending to do homework while we talked in the backyard. I told her how Shirley's family would often eat dinner without me, leaving me to forage in the fridge for leftovers. How Shirley took my books, although she never read anything but gossip magazines about Hollywood stars. Gaby told me about the first time she did it with Earl, assuring me they were careful, that he always pulled out so she wouldn't get pregnant. She laughed at the look on my face and told me that someday I would understand.

Now Gaby asked, "Are you even listening to me?" with a sharpness that warned me her patience was growing thin.

"Sorry." I shook my head. "Why are you bored?"

"If I have to sit through one more lecture on white-guy classic literature, I will kill myself."

"Didn't read the book, huh?"

"I fell asleep. I want to get out of here. Let's go shopping."

"With what? We don't have any money."

"I've got twenty bucks that Earl sent me. That's enough for bus fare to Salvation Army, where we can buy books for you, a new shirt for me, and a malt afterward. My treat."

I hesitated before answering. I didn't want to admit that I had been looking forward to spending the afternoon at the library. I had stumbled onto a book about the petroglyphs at Jeffers, thousands of years old, carved by Indian people from all over the country. I was fascinated by the idea that these symbols told stories, that they held a message for us. I wished I could tell my father about it, ask him if he'd ever seen them. Jeffers was less than a hundred miles from where we were sitting. But I didn't think Gaby would understand. After a brief, silent struggle, I agreed to go along with her plan.

We slipped away from the school grounds without being seen and hopped the city bus to the Salvation Army on Riverfront Drive. Walking in through the double glass doors, I was overwhelmed by the size of the store: dozens and dozens of racks and piles of used clothes, bins of Halloween decorations, furniture, toys, and desks. Gaby pressed a five-dollar bill into my hand and told me to go crazy with it, before walking over to the clothing area. She could pull out an old jacket, add a belt and a bright T-shirt, and look like she stepped out of a magazine. No amount of money was ever going to do that for me. I headed straight to the book aisle.

Looking back, I wish I had paid more attention to the small, perfect details of that afternoon. The way Gaby found me and insisted that I look at clothes with her. She would pull out an outrageous prom dress and tell me to try it on, both of us laughing until I nearly split its seams. We added hats to our outfits, a boa scarf for her, a fake-fur stole for me. Then she got serious, finding a denim skirt in my size and a red shirt that fit the awkward curves of my too-tall body. "Now stand up straight," she ordered, steering me in front of the mirror. "See? You're not the hulk that you think you are." I laughed. That afternoon, I bought clothes instead of books, a first for me.

Afterward, when we were sitting at a table outside an ice cream shop with two full bags at our feet, Gaby said in a casual voice, "Rosie, I have a favor to ask."

"Sure, whatever you need."

"Well, I haven't seen Earl in a whole week. I kind of told my auntie that you invited me over to spend the night."

I wasn't sure what to say. But I had a bad feeling about it. Any time Gaby was around Earl, she turned into someone I didn't know, maybe didn't even want to know. But I was afraid to say that to her.

"It's no big deal," she continued, as if daring me to argue with her. "If my auntie calls—and she probably won't—just tell her I'm in the bathroom or something. And then leave a message at Earl's cousin's house. He'll know where to find us." She paused. "Come on, Rosie, don't look so glum. How else are we supposed to have some alone time? I know how much you hate Shirley spying on you all the time. Well, my auntie is not much better. She hates Earl."

"Earl is a drug dealer," I said. "Look at the mess Anthony is in. He's sitting in jail because of Earl. Think that's a coincidence? Have you thought about how much this will hurt your auntie if she finds out?"

Gaby sighed the way she did when she'd run out of arguments but refused to change her mind. I knew what she was thinking: I had never been in love, so what could I possibly know about it?

"Look," she said, leaning toward me. "If Earl was such a bad guy, would Anthony be his best friend? When Anthony gets back, maybe the four of us can hang out."

Yeah, right. I almost walked away when she said that. She knew I had a bit of a crush on her brother, though I had met Anthony only the one time. He was clearly struggling, trying to find his way, but now it seemed he might be on the right track. Gaby had told me that Anthony was talking to the AIM members who visited the jail. He was trying to get sober, and I wanted to believe he could do it. Maybe we could hang out sometime.

"Okay," I agreed, so we could change the subject.

That night, Auntie Vera called. It was around seven o'clock, after dinner, and I was cleaning up the kitchen, taking my time in case the phone rang.

"Oh, Rosie, this is Auntie Vera. I don't mean to bother you, I'm just calling to see that Gaby has everything she needs. I turn in early, you know, for work."

"Hi, Auntie Vera. Yeah, um, Gaby is in the . . . in the shower. Can she call you back?"

"No, no, just tell her I called. You girls get to bed at a decent hour. Don't stay up all night talking, you hear?"

"We won't. I'm pretty tired," I said, giving my best fake yawn. There was no way I was going to sleep. My heart was pounding and my palms were sweaty from the guilt I felt in lying to Auntie Vera. But I had promised Gaby. I decided there was nothing to worry about.

The next day, Gaby wasn't in class. I tried calling her house after school, but no one answered. She didn't come the next day, either. On the third day, I came down the front steps of the school to find her auntie waiting for me, arms folded across her chest. Vera's eyes pinned me like a butterfly in biology class.

"I know you lied to cover up for Gaby," she said, without bothering to greet me. "I know you must think you were being a good friend to her, so that she could sneak off with that skunk Earl. I also know you don't have a mother or family to teach you how to be a true friend, otherwise I would beat your ass black-and-blue rather than stand here talking to you." I opened my mouth to explain, but she held up her hand and charged on.

"Here's how much you helped your friend. A few nights ago, when she was supposed to be studying with you, she and Earl were busted during a drug deal. He's going away for some serious time, and I'm grateful for that. Because Gaby is still a minor who's never been in trouble before, the judge is willing to be lenient. But she's also pregnant, so she'll spend her time at a residential home for unwed teens."

She took a step toward me, and I shrank back, hearing the rage in her voice.

"I don't ever want to hear your name again. Do not contact my niece."

She stomped back to her car and drove away, taking with her the only friend I had.

CHAPTER NINE

Rosalie Iron Wing
1979

Long, steamy July days created their own slow rhythm as my hands grew calloused from field work. Each morning I woke at dawn and every night I fell into bed before dark, too tired to dream. My skin, roasted to a rich brown, smelled of corn pollen; my hair was streaked by sunlight. I grew even taller, my awkward slump straightened by the act of reaching for the tassels. Corn made me strong. Every day she whispered her greetings in a flutter of green leaves.

Three weeks after we started working, when we were nearly done detasseling the last field of corn, John told us that we would be paid in cash the following afternoon.

Peter and Carl had come back to work, chattering away about dorm rooms and classes and credits. They avoided looking at me, as if certain that I would not be joining them. And they were right. I needed the money to move out, as I'd told John, but my grades were also a problem. The school counselor had told me I scored high on the entrance tests, but ultimately my absenteeism had affected my grades. Before this job, I thought I'd be looking for work at the nearest Hy-Vee store. Or maybe someone would have been willing to pay me to do their dirty work, given my experience babysitting Shirley's younger kids after school and cleaning her house.

But all that had changed with the promise of the hard-earned cash that would be mine tomorrow. That night, I sat on my bed with a nub of pencil and a piece of paper, calculating roughly how much I'd earned. After studying the want ads, I figured I had enough for a down payment on an apartment and the first month's rent, if I could find a room-mate. I would need to find another job, for sure, or maybe some old lady would trade me her basement in exchange for help around the house. Or I could buy a bus ticket to the Twin Cities and rent a room somewhere while I looked for work. Suddenly my life was filled with possibilities, all of them taking me out of this house, never to return. I wished I could call Gaby and share my good news with her. Instead, I hummed to myself and imagined how satisfying it would feel to tell Shirley I was leaving. I almost laughed out loud at the thought.

Then I heard Shirley's heavy footsteps coming down the basement stairs, almost as if she'd sensed my good mood. She rarely came here, instead sending her laundry down with me to be washed, folded, and put away upstairs. Like this wasn't family space, just an empty room to store junk. So why now, why today? Maybe she had a soft side after all; maybe she'd realized that she would miss my unpaid labor when I was gone.

I shoved my paper and pencil into the pocket of my sweatshirt and sat still. Shirley took her time, as if inspecting things along the way, before pushing open my folding vinyl door without bothering to knock. Looked around my room like she was afraid to get dirty.

I'd heard people say that Shirley was a good-looking woman, especially for someone pushing forty. She got her hair done regularly, dyed near black and permed into brittle curls around her head. Painted her nails a color I called vampire red. They didn't see how she let herself go around the house, wearing a shapeless cotton dress and slippers worn down at the heel. But it was the eyes that truly gave her away, that revealed the greedy, openmouthed demon that possessed her. I meant nothing more to her than a monthly check from the state. She used her eyes like razor blades, leaving invisible cuts all along my skin. I waited, every muscle in my body tensed.

"Well, Rosalie, I hear you've been holding out on me," she said, her soft voice like a snake's rattle before the strike.

"I don't know what you're talking about." Damn her, I sounded like a pouting child.

"Oh, I think you do. One of those nice young men that you've been working with told his mother, who belongs to my card club, about the money you all are making on what's-his-name's farm. I thought you were volunteering just to get out of the house. Now I hear that you're getting paid tomorrow."

I jumped to my feet, panicked, feeling her beady eyes on me as I paced the room.

"That's my money. You have no right. I earned it."

"You have no idea how expensive it is for me to keep supporting you," she hissed. "It's only fair that we split that money. You may keep half. Do I need to make a call to this farmer, or can I trust you to do what's right?"

"No!"

I turned toward the door, intent on escape, and she grabbed my braid as if to stop me. Without thinking, I slapped her face as hard as I could, packing all of my rage, hatred, and frustration into the sting of my hand on her skin. And then I ran.

I headed for the river. Plunged straight in, up to my knees, still shaking, my mouth filled with the bitter aftertaste of spent rage. Afterward I curled up on the grassy bank with my arms around my wet knees, head down, feeling an emptiness unlike anything I had ever known. As if the little bit of hope that kept me alive had dried up and blown away. I lay there, shivering, while the temperature slowly dropped as the sun sank behind the trees. I lay there all night, listening to the sounds of the city as it slept. In the early hours, a vole looked at me curiously before creeping toward the garbage can up on the sidewalk.

When the sun's first light finally rose in the east, casting a soft glow across the river, I made my slow way across town to the high school parking lot. I sat down on the curb and waited.

Peter was the first one to show up, dropped off by his card-playing traitor mother. He looked at me and said, "Shit,. tough night?"

I didn't answer.

▭

After one last, grueling day in the fields, we stood around the water jug waiting for John to return from the house with our money. I wondered what was taking so long. I began to pace across the yard, chewing on a strand of hair as I worried about going back home after my fight with Shirley. I knew she would be waiting for me, mad as hell, plotting her revenge. She might have already called my caseworker.

John finally came out and stood in front of us, smiling. He paid in cash, counting the bills slowly into each hand. I had earned a pile of money, more than I had ever seen in all of my young life.

A honking horn broke up our little group. The two boys sprinted to their friend's car, heading straight to their new lives on campus. John would give me a ride back to town as usual. He seemed in no hurry to leave.

"Rosie," he said, startling me with a sudden change in his tone. When had I become Rosie? "If you're not in a hurry to get back, let's sit for a minute."

We sat in a swing shaded by the overgrown lilac bushes on the north side of the house. For a few minutes we sat without talking, looking out at the oak trees on the far edge of the field.

John cleared his throat. "Rosie, this place isn't much, not like it used to be. But it's a start. Two people could make a go of it. You could have a real home here with me." His calloused hands twisted his cap. "What I'm trying to say is, we could get married." He looked like a boy in that moment, with his torn T-shirt and jeans faded nearly white, his knee jiggling from nerves.

"What? Why?" I asked, when I had recovered from my shock. "You paid me. You don't owe me anything."

He thought for a moment, searching for the right words. "Company, I guess. It's a big house to stand empty. You need a place to live. I reckon we could help each other out."

I could understand that. We shared the same kind of loneliness. I had no family, no friends, no community that claimed me. All I wanted was to be safe, to find a place where no one would tell me how unwanted I was, or how ugly I was, how I would never amount to anything. Maybe that was true for him, too.

Still. I barely knew him. I remembered what my father once said to me: "When you're old enough, marry a Dakhóta." When I'd asked him why, he said, "Otherwise we'll end up with water in our veins." He wouldn't have approved of this, not one bit. But I didn't appreciate him dying on me, either. Sometimes we just have to make the best of it, the way things were.

"I can't marry you," I said bluntly. "But I need a place to stay for a couple of months. I can help out with the farm chores, at least until I find a job."

"Good Lord, do you have any idea what people would say if I had a teenage girl living here?"

"That you're a drinker and a fornicator?"

He sighed. "What you're suggesting might work up in the Cities. But out here, people still think that living together is a sin."

"But we wouldn't be living together. I'd be your employee."

"No one would believe that."

An awkward silence fell between us. Finally, he said, "Rosie, there are nights when I don't think I'm going to make it until the morning. I can't sleep. If I doze off, I wake up thinking I hear my brother calling, or my mother rattling pans in the kitchen. I don't want to live here alone anymore."

When he spoke, I could see the black hole of his emptiness, a place I knew well. I felt pity for him. Later on, I wondered if I might have made a different decision had I not fought with Shirley over the money. She was stealing my dream from me just as it was about to become real.

More than anything, I hoped the farm would be a safe place to be for a while. I had no intention of staying long; I assumed he knew that. Marrying was to keep the town from wearying itself with gossip. In my heart, I chose the river. Until I was ready to leave, I would stay here, near the water that flowed every day past the place where I was born. When I nodded, he said, "All right then," and kissed my cheek.

On my eighteenth birthday, we were married at the courthouse. A blustery north wind blew the few remaining leaves from the trees, as a cloud of blackbirds gathered in the top branches, seeming to mock me with their raucous calls. John stared at the floor with his hand clenched around a plain gold band, wearing jeans and a plaid shirt, his cap tucked in his back pocket. I stood at his side in a red wool dress I bought at the thrift store, a dull flush creeping across my neck. We did not speak to each other except to repeat the vows. The judge eyed us with curiosity and called in the secretary next door to be our witness.

I almost left the courthouse when it was made clear to me that marriage carried the expectation that I change my name. I stood there so long without picking up the pen that John grew nervous. Finally, he agreed that I would keep my family name and add Meister, without a hyphen. Just as he could not bear the thought of losing his family's land, I could not live without my family's name, all that was left to me in this new life.

Shirley and I had barely spoken since the summer. When I'd returned to her house on the last day of work, the news that I was marrying John had stopped her cold in the middle of a threat to call my caseworker. Her mouth dropped open and she looked like a fish gasping for air as she struggled to understand how anyone could want me. In one last squeeze, she said I could continue to live under her roof until I was no longer a minor but she would need to charge me rent. I said that was illegal. She gave me a small taunting smile, knowing I would not report her. Half my money was going to her one way or another. She was not invited to the wedding.

After the brief ceremony, John drove in silence back to the farm while I bit my fingernails down to the quick. I shook my head when he offered dinner at the VFW. He carried my bag of clothes upstairs and set it by the dresser in one of the spare bedrooms, mumbling that the drawers were already full in the room where he slept. I followed behind with my box of books. Two west-facing windows glowed with the last rays of the setting sun. A single bed with a white cotton bedspread was pushed against the wall, a table and lamp at its head, a braided rug on the wood floor. After he left, I slowly removed my dress and hung it in the closet next to a half dozen faded gingham dresses that must have belonged to his mother. Two pairs of her well-worn, sensible shoes were lined up on the floor. The room smelled of dust and mothballs.

How strange to move into a family's home and pretend that I belonged there. To walk through these rooms as if their history was now mine. I almost laughed out loud at the thought. As the room filled with shadows, I lay on the bed and stared at the crack in the ceiling, the twining roses on the wallpaper. I fell asleep.

That night, I woke in the blind dark, uncertain where I was for a few panic-filled moments, remembering how it felt to be twelve and alone in a stranger's house. Only by planning my escape could I relax enough to fall back asleep. The remaining half of my summer's pay was hidden in the back corner of a dresser drawer, inside my father's hunting cap. It wasn't enough for an apartment—but it was a start. I would stay until spring, when travel was easier. By then, I hoped, I would have figured out a way to make back the money I needed to start a new life.

Until I did, I would have to make the best of this marriage. I was not so naive as to think there was anything that came without a price. I took pride in sizing up a person and knowing not only what they wanted but what they would settle for. Some people were plain greedy, like Shirley, who could never look at me without dollar signs in her eyes, who sometimes gave in to meanness simply because I had no family to stop her.

The thing is I couldn't tell what John wanted from me. Once I caught him looking at my breasts, but he turned away as if embarrassed to be caught, and he was only twenty-eight. I thought maybe he wanted a housekeeper, an unpaid farmhand when needed, someone in his bed who was obligated to him. In my worst moments of fear, when I watched him drink a half dozen beers after supper, I imagined that as a drunk he would reveal his true mean self with his fists or his tongue, busting me down to nothing like other bullies I had known.

The first few weeks I was ready for him, watching his every move, from the slow way he walked out to the barn, to how he stood at the window studying the sky, holding a cup of coffee and a piece of toast he had made himself. In that time, I did nothing at all, meaning to show him he had not bought himself a cook or a maid or someone to climb on top of whenever he felt like it. I waited for him to come at me, to take offense

at the dishes piling up in the sink, the unswept floor, the way
I wore sweatpants every day and slept in the spare room. He
never said a word. He made himself fried eggs at lunch just
as he always had, politely offering to cook for me, too, then
washed up afterward.

He didn't seem angry or even surprised at my behavior.
More like he was content just to have a living presence in the
house, and the rest didn't matter. Since the farm was dead slow
in the winter, he spent most days out tinkering in the barn. He
spent his evenings drinking beer and watching television from
his daddy's recliner.

Once I realized that John was going to leave me be, I got
tired of the house. One morning after a storm had dropped
nearly ten inches of snow, I added thermal underwear beneath
my clothes, found a pair of tall winter boots in the closet,
and borrowed a barn coat that was hanging by the back door.
When I first walked outside, the air was so sharp I struggled
to breathe. I wrapped a scarf around my face and walked
across the driveway and alongside the barn, where I could see
a bare light bulb turned on over the workbench. When I came
past the corner of the barn, the wind hit me sideways, nearly
blowing me over.

Spread out in front of me was an untouched field of
white snow, a frozen emptiness that dissolved into a pale sky.
Occasional gusts raised up swirling ice devils. Cattle had been
known to get disoriented after a big snow and freeze to death
in conditions like these. I had to shield my eyes from the sun,
so strong was the reflected glare.

I knew where I wanted to go. At the far edge of this field
were the woods we had walked through in summer, leading

down to the river. The trees would block the wind and create a small sanctuary.

What I didn't know was how deeply the snow had drifted across the yard, away from the shelter of the barn. My first few steps sank into snow above my knees, the frozen crust bruising my skin through the heavy layers I wore. Each step meant plunging into the snow and then extracting the other boot. More than once I lost my balance and toppled over. Finally, the last time I fell, I rolled onto my back and stared up at the clear sky, without a single cloud or bird passing by.

Cradled in the snow, I felt the quiet that settles when the land is at rest. It was peaceful lying there. The frantic energy of harvest had given way to the season of long, cold nights, when the few birds that had not fled south were focused on survival, saving their songs for spring. Winter felt like a preview of what it meant to die, to be released from the ties that bind us, to be free of our bodies. When I was growing up, winter had been a time for telling stories, for mending things, for dreaming about the coming spring.

When the cold began to seep through my pants, I got up and struggled through another dozen feet of snow to the edge of the field, where broken cornstalks stood as a reminder of the past season. I would not make it to the woods today. Even this short distance left me sweating and breathing hard, not a safe state for this temperature.

When I finally made my way back to the house and stripped off my wet clothing in the mudroom, I was numb from cold, damp to my skin, and exhilarated by the effort. I planned to make a peanut butter sandwich for lunch, my habit most days. But on the kitchen table was a plate with an egg sandwich and a mug set beside it. A fresh pot of coffee was already brewed. On my chair, the one I liked for its clear view out the window, were a pair of snowshoes and a tall walking stick. The leather bindings were yellowed and stiff but in good shape. That made me pause, it did. What was John after?

The next morning, I strapped on the snowshoes and used the walking stick to propel me through the deep snow. While the going was much easier, I was still not in shape to cover any distance. Within a week, however, I made it to the trees. Wild turkey tracks led through the woods, heading east along the ridge and down the bluff, where they crossed the river to the open field on the other side. I followed the tracks, stepped sideways down the hill, and held on to the branches of small shrubs for balance. With the trees blocking the wind, the only sounds I heard were my labored breaths and the squeak of snow as it flattened beneath each shoe. When I finally reached the edge of the river, I sat down to rest. The water was frozen solid except near the edge, where a tiny mist rose up from the gap and a faint gurgle could be heard beneath the ice.

The slow trickle of water reminded me of home, of a stream that rippled and tumbled on its way downhill, of the times I had stopped there with my father to gather watercress and wild onions. We used to drink from our cupped palms, until the day he said the water was no longer safe. It had been a January morning just like this one, when the frost that lined each branch glittered in the sun, that my father did not come home. If he were with me now, he would have made a fire and a pot of coffee, thrown together a squirrel stew using the last of the wild potatoes to be found at the edge of the woods. He would have told me stories, the old ones, that can be shared only when there is snow on the ground.

I scattered bread crumbs on the ice and pulled an apple from my pocket and set it beneath a dogwood shrub. Broke up the last cigarette I had taken from Shirley. Not stolen but taken, balancing our relationship in ways Shirley had never understood. What I would have given in those days for a kind word.

Much as it pained me to admit it, the snowshoes had been a kindness. And if I were to be honest about my cold silence these past months—the way I refused to cook or clean, how I read my book upstairs in the evening while John watched TV—then even living with me was a kindness. I had come prepared to fight, to defend myself against whatever he thought he might be entitled to. Sooner or later, I thought, he was bound to realize what a mistake he had made in marrying me and he would tell me to leave. Or he would finally reveal the monster he kept hidden, and the illusion of safety would be broken. But while I waited for him to show his ugly side, instead I was undone by his kindness, revealing my skinned self to the bright gaze of the winter sun.

Over the next few days, I started making an effort in small ways, nothing more than what a helpful guest might do. The apple orchard had caught my eye early on, suggesting that here was a place I could be useful. Clearly these trees had not been pruned in years, with branches growing every which way. After spending a morning observing them, I saw how much energy was pulled away by the little sprouts that grew at the joints of larger branches, how the trees needed to be shaped to hold the weight of ripe apples in late summer. Using tools I borrowed from the barn, I nipped and cut and sawed branches until every one of those dozen trees looked cared for. In the spring, the trees would use that freed-up energy to make fruit. Maybe I would even learn to bake a pie.

I found the days went much quicker when I kept my hands busy. John looked so grateful when I troubled myself to cook something for dinner, even if it wasn't much, just a hamburger and some peas I found in the freezer. One night, I felt his eyes follow me as I made my way toward the stairs, sticking to my routine of retiring early to read. I stopped with my hand on the railing, drawn to look back over my shoulder. His beer sat unopened on the tray next to the recliner. John returned my gaze, his eyes unreadable in the shadow. I held out my hand, and like a drowning man, he reached for me.

CHAPTER TEN

Rosalie Iron Wing Meister
1980

A lusty rooster called from the barn in early May, his flock of hens impatient to get outside and explore the yard, searching for bugs and green shoots. A week earlier, tiny buds had unfurled overnight into leaves on the apple orchard, while a half dozen fuzzy, peeping chicks appeared in the barn. In every corner of the farm, new life was sprouting.

The chickens started clucking as soon as they heard my footstep outside the barn. When I opened the pen, they rushed toward me, pecking at my boots until I scattered kitchen scraps and a few handfuls of feed on the ground. After refilling their water trough, I gathered the eggs they had laid. I greeted my favorites by name: Curly Girl, Snowpants, Big Red.

When the rush for food was over, I picked up Curly Girl and stroked her soft feathers. In the dim light of the closed barn, the rafters creaked from a sudden gust of wind, raising up dust from rotted hay and the sharp smell of chicken piss. The barn seemed enormous, built to hold everything a farm needed and other things that might come in handy. A tractor was parked at the back, near a pile of used boards waiting to have their nails removed. A mouse-eaten wool blanket and a cracked leather saddle sat on the top rail of an empty stall. Hanging from a nail in the wall was an old saw, its dull teeth aching with rust.

The door blew open, and Curly Girl flew from my arms with an irritated squawk. John came in with a large sack across one shoulder and kicked the door shut with his foot. He stopped sudden when he caught sight of me in the shadows.

"Rosie," he said, with a short laugh. "You gave me a start."

"Sorry."

"No matter. I just wasn't expecting to see you in here."

He unloaded the sack onto a pallet with a grunt. Swiveled one end so it lined up with the other sacks. He took off his cap and wiped his forehead with the sleeve of his jacket.

"One of these days," he said, "I'm going to clear out some of this junk." He glanced around the barn as if seeing it through my eyes. "All except that saddle. Belonged to my daddy. Back in the day, he grew up using horses to plow the fields. Only time I ever saw the old man cry was when we had to sell those horses."

"Why'd you sell them?"

"Needed the money. We couldn't afford to keep them on, not after we bought a tractor that needed repairs and gas. Horses were another mouth to feed. I don't think my dad liked farming so much after they were gone. Said he didn't like the way things were changing."

"What do you mean?"

"He used to say that farming was about taking care of your family. If you had it figured right, everything worked together. Horses pulled the plow and their manure was used to fertilize the fields. A good farmer rotated his crops, took care of his soil. That's how my daddy learned it, and that's what he taught me and Eddie. But things started changing after World War II. Hybrid seeds, chemical fertilizers, new equipment. Farmers like my dad got left behind.

"But I will say this for the old man. He always paid his debts, so he left me this farm free and clear. That's the only reason I've been able to get by the past few years. And now that there's two of us," he said, smiling sweetly at me, "I figure it's time to start making some changes."

As I washed up the few dishes from breakfast, I watched two rabbits play in the dust, chasing each other before darting away to hide in the long grass. I never considered setting a snare; those days were behind me.

I added water to a twig of apple blossoms that bloomed in a jelly jar, a gift that John had left before I was awake. After a winter of endless nights and slow, cold days, I was learning a new rhythm in spring, the way a farm came alive in the planting season. With John out in the fields before dawn, I had to take on the housework and cooking or it wouldn't get done. Most mornings I still lingered over my coffee, enjoying the quiet. Only afterward did I vacuum the rugs, sweep the floors, fold the laundry, and make two egg sandwiches for John's lunch. I learned the rule of three for making dinner: thaw a piece of meat, boil potatoes, open a canned vegetable.

When the phone rang, I assumed it was a supplier calling for John.

"Hey, Rosie, what's up?" I immediately recognized Gaby's voice and quick laugh, as if she knew she had surprised me. I hadn't seen or heard from her since Casey's store the previous summer. "Yeah, I know, right, it's been too long," she continued when I didn't say anything. "I heard through the rez auntie hotline that you got yourself married. Are you knocked up?" She laughed again.

Same old Gaby. I sighed. "No, it's not like that. I just needed a place to stay for a while."

"Girl, there are easier ways to find a place to live. You should have called me. We don't have much room at the moment, what with Anthony out of jail, but I could have made some calls."

"I know. I should have called. How's Anthony doing?"

"He's sober. For the moment. He said to say hello. You know, he was always kind of sweet on you."

"Who? Anthony? No way."

"He said he watched you that night he got out of the hospital, the way you kept to yourself. He said you were a survivor. But don't get any ideas about him. He's a gone man, just found out he's having a baby with his new woman."

"Tell him congratulations from me," I said, meaning it.

"So how is the marriage thing working out?" Gaby asked, sounding more serious.

I hesitated. Didn't know what to say.

"Well, here's the thing," Gaby said, not waiting for my reply. "I'm sorry about that night, asking you to lie for me. My auntie and I have had some long talks about it, as you might imagine. She didn't come right out and say it, but I know she feels bad for the way she talked to you. It wasn't your fault. So her way of apologizing was to ask me to tell you to be careful. She said the Meisters have always been hard drinkers and quick with their fists, and not just with other men. She also said to ask Meister how his family got that farm you're living on."

"Tell Auntie not to worry," I said. "I'm okay. And I'll tell him to give the farm back." We both laughed, just like the old days.

"You know I had to be the messenger. Anyway, we should get together. My auntie takes care of little Mathó while I study to get my GED. Turns out that my son was the kick I needed to get my life on track. You watch, someday I'm going to be a lawyer, and then I'll get the land back, howah! Call me!" She hung up before I could answer.

I smiled as I set down the phone. Hearing from Gaby was a relief, especially knowing that Auntie Vera had forgiven me. I grabbed the broom and started sweeping the floor, raising a small cloud of dust all the way into the pantry. I rarely entered this little room, not liking its dark corners, the smell of mouse droppings, the many rows of dusty glass jars packed with canned tomatoes and green beans. Pulling the long string that hung from a bare bulb overhead, I studied the jars, wondering if it had been John's mother, Edna, who canned all this food. On the bottom shelf I saw a giant enamel pot, an open box of glass jars, and a bag of rubber seals and lids. Then, as I turned toward the back corner, I spotted a shoebox with "Edna's Seeds" written on it in shaky letters, barely readable beneath a layer of cobwebs and dust.

All thoughts of cleaning were forgotten as I carried the box to the kitchen table and began to rifle through it. Inside were stacked neat rows of small envelopes, each one labeled and sealed. I carefully removed a few of the envelopes, starting with "Edna's German Tomatoes" and "Judith's Early Beans." After reading each name, I poured a few seeds into my hand and admired how unique they were. The smooth white tear-drop of the squash, the dark oval of the bean. We spent the morning together, the seeds and me, and by noon I felt we were well on our way to becoming acquainted.

When John came in for lunch, I spooned a mound of macaroni and cheese onto his plate and added two over-cooked hot dogs. I told him that I'd found the seeds. He said it was a darn shame they weren't being used. His words seemed to hang in the air; a possibility I had never consid-ered. I stopped moving, the spoon suspended in my hand.

"I want to start a garden." I felt a thrill of surprised shock at saying the words. John merely tucked his napkin beneath his chin and nodded.

"I'll get the rototiller out after lunch and run it through the garden out back. You know what you want to plant?"

"Yes." Everything. Even in my casual inventory that morn-ing, I had felt the quickening in the seeds when they were ex-posed to the light, when they felt the warmth of my hand.

After cleaning up the kitchen from lunch, I found John behind the house, admiring a large rectangle of freshly turned earth, black and moist from the spring rain.

"Just look at this soil," he said. "This has got to be some of the best in the county. My daddy worked hard to keep these fields and this garden in good shape. He made sure Eddie and me spread plenty of manure. He used to watch us work, and whenever we slowed down, he'd say, 'The nation that destroys its soil destroys itself.' Franklin D. Roosevelt."

I nodded without really listening, distracted by the fertile smell of earthworms, old manure, and damp soil. After John went back to the field he was plowing, I admired the cleared garden plot, which seemed enormous. Now, somehow, I would have to figure out how to plant the seeds. There were no instructions on the envelopes; Edna must have already known what to do. But I had never met any gardeners. My foster family ate canned corn as their one vegetable, and my father had taught me to gather wild plants, not grow them. I could go to the library, but I didn't want to take the time. The seeds were ready. And the day seemed just right for planting, the morning's cool air turned warm by the afternoon sun. The chickens roamed the yard, scratching, clucking, occasionally fighting. I could hear the faint rumble of John's tractor in the distance.

It was true that I didn't know much about planting. But I guessed that seeds were seeds, whether they came from a pumpkin or fell from a tree. Seeds need soil and water and sun. I thought of something my father used to say: that we watch and we learn from the trees and plants around us. I remembered the coneflower, with its bristly seed head that dries over the winter and scatters in the spring. In the forest and on the prairie, plants were spread by wind and by traveling roots, with trees and shrubs and medicines selecting the best place to thrive, competing with one another while still building a community together.

I knew where to begin. I crumbled the tobacco from one of John's cigarettes, which I had brought from the house, and offered a quick prayer. Then I took a deep breath and began to garden. After selecting one envelope from each kind of plant—tomatoes, green beans, lettuce, carrots, beets, turnips—I poured all the seeds into a bowl, like a miniature forest. Then I walked down the center of the garden and scattered seeds by the handful. I raked each area, making sure the seeds had a layer of soil covering them. Not seeing any clouds in the sky that might promise rain, I hauled the hose over and gave everything a good soak.

That night, I opened one of Edna's jars of green beans and served them with Hamburger Helper hot dish. When John pushed his plate back and lit his after-dinner cigarette, he asked, "So how far did you get with the garden today?"

"It's all planted."

"No kidding?" His eyebrows shot up like two question marks. "The tomatoes and carrots, everything?"

"Yup, it's all done."

He whistled, impressed. His wife was surely the fastest gardener he'd ever known.

"Seeing as this is your first season gardening," he said, "you might want to drop in on Judith and George down the road. Judith is one of the best gardeners I know. It would be neighborly for you to go over and meet her."

I shrugged. John stubbed out his cigarette on his plate and left the table. I heard the squeak of his recliner as it leaned back, the murmur of the television. On evenings when he fell asleep in his chair, I would often slip outside, where the darkness gathered me in like an old friend. Tonight, with the weather so mild, I strolled down the long driveway, past the mailbox, until I could see the sky without any trees in the way. A nighthawk chirped as it swooped past, joined by the chittering chorus of the peeper frogs from the marsh across the road. I thought about walking all night, seeing where I got to by morning. It was spring, and I was still here—planting a garden, even. There was always a reason not to leave; I wasn't wearing my tennis shoes, or I didn't have my money. I didn't seem any closer to a plan than I had been in the winter. But even so I wasn't sure I wanted to meet the neighbors.

I continued to search the sky for familiar patterns. A soft breeze fluttered the leaves nearby, as if my father's voice were whispering in my ear. *Look there, Rosie: the Wičhíyaŋna šakówiŋ, the Seven Little Girls, are connected to Bear Butte in South Dakota. When we take care to do on earth what is happening in the stars, we can open up a connection to the sacred. We call this kapémni—as it is above, it is below.* He believed the old ones coded their knowledge into myths because this kind of under-standing goes beyond words. It can be told only in symbols. I stared down the road at the sharp silhouette of trees against the night sky. My father traveled now with the stars, returned to the vast mystery that had so fascinated him all his life.

The next morning, after John loaded a tractor part into the bed of his truck, we headed east on the gravel road that led to the highway. We were headed to New Ulm, the closest town big enough for a grocery store, a downtown, even a few of the chain stores. He drove with his arm draped over the steering wheel, seeming in no rush to get back to planting.

John slowed when the road dipped slightly to cross the Cottonwood River. As the wheels thumped on the small metal bridge, I glimpsed the water rushing beneath, swollen with spring rain, a handful of trees on either side. Sometimes these little bridges covered nothing more than a drainage ditch that carried away excess water from the fields. Barren of trees, the ditches would be lined on both sides with lush grass. Everywhere I looked, I saw rectangular fields, long rows in straight lines, and square fence corners, land shaped to fit machines.

"How'd your family come by your land?" I asked, casually, my face turned toward the window.

"Oh, I don't know, the usual way. Back in the 1860s, the government was giving out 160-acre allotments to anyone who would homestead for five years. You made a claim on a piece of land, had it surveyed, and it was yours. Family legend has it that Heinrich's son chased more than a few Indians off this piece of land with a shotgun." He paused, seeming to realize what he had just said. "I mean no offense, Rosie. It's just an old story."

No need for me to say anything. I was already familiar with that story.

Over the last six months, I had noticed that every small town in the area seemed laid out according to some master plan. Farm fields ended abruptly at the town borders, where an equipment dealer would display rows of enormous combines and tractors in come-hither shades of lipstick red or harvest green, followed by a cluster of trailer homes. There was always a Main Street, a water tower, and a railroad that ran alongside the big gray bins of grain elevators, each topped by a metal arm that carried grain from semitrucks in the fall. Every town had a school and a baseball field. The larger towns might offer an outer ring of fast food restaurants and big chain retailers.

As one of the biggest cities along the Minnesota River, New Ulm had become a bustling, thriving business center where people came for their weekly shopping. We slowed down as we passed through a neighborhood of small ramblers, with stately elm trees bordering sidewalks that had been swept clean of dirt and leaves. Red and yellow tulips had begun to sprout in tidy gardens. Closer to downtown, two- and three-story buildings filled both sides of the street, their windows advertising real estate, clothing sales, an antique store.

After we dropped off the tractor part for repair, John steered the truck down a street in the historic part of town. The buildings seemed from another era, a time when horses still pulled wagons filled with goods to trade, and women's long skirts were edged with dust from the road. The newly built railroad had been greeted as a sign of progress, a much-needed connection to more civilized areas back east. Turning onto State Street, John parked in front of a brick building with a plaque mounted out front.

"Every student in New Ulm schools learns about the founders," John said. "Even me, a lousy student more interested in girls than history. Actually, I found it kind of interesting. This is one of the few farm towns built around an idea in addition to what the railroad company or land speculator wanted. The founders built this hall as a place for the German community to gather. No doubt there was plenty of beer and polka music. People here are really proud of their heritage."

"This building doesn't look that old," I said.

"It's not. The first one was destroyed in 1862." John glanced quickly at my face before restarting the truck. "There's something else I need to show you," he said.

A few blocks away, we parked near a tall white monument that had been built in the median strip of a busy road. A decorative fence of low posts and a thick chain surrounded pruned shrubs and flowers.

"Go ahead. Read it." John lit a cigarette as I opened the passenger door.

I climbed down from the truck and stood at the base of the monument. I began to read:

THIS MONUMENT IS ERECTED BY THE STATE OF MINNE-SOTA TO COMMEMORATE THE BATTLES AND INCIDENTS OF THE SIOUX INDIAN WAR OF 1862, WHICH PARTICU-LARLY RELATED TO NEW ULM.

HONORED BE THE MEMORY OF THE CITIZENS OF BLUE EARTH, NICOLLET, LE SUEUR AND ADJACENT COUNTIES WHO SO GALLANTLY CAME TO THE RESCUE OF THEIR NEIGHBORS OF BROWN COUNTY AND BY THEIR PROMPT ACTION AND BRAVERY AIDED THE INHABITANTS IN DE-FEATING THE ENEMY IN THE TWO BATTLES OF NEW ULM, WHEREBY THE DEPREDATIONS OF THE SAVAGES WERE CONFINED TO THE BORDER, WHICH WOULD OTHERWISE HAVE EXTENDED INTO THE HEART OF THE STATE.

THE SIOUX INDIANS LOCATED AT THE REDWOOD AND YELLOW MEDICINE AGENCIES ON THE UPPER WATERS OF THE MINNESOTA RIVER BROKE INTO OPEN REBELLION ON THE 18TH DAY OF AUGUST 1862. THEY MASSACRED NEARLY ALL THE WHITES IN AND ABOUT THE AGENCIES . . .

A sudden exhaustion threatened to bring me to my knees. The wind whipped my hair around my face, intensified by the rush of cars that drove past in both directions, ignoring my presence. I faltered, nearly fell, and braced a hand against the cool stone, the inscribed words rough beneath my fingers. Nothing new here, a reminder is all, another old story. Breathe. Slowly I raised the hood of my sweatshirt.

ON THE AFTERNOON OF THE 19TH OF AUGUST, A FORCE OF ABOUT ONE HUNDRED WARRIORS ATTACKED NEW ULM, KILLING SEVERAL OF THE CITIZENS AND BURNING A NUMBER OF BUILDINGS . . .

By the end of the second battle, on August 23, thirty-four defenders had been killed and sixty wounded. Listed on the monument as among those who died in the battles: Heinrich Meister. John's great-great-grandfather.

I climbed back in the truck and closed the door behind me. I sat for a moment in silence. Without looking at John, I asked, "Why did you bring me here?"

"You need to know what you're up against," he said. "Folks around here are friendly, helpful, nice to your face, but they've not forgotten that war. They celebrate this history. It's their way of remembering the family they lost. And you . . . are you."

"That's your family name up there. Do you celebrate this history, too?" My hand was clenched tight on the door handle, ready.

"I figure my ancestors had it coming," he said quietly. "You can't take land and starve families without them fighting back." He shrugged. "I'm not as ignorant as you seem to think. I reckon there's a whole other side to this story."

CHAPTER ELEVEN

Marie Blackbird
1862

I lay awake in the dark, listening for soldiers while Iná slept. Every night, my mother and I took turns keeping watch, even though there was little either of us could do if they attacked. Still, I kept my fingers on the bone handle of my knife, trembling with cold and, yes, with fear. I was old enough at fourteen to help take care of my family, but I had never expected this. Lying awake beneath a makeshift shelter, a lean-to covered in dry leaves and grass, not far from the burnt shell of our family thípi. I was aware of every breath of wind, every snap of a twig. My Até, my father, was still away at the fighting. I counted ten days since we had left him at the camp near Wood Lake.

A light rain began to fall, tapping gently against the cut branches, dripping cold on my face, my thin blanket. In this season of trees shaking off leaves, we should have been hunting, and drying corn, and preparing for winter. My family had always kept a garden, even before the Indian agent tried to make farmers of the men. I could remember when we hunted and gathered plants, before our food was kept locked in a warehouse by the agent. Before it came to us in sacks, shared like handouts, as if we were poor relatives. Waiting in line, Iná had said to me, "Who are we if we can't even feed ourselves?"

With winter almost upon us, I could tell that Iná was worried about how we would survive. Even if we escaped capture by the soldiers, there was no time to prepare for the coming season, and there was no one to hunt for us. When we returned home from Wood Lake, we had found the corn in our garden trampled, the beans uprooted, the dried meat stolen. No food here, and there would be no more rations from the agent. We could not wait many more days for Até to return.

A gust of wind blew through the shelter, raising a swirl of rustling leaves, as Iná huddled closer to my new brother, called Čhaské until he could be given a new name. When the wind dropped, the quiet was broken only by the low rumble of my belly. And then I heard them: a soft keening, the sorrow of voices who cried from the shadows for their loved ones, for release from this world, for revenge. I whispered to Iná, They're back, Iná, they've come back. Before we slept, she had wiped my arms and legs with cedar boughs. She had tucked tiny bundles of čhaŋšáša in my pockets to hold me down, to keep the mist from carrying me away in the still hour just before dawn. I could hear her praying softly, telling our relatives it was time to leave their home and return to the stars. Your memory will live on, she whispered.

Her voice calmed me, but I knew sleep would not come again that night. More than anything, I wanted to wake from this dream, to my life before the fighting began.

When the sun's cold light finally cleared the tree line, Iná rose to tend the fire, uncovering the coals she had kept warm through the night. I watched as she added twigs and blew on the glowing embers, her cheeks lined with worry, a stray leaf clinging to her long braid. When a small flame began to burn, she fed it with the branches we had gathered the day before, enough to keep the fire going a few more hours.

"Marie, I'm going to find more wood," Iná said, using the wašíču name the missionary had given me. She looped her carrying sack over her shoulder. "And to check the snare." Her voice was flat, without hope. We both knew these woods had been empty of game for many months.

Wrapping my blanket around my shoulders, I sat close to the fire while Čhaské slept in his cradleboard at my side. I tucked his čhekpá pouch into his blanket, brushed dirt from the quill pattern my mother had sewn onto his bed. He slept without moving, his round cheek turned away from the glow of the flames. I laid the last piece of wood on the fire, careful to shield him from drifting sparks and smoke. Iná had promised she would return before Čhaské woke, before he cried from hunger. When a hawk screeched nearby, I nearly jumped, clapping a hand over my mouth to stifle a cry. I was tired of being afraid all the time, unable to sleep from the horrors I had seen.

My family was one of many who lived in the woods that run along the Mní Sota Wakpá, the Minnesota River, in a new reservation too small to feed all of us. Iná told me that when I was Čhaské's age, we would come here only in summer, to plant our gardens, pick berries and plums, and gather the plants that we would use as medicines.

Back then, I had round cheeks like Čhaské, but they had disappeared along with our food. I was too thin; my skirt hung limp on my flat belly, my narrow hips. I wished to be more like my cousin, Margaret Thunder, who was tall, with a pleasing face and a quiet way about her. I was too restless, Iná said, and too ready to speak my mind. No man would want a wife who could not control her tongue. At least I was a better gardener than Margaret. That summer I had been trusted to plant the corn, carefully mounding the soil just as I had been taught. Proving my skills brought me one step closer to being ready to marry. Not that any of that mattered now.

I pulled a few twigs from my long braids and wiped the dust from my face with the edge of my skirt. Not so long ago, I cared a great deal about my appearance, especially when young men walked past the garden where Margaret and I would sing to keep the birds away. One man, Whirling Wind, came by more than the others. He even helped carry my basket home when Margaret and I picked berries. I was grateful that he did not tease us, as his cousins did. Before I used to fall asleep, I would think about his kind eyes, the way his strong hands were gentle with his horse. I wondered if he was thinking about me.

Now he, too, had disappeared. Where I used to see the light of neighboring fires, close enough to smell the woodsmoke, there was nothing. Our tiospaye, our cousins and aunties and uncles, had scattered when the fighting broke out. Some, like us, followed the men to battle until it became too dangerous. Others had fled to their relatives out west or farther north. Margaret had disappeared with her family. When I asked Iná what had happened to our village, she could not tell me. But I knew. The settlers had taken the land and allowed us to starve, and now my family was in danger.

The night my father left to join the Soldiers' Lodge, I

had gone to bed with my belly empty, after another day had passed without the long-promised rations. Even my moon had stopped coming, that's how hungry I was. I dreamed of venison dripping its fat into a sizzling fire, of green corn roasted in its husk, of picking gooseberries until the juice ran down my fingers. As I slept, the urgent summons of a drum stole into my dreams. When I woke the next morning, Até was already gone. Now I counted the days waiting for his return.

A dry branch snapped beneath a heavy foot. I spun toward the sound, hoping for my mother's return. But it was not my mother. A wounded Indian, no one I knew, walked slowly toward me, leaning on his hunting bow, using it as a walking stick. A rag was tied around his thigh, and his deerskin leggings were stained with dried blood. He wore an ill-fitting soldier's coat and a black hat that shadowed his face. I drew in a quick, sharp breath, gripped the handle of my knife. He stood just outside the clearing, not moving. When he spoke, his voice was gentle.

"Don't be afraid, thakóža."

"I'm not afraid," I said, unable to keep my voice from wavering. "I can take care of myself. And my brother."

"I believe you." He removed his hat and rubbed his forehead. "My name is Two Bears. Can you spare some water?"

I hesitated. I had been raised to always offer food and drink to any visitor, no matter if they came limping in bloody and dirty, smelling of sweat and something worse. But the war had changed everything, reshaped my world into a shifting mass of confusion and death and hunger. Sometimes the enemy wore the uniform of soldiers, sometimes the skin of my relatives. I dipped a gourd into the water pail and set it on the ground halfway between us. Never taking my eyes off the stranger, I backed away until I stood in front of my brother.

Two Bears grunted his thanks—or maybe his pain—as he bent to lift the gourd, drinking it so quickly that water spilled down his chin. Wasteful. He wiped his mouth on the back of his muddy sleeve. Hobbling to the large stump we used for chopping wood, he leaned on his walking stick and slowly eased his body down, then stretched his injured leg out in front of him. He stared at the fire for several minutes, not speaking. His chin dropped to his chest and he began to snore.

I did not dare move. Instead I stared at Two Bears, glancing back at the trees where my mother had disappeared over an hour ago. What was taking her so long?

"Thakóža, do you have a name?" He was awake.

"Zitkádaŋsapa. Marie Blackbird."

"And your parents?"

"My Iná is Maȟpíyamaza. My Até is Mázakhoyaginape. He's away at the fighting."

"Was he at Wood Lake?"

"Haŋ. We followed him and helped to make camp. After that battle, he sent us away. We're waiting for him to come back."

"Thakóža, you might have a long wait. Many of the warriors who survived have been captured and taken away."

"Did you see him? Did you see my Até?"

"No."

"Then he's coming, I know it. My mother said we'll head west to see our cousins, where we gathered thípsiŋna this summer."

"That's good. You're not safe here."

He gestured toward the water bucket. This time, when I

filled the gourd, I handed it to him. He drank slowly, returned the gourd to me, and struggled to his feet.

"Thank you, thakóža. Tell your mother that the soldiers are coming this way. They're rounding up families and taking them to a camp. They'll be here by morning."

He turned and walked back in the direction he had come, slowly disappearing into the woods, a ghost man limping toward home.

Not long after he left, my mother returned, carrying a heavy bundle of branches in her arms, bent over from the weight of the carrying sack on her back. Enough wood to last the night. Dropping her load to the ground, she staggered and nearly fell before bracing her hand against the nearest tree.

"We'll eat," she said, placing a kettle on a hook over the fire. After partially filling it with water, she threw in handfuls of corn and beans and dried squash, crumbling in a few herbs from her pack. While the soup cooked, I told her about the warrior's visit and his warning of the soldiers. Iná stared in the direction that Two Bears had gone. Finally, she sighed. "We can't outrun them. We'll have to survive until your father can find us."

After we had eaten the soup, my mother lifted Čhaské to her back, told me to bring her carrying sack, and followed a deer path into the woods. I took a deep breath, smelling earth and rain and dying plants. As we walked beneath the towering red oaks, I could feel acorns pressed beneath the thin soles of my moccasins, and I wondered if we should gather up them up for flour. When I was a child, I had used their little caps as baskets when I played in the long grass with my corn-husk doll. But Iná did not slow down, nor did she even glance around her. She walked so quickly that I had to hurry to keep up.

This time of year, we would usually be gathering nuts, drying venison, and tanning skins for new moccasins. We were one of the families that kept the old ways, leaving the reservation to hunt for deer and working long days to prepare for winter, with Iná drying strips of squash from the garden and wild plants and berries in the sun. She was known as one of the best gardeners in the village. And Até had been a good hunter, back in the days when there was game in these woods. I was afraid to ask her how we would survive the coming winter once the soldiers came.

I knew families who had built wood houses like the settlers, and who had become Christians, cutting their hair and wearing trousers. Even Iná liked the fabric in the traders' store, using it to sew our summer skirts. But she was afraid of the food they handed out. She worried about what would happen when the women no longer knew where to find medicines, when the men gave up hunting, if they began to drink instead. She said our food was sacred because it made life. "This food has no spirit," Iná had told me, dipping her hand into a sack of flour. "What will become of us when this is all we have?" Me, I would have gladly eaten it, if I was hungry.

Iná walked with her head down, following a path covered with dry leaves and pine needles, as a brisk wind tugged at her shawl. After a short distance, she stopped, looked around, and poked at the ground with her walking stick. When she tapped something solid, Iná grunted, pleased.

"Marie," she said, pointing to a large stone. "Move that rock."

Underneath was a thick layer of decayed leaves. Iná pulled a bone hoe from the carrying sack and handed it to me. Within a few minutes, I had dug a shallow hole, about two feet wide, revealing a layer of deer hide. Following my mother's instructions, I pulled up the hide, and then a crosshatch of sticks. A pit was exposed. I smelled the dry breath of seeds that had lain dormant for the past year. I knew this place: I had helped to dig the pit, helped to fill it with last year's harvest, with long braids of dried corn, ropes of squash, deer-hide sacks filled with beans. With medicines we gathered to treat winter colds and bad stomach, to bind wounds, and to soothe toothache. In the spring, some of these reserves had fed us when the annuities ran late. We had even had enough to share with Margaret's family.

"I kept this in case we had a poor harvest," Iná said. "We'll carry what we can with us. We'll need food for the winter and seeds to grow in the spring. We'll leave the rest for our return."

Iná leaned the cradleboard against the trunk of a nearby tree. She squeezed through the neck of the pit, loosing a layer of soil from the walls as she dropped to her feet, her head just visible above the lip. Using her hands as her eyes, she felt all around her, her fingers recalling the corn they had shelled, the squash they had sliced thin with her knife. She lifted a bag of corn to me, followed by a smaller bag of beans. She searched the walls until she found a packet of squash seeds. Grasping her hand, I helped her climb gingerly out of the pit, until she lay on the ground, breathing hard.

"Marie, do you remember how we covered the pit last fall?" she asked, still trying to catch her breath.

"Haŋ, Iná."

"Do it now, while I feed your brother."

I laid the sticks back across the opening, covered them with the deer hide, added a layer of soil, and buried everything in a thick pile of leaves. When my mother nodded her approval, I rolled the large stone back on top. Iná scattered a pinch of čhaŋšáša across the leaves and whispered a quick prayer asking for the seeds' protection, for their safety.

"Look carefully at this place, Marie, so that you can find it again."

I turned slowly in a full circle, seeing the twin boulders to the west, the hill behind them. The stone marker had a flat top with alternating bands of dark and light gray that gleamed in the sun.

As we turned to leave, Iná stopped and pulled the bone hoe from her sack. Her fingers tenderly brushed the coarse edge of the bison scapula before she passed it to me. "This belonged to my mother. It's all she would use. She said that the wašíču steel tools scar the earth. We cannot carry it with us. Bury it with the seeds, not too deep. Be quick."

I hurried back to the pit, rolled the stone slightly to one side, and dug just deep enough to cover the bone with soil. After smoothing the leaves again, I replaced the stone and ran to catch up with my mother.

That night, Iná showed me how to sew rows of seeds into our skirts, along the edge of our blankets, in the hem of Čhaské's warm baby dress. My fingers trembled from cold and hunger as I sewed quick, uneven stitches along my skirt, folding the fabric over a double row of corn, seeds that were blue, rose, and cream. Wamnáheza, the corn for our traditional soup. My mother was afraid the soldiers would take everything of value left to us. She knew, too, that if the food ran out, these seeds would have to be hidden from her own people, who would be desperate to feed their children. She had to keep safe enough seeds for planting. No matter the cost.

I tied a double knot at the end of my thread and cut it with a quick slice of my knife. We worked long into the night. I would have fallen asleep early on, but Iná said we could not take time to rest. She showed me how to quickly stitch a small deerskin pouch and fill it with corn from her sack, making a second pouch for the beans. She placed each pouch inside a willow basket that I would carry. Iná would have Čhaské on her back in his cradleboard and the rest of the food hung in sacks around her neck.

From a beaded pouch she kept near her sleeping place, Iná unwrapped a small object with great care. Taking my hand, she placed a wrinkled cob with faded bloodred seeds on my palm.

"This was a gift from your grandmother, your Khúŋši, who gave me these seeds when I married. You must keep them safe." Iná rewrapped the little cob and placed the pouch around my neck, where it lay heavy on my thin chest. I understood, even at my young age, the responsibility that my mother had just shared with me. No matter what happened, I must be strong enough to protect this pouch and the willow basket I would carry in the morning. With no men to hunt for us, forced to leave behind the medicine plants we had relied on for generations, we would have only these seeds to help us survive.

When I finally went to bed, I did so fully dressed, still wearing my moccasins, and waited for the sun to reveal the new life that lay ahead.

CHAPTER TWELVE

Rosalie Iron Wing Meister
1980

For the first two days after I planted the garden, I checked anxiously each morning for signs of life. Nothing. Bare soil greeted me each day. Was this normal? Did I need to replant? Uncertain, I decided to follow John's advice and go meet Judith.

I wrapped a dozen slightly scorched muffins with a cloth and walked the mile to her farm. A winding driveway led toward a two-story farmhouse that had been partly painted sunflower yellow. Blackberry vines grew along the fence; tall stems from last year's asparagus moved gently in the breeze. Unlike the orderliness that John insisted on, Judith's farm seemed to be coming gloriously apart, almost as if bursting with too much life, too much abundance. The barn leaned to one side, and the apple trees dripped with white blossoms, scenting the air with sweet nectar. Chickens wandered through the yard. An elderly mutt wagged his tail slowly as I approached.

"Halloo, neighbor, come join me in the garden!" I looked around and saw an older woman kneeling between two raised beds, waving me over. Judith was wearing a flannel shirt with the sleeves rolled up and unlaced men's boots. Wiry gray hair peeked from under her wide-brimmed straw hat. She looked old enough to have children my age—but tough, with strong arms and short, powerful legs. Even from a distance, her blue eyes appeared sharp, observing everything with quick sideways glances.

Strangely, it looked as if each of her beds held a crop of plastic milk jugs, necks removed. As I got closer, however, Judith lifted one of the jugs, and I saw what was beneath. A seedling! Signs along each row identified the plants: tomatoes, broccoli, squash, green beans, eggplant. When I paused by the edge of one bed, she stood up, placing her hand on the small of her back and shading her eyes with her hand. There was something brisk and no-nonsense about her, like a schoolteacher, someone who will always tell you what she thinks. I liked that she didn't wear gloves in the garden.

"You must be John's wife," she said. "My name is Judith. I didn't want to drop by too soon, you two being newlyweds and all." She laughed. Even worse—she winked. Then, without waiting for an answer, she beckoned me to a lopsided picnic table that held trays of seedlings to be planted. "If you don't mind, let's talk while I work."

Judith carried two trays back to a row she had already started. After digging several small holes with her trowel, she pulled a carton from her bucket of tools.

"This is the magic ingredient," she said, shaking a spoonful into one hole. "Epsom salts. If you don't have any, I've got an extra carton. Just pick up another when you're in town. If you'd like, I'll also give you some cuttings from my raspberries. John said he mowed yours down last spring. That's men, for you.

Hardly pay attention unless it's got a motor or boobies." She glanced at me and smiled. "Does that shock you? Guess I've gotten too used to saying what's on my mind."

"And don't I know that!" came a deep voice from behind us.

Judith laughed and called over her shoulder, "Now how long have you been standing there, eavesdropping?"

"Long enough to hear more than I care to."

"In case you haven't guessed yet," Judith said, "this is my husband, George."

George walked over to me and carefully wiped his hand on a kerchief. He must have been a full foot taller than Judith, with the round belly of a man who loved his mashed potatoes and gravy, his farmer overalls straining at the side buttons. He wore a red bandana tied around his neck, and a wide straw hat with a turkey feather that somehow looked just right on him. When he smiled, there was genuine kindness in his eyes. He extended his hand, held my fingers lightly, and bowed, murmuring, "Enchanté."

"Oh, for Pete's sake," Judith said. "Keep the bullshit for the fields."

"Pay her no mind," George replied, still holding my hand. "She is eaten up with jealousy."

I couldn't help but laugh, and they joined me. Soon we were all sitting together at the table, drinking lemonade and picking the burnt edges off the muffins. Judith worked in town as a middle school principal, a job that allowed them to farm as they pleased. George had inherited their 320-acre farm from his father, who had made a good living raising beef cattle. Ten years previous, after a mild heart attack, George had sold the cattle and leased half of his land to neighbors.

"I consider myself to be an 'artist of the land,'" George said, while Judith rolled her eyes. "Laugh all you want, dear wife, but I pay attention to the process. Not for me are your designer crops and fad-of-the-moment chemicals and million-dollar pieces of new equipment. Give me a horse and a plow and I'll be content the rest of my days."

"Don't you mean a hammock and a beer?" Judith asked. "If it weren't for my job, you would have gone broke as a farmer ten times over."

"True, my dear, very true. I was not made for the danger-ous game that farming has become. There's very little room anymore for the family farm to survive. Costs have continued to spiral up while crop prices ride a roller coaster. I don't know how John gets by." He threw a curious glance at me, as if ask-ing a question. I had no idea what to tell him.

"And now I must leave you ladies to your work," George said, tipping his hat to each of us and getting up from the table.

"Have you had time to get your garden in yet?" Judith asked once he'd gone. "Edna always had the best tomatoes."

"I'm working on it," I said. Seeing Judith's tidy rows, each one growing a single vegetable, had provided a shock I hadn't quite absorbed yet. Maybe I *should* get a book from the library. Maybe it wasn't too late to start over.

⸺

When I confessed my first gardening attempt to John, he did his best not to laugh. That night, I read my first book on the subject. I learned that the seeds would be dependent on me, the gardener, for many of their needs. In exchange, we'd have a bounty of food to eat and can. Hmm. That seemed fair, although a lot of work.

Over the next week, I lined up my rows like the book told me to. I marked each one with a stake and the crop's name written on a plastic tie. Then I planted a second round of seeds, grateful that I hadn't used all of Edna's envelopes.

About ten days later, as I was hauling the hose to the middle of the garden, I saw it: a slender green being had broken through the thin crust of soil, with a tiny leaf just beginning to unfurl, still wearing a brown cap from its seed shell. A few inches away, another green seedling—and another, all the way down my crooked row of beans. Here was new life that I had helped bring into the world. Here was food that I had planted. In that moment, I was hooked.

Unfortunately, my first scattering of seeds also came up every which way around the garden. I had broccoli in with the beans, lettuce popping up between rows, scraggly tomato seedlings growing at random. The book had no solution for my situation. It didn't seem right to just pull out the extra plants. That would be a terrible waste of food and disrespectful to the seeds.

With everything all mixed up, that first season was something of a disaster. The broccoli drowned when I overwatered, and the green beans withered on the vine when I went too far the other way. I didn't know about potato beetles until it was too late. The first time I tried to thin carrots, I pulled out all the seedlings in one long row before realizing my mistake. I tried to quickly replant them, but they all died.

Still, the season was not a complete loss. I felt a thrill of pride the first time I filled my basket with ripe tomatoes. The beans dried beautifully on their slender branches into long, withered pods filled with perfect seeds. When I wrote "Rosalie & Edna Soup Beans 1980" on an envelope, I felt a connection to Edna, who had kept these seeds to feed her family and left them neatly organized and labeled for the next gardener to care for them.

With all the planting and weeding and harvesting, I told myself I was too busy to think about leaving. The garden's needs carried me from one day to the next. I decided there would be plenty of time in winter to plan my departure. While I had not forgotten Gaby's advice to be careful, my feelings toward John had softened. I liked sleeping with him. It was easy to be around a man who knew the value of silence.

Over the summer, I had grown more attached to this land and the river that ran alongside it. Some days I thought I heard singing, only to realize it was the cottonwood leaves rustling in the wind. Or I glimpsed a movement at the edge of the woods, but my eye was never quick enough to catch it. Even the ground felt strangely familiar, as if my boots were following an old moccasin trail.

Then the rumble of the tractor would scatter my thoughts like a flock of geese after a gunshot. All that remained was the memory of generations of my family, buried somewhere across this river valley, whose stories had disappeared. For now, it was enough to be on this land again, to walk where they had walked. I was soothed by plants, comforted by the long patience of trees. I knew with certainty that just as the seasons would always change, I would one day find my way home.

One Saturday evening in midsummer, I was sweeping the kitchen floor after supper when John called me from the living room, raising his voice over the baseball game he was watching.

"Rosie," he said. "Come here a minute."

I finished emptying the dustpan into the wastebasket, replaced the broom in its narrow closet, and hung my damp apron on the cupboard knob. I stood in the kitchen doorway, where he could see me. I was wrung out from a day of gardening and cleaning and wanted nothing more than a bath and my bed.

"I think you and me should go to church tomorrow morning," he said, his eyes still focused on the television. "I ran into Pastor Bob at the hardware store yesterday. He badgered me until I about had to swear that we would be there. Said it was a shame the family fell away after Mama passed. People want to meet my new wife."

I had been dreading this moment. Without looking at John, I nodded.

In the morning, I put on my red wool dress, the one I had bought for our wedding, despite early warmth that promised a sweltering day. I must have filled out some, I thought, noticing the fabric pulled tight across my breasts and belly. Our finances did not allow for new clothes beyond what was strictly necessary, but I was not much on dressing anyhow. Braiding my long hair, wearing my one pair of town shoes was the best I could do. Even so, John raised his eyebrows when he saw me waiting by the door and gave a quick nod of approval. All cleaned up in his best shirt, his face red and smooth from a recent shave, he looked hopeful and young.

Pastor Bob's white-clad Lutheran church stood one block off Main Street in New Ulm, past the hardware store and a healthy distance from the Catholic church. Its radiant stained-glass window and tall steeple were a testament to the strong faith of the community. When the old church had burned down ten years earlier from faulty electrical wiring, the men had pooled their talents and raised up a church just as they used to build barns in the old days. Their wives had loaded the picnic tables with hot dishes, Jell-O salads, and rich cakes heavy with homemade frosting. Two years of bake sales bought the organ, the finest in the county. Volunteers kept the church sparkling clean and provided a lunch after every funeral.

On warm mornings like this one, people gathered outside the church to exchange greetings until the first chords of the organ announced it was time to go in. John and I had come early so I could be introduced before the service. I wiped my damp palms on my skirt, feeling a knot of tension in my neck.

As we came up the steps to the sidewalk, our arrival attracted several quick glances and lowered voices, and a few folks looked their disapproval at us. Having seen the war monument, I knew that some must still carry stories of relatives who had died defending their homes from my ancestors. Along with these stories, their families had passed on distrust and long-simmering hatred. They would not confront me directly, of course, but they would find ways to let me know their true feelings. My presence, like the monument, was a reminder of old wounds.

Standing behind John, I felt the shift around me, the way an animal knows when it's been cornered. I squared my shoulders, stared past the parishioners toward the cemetery, and gave my best stoic Indian. John seemed unaware as he scanned the crowd for familiar faces.

Fortunately, the first people we met were Lester Thompson and his wife, Elly Mae, an older couple whose warm welcome seemed to rise from innate decency. To them it was only right that I should be considered as family, having married a member of the congregation. Lester gave me a calloused hand to shake, while Elly smiled and clung to his elbow, her thin legs seeming ready to give way. John had told me Lester owned a large farm several miles south, where his son had taken over much of the daily operation.

"Pleased to meet you, young lady," Lester said, giving my hand a vigorous squeeze. "John's family has been here almost as long as mine. I hope you feel welcome. Let me and Elly Mae know if you ever need anything at all." With that long speech behind him, he nodded and led his wife toward the church doorway.

We had almost made it inside, after fielding a few more friendly greetings and cold stares, when a large hand was clapped down on John's shoulder. "Now hold on a moment," a gruff voice said. "Aren't you going to introduce me to your new wife?"

John turned slowly, pulling his shoulder away, and I turned as well, to see an older man standing a little too close to us.

"Hello, Mayor Jackson. I guess I didn't see you there. This here is Rosalie."

"Well, well," he said, giving me a quick once-over before extending his hand to shake. "Well. We're all glad to see that John has finally settled down. He had us worried for a while." He laughed heartily at nothing, his broad belly shaking beneath his striped tie, his white shirt already stained with sweat.

"Excuse us, Mayor, we're just on our way in . . ."

"Of course, of course. Don't be a stranger, now," the mayor said, shining his practiced smile on us. Just before we turned away, he touched my shoulder so that I stopped. "Mrs. Meister—Rosalie—you let me know if you need anything, anything at all. Or if anybody gives you trouble on account of you being an Indian. I don't have a racist bone in my body, but there's people around here who don't share my feelings. Folk are just folks, I like to say." I turned away without replying.

The chapel was warm and airless, with so many bodies packed together. Looking around the crowded room, I wondered what my father would have thought if he could see me there. He had blamed churches for supporting boarding schools and refused to set foot inside one. He said boarding schools had broken up families, including his own. He could not forgive the stealing of generations of children.

Gaby's auntie Vera, who was a Christian, had explained things to me differently. She told me to think of the boarding schools as mistakes made by the people who ran churches, not by the faith itself. Prayer is prayer, she'd said, whether it's spoken out loud in a big white church or whispered in private at the edge of a river. I just wished more Christians felt like Vera did. Maybe they wouldn't have tried so hard to convert us.

As we settled into the middle of a long wooden pew, the air seemed to close in around me, carrying an uneasy blend of musty hymnals and cheap aftershave. I tried not to breathe as Pastor Bob climbed the steps to his pulpit and announced the first hymn. Between the loud clamor of the organ and the itchy nightmare of my wool dress, I began to feel panic rising. Cold sweat beaded on my forehead and prickled my armpits, sending a slow drop rolling down my stomach. I felt queasy and regretted my breakfast. But I made it through most of the sermon before I had to stand abruptly, causing Pastor Bob to pause in surprise. I squeezed my way across the sharp knees of an old couple who were too shocked even to glare and ignored the flock of heads that turned as one to watch my flight up the aisle. Passing through the door, I headed down the hall, straight for the blessed sanctuary of a bathroom.

I slammed open the door, rushed past a woman standing at the sink, and barely made it to the toilet before throwing up. When my stomach was empty, I wiped my mouth on the back of my hand and leaned against the stall partition. Closing my eyes, I whispered a desperate prayer that the woman at the sink would have the good sense to leave me alone. Go away, go away, go away . . .

"Honey, are you all right?" I had forgotten to latch the door on my stall. The woman leaned near me, her breath reeking of stale cigarettes. She had the frizzed hair of a blond poodle. "I know that Pastor Bob can be deadly dull, but he doesn't usually make a person sick. Unless . . ." She took my chin in her hand and turned my face up where she could study it closer. "Any chance you could be pregnant?"

I stared back at her in shock and struggled to my feet. That would explain the tenderness in my breasts, the nausea I had felt all morning. I had not meant for this to happen. I moved to the sink to wash my hands, hoping she would get the message and leave. Instead, she followed me and patted my shoulder.

"Don't you worry. Do you know who the daddy is? We have a Catholic Ladies Society that can help place an un-wanted child."

I was reaching for a paper towel when she said this, after splashing cold water on my face. I might have slipped—I couldn't remember later—but regardless my fingers caught the top edge of the towel canister and ripped it from the wall, the force of my weight slamming it to the ground with a loud bang. Unwanted child! The woman clapped her hand to her mouth and fled the room.

I kicked the box under the sink with my foot and stomped out to the hall. John was standing there with Pastor Bob, who turned toward me with an expression of concern. John turned, too, his worry shifting to surprise as I marched past them both, ignoring the pastor's outstretched hand. I kept moving straight out the door, down the church steps, and to the parking lot.

John ran along behind me. "What the hell!" he spat, grabbing my arm.

"I'm pregnant." I pulled away from his grip and headed to the truck.

"How do you know?"

"I just know."

"Well, goddamn." John whistled under his breath all the way to the farm.

⸻

My father once told me that women keep their hair long because it's part of their spirit. He told me never to cut my hair; he said it was the color of crow's feathers. He used to help me brush it after the bath, when it was tangled and pulled at my scalp. Sometimes he sang while he worked, combing with slow, patient strokes, and then braided it exactly right, not too tight, and wrapped the ends in red cotton string. To keep me safe.

By the time I turned eighteen, I had hair that hung near my waist. The afternoon John and I returned from church,

I stood in front of the bathroom mirror, a scissors close at hand. There was the face I avoided each morning, just as I had avoided the truth that I was already making my choice. I had fooled myself into thinking I would wake up one day, take my money, and start my real life. That I would move to the Cities, find a job, rent my own place. Or maybe return home, to see if my family's cabin was still there. Now my options had shrunk to a single, narrow path.

I knew that if I hesitated too long, I would lose my courage. Taking hold of my braid with my left hand, I picked up the scissors and began to cut. Strand by strand, the braid unraveled, its weight lifting from my back as black sheets fell away onto the floor. The rasp of the metal blades was the sound of a door being nailed shut, once and for all. When I finished cutting, the girl who was born in the woods was gone. In her place was a new self, a woman who was harder and stronger, who was ready to become a mother and raise a child.

My shorn hair was the last reminder of all that I had lost. Since I'd never mourned my father, cutting my hair was a gesture to him, my Dakhóta way of grieving for a lost family member. I would carry his memory as long as I was alive. The eyes that stared back at me in the mirror were filled with doubt. How would I hold on to what my father had taught me when everything around me insisted on another story, another way of life? I was a small stone on the bank of a river whose current would surely wear me down over time. Still, this child carried Iron Wing blood, the hope of another generation in a family that had almost disappeared from this land. I knew what it would have meant to my father to see the family continued, even if the child carried a white man's name.

I laughed once as I realized how vulnerable I had become. No longer the untouchable ghost who had nothing to lose. Somehow, despite the legacy of my troubled family, of the generations who had suffered and disappeared without a trace, I would keep this baby safe. This child would be born into a hostile world, instantly marked as a threat. With the first stirrings of life, I finally understood what it meant to be afraid for the future.

I closed my eyes. The dream of following the river upstream to my home was nothing more than a thin mist on water, burning away in the sun's bright light. Already I knew that this child's first name would be Wakpá. River. A child born of water that is always moving.

germination

a seed awakens

———(■)———

‡

CHAPTER THIRTEEN

Rosalie Iron Wing Meister
1981

As new life took root in my body, as my breath became breath for this child, I began to transform from the inside. At first, I threw up everything, as if purging all that had come before me, that had made me who I was. And then I slept, lying in bed well after John went to the fields, napping in the afternoon, and returning to my bed before dark. The earth and I would go through winter together, biding time, as we waited for our rebirth in spring.

While I sank deeper into lethargy, John threw himself into his work, determined to support his new family, to prove himself. He was on fire once more with dreams for the farm, seeming to change overnight, just as I had. After one last night of drinking beer in his father's recliner, he announced the next morning that he was quitting. From that day on, he said, clutching his coffee cup like a rope thrown to a drowning man, he would be sober. He lit a cigarette with trembling fingers. Without a word, keeping my doubts to myself, I refilled his cup.

The next few weeks were a torment of withdrawal. John began smoking two packs of cigarettes each day, while floating in a stream of coffee. Exhaustion was his remedy, but even that was not enough for the ghosts that haunted his dreams at night. He was restless, sweating, rising at dawn with a drawn face. But he kept his word. After a couple of months, his craving seemed to ease. His face was less bloated, his appetite increased, and finally he slept. The evenings remained his greatest challenge, when his shadow called to him to crack open a beer.

To calm his restlessness and ease the swelling in my ankles, we began taking walks on the gravel road just before sunset, when the dust had settled. I walked with one hand resting on my belly, feeling the occasional small movement of the child I carried. In the falling light, John would tell me his hopes for his son; he was already certain this child would be a boy, one who would carry on his family name. Thomas Meister, named for his grandfather.

John's words formed a wall around my family, around my own name, as if I was part of a past that no longer mattered. I had become invisible to him. I could already see the road he had paved for the child, the naive dreams of a father who thinks he can control the future. I felt the undercurrent of his fear, of his need to protect. But I knew the power in a name. I knew how a name would draw its strength from the child; how the child would grow into that name.

"Our child's name is Wakpá," I said.

John did not speak for a few minutes. I felt his utter surprise that I would even suggest a Dakhóta name. He knew that his small-town community would rise up against it. I was sure he was picturing the response, feeling again the criticism that had followed him as a young man who drank too much and rebelled against his father. The minister would offer unwanted advice, and a matron would be sent to have a talk with me. I waited. He would have to choose his path, as we all did.

"I think," he said, stopping to light a cigarette and gaze at a wide sky filled with stars, "that name would not be good for the boy. You know how people are." I know how *your* people are, I might have said. They're so afraid of stirring up the past that even a name is too much of a reminder.

Instead, I replied, "I'm not asking." I didn't need a paper to name my child.

⸺

Early in spring, when the geese had begun to follow the river north, when I dreamed of pasque flowers pushing up through melting snow, my son was born. His perfectly round head was capped with bristly black hair that delighted the nurses. Tiny brown fingers grasped at this new world and at my breast, now swollen with milk. I was completely consumed with this being, with the way my body responded to his needs. The miracle that John and I had created together deepened the bond between us. One of the nurses took a picture of him holding his son, Thomas, with a wide smile on his face and an unlit cigar between his teeth.

But by the end of the first month, the days had blurred into sleepless nights, wet diapers, and endless rocking in a chair holding an infant who refused to be soothed. John and I grew irritable from the lack of sleep, the constant noise of a squalling, colicky, demanding baby. I had no experience with this. No family to turn to for advice.

One afternoon, when John had fled to the fields, I found myself alone with this stranger who had taken over my life. I wanted to drive away, to go back to the time when I'd had only myself to worry about. I couldn't get anything done, not the dishes, not the laundry, and certainly not the garden. My hair was unwashed, my shirt dribbled in spit-up, my sweatpants lived in for too long.

A knock on the door. Goddamn it, I said to myself, if this is one more asshole salesman or door-knocking evangelist, I will punch him in the mouth. Holding my shrieking infant in one arm, bouncing him in ways that seemed only to enrage him further, I threw open the door.

And there stood Gaby, with perfect hair, perfectly dressed in a leather jacket and long skirt, holding a blanket wrapped in a baby-blue ribbon. We stared at each other for a moment, and she began to laugh. Before I could explode, she stepped into the house, set down her gift, and took the baby from me without a word. She nestled him in the crook of her arm, rocking ever so gently as she murmured compliments on his handsomeness, his healthy voice, his strong body quivering with anger. Carrying him to the couch, she pushed aside a pile of unfolded laundry and laid him down. After changing his wet diaper, she showed me how to swaddle him snugly in the new blanket so that he felt safe, his arms no longer flailing at the cold emptiness of the world. As she began to slowly walk the room with my now quiet baby, she waved her fingers at my sweatpants and pointed upstairs. "You go deal with that," she whispered. "I've got this."

Later, when I had become human again, she told me that she had been accepted into a community college in the Twin Cities. She planned to live with a cousin and come home on weekends to see her son, Mathó, who would be living with her auntie Vera. She didn't know when she'd have a chance to visit again. Seeing my face, she told me that I wouldn't have time to miss her, that having a child was a beautiful gift. It was only the first month or two, she said, that really sucked. And we laughed together, just like old times.

Gaby was right, of course. In time, the three of us—me, John, and Tommy, whom I still called Wakpá in private—learned a new way to be together, a rhythm that settled around the needs of the baby. His birth seemed to bring a time of prosperity for the farm. Finally, there was money in the bank. John's confidence soared as he earned the respect of other farmers in the area, even joining them in the slow season at a coffee shop in New Ulm, where they passed the time by joking, talking politics, and swapping stories.

On days when winter had closed us in for too long, I bundled up Tommy and rode into town with John. He insisted on carrying his son to meet the guys, to show him off. As fathers and grandfathers themselves, they all admired how much he had grown, how much better looking he was than his father. To me, they were painfully polite, offering a nod from each farm cap, as they kept their eyes turned toward John and the baby. Finally, I would escape with Tommy to do the shopping. John would catch up with us at the drugstore, where we strolled the aisles, picking out new toys, and shared a malt at the fountain center.

But farming is a fragile partnership with an ever-changing world. In the mornings, while Tommy napped, I began reading the newspaper that was delivered to our mailbox. From what I could see, John had a gift for plants, for knowing how to read the weather and understand the soil. He loved the land like a brother, worrying about every small sign of distress. But when it came to the bigger picture of what was happening around the country and how it affected farmers, he was sometimes at a loss. He'd say, There's probably a good reason why the president decided to do this. I'm just a common farmer; I have to trust our leaders in Washington.

I could only shake my head, thinking that trusting the leaders hadn't worked out so well for Indians. Before marrying John, I had never thought much about farming. And now that I was reading the news, I couldn't understand why President Carter would declare a grain embargo against the Soviet Union. By the time Reagan lifted the embargo a year later, the damage had been done; farmers lost a big market and prices dropped. To make things worse, interest rates had begun to climb. The low rates of the past decade had enticed many of the big farmers, like Bill Daly, to buy up all kinds of expensive equipment. With land values dropping, it seemed there was a storm gathering on the horizon.

Of course, our luck turned when everyone else's did. First came a leak in the roof that we couldn't fix, leaving out pots to catch the drips when it rained. Then the tractor broke, the truck needed a new engine, and of course Tommy just kept growing. John filled one credit card and opened up another. I had to start throwing away the shiny envelopes with their offers for zero interest before he could see them. I began to realize that if we didn't figure out a better plan, we weren't going to keep the farm.

CHAPTER FOURTEEN

Rosalie Iron Wing Meister
1986

We celebrated Tommy's fifth birthday with a homemade cake decorated with white frosting and sprinkles, just how he liked. He puffed out his round cheeks to blow out his candles, his father encouraging him not to spit all over the cake. After three moist breaths, and a little help from John, the candles were finally extinguished. While Tommy was busy scooping up cake and ice cream, John disappeared into the other room. He came back pushing a shiny red bike with black handlebars and a set of training wheels. He rang the bell and Tommy spun around, staring at the bike while a spoonful of ice cream dripped into his lap.

"Is that mine?" Tommy asked.

"It says here on the card this bike is for a Mr. Thomas Meister," John said. "Do you know anybody by that name?"

"That's me! That's my bike. Can I ride it?"

"It's too late tonight, kid. How about you and me take it for a spin tomorrow?"

I had begun making birthday cakes at John's request, since

his mother had always made them for him and his brother. As I covered the cake with tinfoil, I tried to remember ever having one of my own. The fall before my father died, he took me fishing for walleye up on Big Stone Lake, where we caught our limit and fried it over an open fire. Best birthday I could imagine, lying in my sleeping bag, looking up at the stars.

After putting Tommy to bed, John came back into the kitchen and sat down at the table to finish his cake. Without being asked, I refilled his coffee cup. After five years of mostly not drinking, evenings were still a struggle for him. I kept the coffeepot going right up until bedtime.

"Now, I know what you're going to say, Rosie, so don't even start," John said. "The bike is secondhand, and Gordon gave me a good price once he knew it was for my boy's birthday. I gave him twenty dollars down. He said there's no rush for the rest."

"He always says that," I replied. "And then he's asking for his money every time I stop at the hardware store."

"I just wanted the boy to have something nice, is all."

"You're the one always saying there's no money. Tommy needs new shoes a lot more than he needs a bike."

"And I said don't worry about it," John stated, his voice flat. "I'll take care of it." He ate in silence, the scrape of his fork the only sound in the room. "Besides, I've got a plan. I mean to lease that one hundred sixty acres from George."

"Seriously?"

"Yeah. George lost Bill Daly as a tenant when he went under. He's already agreed to let me have it."

Ever since I had met John, he had told me that farmers needed to own more and more land just to survive. Economies of scale. But leasing land seemed like a big gamble when the headlines in the morning paper were all about the worst farm crisis since the Great Depression. Recently, a bankrupt farmer and his son had murdered two bank officials in Parker, a small town just a hundred miles west of us. A few weeks earlier, a farmer had killed his wife, his banker, and his neighbor before committing suicide. Seemed like there was violence happening all around us. Local bars were thriving, and wife beatings were on the rise. Everybody knew somebody who had lost his farm, his family, or his life.

John left early the next morning, dressed in his one suit, his hair slicked down, his eyes bright with hope. When he came home that afternoon, his suit limp and his tie hanging loose, something in him had changed. At the bank, he had asked to speak with his banker, the man who had lent money to his family every spring for as long as he could remember. John's family could always count on getting the money they needed for planting with little more than a handshake, since his dad had always paid back his loans after fall harvest. His banker, he learned, had retired. In his place was a smart-talking college fellow who didn't know much about farming.

"I told him that I had already spoken to George about leasing those acres," John said, his face flushed in anger. "So, this shit-in-a-suit—pardon my language—tells me that I don't qualify for a loan. He said my methods were outdated. I wanted to tell him to leave the farming to the men. But I held my tongue; we need the money too badly. Finally, he said that my family's long history with the bank would qualify us, provided I show him a contract that someone was going to buy my corn. I said, Give me the loan and I'll get you your proof. We went round and round until finally he brought in the manager.

Somebody from around here, who knew my family. He gave me the loan. Not as much as I had asked for, but enough for the lease."

When the rains came that spring, they came too early and too hard. The young seedlings drowned in the fields. John reseeded, his face lined with worry at the extra expense. Then the warm weather stalled, and the plants waited for the heat to arrive. It came in a rush, as if bloated with a thousand farmers' prayers. The clouds dried up, and the plants roasted in the fields, their leaves edged with brown until eventually they stood hollow and dry, as the topsoil began to lift up and blow away.

John left each day before dawn and stayed in his fields past sunset, as if his determination would be enough to bring the rain. Tommy learned to be careful and quiet when his father was in a mood, doing his best not to spill his milk at the table or bang his truck while he played. I stayed out of John's way. We began strict rationing of water so the well would not run dry. Showers were a weekly luxury. Clothes were hung outside between wearings to air out. Salt stains rimmed the neck and armpits of every shirt.

One night, after I had already gone upstairs, I heard the distinct sound of a bottle cap being pried off. A short time later, another. And another. Then I heard John's low voice, anguished, almost angry, arguing with a God who refused to hear him. As the drought continued, so did the drinking. He would wait until I had gone to bed before opening his first beer, refusing to do so in front of me or Tommy. Often, he fell asleep in the recliner. Once I found him still asleep there in the morning, shoulders slumped, chin stubbled, defeated. I wished there was something I could do that would help.

⸺

After leaving a package of hamburger on the counter to thaw, Tommy and I went outside to work in the garden. Before he could walk, I used to set him on a blanket with a pair of spoons and a cracked bowl to bang on. Now, as a curious young boy, he was more frequently at my side, wanting to help pick off potato bugs or pile mulch around the plants. As he bent to fill his bucket with mulch, a strand of dark hair covered his forehead. When he looked up at me, proudly displaying his work, I felt the slow tug of memory, seeing my father's features emerge on his young face. Strong brows, deep-set brown eyes, a lopsided smile. Skin that darkened easily in the summer sun. I closed my eyes, trying to hold that image.

I sat without moving, my hands idle in my lap. When Tommy touched my shoulder, I was startled awake. He turned his head to direct my attention toward his arm. There, its wings moving ever so slowly, was a monarch butterfly. Tommy was stiff with joy, afraid to move lest his new friend fly away. "Can we keep him?" he whispered. I shook my head. He didn't argue. The butterfly rested a full minute before rising up with a fresh gust of wind, its wings fluttering as it flew quickly beyond reach. Tommy watched it go until it was out of sight.

When the sun was high enough to bring on the full heat of day, we drove to New Ulm to run errands and return our library books. On Main Street, the only women's clothing store,

Dee's Boutique, had its windows boarded up, although the thrift store on the next block seemed to be thriving, its parking lot half-full. At the stoplight, I pulled up behind a pickup truck with a loud, rumbling muffler and a bumper sticker that read "Crime Doesn't Pay . . . Neither Does Farming."

I parked in front of the newspaper office, next door to the Pit Stop, the local bar where gossip was swapped over beers. Since Tommy was starting school in the fall, I thought I could help out by bringing in some money, and with a little bit of persuading, John had agreed that I should find a job, if I could. I had seen an ad in the New Ulm *Dispatch* for someone to work part-time writing obituaries. I had a knack for stories—or so an English teacher had once told me—and decided to follow up right away.

A bell jangled over the door as we walked in. An older man with caterpillar eyebrows, wearing a limp tie over his faded cotton shirt, was sitting at a desk by the front window. He peered at me over his reading glasses.

"Can I help you?"

Letting go of Tommy's sticky hand, I pulled the application out of my back pocket and placed it on the counter. My thumb left a raspberry-jam print on the corner.

"I'm here to apply for the job writing obituaries."

No response while he stared at me. As I waited for him to decide if he should talk to me or not, I looked around at the piles of paper stacked on empty desks. A single computer, two typewriters, phones, a jar filled with pencils. Bundles of last week's issue were pushed against the wall. The smell of dust, ink, paper. The phone rang. The man ignored it.

"You have a high school diploma?"

"Yes, sir."

"Can you type?"

"Hunt and peck is all."

"What's the last book you read?"

"*Curious George.*"

He grimaced. "Job pays a nickel a word, most run between fifty and a hundred words. Except for politicians."

"Fair enough."

He beckoned me through a swinging gate, pointed at a desk, and handed me a sheet of paper covered with scrawled, barely legible notes.

"Show me what you can do," he said. "The owner of a local feed mill dropped dead of a heart attack at a motel last night. Not there with his wife, according to the sheriff's report."

I got Tommy set up with a piece of paper and pencil at another desk. I rolled a sheet of paper into a typewriter. Then I pushed my glasses up on my nose and thought for a moment, before starting to type.

"Family Mourning Sudden Loss of Community Leader Earl James Wilkinson. On August 12, Mr. Wilkinson had a heart attack while traveling on business for the local feed mill. On his way home to his family, he was forced to stop at a motel due to the pain. He will be missed by many." Followed by information about the service.

I pulled the sheet from the typewriter and handed it over. The man read it and dropped it in his overflowing inbox.

"Okay. I'm the editor. Ralph Lindquist. And you're hired. Someone will call you when we need you."

"Do I get paid for what I wrote?"

Ralph gave the first hint of a smile. He nodded, turned back to his work.

═

We walked a long block to the library through the stifling heat, the air heavy with humidity as it shimmered above the blacktop. The morning breeze had died away, the birds had gone quiet, and not a single leaf moved on the nearby trees. Tommy's hair was plastered to his damp forehead. My shirt stuck to my skin; my heavy braid clung to my neck. For people accustomed to the punishing cold of winter, these brief heat spells seemed intolerable. We survived by finding shade, or, better yet, air-conditioning. Like in the library, my favorite refuge.

We handed over our stack of books to the librarian, Mary Watson, who greeted us with a friendly smile.

"Well, hello, Mrs. Meister and Tommy. Is it hot enough for you?" The weather was a favorite topic in town any time of year. The right weather at the right time made all the difference for farmers.

Across the room, a reading circle for kids near Tommy's age was about to start. Tugging on my hand, Tommy pulled me toward it. The volunteer reader looked at us for a moment in surprise. Seemed at a loss for words. Finally, as if remembering her manners, she said, "Please join us." The circle of women and their children created a wide-open space for us, far more than we needed. The other kids stared at Tommy with unabashed curiosity. "Mama, mama," one little girl whispered. "Is he a real Indian?" The volunteer picked up her book and began to read. Tommy was entranced by the story, his small brown hand resting on my knee.

Our last stop was a visit with George at the Corn Museum, where he spent two mornings each week explaining the miraculous story of corn to a handful of tourists. George had taken a special liking to my son. When Tommy was a baby, George had insisted on holding him while I visited with Judith; now that he was older, George would bounce him on his knee.

Tommy ran down the sidewalk ahead of me, threw open the front door of the community center, then disappeared into the cool darkness. George was sitting at a card table, his reading glasses perched on the end of his nose, a paperback in his hand. He steadied his coffee cup as Tommy ran up and grabbed his knee.

"Well, good morning, young man. What a pleasure to have a visit from you and your mother. Rosalie, help yourself to a cup of coffee. Now, how can I help you today?"

Tommy slapped his Curious George book on the table. "Read, please." He pointed to the monkey's face on the cover. "That's you!"

While George kept Tommy busy, I picked up the Minneapolis *Star Tribune* that had been lying in an untidy heap on the table. I felt a surge of pride that I myself was now working for a newspaper, humble as it was. Buried in the back section, next to the classified ads, I found a photo of Gaby Makespeace speaking at a community event, her hand gesturing to the river behind her. Smoothing the newspaper crease, I studied her strong face and long hair.

We talked by phone every few months or whenever she

stole a quick break from studying. She was now a first-year law school student, the only Indian woman in her class, paying for it with money from the tribe, a scholarship, and student loans. When she called to tell me that she had been accepted, she said, "Imagine that, Rosie! Me, a C student, here at this school. Wish Mr. Warner could see me now."

The accompanying article quoted Gaby speaking about pollution from farm chemical runoff in the Minnesota River. Gaby claimed that farmers were destroying the river, which was on Dakhóta homeland. "Water is life," she'd said. "We need to protect this river for our children." In the photo she looked older, tired. I knew what John would have said about her argument. That if the chemicals he used weren't safe, the government wouldn't have approved them.

George finished reading to Tommy and turned to me. "That's a smart boy you've got there. Tell me, how's John holding up in this weather?"

I shrugged. "About the same as everyone these days." I paused, hesitating to ask George about the article. Some farmers were touchy when asked about their farm practices. Well, I thought, best to come straight out with it. "Do you think it's true, about the farm chemicals?" I pointed to Gaby's photo.

George sighed and stayed silent a moment before answering. "Good question, Rosalie. Nobody really knows what those chemicals are doing to us. We do know they're showing up in our water. There's a lot of farmers concerned about how these chemicals might affect their families. But if a farm is managed by someone else, like a corporation, then it's just one more calculated business risk. You keep spraying your fields until someone sues you and wins."

"Why don't they sue?"

George laughed. "Who? Our migrant brothers who need these jobs to survive? A poor farmer like me, who depends on his wife's income? It's easy to criticize, Rosalie, and much harder to fix. Who can say no to a higher yield when it might mean the difference between breaking even and losing the farm?"

I watched Tommy draw a tree on George's napkin. "I was taught that we have a responsibility to take care of the water. To protect it for our children and grandchildren."

"Me too, Rosalie, me too." George drained his coffee cup. "Well, it's time to go feed the world."

———

After debating for a day, I called Gaby. The house was empty; there was no one home to question what I was doing.

"Rosie, it's been too long," Gaby said. She told me about law school and her internship with the Save Our Rivers task force, which was working to clean up rivers in the state. When she asked me what I was up to, besides farming, I said, "I'm working for the *Dispatch* . . ."

"A journalist! I'm impressed. You really should get onto this river pollution story, it's going to be big," she said.

"Writing obituaries," I added quietly.

"Oh. For dead white people?"

"Mostly." In an area that was about 98 percent white, it stood to reason they would claim more space on the obituary page.

"Well. You always did good in English class." An awkward pause. "So, Rosie, what's up?"

"I read the article where you talked about chemicals in the river. I'm wondering about my son. Is it safe for him to swim and eat the fish he catches?"

"I don't let Mathó play in it or fish, unless he releases them. It's not just the river, Rosie. Those chemicals leach into the groundwater. And if you're downwind when they're spraying, they're on all those nice vegetables you grow. Think about the migrant workers who spend all day breathing this stuff." She paused, as if considering an idea. "Hey, the Mankato powwow is in a few weeks. Why don't you come, and I'll explain more about my work? Besides, it's about time our sons get to know each other better. I told Mathó that Tommy is his cousin."

I heard the front door open as John and Tommy came back from the store.

"I'll try to come. I have to go. Goodbye."

$\dagger$

CHAPTER FIFTEEN

Gaby Makespeace
1986

Walking up to the Mankato powwow grounds at midmorning, I took a deep breath of woodsmoke, frying bacon, and coffee percolating over the fire. This smells like home, I thought, feeling my shoulders relax for the first time in weeks. Tents and trucks and RVs were set up all around an open field, along with a couple of thípis, as families cooked breakfast at their campfires. A grandma was already making fry bread, each ball of dough sizzling as it dropped into a pan of hot oil, and my mouth watered as I walked past. I moved slow, enjoying the warm sun on my face, the sweet smoke of burning smudge from a morning prayer.

I remembered weekends waking up wrapped in a blanket next to Anthony, smelling the campfires, and falling back asleep, feeling content and safe. On Friday mornings, Ma used to tell us to check our pockets and look under the sofa cushions for loose change to buy gas. We used to pitch a tent at whatever powwow we had enough money to get to. While Anthony and I scrounged for wood to make a fire, Ma took off, telling us not to wait up. I never asked where she went.

In the morning, Anthony and I would roam the campground looking for someone to give us breakfast while Ma slept it off in the tent. At one of the powwows, I watched Anthony steal a purse for the first time, taking some white woman's money while she was looking at turquoise rings. We do what we have to, to survive.

Since I was not much of a camper anymore, Mathó and I had a room at the nearby hotel. I made sure he was well-fed at the buffet before we showed up at the powwow grounds. We made the rounds, visiting and drinking coffee, while the vendors set up their tents with jewelry, blankets, hats with Native insignia, T-shirts, ribbon shirts. Fry bread tents competed for the longest line as word spread about who made the best, freshest, biggest wheels. Or the tallest, meatiest, greasiest Indian tacos. At some powwows you could still find pasdayapi soup and elk burgers, sometimes right next to the mini-doughnut tent. We were civilized, all right.

That day I was dressed for Grand Entry, my hair combed into a French braid and held in place with a beaded barrette. My favorite dance regalia was snug from too many fast-food meals and late nights studying at the law school library. But those sacrifices would eventually be worth it. Or so I hoped.

I reached over to straighten the long yarns on Mathó's new grass dancer outfit, finished two days prior by Auntie Vera, after she had seen how much he'd grown over the summer. He pulled away from me, seeming too old at eight for a mother's fussing. Especially one that had been gone as much as I had. While we waited for Rosie and Wakpá, Mathó spun in place, making the yarns twirl around him. His short legs were as sturdy as young trees, his round belly already pressed against his waistband. He had never met his dad, and I had no plan for us to visit Earl in prison. Mathó never asked, either.

I saw Rosie looking for us from the other side of the circle. She was tall enough to see over the crowd, so I waved until I caught her eye. Her hair was grown out again. I had never understood why she cut it before her boy arrived. Seemed like a strange way for him to come into this world, like he was born from grief. Maybe that explained why he was crying so hard the first time I came to visit, why no one could console that child. Rosie held him like he was made of glass. I had no choice but to take him, wrap him up snug in the blanket I brought as a gift, and sing him to sleep.

Now he walked alongside her like a little old man, afraid to cut loose and run like a kid. See how tightly he held on to his mama's hand, how they already looked so much alike. Rosie herself never changed: same glasses, held together now with tape; beat-up boots; some ugly straw thing on her head. Wakpá stared around him at everything, but especially at the spinning blur of yellow yarn that was Mathó. When Mathó finally stopped and lurched with a crazy, dizzy smile, Wakpá laughed. That's all it took for the two of them to run off and see the beaver pelt at one of the vendors' tents.

Rosie and I shared a hug, me feeling conscious of my law school bod, while she was one tall, lean muscle. Seeing her again was like a reunion with a favorite sister, someone I could talk to about anything. She had obviously not come dressed to dance, but we could talk to Vera about getting her an outfit. We sat at a picnic table, and I poured her a cup of coffee from my thermos.

"So, Rosie, how long can you stay?" Always the question with her. Like dealing with a skittish colt.

"Oh, you know, through Grand Entry," she said, vague as usual about the details.

"What's John think about Wakpá coming to powwow?"

Rosie shrugged. "He can't really think about much else besides the drought. He's worried sick that he'll lose his entire crop. We were already getting in the truck to come here when he yelled to Tommy, 'No mohawk!' I'm not sure he even knows what a powwow is."

That was probably true of a lot of people in the area. Despite the work of a few families raising awareness about Dakhóta history through the powwow, I would guess that your average citizen wouldn't have any idea what we were doing. A powwow is a social gathering, but it's also a way of honoring your ancestors, and dancing for those who can't dance. I can't describe the feeling that comes through the drum, the energy I get when I'm dancing to a good song. It's like flying.

"We start lining up for Grand Entry in about fifteen minutes," I said. "That doesn't give us much time."

"I'm sorry to be so late. I had to check a few things in the garden."

"Rosie, I just don't get what the fascination is with you and farming. People still remember how the government tried to force us into becoming farmers."

"I'm not farming, at least not the way it's done in the big fields. Gardening is different. It's a way to feed my family."

"I know all about feeding a family. It's called Auntie Vera. And McDonald's." I patted my soft belly. We both laughed.

"I like being with plants," Rosie said, seeming a little embarrassed about admitting it.

"Do you talk to them?"

"Of course. Sometimes I sing."

"So you hardly ever go to powwows or community events. Instead, you stay home singing to your plants. That's like the stereotype that white people have about Indians, that we're all plant whisperers."

"I don't whisper," Rosie said, completely serious. "They tell me what they need. Or they show me. When Wakpá and I are in the garden and the birds are singing and the wind comes up, I'm happy. I don't know what else to tell you, except that it reminds me of home. If I go someplace where people are drinking or being unkind to each other, it makes me feel bad and remember things I don't want to think about."

"I get that. Just remember, there's a lot of people who are working hard to change things."

"I know." We fell silent for a few moments. Whenever Rosie and I got together, it seemed like we helped each other see things in a new way. I knew she wanted to learn more about the river, but I wasn't sure where to begin; there was so much to say. I wanted to tell her how some days I had to escape the office, driving upriver until I found a quiet place to sit in the long grass on the bank, to remind myself why I did this work. With my eyes closed, I would listen to the water, maybe hear the slap of waves against a passing canoe. Sometimes a big fish would jump near the shore, or a blue heron would step out from the tall cattails that grew in the shallows. I would picture my ancestors in that canoe, the grandmothers and the babies, and that's when I would get mad all over again. Thinking of this, I decided to give Rosie all the facts I could—because that's how the corporations work against us, twisting the truth till we're at war with each other.

"Okay, Rosie, we only have a few more minutes. I said I'd tell you more about the work I'm doing." I took a deep breath. "When Mathó was born, I realized that up until then I had been a complete waste of space. I started to think, What kind of life will my little čhiŋkší have? What kind of fucked-up world is he going to inherit? And what can I do about it? Then I had a dream. You know me, I'm pretty hardheaded, but that dream meant something to me. I dreamed the river was crying, that she had no one to help her. The women, the water carriers, had disappeared. There were no trees, no animals who came to drink. And when I woke, I knew what I needed to do. I would help our sister recover. That's why I'm in law school."

I leaned toward her, wanting so badly for her to understand why this was important. "Here's what you need to know, Rosie, since you're a farmer. I'm assuming you're familiar with the miles of drainage tiles and ditches that help keep fields dry?"

"Yeah," Rosie replied. "John added a new ditch this past spring. He was pleased with how early he could get in that field."

"Did he say anything about where the water goes?"

"No. I didn't think to ask."

"As water drains from the fields into the ditch, it also carries off a heavy load of chemicals, fertilizers, and pesticides. The water flows from the ditch to little rivers like the Cottonwood, and those connect to the Minnesota River, and that goes into the Mississippi, where the runoff goes all the way downriver to the Gulf of Mexico, creating a dead zone where nothing can live. Some of those chemicals are linked to cancer. But that's not all. Think about this, Rosie, the next time you're in your garden: These chemical manufacturers are in bed with the seed companies. Nowadays these big seed companies are the same ones selling us the pesticides and herbicides that you use on your fields. What a racket." I checked my watch. Almost time to go.

"You may be living on a farm, Rosie, but you still have to think like a Dakhóta. You can't sit back and let others poison the river or the land or fuck around with our seeds. Think about the sacrifices our ancestors made. You have to make a choice."

Before Rosie could respond, Mathó and Wakpá came racing toward us, slapping the picnic table to declare a winner, both of them out of breath. "Mom, Mom," Mathó said. "They're lining up. Let's go!"

With a quick hug to Rosie and Wakpá, we hurried to find our place in line, Mathó joining the other grass dancers. I still danced fancy shawl, but I was not the high-stepping dancer I once was. It didn't matter; at these traditional powwows, most of us were there because we danced from the heart. Of course, some of us were there for the snagging . . . howah!

With the first beat of the host drum, the long line of dancers began to move forward. We followed the veterans and the color guard, the flag bearers and the eagle staff. Each group took its moment as it entered the arena, all of us putting our best energy into our moves. I felt such gratitude to be there with my son.

Mathó danced his way past Rosie and Wakpá, showing off his finest steps, bending like the grass moving in the wind. Unable to resist the drum, Wakpá ran into the circle, bouncing and jumping, trying to imitate Mathó. I thought at first that Rosie would come after him and dance with us. But she didn't. She waited in the shade, hidden in a shadow where I couldn't see her face. Always watching and listening, her fear a living thing matched only by whatever it was that kept her moving forward.

When the dance ended, she and Wakpá melted away in the slow-moving crowd.

CHAPTER SIXTEEN

Rosalie Iron Wing Meister

1986

The fire was started by a cigarette left burning in an ashtray on the kitchen table. The homemade rub Edna had used to polish the wood with such loving care turned out to be highly flammable, especially when a light breeze blew in through the open window and fanned the spark that jumped quickly to a pile of unopened bills.

Upstairs, I woke coughing, tasting smoke. My eyes burned. A shrill alarm bleated in the distance. Was I dreaming, or was this real? A rough shake of my shoulder brought me abruptly to my senses, and adrenaline instantly flooded my body. John coughed as he got out of bed and yelled to me over the din of the alarm. "I . . . Tommy . . . hurry!"

I jumped up, grabbed my robe, and ran downstairs. Since John would get Tommy, I rushed to the hallway closet, where we kept a fire extinguisher that I prayed was up-to-date. A cloud of smoke was rolling through the open door of the kitchen. Inside, I saw that flames had already consumed the curtains and were climbing the walls. Desperate to stop the fire from reaching the propane stove, I squeezed the nozzle and held on as a spray of white foam streamed across the room, over the table, onto the walls. The flames refused at first to give way. But I held on, spraying and spraying, until I was left with a blackened wall, a smoking table, and an empty canister.

Dropping the extinguisher, I ran to the pantry. I grabbed the box of seeds, my body moving instinctively. As I ran out the front door, I nearly crashed into John, who was rushing up the steps with the garden hose. We looked at each other in shock, a growing horror on each of our faces. Tommy! Where was Tommy?

John pushed past me into the smoke-filled hallway, tearing up the stairs two at a time. In seconds, he came pounding back down, carrying Tommy, wrapped in his blanket and rubbing his eyes. John stomped over to where I stood frozen with fear, still holding my box.

"What the hell, Rosalie? What were you thinking? I told you to get Tommy. And you come out carrying this? Seeds? Is that all you care about?"

He stared at my face with such rage that I barely recognized him. In that moment, I believed he would have hurt me had any harm come to his son. Instead, he could hardly take a breath, the veins on his forehead popping out with the force of the blood pumping through his body.

"I thought . . . you said . . ."

"I said to get Tommy. I said to get Tommy!"

Alarmed by his father's shouting, Tommy reached for me. John's grip tightened around his son's body, and I knew it cost him when he let Tommy go.

"How am I supposed to trust you?" he spat, before turning

and marching back into the house. My knees gave way, and Tommy and I sank to the damp grass. I began to shake so badly that Tommy asked, "Mama, what's wrong with your hands?"

Within a few minutes, John returned to the yard, carrying a blanket and an overnight bag. He dropped both in front of me and handed me the truck keys.

"I called Judith. She's expecting you. I'll stay here and keep an eye on things."

He walked away without another word. Somehow, I loaded Tommy in the truck and drove to Judith's house, where the lights were blazing. She and George came out to meet us and took charge without asking a single question. Judith took one look at my face and wrapped me in the blanket we'd brought, telling George to take Tommy up to bed. She led me into the kitchen and filled the coffeepot. I put my head down on my arms, turned my face toward the wall. When the coffee was ready, Judith placed a steaming mug on the table and added a dollop of whiskey.

"You're in shock," she said. "Drink this, it will help."

We sat in silence for what seemed like a long time. Eventually a lone bird sang out, calling the others to wake. The darkness began to shift to gray.

"You need to rest."

"Not yet."

"Well, then, I may have to put you to work in the garden."

I laughed, and Judith laughed along with me.

"Judith," I said, and then stopped. I took a ragged breath. "Judith, he could have died because of me."

"Nonsense. From what John told me, it was you who put the fire out. What was he thinking, dragging in the garden hose?"

"He thought I had Tommy. And I thought he did."

"There was no harm done. The boy is fine, although Edna's probably rolling in her grave over that table. John was just scared, that's all. People say terrible things when they're upset. Get some rest. You'll feel better."

Upstairs, in Judith's spare room, I fell into a deep, uneasy sleep. I dreamed a woman's voice that sounded like wind, like water over rocks. She whispered:

The first sign came from the west, a thin trail of smoke against the deep blue of the sky. The wind carried the smell of burning, draped it on my hair and across my shoulders. Fear rustled the leaves on trees, woke memories of sacrifice when fire had swept through the prairie, sparked by lightning from the thunder beings. Fear quickened the footsteps of those who could flee. I was running with them, moving without hesitation along unmarked paths, my feet reading the land far better than my eyes. And then I stumbled and fell, rolling down a steep hill to the water, where I knew I would be safe if only I could cross to the other side.

I walked quickly on trembling legs, carrying a bundle that I held tight when I fell. My arms were so tired. The sun was shrouded in ash; even at noon I had trouble finding my way. My eyes stung from the smoke. Behind me, I heard a roar of voracious appetite, the earth consumed as hunger fed hunger, the flicking tongue of engorged flames climbing higher as the smoke became a cloud that hid us from each other. I heard a cough nearby, and another. It seemed we were many. We hurried along the river, seeking a safe place to cross. The old ones dropped behind and we could not stop to help. When my mother fell, I knew it from the pain that crossed my heart. I called for her, Iná! Iná! But she did not come . . .

I woke with a start, my breath coming in gasps as if I had been running. Without thinking, I grabbed the phone and dialed Gaby's number. She answered on the second ring.

"This better be good," she said. In a few brief sentences, I explained what had happened. She grunted. "What's the problem here, Rosie? Seems like things turned out okay. John will calm down."

"I know that. But, Gaby, I don't know what came over me. I just knew I had to get those seeds out, no matter what. I never stopped to check that Tommy was truly safe. All I thought about was the fire, and then those seeds."

The silence that followed was so long I finally asked if she was still there.

"You can believe this or not," Gaby said, choosing her words carefully. "But there are times when women have to make hard decisions, choices that are sometimes unforgiveable. We have to see beyond and be prepared to do whatever is needed to save our people, even if it breaks our hearts. My grandmother had a soul of iron from what her life cost her. It takes courage to do what you did. In another time, that act might have saved your family, or even your tribe."

I stared into the darkness as Gaby continued, "Think about this. Fire is a purifying force in the world. It cleans forests of dead wood, sterilizes as it scorches, and consumes us all if we let it. Some seeds need fire to sprout. What if you're that seed?"

That made no sense at all, though I didn't say so. I was beyond tired. I thanked Gaby and got off the phone.

John came by later that morning, while I was sleeping, and Judith explained to him why I had not looked after Tommy. He seemed to accept this, and we came home that afternoon. John never apologized, exactly, but he did acknowledge to Tommy that I had put out the fire.

Nevertheless, we had crossed a line. I knew, despite Judith's best efforts, that a part of John still wondered why I hadn't gone to Tommy first. The question lived between us, small and nagging, contested ground in an old war.

CHAPTER SEVENTEEN

Rosalie Iron Wing Meister
1987

Tommy knelt in the grass as I showed him how the delicate vine of the wild bean grew by wrapping itself around the stems of taller plants. Close up, he smelled like a sweaty young boy, salty and earthy and innocent. His dirt-rimmed fingernails followed the vine back down to the soil, through a tangle of green leaves and grasses, just as I had shown him. He pressed the sharp tip of a trowel a few inches deep and popped the plant free. Pulling away the residue of dirt that clung to the roots, he uncovered the tiny bean that we were gathering.

"Look! I found one!"

"Nice work. Sometimes this bean is called a hog peanut. In the fall, mice gather these beans for their winter food. My father, your Uŋkáŋ, told me that Dakhóta women used to always bring some corn to trade for beans with the little mouse."

"Why?"

"So the mouse children would not starve. No one wants children to go hungry. That's why we always share our food."

Tommy thought for a moment. "Is that why we bring potatoes to that one store?"

"Yes. We take care of each other."

Tommy added his bean to the bag we carried on our gathering trips. He pulled out the apple I had brought for him and laid it on the ground. "This is for the mouse people."

I had begun teaching Tommy about the plants I had learned from my father when I was a child. The two of us foraged in the woods at the edge of the field and farther along the river. He helped me gather wild ginger, for a tea to soothe his stomachaches, and heal-all, a mint that we used for poultices. He grew skilled at spotting bearberry and knowing when the chokecherries were ripe. And in the spring, I had shown him the crimson source of bloodroot's name.

We gathered enough beans to cook a small dish for supper and headed toward the river to cool off. At seven, Tommy was tall for his age and fast, running down the hill ahead of me and stripping off his shoes so he could wade into the slow-moving water. While I watched him throw rocks almost to the other bank, I remembered my own days as a child, spearing imaginary fish and catching minnows. Skipping rocks and hunting for turtles. Back then, I had wondered why my father would not fish in the river, why he stayed so far from the water. When I asked him, he had turned his head away with a silent shake, his mouth set in a firm line.

When it was time to go home, Tommy climbed the hill like a young goat, leaping between rocks and chasing after a skittering bull snake, roused from its nap on the warm rocks. At the top, we came around the wide trunk of a tree to find ourselves face-to-face with an enormous buck, who seemed as surprised to see us as we were him. Tommy froze. I placed my hands on his shoulders and we slowly backed up, one step at a time, until the tree stood between us and the deer. Losing interest once we were out of sight, the buck chuffed twice and then bounded across the field, his white tail flashing as he ran.

"Mama, where did he go?" Tommy ran out to look in the direction the deer had vanished.

I could not answer him for a moment. Suddenly I was lost in the dream of my mother tending the fire, the buck hanging from a branch overhead. Her voice calling my name. In the pattern of routines that had become my world, I had almost forgotten that dream.

"That was a male deer," I finally said. "This is his home. He was more afraid of us. See how quickly he ran away?"

"Yeah."

"If we were hunting today, and we had prayed first and offered čhaŋšáša, then he might have given his life so that we could have food."

"Why?"

"We all depend on each other to survive. The plants we gather give their lives; the deer gives its life. Someday we will give ours, too. You have to be respectful, knowing that a plant's or animal's life is a gift that allows us to live. You never take more than what you need."

We were so late getting back to the house that John was waiting for us, sitting at the new kitchen table. I dropped my gathering bag in the pantry and sent Tommy upstairs to change his clothes.

"I thought we had a teacher conference tonight," John said,

not looking at me. After the fire, he had begun checking up with me on Tommy's activities, like I couldn't be trusted.

"We do. I've got leftover hot dish that will take a minute to heat up."

Silence filled the kitchen, broken only by the sound of my knife chopping lettuce for a salad.

John stood up. "Tommy is old enough to start helping out with a few chores after school," he said, as he reached into the refrigerator for a beer. I did not reply.

Tommy's second-grade teacher, Mrs. Gunderson, was an older woman a few years from retirement, who was loved as a grandmother by her young students. While Tommy colored at his desk, we sat in two small chairs facing her.

"Tommy is a very bright student," she said, beaming at us. "The only assignment he had trouble with was drawing a picture of his family. When I asked him about his grandparents, he said he didn't have any. Is that true?"

"Yes, it's true," John responded. "My folks both passed away before Tommy was born. And Rosalie—well, she can tell you about her family." He looked at me with his eyebrows raised, clearly inviting me to share my story. I kept my mouth shut. An awkward pause bloomed between us.

"I see," Mrs. Gunderson said. "I told Tommy that we could just write their names if they're no longer living. But he never brought the names to school with him."

"Oh. Most likely the assignment was misplaced," John said, glancing at me. "My folks were Harlan Meister and Edna Horst."

"Of course, I knew their families," Mrs. Gunderson said as she carefully wrote down the names. "And Rosalie, who were your parents?"

It seemed that she turned to me with more than casual interest.

"My father was Ray Iron Wing. And my mother was Agnes Kills Deer."

I waited as Mrs. Gunderson's pen did not move.

"So, it's true, then, that your son is . . . part Indian. I wondered, you know, because he looks so . . . like you . . . and, of course, other children can sometimes be unkind."

"Unkind?" I asked, with a rising edge in my voice.

"You know how kids are. They like to tease, call each other names."

"What names?"

"Like 'Chief' or 'Crazy Horse' or 'Redskin,' things like that. 'Savage.'"

"And you allow it?"

"Oh no. No, no, no. More than one boy has found himself in the principal's office for calling names. I just don't always hear them. And your son is not one to tell tales."

I felt the heat rising in my body, a dangerous sign. I could still hear voices from high school singing out—*squaw, Pocahontas*—as I walked down the hall. I felt an old familiar rage prickling the skin on my arms and across my chest. Stinging nettles.

"Mrs. Gunderson," I said, and she turned to me with a smile that faltered just a bit as she met my eyes. "I want to talk to the parents of these children."

"I'm afraid I can't . . ." she started to say, until I slammed my hand down on the desk hard enough to scatter Tommy's papers.

"I want to talk to the parents of these children!" My voice had grown louder, as if that would help her understand what I was saying.

"Rosie, I think you've said enough. Let's go," John said, grabbing my arm and gesturing for Tommy to get up. I was hustled out of the room as if I was about to start making threats. Mrs. Gunderson stared after us, her hand pressed over her heart.

John kept shaking his head as we strode back to the car. Perhaps because he never saw brown skin when he looked at his son, he hadn't realized that the world had already marked him as different. Knowing the history, understanding how some of his neighbors regarded Indians, had not prepared him to see his own son treated that way. He didn't want to admit, even to himself, that a thin veneer of nice covered a dormant hostility in this community. He wasn't there when store clerks suddenly appeared in whatever aisle I was shopping in, or to see the way mothers pulled their children to the side when we joined the reading circle at the library. He didn't hear the silence that fell when Tommy and I walked into the coffee shop. From his family, he knew how it felt to be the object of gossip, but he didn't know the first thing about being brown in a white Christian community living on Dakhóta land.

When Tommy was asleep upstairs, I went to the living room, where John was watching television in the recliner, a can of beer on the table next to him. I sat on the couch and waited until he turned off the TV. There was much that needed to be discussed.

"I want to teach Tommy at home," I said.

"I don't think that's a good idea," John replied. "He needs to learn how to stick up for himself. If kids are picking on him because he's Indian, he can't just run away. That will make things worse when he gets older."

"No, it won't," I said, feeling my face flush. "Knowing who he is will give him the strength he needs to put up with all the crap he's going to face in life."

"He knows who he is. He's my son, he carries the Meister name. If that was good enough for me, it's good enough for him. I'll teach him what he needs to know to be a man."

Silence.

"Rosie, I know you're worried about him," John continued, speaking in the calm voice he used whenever I got upset. "I'm worried, too. If he's going to run this farm someday, he needs to learn from me. Can't you see that? Your way will make him more of a target."

"Why can't we both teach him?"

"We have been. You take him to powwows and show him plants. Now that he's older, he needs to spend more time with me, learning about the farm. When I was his age, I knew how to run the tractor." Hearing nothing more from me, he turned the television back on.

I escaped upstairs and lay awake, staring at the ceiling, shaken by our conversation. How naive I had been, years ago, to think only about needing a home. Now I understood why my father had told me to marry a Dakhóta. He had been trying to warn me about exactly this moment, when a child's heart was at stake. He had believed that growing up in a mixed family made it easier to turn away from Dakhóta values.

My conflict with John was rooted in the essence of who we were, and an unshakeable belief we each had that our own way was best for this child. My fear was that Tommy would grow up confused, unable to reconcile the two sides of his blood. As our son, one day he would have to choose which road to follow.

Generations before me had been silenced, forced to hide their ceremonies and language underground, deep in the woods, carrying this knowledge as a lifeline to the culture. I wasn't giving up on my son. Every time we gathered plants, offered our čhaŋšáša to the water, or said a prayer as we watched the sun rise above the trees, Tommy was learning from me, just as I had learned from my father. Without words, without books, I would do my best to teach him what he needed to know to live in this world.

The next day, Tommy and I went out to the garden as usual, but it seemed more important than ever. After a sleepless night, I needed the comfort of plants around me, the language of their mute endurance, their ability to survive and thrive and adapt. My father had once pointed out a chokecherry tree that had dropped most of its leaves, while a young tree nearby was thriving. The mother tree had chosen to sacrifice its own health for its offspring, sending its share of nutrients to help the other tree battle a fungus. The young tree recovered and, over time, the mother tree also regrew its leaves.

In the garden, I showed Tommy how the withered pods should feel dry like paper, not soft or damp. I cracked one open to show him the tidy row of black beans inside, now dry enough for us to store for the winter.

"Like the bean mouse?" he asked.

"Like the bean mouse."

While Tommy filled his basket, I told him that we would save the very best beans to plant in the spring, so we would have plenty of food every year. He could fill his own envelope with seeds and write his name on the outside.

As we picked, a large flock of blackbirds appeared. At first dozens, then hundreds of birds landed in the upper branches of the oak trees across the field. They called and called in their rough voices before taking off again, their black bodies punctuating a pale blue sky, wheeling and turning as if connected by a single thought. When they flew low overhead, I could hear the murmur of wings, feeling the blessing in that sound. Tommy was just as entranced as I was, sitting completely still, almost forgetting to breathe as he gazed upward, his mouth half-open.

The birds had barely disappeared when we heard John, home early from the fields, calling for Tommy. Hearing his name, Tommy looked at me, as if unsure what to do. Neither of us moved for a moment.

"Go on, then, your father wants you." Wiping his small hands on his jeans, Tommy ran toward the barn. At dinner that night, he chattered about his afternoon with his dad. "I'm to help feed the chickens. And on weekends, I can ride in the tractor."

At bedtime, John announced that he would read a book to Tommy. Stopping in the hallway with an armload of laundry, I overheard John's halting voice reciting the tale of David and Goliath. What next? I muttered to myself. Church? Sure enough, while John never made it back to a service, he began regularly dropping off his son for Sunday school. Tommy learned to sing hymns in his sweet, high voice, to memorize the

Ten Commandments, and to understand heaven and hell. He asked questions about the devil and baby Jesus. Surrounded by approving adults, he learned that his father's beliefs were blessed by God and church and community. Eager to please him, Tommy began spending less time with me, until I finally stopped asking if he wanted to help in the garden or gather plants in the woods.

Because this is what he remembers, Thomas grew up believing that I had given up on him. And that is what he cannot forgive.

CHAPTER EIGHTEEN

Rosalie Iron Wing
2002

Seventeen days after I first met Ida in the woods, my attention to the world began to slip. After so many days of not speaking, of not hearing another human voice, my skin seemed to peel from my body, layer by layer. Images from the past rose and dissolved, my story unraveling into a blank, raw emptiness. Leaving was no longer an option. It was as if I was being gradually reshaped by winter's isolation, by the death grip of cold, by the insistent darkness. This longed-for solitude slowly turned into my great challenge, the sharp edge on which I balanced.

As the days blurred together, I became careless. I nearly froze one night when I accidentally let the fire go out. I woke from a dream sometime after midnight, my feet numb, my fingers stiff with cold. Suddenly alert, I realized that staying alive was a choice I had to make every day if I wanted to survive the winter. I had to keep the fire going at all times—otherwise I would freeze to death, simple as that.

Staying alive meant I had to stoke the fire before drifting

off to sleep, wake in the night to add more wood, and leave my warm bed at dawn to reload the stove and heat water for coffee. There was no backup oil furnace to kick on when the temperatures dropped well below freezing, a luxury I had never fully appreciated at the farm. Or the lifesaving efficiency of a chainsaw, a tool I had not thought to bring with me. Instead, I had to make do with what I had.

Taking stock the morning after my close call, I realized I had already burned through much of the woodpile behind the cabin. I thought of the long walks I used to take with my father, searching for fallen branches and logs not yet rotted and hauling them back to the cabin, where he spent hours chopping each load into pieces that would fit into the stove. Back then, we had a sled that I used to ride before we filled it up. He had added hinged sidewalls and replaced the metal runners with wide, flat slats to allow the sled to glide across snow and fallen leaves.

Beneath the mound of snow near the woodpile, I knew I would find my father's hardware store, his treasure mound, his might-need-it-later collection of car parts, broken tools, chicken wire, wooden crates, whiskey bottles, lampshades, an armchair, and a hand-crank washing machine. A rusted-out Ford truck rested on four flat tires, nearly buried in snow, cobwebs fluttering across a half-open window. After a brief search, I found the sled, in surprisingly decent shape, aside from its mostly rotten wood slats. With a hammer and a couple of nails, I attached the remaining bits of solid wood to a sheet of metal that had once been part of the roof, curving one end so it would glide.

I strapped on my snowshoes and strode into the woods, hearing the distant echo of Šúŋka's happy bark, my father's whistle. Sunlight broke softly around me, stray beams catching on snow-lined branches, reflected by the white until the woods shimmered with light. As I squinted against the glare, I remembered that my father had once mentioned that the Dakhóta name for March meant "sore eyes" or "snow blindness."

Once the sled was loaded with branches and remnants of logs, I hauled it back to the cabin, working up a sweat as I trudged through the deep snow. After unloading the wood straight onto the front porch and covering it with a ragged tarp, I made one more trip to gather kindling and a bucket of fresh snow that I left on the stove. Tired, sweaty, and wanting only to sit with a cup of tea, I had one small chore left to do. Every morning when I was a child, my father and I would leave leftover food for local scavengers beneath the ancient red oak behind the cabin. Now I picked up a bowl of meat scraps from the previous night's dinner and carried it to the same tree, its massive branches spread wide, a handful of acorns still clinging to small twigs. I dumped the scraps in a pile and used a handful of snow to scrape the bowl clean.

When I turned back toward the cabin, I was startled to see a feral cat perched on the hood of the old Ford. His yellow eyes watched me with a flat, predatory gaze. Matted orange fur covered his gaunt shoulders, rippled across his bony ribs. He was taking a risk feeding in the yard; I'd seen fox scat around recently. He must have been starving to show himself to me, especially in daylight. I wondered how he had made his way here. Maybe, like me, he had found himself snowed in after a storm, surviving on voles and rabbits.

I turned away and walked slowly back to the cabin, not wanting to spook him. I'd seen enough feral cats to know they had no interest in getting close to people. But perhaps I could help him survive the winter. I wouldn't mind another living being nearby.

That evening I made a simple soup from a package of Ida's venison sausages, adding a jar of carrots from the farm and potatoes from last fall's harvest. When the broth cooled, I spooned off the layer of congealed fat and set it aside in a dish, to mix with a scoop of meat and vegetables. With regular meals, my new neighbor—whom I'd already dubbed Šazí, or "Orange"—might have a fighting chance.

We quickly fell into a routine, Šazí and me. At night I cooked for us, separating his portion into a bowl that I left each morning under the oak. He was usually in the same place, on the hood of the truck, waiting until he heard the cabin door close before approaching the food. I watched him from the bedroom window as he made a leap from the truck to the woodpile, picked a careful path from one log to the next, jumped to the roof of the outhouse, made a final, desperate leap to a low-hanging branch of the oak, and clawed his way down the trunk to the food. He wolfed it down in a few hurried gulps, his eyes scanning the trees around him with furtive, paranoid glances.

I could almost hear John's skeptical grunt at the waste of time and food. "Those cats are plain wild," he would have said, "just good for nothing." John wouldn't have gone so far as to drown a litter of unwanted kittens, like some farmers we knew, but he wouldn't go out of his way to keep one alive, either. Animals had to earn their keep, like our old hound Boomer, who was a good hunting dog in his day and kept an eye on the place whenever we were gone. Boomer knew how to ride in a truck and sit on command, and he finally died in his sleep of old age, as a dog should. He knew his place in the world.

This cat, on the other hand, wanted only enough scraps to keep from starving. He made it clear that he owed me nothing, keeping his distance and watching me with an air of repressed hostility. But in the long, dark hours of those early weeks at the cabin, when I was still adjusting to the silence of loss, Šazí was the one spark of life that kept me tethered to the world. His hunger gave me purpose. I think he sensed that I had little to give him beyond the scraps in my bowl. Nor did I need his affection, avoiding any temptation to draw him closer, a connection that would only come at the cost of his wild, untamed self. I wanted him to survive on his own terms, getting nothing from me other than a helping hand. I still carried my childhood yearning to run through the woods, to feel the freedom of wild things around me.

But we had not counted on our mutual loneliness, the way it slowly pulled us closer together when it seemed he might survive after all. A week later, when the March thaw started the ice melting in leisurely drips along the porch, I chopped kindling on a large stump near the woodpile, at a safe distance from Šazí's tree. He had grown used to me moving around the yard, trusting that I would not come near him. When he was done eating, he cleaned his fur before yawning. He watched me work for a few minutes, studied the shrubs nearby, then sauntered back to his lair inside the truck, where I had snuck an old blanket.

I found myself looking forward to Šazí's occasional appearances outside of mealtime. Watching him step carefully across the snow-covered field, the way he studied the world around him with fixed attention, started to teach me a new kind of silence, one not made from dying and loss. I remembered how it felt to be connected to each season, to listen deeply, to find a resting place within winter's isolation.

I studied the patience of the red oak, so perfectly formed over many years, as she endured the cold. In the fall, she prepared by pulling the energy of sunlight belowground, to be stored in her roots, much as I preserved the harvest from my garden. Through a season that seems too cold for anything to survive, the tree simply waits, still growing inside, and dreams of spring. Without fully understanding yet why I had come back, I began to think it was for this, for the slow return of a language I once knew. The language of this place.

The next morning, I rose at dawn, unable to sleep, sensing the distant rumblings of spring. As I stood at the front window, rubbing my arms to keep warm, I saw a cottontail slipping out between two loose boards under the steps. Rabbits rarely sought shelter this close to a house, preferring to hide their nests out in the open. How desperate she must have been to risk encountering a human, not to mention Šazí—or the fox, whose tracks I'd seen around the oak tree again the day before.

My father would have told me not to worry, that this was how nature took care of itself. "Did I ever tell you the story about the rabbit and the fox?" he had asked me one day, over lunch. It was an afternoon when I had little patience for my father's tales.

"No," I said, not wanting to listen but knowing I had no choice.

"Well, that old fox, he thought he was smarter than the rabbit, and he boasted that he planned to eat her, probably with pickles and mustard, just like you have on your sandwich."

"He did not say that."

"You're right—maybe it was ketchup. Anyway, the rabbit turned herself into a dead tree and fooled the fox, who broke off a branch to be sure and trotted away. When rabbit turned herself back, she had a short nose, where the branch had been broken. The next day, after fox realized he had been fooled, rabbit hid behind a dead tree. Not wanting to be fooled again, fox ate the whole tree and crawled away, not feeling too good. Rabbit laughed and laughed and lived to raise her babies."

I narrowed my eyes at him, unconvinced. "That old fox is going to eat those babies when they grow up, isn't he?"

"Probably. But if he didn't, then pretty soon we'd have too many rabbits running around, eating all the grass and the berries and the plants you like to pick. When there's nothing left, we all starve. You don't want that, do you?"

"No."

"See, that's why we need the fox *and* the rabbits. That's the law of the land, how nature keeps the balance between all of our relatives."

To be sure I understood this lesson, a few days later he showed me how to make a snare, catch my own rabbit, skin it, and make stew. I must have been ten or eleven years old. That first time was hard, even though I had already learned that hunger was a powerful teacher. I knew that if I had to choose between the rabbit's life and an empty belly, I was willing to play the fox. The night I told Gaby and Anthony about killing the rabbit at my foster family's house—the night they laughed—I could tell they had never known hunger like I had. It changes you.

When the cottontail disappeared into the woods, I walked into my father's room and looked around. On the wall, near the photos and articles about space, he had tacked up his own star map, with the word "Wičáŋhpi" written across the top in crude block letters. Then he began staying up for nights at a time staring at the sky. He would show me the North Star, tell me its true name was Wičáŋhpi wazíyata, and ask me to repeat this over and over until I had it memorized. Or sometimes he would wake me from sleep to come watch the stars with him.

On and on he would talk, but he always came back to the same place, the same argument he had used against the school board that fired him for teaching Native science. "Proof?" he would say, and I knew what was coming next. Nothing I could say or do would stem this flood of words. I closed my eyes.

"You want proof? What more do you need than thousands of years of astronomy that Western scientists are only now beginning to understand? Indians have used the stars to guide our food gathering and ceremonies since the beginning of our time here. That's right: star knowledge was a way of life that included our spirituality. You can't have science without caring about how it's used. You have to be a good relative.

"Can't they see that the earth is dying? It's time people stop pretending there's no limit to what they can take . . ."

As he ranted, my head would dip lower and lower until I fell asleep. I always woke back in my own bed, dreaming of stars and animals and thunderbirds. The first thing I'd do was check to see if he was still home. Sometimes, when he stayed awake all night, he'd disappear. One morning I woke and the front door was standing open, the wind blowing his papers around the room, a half-empty whiskey bottle on the table. I poured the rest out in the snow, hating the smell, what it did to him.

My father always said it wouldn't happen again, each time he returned. But he couldn't always afford his heart medication, or he'd bury the pills in the woods after starting to feel slow, to have trouble finding words. I always knew when he stopped taking them. He would either stay in bed and sleep for days, or he would stop sleeping entirely, spending hours with his star charts and maps and books.

When I think back, I tell myself that he taught me to be a survivor. Even as a child, I knew how to snare my own food, build a fire, and busy myself with books until he finally came home, sometimes days later. I was proud that I could survive on my own. I never said to him, There have been times when my snare was empty, when you left me with nothing in the cupboards but a bag of moldy flour. When I started to believe that the coyotes were yipping for me, coming closer and closer to the cabin. Do you know how long a fire will burn when the wood runs low? Especially on winter days like this one? I was too small, then, to swing the long ax for chopping wood. I was cold and hungry and so scared that I hid beneath my covers and cried myself to sleep, trying to forget the pit that burned in my stomach. I wished I could say, I always knew a day would come when you wouldn't return. That you would leave me alone and expect me to figure it out.

I have my own son now, the grandson you never met. He's tall, like you, with the same deep-set eyes and strong, stubborn chin. But I'll tell you this: when he was a little boy, I thought the most important thing I could give him was a safe place to grow up, a home where he would never be hungry or left alone for days at a time. Now I'm not so sure. What you taught me helped me get through the hard years, after I was taken away. I know it made me tough enough to survive. Whether I passed that on to Thomas, I don't know. Time will tell.

My father had covered his star map with drawings of thunderbirds and turtles, bears and snakes and salamanders, which showed the constellations in meticulous detail. As I smoothed a wrinkled corner of the map, I read an inscription in his handwriting.

"Find the place that Indians talk about," he had written. The place of spirit where all things are created. I wondered if he ever found it.

CHAPTER NINETEEN

Marie Blackbird
1889

A lone sandhill crane landed in the field across the road, making a slow circle before deciding it was safe. I might have told him different, but that's my old self talking, the one that sees danger behind every tree, that jumps when the wind blows the door shut. I had watched him spread his wings, riding the wind better than any man has ever ridden a horse, and pull up just before his heavy body settled on two long, skinny legs. Like mine, I said to myself, the meat on my bones used up in the hungry years at Crow Creek.

The crane took a step or two, walking like a man, a different bird now, almost as tall as me. There was a time, long ago, when we might have visited with each other, trading stories of things we had seen. But today when he called, *kar-r-r-r-o-o-o*, I could only wonder at his meaning. It was that sound that got to me, as if he had called up the past in a circle around us. Like he was telling me that he had always been here, would always be here, despite the fences, the cutting down of trees, the wood and brick buildings that were springing up across the land.

His raspy cry said the Missouri River still winds its way south and the wind still sings across the open plains. We are still here, the crane called to me, and this land is ours.

Maybe so, I thought, and maybe not. What the white settlers called progress was a storm of fury thundering its way across the land, and none of us were strong enough to withstand it. How else would the Dakhóta have become so scattered, shipped here like sacks of flour or fleeing far to the north, blown in every direction like milkweed seeds in fall?

After more than twenty winters in this place called Santee, another reservation meant to pen us in like the white man's cattle—after learning the harsh lessons of the plains, of a new river, of plants that had been a mystery when we first arrived—the thought of leaving filled me with fear. To me, Nebraska wasn't home, but it was beautiful in its own way. Still, I had promised Iná, my mother, that one day I would return to Mní Sota.

Seeing the sun move higher above my neighbor's roof, I picked the last ear of corn, pulling down quick to snap it from its withered stalk. The corn was nearly as tall as it had grown back home, where we used to roast it over the fire and dry the seeds for spring planting. Here the dirt was not as good, and there wasn't so much rain, but the corn had learned to survive, just as we had. A long time had passed since the night I spent sewing seeds into my skirt. Every day I offered a prayer of gratitude for my mother's quick thinking, for the corn that had helped feed us through the winter.

I left the last row for the deer and the hungry magpies who perched in nearby treetops. And for my neighbor, whose corn did not grow so well as mine, even though I had shared my seeds with her. She did not know how to sing to them.

Hoisting the basket to my hip, I carried it to my small house and set it down just inside the door. That evening, I would braid the corn so it could be hung up to dry.

The main room of the house was big enough to hold two beds, a table and chairs, and a wood-burning stove for heat. I washed my hands in a bucket I used for cleaning vegetables. Then I faced the small mirror that hung from a nail on the wall. The face that stared back was not me; a stranger had taken my place. Deep lines pulled down the corners of my mouth, as if holding back my anger. My eyes were black with sorrow and shame, my face framed by silver hair that made me look older than my years. My dreams always came from war.

As if living on this reservation was not enough, I had to dress like a white woman, too. This was one of many rules at the Santee Normal Training School, where I helped cook for the Dakhóta students who were learning to be teachers and ministers and farmers. Pulling my long hair back just as Miss Williams had shown me, I struggled to wrap it around my clumsy fingers and pin it snug against my head. I couldn't get it smooth, as the white teachers did. Most days I didn't worry so much, but today was different. I wanted nothing that could be criticized. I pulled the pins out and tried again, this time getting most of my hair tucked inside a large bun. Well, it would have to do. After slipping off my moccasins, I squeezed my wide feet into a pair of tight button shoes and covered my head with a bonnet that tied under my chin. My father would not have known me.

I heard a sharp, playful yip from the stray dog that roamed between houses, searching for kitchen scraps and slow mice. At least I knew where to find my daughter, Susanne, who would spend all day running through the woods if she could. The door banged open and she rushed in, breathless from her games with the dog, a strand of black hair stuck to her sweaty forehead, her brown skin a startling contrast to her blue eyes. Now that she was a first-year student, she walked to school with me every day. I was proud of her quick learning, the way she could already speak wašíču and read their books. If only she was as quick to be ready in the morning. These teachers were very strict about time.

Even so, we couldn't help dawdling on our long walk to school. The air was crisp and clean, a welcome relief from the parched heat of summer. Trees did not grow so tall here, except close to the river, or in the cooler hills that trapped water in ravines. When we came up over the crest of a low rise, I could see the school sprawling out in front of us, with tall buildings made of brick, a dormitory for students who traveled far, a church, a smithy, even a garden. Susanne became more subdued and walked quietly next to me, squeezing my hand tightly before I left her at the classroom.

By midmorning, breakfast dishes for nearly two hundred students had been cleared away, washed, and left to dry on the long tables. I had already filled the big soup kettle with water and a few beef bones to simmer for lunch. The floor was swept, the slop buckets emptied. There was nothing that Cook could criticize. Except my news. After smoothing my skirt with damp, anxious hands, I waited for a calm moment to speak to her.

"Excuse me, Cook, a word, please, when you have time."

She stared at me for a moment without saying anything, her eyes narrowed in suspicion. Finally, she wiped her hands on her apron.

"What is it?"

"In three days, I plan to marry the farm teacher, Oliver Bordeaux. He was offered work back home, teaching farming to Dakhóta families who have returned to Mní Sota. We leave at the end of the week."

What a fierce look she gave me then. Because she was Ho-Chunk, she blamed me for what had happened to her people after the war. They had nothing to do with the fighting, but the government removed them anyway, because the whites demanded it. She shrugged and turned back to the bread dough she was kneading. The rest of the morning she ignored me, speaking only to the other women. That was fine; I was used to her. Besides, in a few days, I would be gone. I was returning to my home, the land I had not seen since I was a young girl. Oliver and I thought we might even get a piece of land on the old reservation, by the river, near where I once lived.

I had been working at the Training School since 1870, when it first opened to teach a handful of Dakhóta students. The boys learned how to farm, shoe horses, make their own tools. The girls learned housekeeping and sewing. I was too old myself then to be a student, but they hired me to help cook. In truth, I liked working there, because the students were allowed to speak Dakhóta, unlike in the boarding schools, where they were punished if they used their own language. We had heard stories of the Carlisle School out east, where some of the chiefs had sent their children. It was said they returned as wašíču in the way they talked, the way they looked down on their families. Some didn't return at all. In Santee, however, we even had a Dakhóta Bible and hymnal. I could not read, but Susanne was already learning. She gave me such pride.

No matter what Cook thought of me, she must have passed the word of my leaving to the people who ran the school. The next day, the headman told me a wašíču teacher and a Dakhóta student wanted to ask questions for their journal, the *Iapi Oaye*. I didn't know what I could tell them. All I could say was that it made me happy to feed the students, to see them laugh with each other. We had all known too much sorrow for one lifetime.

They told me to wait in one of the empty classrooms. I was grateful for a few minutes to myself. I was just past forty winters, but I felt much older. This was true for everyone who had survived the years at Crow Creek, before the government moved us to Santee. Even now it was hard to think of those days. So little to eat, the meat rotten, no woods nearby to gather plants. The hills were covered with small graves, including that of my younger brother, Čhaské. We never spoke of those days, my mother and I, before she died. We had wanted Susanne to grow up without that shadow in her young life.

I sat down at one of the student desks and wished I could take off my shoes. It was a long walk home after standing in them all day. I smoothed my skirt, my fingers restless for work, and briefly wished I had my quilting box with me. I could have filled this time by stitching a few more pieces for the quilt I was working on—a morning star, my favorite design—made from donated clothes I'd found in the church box.

Finally, a young woman, Esther Langley, walked in. She had been hired the month previous to teach home skills.

Behind her was a shy older student, Sarah, who carried a pencil and paper for notes. After they had settled into nearby desks, Esther thanked me for my time. I told her I didn't know much about anything.

Esther smiled and said, "We'll just ask a few questions and you can answer, or not. Your name is Marie Blackbird, is that correct?"

I gave a slight nod.

"And does your family live here as well?"

"My mother, Maȟpíyamaza, passed on last year. We think my father, Mázakhoyaginape, died at the prison in Davenport, Iowa."

We did not know precisely when or where my Até had died. Two years after he was taken prisoner, while we were living in that place not fit for animals, a letter came, written in Dakhóta by a missionary at the prison. I asked Reverend Williamson, who knew our language, to read it to us. I kept the words in my heart. *Mitakuye hécen eha wówapi cicaǧe...*

What joy we felt to know that my Até was alive and searching for news of us. The letter restored my mother's hope that he would return. We kept it safe inside a small piece of deerskin, tied with sinew, tucked away at the bottom of the willow basket. She prayed for him every day.

When the surviving warriors were released the next year, in 1866, they joined us at Santee, but he did not come with them. What little was left of my mother's spirit broke down. At night, I heard her whispering to him as if he lay next to her. Telling him how the soldiers had taken us from our home, then sent us on boats to a land where nearly half our people died from hunger and sickness. Our dead were left behind, some in shallow, unmarked graves, others alone in the woods or surrendered to the river.

I was so lost in my thoughts that it took a moment before I realized Esther was speaking again. "Excuse me, Marie, should I repeat that? We thank you for your many years working at our school. Since the beginning, I understand."

Another nod. I was tired. I did not wish to remember all this.

"And in that time, you have become a Christian and regularly attend the Episcopal church?"

Nod. In the desperate years following the war, many of us converted.

"Good. You are also a member of the Wíŋyaŋ omníčiye—did I say that right?—the women's church society that meets every Wednesday. I hear that you have become an accomplished quilt maker. I had the pleasure of seeing the quilt you made for the last church auction. Truly beautiful."

She waited for a reply while continuing to stare at me. There was nothing to be said. Sarah kept her eyes on her paper like a proper Dakhóta wíŋyaŋ.

"I'm sure you're happy to be going home," Esther continued, prodding. "Is there anything that you'll miss here? Anything you are sorry to be leaving behind?"

That's when I understood. This new teacher was from the East and did not know the story of what had happened to us. For reasons I did not fully grasp, this filled me with rage, a feeling that rarely stirred beneath the heavy weight of my grief. I opened my mouth to reply and then stopped. Years of being afraid to speak out had become a habit. The silence grew long while a torrent of angry words threatened to push their way to the surface. I was too tired to hold them in any longer. And so, speaking only in

Dakhóta, I gave the one speech of my entire life, to a woman who could not understand me, and to a student whose heart I broke.

"I am leaving behind the bones of my Iná in your cemetery for Indians. I am leaving behind the absence of my Até, who died alone in a prison far from here. I am leaving behind the grave of my only brother, Čhaské, who did not live to see his second winter. Maybe you can see the wanáǧi who follow me still, crying for their loved ones, lost in a land that is not ours.

"The wašíču do not know what it means to be from a place that has shaped us like the river carves its path through the land. They are blind in their certainty that their God, their civilization, is worth the sacrifice of so many lives. We are treated as children, ignorant and in need of teachers. I have watched my brother starve to death and my relatives carried off by sickness. No matter what salvation they say is waiting for me, I cannot forgive the death of so many children."

A pause while I struggled to control my anger, the blood rising in my face, my fists clenched in my lap. The teacher had asked me a question, but I could not give her the answer she wanted. Not yet. Not until I said what had been left unsaid for too many years.

"The minister says it is a sin to hate; well, then, I am a sinner. He says we must forgive each other for what cannot be undone. I ask, What does he know of forgiveness? Now that they have our land, do they forgive us for defending our families? Do they forgive the babies who died of hunger, when their only crime was to be born Indian?

"Let me tell you what I know of forgiveness. It came with sharp teeth and the bluest eye, with a breath that stank of whiskey, and a fist that knocked me to the ground. The bluest eye follows me now, sits in your classroom learning to read. In a few days, we leave for my home and she will ride in the back of the wagon, this bluest eye, this reminder, this half-breed child. My mother, Maȟpíyamaza, taught me forgiveness when she said, You must love this child, that's the only way you can survive. Over time, I knew the wisdom in her words. This child is innocent, she is sacred, no matter how she came to be. My mother said, Raise her to be a Dakhóta wíŋyaŋ. Let love be your vengeance, your honor restored because you did not surrender to their violence. Most days, I do. I try. I pray, holding the book I cannot read, calling on Wakháŋ Tháŋka, on God, on Jesus, to help me forgive.

"That is what I leave behind. The memory of all that I have lost."

When I finished speaking, Sarah was weeping in silence, wiping her eyes. Esther looked from her to me, a question dying on her tongue, hearing my story only through the tone of my voice, in my eyes that would not meet hers. But she knew, she knew.

Afterward, Susanne and I walked home together and cut across a field to the cemetery where Maȟpíyamaza was buried. While Susanne picked wildflowers to leave for her grandmother, I sat at the grave and told my Iná—until we meet again in the next world. I knew she would have been happy that I was going home with her only granddaughter, her beloved thakóža.

We would travel in a wagon packed with our clothes, Oliver's tools, a few pots and pans, and enough food to last us for several weeks. I would carry the willow basket of seeds that Iná had given to me many years earlier. It was always her wish to return home, to be buried with her ancestors. I carried a lock of her hair that I had promised I would one day place beneath the cottonwood trees near the river. Hearing her last words to me: "Find them, mičhúŋkši, tell them they have not been forgotten."

$$\maltese$$

CHAPTER TWENTY

Rosalie Iron Wing Meister
1987

Before my father died, he told me that we each had a path, a purpose that the Creator had chosen for us. Just as a warbler knows to sing, and build its nest, and fly south in winter, I was supposed to learn my purpose through the choices I made. But my father's death, the birth of my son showed me how random life can be, blowing us adrift like the winged samara of a maple tree, a wind-borne seed searching for a place to set root.

The newspaper had become one such landing place, providing a space for me to grow. After a year of writing obituaries, I was promoted to copy editor, saving Ralph the trouble of having to hire more staff. He had landed a big advertising account, Agri-Tech, that brought in enough revenue for me to work at the office two days each week while Tommy was in school. Ralph gave me my very own scratched-up desk, with only one broken drawer, an electric typewriter that he insisted I learn how to use, and a dictionary. I added a photo of my son and brought my own coffee cup from home. Now that we had a mortgage on the farm, my paycheck made a big difference. John even said he didn't know how we would have gotten by without it.

Ralph began to encourage me to write short pieces in addition to my other work, provided I could get them done in my regular hours. The first time I saw my name in the newspaper was one of the biggest thrills of my life. I felt like a real journalist, even if I was only writing about the crowning of the Corn Days princess. A person had to start somewhere.

Today I was waiting for Ralph to get off the phone so I could show him what I had been working on in my own time. Since the powwow the previous year, when Gaby had talked to me about the river, I had been researching farm chemicals and drain tiles and oil spills and toxic fish. I read until my head ached, staying up long after John had gone to bed.

Everything I read confirmed what I had learned from Gaby, but also from my father, from my garden, and from the unspoken teachings of wild plants. The oak trees along the river dropped their acorns in fall, some to reseed the woods, others to be eaten by wild turkeys, who then became food for our table. If I take care of the oak trees, I am also taking care of my family. We all need the river to survive. As my father had often reminded me, water is our first medicine, allowing us to live, and that makes her sacred. The chemicals used in farming were a risk to all of us.

When I tried to talk to John about it, he wasn't interested, dismissing me as if I had no real understanding. Gaby, on the other hand, was like the coyote I'd seen in Tommy's cartoons, always chasing after the roadrunner: me. She called a couple of times each week to talk about the task force or to tell me about a new article she had just read, about the endangered status of the peregrine falcons, or to recount how the tribal council meeting went. When I attended one of her task force meetings, I was pressured by the group to promise that I would get the newspaper to cover the story. Why us? I asked them, not understanding how a small rural paper could make much difference.

"Because farmers read it," Gaby said. "Most of these papers outside the Twin Cities are afraid to say anything that might jeopardize their advertising revenue. You're the only reporter we know who gets it."

Gaby seemed to believe that I couldn't possibly fail, because the river was so important to the area. I tried to warn her that there was no guarantee. She just kept sending more information my way. Like John, she heard only what she wanted to.

When Ralph hung up, I gathered my notes and took a deep breath. He was not an easy man to get along with, especially not on cold days like this one, when he sat as close as he could to the clanking radiator with a wool scarf wrapped tightly around his neck. He even wore gloves with the fingertips cut off. Every morning, he came in complaining about the cold, slamming the door shut as fast as he could, while his glasses fogged in the sudden warmth. He frequently threatened to take the next bus back to his home state of Texas. He had married—and divorced—a Minnesota girl but stayed in the area so he could be close to his two daughters. There were days when I wanted to buy the bus ticket for him.

"Ralph, can I have a minute with you?"

He peered at me over his reading glasses, hating to be interrupted, assessing my willingness to be shooed away. I'd seen him bark orders at the intern and then apologize later, in a whisper, as if to keep me from hearing. I was not fooled by his Texas bluster. He sighed, the busy editor bothered by the cub reporter.

"I'll give you five minutes, and then . . ." Not bothering to finish his sentence, he gestured at the sloping pile of papers that covered his desk.

I had prepared a brief speech that I hoped would convince Ralph that this was a story that had to be published. Farmers needed this information. How else would they know what these chemicals were doing to the river? But about thirty seconds in, Ralph put up his hand to tell me to stop. Without a word, he reached for my notes and scanned them quickly. Then he handed them back to me.

"Not a chance," he said. "I'm not saying it's not a good story. And you've put in the time on the research. But this would scare the hell out of people. Worse yet, you know who pays our bills? Agri-Tech. They buy a full-page ad each week. And what do they make? Fertilizers. They would drop us like a sack of shit."

"But . . . what happens if we don't say anything?"

"We leave it to the scientists and politicians. Somewhere down the road, somebody will have to figure out how to fix it. And when that happens, we'll make it our goddamn headline. Until then, I have a newspaper to run." End of conversation.

I went back to my desk, stunned by his abrupt dismissal. Every now and then, I felt his guilty glance slide in my direction. I refused to speak or look at him. Finally, he came over to my desk and dropped a press release in front of me. Months earlier, Governor Perpich had declared 1987 as the Year of

Reconciliation between the Dakhóta and white communities. I had asked repeatedly that we cover the story. Evidently, he was throwing me a bone.

Ralph cleared his throat. "I was thinking that maybe we should do something with this Year of . . . uh . . . Reckoning story." Oh, so now it was his idea? I shrugged. The year was almost over, so what else needed to be said at this point? I told him I'd think about it.

That evening, I kept finding reasons to not call Gaby. There were the dishes to be done, homework with Tommy, bedtime, tidying up. Just before nine, I ran out of excuses and picked up the phone.

"Rosie, perfect timing, I just came in from our meeting. Any progress with Ralph?"

"That's why I'm calling. He didn't go for it. Said he'd lose his biggest advertiser."

"What? You're kidding. Did you tell him about . . ." And then she was off and listing a million reasons why he had to publish the article, there was no way he could refuse, maybe she should talk to him herself as a subscriber, as a local citizen . . .

"Please don't," I said, unable to imagine the two of them having a productive conversation.

"Why not?" she snapped. "Since clearly you couldn't get it done."

"Because I need this job."

"Is that all you care about? You can't let him win. People have to be held accountable for what they're doing to the river. Can't you see that?"

"I'll keep trying," I said. "That's the best I can do right now."

A silence fell between us. I knew that Gaby had met with

stiff resistance from all of the newspapers she had approached. Finally, in a flat voice that didn't sound like her, she said, "We'll just have to figure something else out." She let out a big sigh that we both knew meant *she* would be the one to figure it out. I had let her down. "By the way, I wanted to tell you that Anthony will be running later this month to honor the thirty-eight Dakhóta warriors. They run all night, from Fort Snelling to Mankato, finishing at Reconciliation Park for a ceremony." Only when Gaby talked about Anthony did she sound like her old self, the girl I knew at school. "He's back home. Swears he's clean. I believe him, Rosie. I think this time he's beat it." When we hung up, I felt like she had forgiven me.

On the morning of December 26, Tommy and I rose early and drove to Mankato, telling John that we had errands to run. We parked at the side of the road and watched quietly as the runners went slowly past. Behind them came a procession of powerful horses, their breath a white cloud on the cold air, with several riders carrying a staff or tribal flag. A young man with a hand drum sang as he walked, followed by a large group of people running slowly or walking, and an even larger line of cars. I recognized Anthony, his hair in a long braid, leading the runners and carrying a beaded wood staff with thirty-eight feathers that fluttered in the wind. He ran with a limp, his face whipped red by the wind, yet I could see his determination to carry the staff to the park, where the elders were waiting to welcome them.

I knew then what I could write about the Year of Reconciliation. On the way home, we stopped at the newspaper office, even though it was closed for the day. I settled Tommy at a desk with crayons and rolled a blank sheet of paper into the typewriter. I thought about the aftermath of the 1862 war, when thirty-eight hastily condemned warriors had been hung in Mankato, in the country's largest-ever mass execution. Their bodies were buried in shallow graves and then dug up for study by local doctors, including Dr. Mayo, who kept the body of Cut Nose for his personal examination.

I thought about my father losing his teaching job, about his struggle with depression and drinking. About how angry he was that our history was not taught in schools. Instead, we had to battle sports mascots and stereotypes. Movie actors in brownface. Tourists with cameras. Welfare lines. Alcoholism.

"After stealing everything," he would rage, "now they want to blame us for it, too." Social services broke up Native families, sending children like me to white foster parents. Every week, the newspapers ran stories about Indians who rolled their cars while drunk or the rise of crack cocaine on the reservations or somebody's arrest for gang-related crimes. No wonder so many Native kids were committing suicide.

But there was so much more to the story of the run. What people didn't see because they chose never to look. Unlike the stone monument in New Ulm, built to memorialize the settlers' loss with angry pride, the Dakhóta had created a living, breathing memorial that found healing in prayer and ceremony. What the two monuments shared, however, was remembering. We were all trying to find a way through grief.

My fingers hovered over the typewriter keys as I searched for a way into the story. Finally, I wrote about Anthony, how he carried the staff with fingers that were numb from the cold and an ankle twisted while passing Traverse des Sioux, where the treaty was signed that took away Dakhóta land. Anthony carried the blood memory of the men who died in the war, who starved in prison, who could not keep their families safe. His struggle with drugs and alcohol was the only way he knew to quiet the voices that would not let him rest. He tried so hard to be strong, and instead, he had to learn how to grieve.

During the run, his son, Hiŋháŋ, and his nephew, Matȟó, rode in the car behind him. As young boys, they saw how he ran for them so they could grow up happy and healthy. The Year of Reconciliation, I wrote, is about healing from the harms of the past. It's about remembering the prayers and the love that helped us survive. It's about the tough, deep work of forgiveness.

I left my article in Ralph's inbox, and we walked out the door. A light snow was drifting gently toward the sidewalk, plump flakes that caught light from a hazy sun. Peaceful.

My story never did make it into print. Instead Ralph grabbed a few quotes from the press release and left it at that. I don't know if he understood what I was trying to say. He must have known I wasn't really writing it for the newspaper. It was a prayer, I think, for Anthony. And for Gaby, who waved when she drove past our truck with her son. And for Tommy, who leaned against my shoulder as we watched the runners pass by.

pollination

and the Corn said
know me

———(▪)———

CHAPTER TWENTY-ONE

Rosalie Iron Wing Meister
1996

The screen door slammed open hard enough to startle the birds who were perched on the feeder outside the kitchen window. Tommy stomped into the room and slumped in the nearest chair, his long legs sprawled in front of him. I closed the book I was reading.

"I thought you were working with your dad today," I said.

"I was. He got mad and told me to go wait in the kitchen like a girl."

Tommy was still spending his weekends helping out in the fields. But by the time he turned fifteen, it had become clear that he was not much interested in farming. More than once, my husband and my son had come in for lunch barely speaking to each other. No longer the sweet child he'd once been, Tommy had grown into a moody, resentful teenager, who spent long hours reading and playing video games in his room. When he joined the cross-country team the year prior, spending long hours training, I had wondered if it was an excuse to get away from the farm.

Tommy had grown tall and slender, his gawky teenage limbs ill suited to heavy farmwork. He could barely lift a hay bale. He had become so like my father, with his deep-set eyes and strong cheekbones, that I was sometimes startled when I came upon him unexpectedly. His black hair bristled in its short cut, accentuating large ears that protruded slightly. Even his rare laugh, his long fingers seemed familiar.

Now he sat chewing a fingernail, waiting for his dad to appear. When John arrived, he stood in the doorway, looking at his son's hunched, narrow shoulders. Tommy looked more like a whipped dog than a farm boy. Without a word, John disappeared into the room we had turned into his office. After a few minutes, he called for Tommy, who hesitantly got up. I stayed in my chair and listened.

"Since you're no damn good as a farmer, you may as well do something useful." I heard John slide a pile of papers across his desk—the invoices, receipts, and unopened envelopes that tended to accumulate in his office. "Put everything we earn in one column. Put everything we spend in another column. Make a pile of bills to be paid." With no more explanation, John left the room, walking by me and out the door, to return to his fields.

I braced myself for the flurry of complaints I was sure to hear from the office. Instead, there was silence. After an hour, I peeked through the open door. Tommy's head was bent over his work, an expression of contentment on his face. That evening, when he showed his dad what he had done, John gave a low whistle of approval. He patted his son's back, told him he had done a good day's work. Within a month of working like this, Tommy convinced John to let him put everything on the computer. He taught himself simple accounting and showed an interest in farming for the first time. I could tell he was pleased with the praise he was finally hearing from his father.

I had become accustomed, over the years, to silent meals, while John browsed the newspaper and Tommy read a book on his lap. As Tommy became more interested in the family business, however, our dinners became filled with lively conversation. The two of them talked about yields, futures, delivery prices, inputs, subsidies, and how best to spend the money they anticipated from the highest prices anyone had seen in a decade. If I offered an opinion, they listened politely and then continued as if I had not spoken. As if they knew how short-lived these dreams could be, and they wanted to hold on to these moments, where they could see their best selves reflected in each other.

⸻

John called from the mudroom as he pulled off his work boots. "George said there's a meeting tonight with the sales manager for Mangenta."

I was sitting with Tommy at the kitchen table, drinking coffee while he did homework. Without looking up from his math textbook, Tommy asked, "What's Mangenta?"

John came into the kitchen, touching my shoulder in greeting. "It's the company that's building a new research plant outside of town. There was an article about it just last week in your mother's newspaper."

Tommy snorted. "Like I read that."

Lately, I wasn't too pleased with it myself. Ralph had written a glowing editorial praising the new mayor, Jerry Gustafson, for enticing Mangenta to build its facility in the area. I had tried to talk to him about my concerns, but they went right over his head. He had accused me of being afraid of progress.

"The guy wants to talk about starting a seed revolution," John added. "Sounds like another sales pitch to me. Still, no harm in hearing him out. I thought we might all go, since most of the town is likely to be there."

I made an early supper while John changed into his last clean shirt for the week, wiping his face with a damp cloth rather than running water in the sink. These last two weeks in August had brought unrelenting heat and no rain. Even the best fields were dry, dependent on whatever irrigation a farmer could afford. The meeting would provide a welcome distraction from the worry of what might happen if the drought continued much longer. After a quick meal of hamburgers and fresh green beans, we drove to the community center and parked in the nearly full lot, with more cars and trucks pulling in behind us.

The room was loud with boisterous greetings among farmers who hadn't seen much of one another since planting season had started. John was called away almost as soon as we walked in, with Tommy trailing along behind him.

I looked around the room and saw George, who gave me a quick nod as he supervised two young men setting up more folding chairs to accommodate the large crowd. I was on my way to greet Judith, sitting at the back of the room, when I heard Ralph calling my name. I turned to see him barreling toward me, his face flushed from the heat.

"Rosalie, thank God I caught you," he said, wiping his face with a handkerchief. "My daughter's car broke down on some back road and I've got to go pick her up. Take notes, will you, and write something up for Thursday's edition. Nothing too complicated. You're a peach."

Luckily, I had started to always carry a notebook and pen in my purse. "That's fine," I called after his retreating back. I pushed my way through the crowd and found a seat next to Judith, who looked pale and tired. I told her I didn't recognize her without her big garden hat.

"I've got one of my headaches," Judith said. "I swear they come on after the Petersons spray their fields, but George says there's nothing we can do about it. Anyhow, I've got some raspberries ready to pick tomorrow, if you care to stop by."

Shortly after six o'clock, George called the meeting to order. John sat in the second row with Paul Johnson, one of our neighbors, a soft-spoken farmer who held his coffee cup carefully with thick, calloused fingers, his denim-clad legs spread wide, dusty boots planted firmly on the floor. Tommy sat on John's other side, his nose buried in a book. In front of them sat Mayor Gustafson, one of the big landowners, who had also just come in from his fields.

"Evening, folks," George said, peering around the full room. "As most of you know, I'm George Hansen, a local farmer and lifelong historian for the Corn Museum. Now, I don't want to take much of your time, because I know you farmers need to get up early tomorrow. We've had a request from this young man, Mark Schafer, who wants to tell you about Mangenta, the seed company that's building a new plant out west of town. He seems pretty excited about what they're doing, so I hope you'll hear him out."

As Schafer stood up and waved to the crowd, a voice called

out, "Can he make it rain?" A chorus of cheers rang out in support of the heckler. Something about the young man's casually loosened tie, the sleeves neatly rolled up on a clean, white shirt seemed to set the audience on edge. He looked like just another suit come to tell us how to run our farms. Everyone had chores waiting at home. Unpaid bills piling up. A few people were already throwing glances toward the door.

Schafer held up both hands, palms out as if in surrender. "I can't promise to make it rain," he said, turning his smile from one side of the room to the other. "But what if I could promise you a season without any worry about the corn borer? What if I could cut your pesticide bill in half and increase your yield at the same time?"

"I'd marry you!" called out the same voice from the back.

After the laughter died down, the farmers gave Schafer their attention. Even Tommy closed his book and pulled a notepad and pencil from his pocket.

Schafer paced the front of the room as he described a seed revolution, a new product that was going to change the lives and incomes of farmers everywhere. After years of research, Mangenta had combined a seed with the genes of a soil bacterium that would control the corn borer, the bane of farmers everywhere. Other genes made plants tolerant of Mangenta's most commonly used pesticide, so farmers could just spray and go. Less time in the fields, lower costs for the farmer. How could you say no to that?

Around the room, a few heads nodded in agreement as they figured what that would mean to the bottom line. John and Tommy exchanged a glance, and Tommy bent over his notebook as he quickly made his own calculations. He showed the page to his dad before turning his attention back to Schafer, leaning his elbows on his knees as if to make sure he didn't miss a single word.

I knew as well as anyone in that room what the increase might mean. For families accustomed to barely getting by in years when the harvest was hit by disease or drought, suddenly there would be hope that they could replace a tractor or buy a new combine or even put something aside for their kids' schooling. These families were not only thirsty for rain; they were hungry for a life that held a bit more ease, a lessening of the anxiety that gripped every one of them from seed planting until the safe delivery of the harvest to the grain elevator. Most of them—if they'd been farming long enough—knew what it meant to lie awake at night worried about how to pay the mortgage and the loans on their equipment. A lot of the wives, like myself, had jobs in town to help make ends meet. Money that meant we could survive the long winters.

In the second row, a silver-haired old man slowly got to his feet, holding on to the back of the chair in front of him. Lester Thompson. I remembered meeting him and his wife, Elly Mae, at church years ago. They had been kind, and it pleased me to return the favor as best I could when I had written an obituary for Elly Mae the year before. Schafer paused, still smiling.

"My family has been farming here for four generations," said Lester, "back to my great-granddad, who settled here in 1865. We've raised wheat, corn, cattle, soybeans, hay—you name it—and somehow managed to make a decent living, despite everything that can go wrong on a farm. Now you're telling me, young man, that you've got a magic seed that's going to fix everything. Unless your name is Jack, I need to ask you this question: What's the catch?"

"Ha ha, yes, sir, good question," Schafer said, addressing the whole room. "The one catch, as you put it, is that you have to sign a contract with us to grow our seeds. And you have to buy new seeds each year. But we guarantee you will still make money, despite that extra expense."

"New seeds? We do that now with hybrids. Why do we need a contract?"

"We, Mangenta, feel it's important to protect the patented process that went into making these new varieties."

"Not sure what you just said, young man. Tell me this: What happens if old George here decides to grow this new seed, and it finds its way over to my field? I can't control the wind, you know."

"With all due respect, sir, that would be a violation of the patent, which gives us complete control of the corn's genetic material. Mangenta would be well within its rights to prosecute anyone who violated our patent."

"You mean to say I can grow your corn only if I sign that contract."

"That's right."

"So that's where Mangenta makes its profit."

"Yes," Schafer replied, wiping sweat from his forehead with a napkin. "But you farmers are also increasing your profit, don't forget that. The company has to recoup its investment in developing this new technology."

"Technology? I thought we were talking about seeds." Shaking his head, Lester sat down, as a number of voices broke out all at once, shouting questions and making comments.

George stood up, requesting quiet. The mayor eased up from his chair and joined George at the front of the room as the clamor slowly died down.

"I agree with Lester that this young man has given us a lot to think about," Mayor Gustafson said. "Every one of you needs to decide what's best for your own farm. But while you're busy with your calculators, I want to add this thought. Mangenta is breaking ground on its new research facility right outside town next month. Not only will we have access to the best research these desk farmers can come up with, but they've promised this plant will bring in new jobs. You all know that we've lost more than a few farmers these past couple of years. We need to think smart and look down the road. That's all."

"Mayor," John called out, before Gustafson could sit back down. "Will you be using these seeds on your own land?"

"I already am."

As a hum of conversation began to rise following this revelation, a woman's voice struggled to be heard above the noise. "Mayor, Mayor, a question, please."

On the far side of the room, Gaby Makespeace stood up, surrounded by men who looked at her with curiosity. The last time I'd seen her was earlier that year, for a quick coffee between her meetings; she was so busy suing people that our paths rarely crossed anymore. That night, she was dressed in a suit and high heels, as if she had just come from the courtroom. Her dark hair was pinned in a loose bun, and she wore long, beaded earrings that caught the light. A few of the farmers leaned back in their chairs, arms folded across broad chests, and regarded her with open hostility.

"What is it, Miss Makespeace?" the mayor replied. "We're about done here."

"Mayor, how do we know these seeds are even safe? Can you trust . . ."

"Not now, Miss Makespeace," the mayor said. He glanced around, checking to see if there were any other, safer questions to be answered. When he looked my way, my hand shot up.

"Well, hello, Rosalie. I see the whole family is here tonight. What can I do for you?"

"I think what Ms. Makespeace was trying to ask was if you can trust a chemical company to sell you seeds. Mangenta manufactured Agent Orange during the Vietnam War, and now they're buying up the patent rights to our seeds. What about all the farmers and migrant workers who are exposed to these chemicals every day? What happens to our rivers from the runoff?" I made a point not to look at John or Tommy, who had turned toward me with their mouths open in surprise.

"Excuse me, Mayor," Schafer said, holding up his hand. "I think I can help answer her questions. With these new seeds, you apply your pesticide once, instead of in multiple applications. Farmers don't need to spend time and gas tilling for weeds. That means fewer chemicals end up in the runoff from the fields. That should help the river. You can clean up the water *and* improve the bottom line. You can't beat that!"

"But Mayor . . ."

"Thank you, Rosalie. That's all for tonight, folks," the mayor said. He pointed to a table against one wall. "Mr. Schafer has got a table set up with brochures about his company. I'm sure he would be more than happy to answer any questions you have. Thank you all for coming tonight. And let's pray the rain comes soon."

"Amen!" came a chorus of voices. As the meeting broke up, many of the men filed past the Mangenta table, picking up brochures and asking questions. Gaby exchanged a few heated words with the mayor before striding toward the door, not looking at anyone. Her hair was streaked with gray at the temples, and deep circles were etched beneath her eyes. She looked tired, like she ran on coffee and little sleep.

The woman seated next to Judith leaned over and said, "My husband calls her Gaby Makes-men-shrink. He wishes someone would tell her to stay home and mind her own business."

Judith said, "Shut it, Maybelle, you sound like a goddamn fool."

But I had no interest in Maybelle. I was already moving toward Gaby, who had paused to throw away her cup in the wastebasket near the exit. When she saw me, she smiled and wrapped me in a big hug.

"Thank you," she whispered, stepping back but still holding my arms. When she saw the notebook I was carrying, she said, "I always knew you'd come through. Let's get together soon, we have so much to catch up on. I'm late to a meeting. Gotta run." She disappeared through the door, into the humid evening air. I turned as if to follow her.

"Where are you going?" Tommy's hand on my shoulder stopped me. His dark eyes were smiling, curious. "Whoa, what's that look for?"

"Nothing," I said. I took a deep breath.

He looked in the direction Gaby had just gone. "Was that Mathó's mom? She sure has changed. Mom, I know she's your friend, but you should watch out. Dad says she's a radical who doesn't understand farming."

Before I could answer him, John walked over to us, a couple of brochures tucked into his back pocket. "My daddy would have had a fit at this meeting," he said. "He and Lester would have run this guy right out of town. Times have changed, that's for sure." He looked at me. "Rosie, I know you're working for the paper, but did you have to speak up like that? We're all doing the best we can."

"Yes, John, I do have to speak up. Do you have a problem with that?"

He started to say something and then stopped. Instead, he gestured toward the door. As we walked out to the parking lot, George caught up to us. "John, can I have a word?"

"Sure thing, George."

"I'm not sure about these new seeds. Maybe I'm just getting too old for new tricks, but I'd like to study on it before anything gets used on my land. I don't mean to tell you how to farm, I'd just like to go slow, is all."

"No problem. I'm still trying to survive this season. I'll start worrying about next year's seeds when I've got this harvest out of the fields."

After a silent ride home with the windows rolled down to catch the cool night breeze, each of us deep in our own thoughts, Tommy went straight to his room. I carried a warmed-up cup of coffee into the spare bedroom that I sometimes used for work. John stopped at the doorway and said he was turning in, needing an early start in the morning.

"I won't be long," I said. "I'm helping Ralph out with a last-minute story."

He hesitated. But all he said was "Be careful, Rosie."

As soon as he was gone, I pulled out the big file I'd started years earlier, when I had tried to run the story about farm chemicals and the river. I was grateful that I had kept it updated with current news from the library. I knew all about the long list of lawsuits pending against Mangenta for Agent Orange, the risk of buying seeds from a company that wanted to sell you pesticide.

Now, if I could make a connection between these chemical manufacturers and the danger to our seeds and our water, Ralph would have to run my piece. Agri-Tech had stopped buying ads years ago, so he couldn't use that for an excuse anymore. I worked all night, finally crawling into bed just before John got up at 4:00 a.m. While the article was still rough in places and would require Ralph's editing, I believed it was the most important story I had ever written.

I slept only a few hours, too eager to get to the office to stay in bed. After dropping Tommy off at a friend's house, I drove straight to the newspaper, hoping to catch Ralph. He wasn't in, so I left my story in his overflowing box, with a note to call me if he had questions. I couldn't wait for him; I had promised to help Judith harvest her raspberries.

On Thursday morning, I was waiting when the newspaper was delivered. John had already left, Tommy was still asleep, and I had a few minutes to savor my article. There it was on the front page, with my byline. Only it wasn't my story at all. Ralph had gutted it; all of my research was gone. All that was left was a fluff piece about the meeting that prominently featured a quote from the mayor, saying he was happy to welcome Mangenta and their fine products to our community.

I called Gaby immediately and left a message on her machine asking her to please call me. The article in the paper was not what I had written. Ralph did a hack job, I could show her the original story . . . and then my words ran out. I left five messages over the next three days, and she never called back.

My second call that morning was to Ralph.

"I quit, you fucking piece of shit."

CHAPTER TWENTY-TWO

Rosalie Iron Wing Meister
1998

Looking back, I don't know that publishing my story would have made any difference. Mangenta was a freight train rolling downhill, gathering speed as farmers decided when to jump on board. We became one of the first to adopt the seeds. Tommy showed his dad a spreadsheet that promised better days, and after studying the numbers, John was persuaded the change was coming, whether he liked it or not. He still heard his daddy's voice in his ear, telling him he would lose the farm with his crazy ideas, but John wanted to be proved right about this new way of farming.

After I quit my job, we felt the loss of my paycheck. John never complained, though I saw the worry on his face, the way he drank at night in order to sleep. He agreed to grow the new corn under contract to the ethanol plant, feeding the country's voracious appetite for fuel. The company would provide the schedule, the seeds, the chemicals, and even help with the harvest. They gave John a list of equipment he needed to buy and changes that had to be made to the fields and buildings.

Tommy helped negotiate the loan we needed from the bank, more money than John used to make in an entire year.

A few months before the first shipment of seeds was due to be delivered, I knocked on the door of Tommy's room. He was a young man now and kept it closed all the time. His deep voice cracked as he called out for me to enter. Inside, clothes were strewn in untidy heaps, a math book was open on his desk, and he sat playing his favorite video game. He looked at me with curiosity, so seldom did I come to his room except to put away laundry. "What's up?"

"Tommy, your father listens to you. If you tell him not to use these seeds, he'll pay attention."

"Why would I do that?"

I told him my fears. Then I added an argument that I hoped would spark a memory of what he had learned as a boy. "It's not right what they've done to these plants. It's not right to take life apart like that, just because it will make money. You remember when you were younger, and we talked about how the corn feeds the little voles, who become food for the hawks? How the sandhill cranes eat the leftover seeds when they stop here to rest during their fall migration? Even the crows rely on field corn to survive. What happens to the birds when they eat these seeds? What happens to us?"

"Nothing, Mom. Nothing is going to happen to the birds or to you and me and Dad. Except that, for once, we will make some good money. Even you can't argue with that. You might even buy yourself something decent to wear."

After that conversation, I barely listened when Tommy and John talked about the farm. I didn't want to give up, not when the Minnesota River was already one of the most polluted in the country. But I wondered if there was a different way for me to do this work. I had tried to be like Gaby, who used her skills as a lawyer to fight threats to the river and the land. Maybe it wasn't my way to fight from anger. Maybe I needed to learn how to protect what I loved instead.

For now, at least, that left me with my garden. I poured my time and energy into caring for her, feeding the soil with manure I spread with a shovel, watering the plants by hand. Some days I sang to them, serving up a mix of my father's old powwow songs. Once John offered to spray his pesticide to kill the weeds, thinking to save me time. I glared at him until he threw up his hands and said, Okay, okay, do it your way. And I did, sweating for long hours under the hot July sun as if my pain was nothing compared to what had been done to the earth and water around me.

When all this tender care resulted in an overflowing harvest, I canned everything, refilling the pantry shelves with enough food to last a year or more. After so many years of hot dogs and Hamburger Helper, I learned to be a better cook by reading recipes and experimenting. The rule of three that had once dictated our meals—meat, potato, canned vegetable—gave way to homemade soups, stews, roasted vegetables, marinated meat that fell apart with the prodding of a fork, fresh-baked bread slathered in jam from my raspberries.

With the exception of beans, I'd run out of Edna's seeds years ago, buying my garden supply from the feed store instead. I had always believed that John's mother must have been taught how to save her seeds—or maybe she was just smarter than me. Anyone could figure out how to save beans, an easy seed that needed nothing more than shelling and drying, but other plants, like tomatoes, were more complicated. Now, I thought, after nearly two decades of gardening, I could save money if I learned how to save my own seeds. And, in a small way, push back against our partnership with Mangenta.

A library book showed me that the tiny seeds I had taken for granted were actually unique living beings with their own history, story, and family. Each seed was made of an embryo, a seed coat, and something nutritious, almost like a packed lunch. The Mother Plant, like me, wanted only the best for her babies. Some plants, like dandelions, scattered their seeds in the wind, while others, like some pines, needed fire to open their cones. Somehow, the Mother knew to dry her seeds almost completely so they would sleep until the time was right to wake. Each seed held a trace of life that would spark when given water, when given the appropriate conditions.

Everywhere I looked, I saw how seeds were holding the world together. They planted forests, covered meadows with wildflowers, sprouted in the cracks of sidewalks, or lay dormant until the long-awaited moment came, signaled by fire or rain or warmth. They filled the produce aisle in grocery stores. Seeds breathed and spoke in a language all their own. Each one was a miniature time capsule, capturing years of stories in its tender flesh. How ignorant I felt compared to the brilliance contained in a single seed.

I started with tomato seeds because I used so many of them. First, I learned to ferment them to remove the film that prevents growth. I kept the book open in front of me as I sliced a heavy ripe tomato and squeezed the inner gel that held the seeds into a five-gallon bucket. When it was full, I covered the bucket with its lid.

Three days later, I poured off the pulpy water, leaving the seeds at the bottom of the container. After a thorough rinse, I spread the seeds onto a clean screen, where they dried for about a week. It was satisfying to fill a clean white envelope with them, labeling it with my name and the date. Then I looked around at the rest of my garden. I had begun to see that when we save these seeds, when we select which ones will be planted again, our lives become braided into the life stories of these plants.

As I grew to know the seeds in my garden more deeply, I worried about the Mangenta seeds that John was using on the farm. But my concerns went unheard as the corn grew tall and soldier straight, each plant an identical clone of the one next to it, providing almost three times the yield John's father had once grown. John announced this figure with great pride to anyone who would listen. Very little was lost to the corn borer, and prices were as high as they had ever been. We bought a new truck, patched the hole in the roof, paid our creditors. I bought a new coat to replace one Judith had given me years earlier.

I told myself there was nothing I could do. I simply watched and waited to see what would happen. Mangenta's salespeople reminded us often that we were growing corn for fuel the country needed, even helping the environment. It seemed there was no end to the use scientists could make of field corn, from feeding livestock to creating the corn syrup that flavored so many foods.

And yet each spring when the new shipment of seeds arrived, John would be distracted, restless, silent. He had become increasingly withdrawn. I suspected that he questioned whether he had made the right decision. This new way of farming was so different from that of his boyhood, from what his father had taught him. A country that destroys its soil . . . I believed that in his heart John was an old-school farmer, like his dad. He loved the land. And no one knew what these chemicals would do to the soil, or to us, over time.

CHAPTER TWENTY-THREE

Marie Blackbird
1920

My thakóža, my granddaughter, took my elbow even though I didn't need her help. "Watch out for that tree root, Khúŋši," she said. "Let me hold your arm so I don't fall."

I'm not an old woman yet, I wanted to reply, even if I've survived more than seventy winters. If you knew what I've seen and lived through, you would know that I'm made of iron. But I held my tongue. After all, Darlene, the second-born girl, seemed to understand me better than even my own daughter, Susanne. She didn't fool me with her tricks, but they allowed me to keep my pride. Of all Susanne's children, little Darlene was most like me, always ready for a walk in the woods to see who's awake. The eldest, Lorraine, stayed close to her mother's side and liked to help with the garden. The young boys, Frederick and Harry, would rather throw stones in the river and fish with the long poles that Clayton had made for each of them.

I was none too pleased when Susanne decided to marry him. I said, You can do better than this Clayton Kills Deer. Who's his family? I don't even know them. If my husband,

Oliver, had still been alive, maybe she would have listened to him. But he died on me a few years after finishing the cabin we were all sharing now, with me sleeping in the big room like it wasn't even my own house.

"Khúŋši, look, look!" Darlene said, her high voice squeaking in excitement. She pointed at a clump of nearly ripe wild strawberries, their crimson flesh peeking through a cluster of green leaves. I smiled and nodded at her. There was something in Darlene's wide eyes, shining with happiness, and strong, stubborn chin that reminded me of my Oliver. They may not have been blood related but she was always ready to help, just like him.

"Wašté, Darlene. It's time to plant."

Oh, how I remember the way Oliver couldn't sleep at planting time, his excitement when he first saw how green and fertile the land was in Mní Sota. At Santee, you always had to be aware of water, how precious it was, especially when the summer sun baked the land into a hard pan, sending scrub brush rolling across the hills. When we finally came home in 1889, we saw more lakes and rivers than we could count, streams and marshes, cattails growing in puddles along the side of the road. Even the leaves on trees seemed plump and ready to burst from all the rain. And then he saw open fields of fresh-turned black soil that called to his farmer's heart.

Me, I couldn't hardly find my way back because so much had changed. I remembered forests that filled the land between rivers, not all these empty, dug-up fields. Not until we reached the banks of the Mní Sota Wakpá did I truly believe that I was home. When the wagon finally stopped, I climbed down and knelt in the long grass, my palms pressed into the earth as I prayed. It was all so different, and yet my beloved river was the same. The next morning, I made my way to the tallest cottonwood I could find and buried my mother's hair. I gave a pinch of čhaŋšáša to the river, with a prayer of gratitude. In that small way, my Iná returned home with me.

Within the first year, Oliver began building our cabin on a rise overlooking the river, on the same land where my family had lived nearly thirty years earlier. The hills and fields where I had run as a child, and then known as the reservation where war had destroyed everything, were now broken into 160-acre pieces that we were allowed to purchase. Other Dakhóta families had begun slowly moving back, drawn here by our makapahas, our earth-hills, where our relatives were buried. The government helped a few families who had stayed, the loyalists, the ones who hadn't fought against the white soldiers, while the rest of us scrimped and saved to buy back parcels that belonged to us as our homeland, and by treaty. No one complained, however, because we had all learned the lesson of acting like "good" Indians. We knew the vengeance of the wašíču had no limit.

Some of us still remembered the bounties that were offered after the war for any Dakhóta scalp. Then the government passed a law that stole our land and sent us to Crow Creek, making it illegal for us exiled Dakhóta to come back home. Once there was money to be made, the government ignored its own laws. Even so many years after Oliver's death, it was still illegal for us to be on the land we owned.

And even to pray. The government had passed another law in the 1880s saying it was a crime for us to pray in our own way. A few families held ceremonies in secret, speaking the

Dakhóta language only to one another. Just as some women—
like Iná and me—had kept the seeds, others took care of the
ceremonies and the language until it might be safe again. No
one spoke of the war or what followed afterward. When we
heard stories whispered of the massacre at Wounded Knee, it
was as if a long winter had settled into our hearts.

When we returned, we learned that no one had yet made a
claim to our old land along the river, because it was too steep
for farming. Oliver had had his eye on a piece of flat land that
would be better suited for crops. But that was one time when
I had to insist, when I said, I will live nowhere but my family's
home. He was a good man, my Oliver, and he bought that land
for us, renting his own farm acreage a few miles west.

He chopped down trees for logs to build our cabin and
added real glass windows and a wood-burning stove. Two
bedrooms opened off the kitchen, with a long room for eating and visiting. Off the back porch he dug a well where we
could draw water with a hand pump, keeping a full bucket in
the kitchen with a ladle hooked to the side. This was much
easier than hauling water from the stream every day. When
he was done, our cabin was warm and plenty big enough for
the three of us. I never imagined it would one day also hold
Susanne, her husband, and their four children. But we made
the best of it.

There were better times when Oliver was still alive. He
was a steady man, a hard worker, who believed that farming was the best future for the Dakhóta. He helped build
the new Episcopal church, and we both went to service most
every week. He raised Susanne like she was his own daughter
and never asked where her blue eyes came from. On summer

evenings, when sunlight danced on the slow-moving river, I began to feel less afraid for the future.

My daughter grew tall, with dark hair, a handsome woman with a strong mind. I had hopes for her to become a teacher. Instead, she married Clayton Kills Deer, a man who was not nearly her equal. If my Iná had said to me what I did to Susanne, I would have listened with more respect. It was the influence of the school, I think, that gave her different ideas about her place in her family and community.

That night, as a raw spring wind blustered around the corners of the cabin, I asked Susanne to bring the willow basket from her bedroom, where she kept the seeds in cool darkness. The basket was hers now, a gift from me when she married. But I still liked to visit with the seeds, to feel once more the sacks and antler that had belonged to my mother. I had taught all the children, even Frederick and Harry, how to select the best corn to be saved for planting. Those seeds were kept in the basket and replaced each season; everything else we used for food.

"They should look like strong young men, long and muscular," I told them. "Keep the seeds from the center of each cob for planting. The seeds near the tip can be used for cooking; seeds from the other end, share with the animals. Keep a sharp eye open for any kernels with a black heart. Those cobs were picked too early and will not grow."

Lorraine was sitting next to her mother, as she did whenever we sorted seeds or planned the garden. At twelve years old, she was tall for her age, with a quick tongue that she used to keep her younger brothers in line. Lorraine shared her mother's gift for knowing what the plants needed. She was already skilled at braiding corn, and her broad shoulders were capable of hauling a man's load back to the cabin. Yet she could be surprisingly delicate when she planted a seed. As the eldest daughter, and especially with her gift for gardening, we all knew that she would be the one to inherit the family's seeds, to become their keeper and protector. Just as Iná had given the seeds to me, and I had given them to Susanne, my daughter was teaching Lorraine to care for them in her turn.

I remember it was cool that night because we needed a fire in the stove. Clayton was off in the woods, drinking—I suspected—with his friends. As the oldest boy, Frederick was supposed to keep the fire going, but he and Harry had fallen asleep on the floor, wrapped in a quilt from their daybed. It was a pleasure for us women to be alone together.

Reaching into the basket, I picked up a piece of deer antler. "In my grandmother's garden," I began, speaking softly so I wouldn't wake the boys, "she used this antler to clear away the dead leaves in spring. When the traders brought iron rakes and hoes, our people quit using these tools. My mother saved this bone so we would remember the old ways."

I pulled out several deerskin bags, each one filled with seeds of many colors and sizes. I rolled a few seeds on my wrinkled palm as if I held precious stones. Lavender and rose corn, red-and-white speckled beans, and teardrop-shaped white squash. I passed the seeds to the girls to hold. I explained, as I had in the past, that my family had cooked these foods into special dishes, some that were used for ceremony. These stories were repeated often so that children would remember them.

As I carefully replaced each bag in the basket, my fingers brushed a piece of rolled-up deerskin tucked away at the bottom. My old heart skipped as I remembered the letter from my Até, written all those years ago from prison. I wanted to unfold it, to ask Susanne to read it to me, so that I could hear his voice once more in his words. But as I looked at the innocent faces around me, I decided there was no need to speak of that time. Better that these children should grow up without the weight of the memories I carried. Better that those memories should die with me.

Instead, we talked about the garden. I told them how the stray dog at Santee would come around when the tomatoes were ripe and steal them. What a sneaky devil he was. I used to rise early to catch him in the act, but he knew how to wait until I dozed off again in my chair. I would wake just in time to see the tail end of that flea-bitten mutt, running off with my prized tomatoes. How we all laughed together, the girls loving the story of their Khúŋši fooled by a dog.

We kept busy all summer with planting, weeding, and watering, so the days went by quickly. Before I knew it, the time had come to harvest the corn. That day we rose just after dawn, when the air was still cool, before the late-summer sun reminded us that the season was not yet over.

Susanne led the way to the garden, followed closely by Lorraine, with me on her heels, trying to keep up. Behind me, Darlene carried a sack of gabúbu bread, several strips of dried venison, and a bag of coffee. When Darlene accused her sister of not carrying her share, Lorraine whispered, "I have to help Khúŋši Marie." I pretended not to hear her, leaning on my walking stick as always. At the end of this short line, Frederick whacked the long grass with a stick until Darlene told him to stop, and then he threw twigs in her hair. Harry came last, still wiping the sleep from his eyes, his short legs struggling to keep up.

Harvesting the corn was a favorite time for all of us. I was reminded of my family when I stepped out of the shaded woods into the soft light of a new day. Across the clearing, we had planted young cedar trees that would grow tall enough to help protect the garden from deer. A dense stand of maple trees gave us syrup each spring. Sunflowers lined the north side of the garden, their broad faces turned toward the sun. Our corn grew from low mounds, the slender stalks wrapped by vines loaded with dry beans. Nearby, the round shells of pumpkins and squash peeped out from beneath wide leaves. Before anything else, we offered čhaŋšáša, and I spoke a prayer in Dakhóta, thanking the Creator for the abundant harvest.

Then we got to work. Frederick and Harry gathered wood for the fire while Darlene filled a coffeepot at the stream. When the fire was going strong, and the kettle hung on its hook, we spread out in the garden with our baskets. Susanne and Lorraine each took their own row, twisting and removing the ears of corn with practiced, sure hands. When our baskets were full, we would empty them in a shared pile, and the next day we would braid the largest ears together so they could be hung up to dry.

As I picked, I looked around, appreciating how much the garden had grown over the years. At the far end stood a small watch platform, built by Oliver, where Susanne and

I used to shoo away birds when she was young. We used to sing to the corn, partly to pass the time, but also to help it grow. For the rabbits and deer, Clayton had built a fence of alder branches. And I had promised that after harvest I would teach the girls how to make a new cache pit for our seeds. Although I had searched many times since returning home, I had never again found my mother's pit. I felt bad about it, like I had failed her.

"Darlene," Susanne called out. "Help Frederick and Harry get started."

Darlene sighed, but not so loudly that her mother could hear her. She was nearly eleven, and I could see that she wanted to be with the women. Not with Harry, who was too little to be of much help, easily distracted by the bugs he found or by watching the birds that perched in nearby trees, hoping for a share of the harvest. And especially not with Frederick, who continued to toss things at her when their mother was not watching. At nine, he was full of energy that would have been better spent with his father. But Clayton was working at a nearby farm, earning some much-needed cash. Corn was always picked by hand, and skilled farmworkers were kept busy during harvest. When a clod of dirt exploded at the back of Darlene's head, she turned in a fury and hurled the freshly picked corn she was holding. It smacked Frederick on his shoulder and bounced into the dirt behind him. He laughed, pleased at having stung her into such a strong reaction.

In a few quick strides, Susanne had reached Darlene, grabbing her arm and spinning her around. She stared at Darlene as if not believing what she had done. "Pick up that corn," she said, sternly.

"But Frederick . . ."

"Pick up that corn."

Darlene half stumbled to pick up the corn. She did not cry, although I could tell she felt sorry for herself, hanging her head to hide the tears. Darlene stood in front of her mother and held out the corn. Susanne took it from her calmly, her anger spent as quickly as it had flared up.

"Would you throw Khúŋši in the field?" she asked, and they both turned to look at me. I gave a little hop like I was flying across the grass. They laughed. "Remember that next time. You're old enough to ignore Frederick."

Darlene nodded.

"Why don't you and Khúŋši check to see if the hazelnuts are ripe?"

My helper gave a jump for joy. I knew how she felt. Neither of us minded garden work, but it was best left to Susanne and Lorraine. Darlene and I loved the woods and the plants that grew wild, the berries and roots and nuts that added such good flavors to our foods. Maybe we could find a few grapes or plums the birds had missed.

We hurried away as fast as I could move with my stick, not waiting for anyone to change their minds about needing us. Darlene carried a piece of jerky and bread for us in her basket. After a brief discussion, we decided to check one of our favorite berry patches, a short walk from the garden. We could pick wild bergamot if it was still blooming.

As the sun rose higher, our pace slowed, and we explored, finding low-growing gooseberry shrubs and a few chokecherry trees for harvesting next summer. Darlene gathered a handful of sumac berries to make a drink that was tasty on hot days.

I was partial to rosehip tea, myself, but we were too early; the fruits were not yet ready.

Once we found a small grove of ripe hazelnuts, we picked until we had one mostly full basket between us. I was tired then, needing a rest even more than I needed food. While Darlene ate the bread and jerky, I lay down on a soft bed of old leaves, beneath an oak that had seen more winters than I had. I must have slept for a long time. When I opened my eyes, the sun was already at midafternoon.

"Thakóža, wake up," I said, rising onto my elbow, a few leaves still clinging to my hair and my shirt.

"I am awake, Khúŋši," Darlene replied. She was watching me, sitting with her back against the tree. "I've been waiting for you. You've been snoring so loud I didn't know how you could even sleep. At least you kept the bears away."

"Tssst, I do not snore," I said. "Let's just be grateful we have something to show your mother for all our time away."

Since my old bones refused to hurry, we walked slow on our way back to the cabin. I liked to smell the pine needles warmed by the sun, to listen to the high-pitched hum of the cicada. We stopped to drink from the stream, cupping our hands to splash water on our flushed skin.

As we came around the bend in the path, we saw Clayton sitting at the outside table. He sat with his back to us, holding his head in his hands. I thought he must be tired. Darlene looked a question at me, and I nodded, pushing my lips toward her father. She hurried to the table and set her basket down with a thump, waiting to see him raise his head and smile, but he didn't move.

Something about the way he wouldn't look at Darlene sent me at a faster walk toward the house, where I expected to find

Susanne cooking dinner in the kitchen. Inside, it was dark, without a light or a fire burning. Susanne was in her chair, not moving. I sat down next to her and said, "Susanne, what is it? What has happened?"

"They're gone," Susanne said. "The agent came by at noon and took them away to the school. They're gone."

═══

That night, I shared Darlene's bed with her so she would not be alone. She lay beneath the blankets trembling, unable to sleep. From the darkness, her timid voice asked, "Where did they go? When are they coming home?"

I had no answer. I stayed with her—that was all I could offer. At Crow Creek, I thought I had seen the worst a person could do to another. But now this.

Susanne and Clayton were awake the entire night, talking in low voices. Sometimes I dozed and woke to see the fire-light throwing shadows across the doorway. I dreamed of wanáǧi crying at the edge of the woods. Long before sunrise, Susanne came into the room and sat down on Darlene's side of the bed. She stroked her daughter's hair, her cheek. I felt her heart breaking as she sat there in silence. Old memories came flooding back to me: the way my brother, Čhaské, cried from hunger, before he stopped crying at all.

"Darlene," Susanne said. "Wake up. We need to pack your things."

"Why? Is the agent coming back? Am I going with Lorraine?"

"Shhh. Father and I have talked this over. We don't know if the agent will come back. We can't risk keeping you here.

We're sending you to live with my cousin Pauline and her husband in Mankato. They have a baby and will be glad to have the extra help."

As she talked, Susanne moved quietly around the room, gathering up Darlene's clothes in a sack. Darlene dressed with clumsy fingers, trying not to cry, while I went to the kitchen and wrapped bread and venison in a cloth for the road. When all was ready, Susanne stood at the door with her daughter, no longer tender, speaking in a brusque, almost harsh tone. "Your father is waiting in the wagon. Be a good girl. Always remember who you are." She handed Darlene the bundle of food and tucked a small medicine pouch into her pocket. Then she pushed Darlene through the open door and closed it quickly behind her.

When the last creak of wagon wheels had faded away, I lay down on my small cot and turned my face to the wall. I had no words left.

CHAPTER TWENTY-FOUR

Rosalie Iron Wing Meister

2000

Two long lines of farm trucks and family sedans were parked along both sides of the road for a quarter mile, leaving only a narrow lane for traffic to drive through. Though I had prayed for rain, to discourage the mob of people typically drawn to the spectacle of a farm auction, the morning was bright and crisp, a perfect fall day.

As John and I walked along the shoulder of the road, he unexpectedly took my hand. Many times, I had traveled this same path on my way to visit Judith and George. Today Judith was staying at the little apartment they had rented in town; only George would be there to witness the dismantling of their farm.

Everything was to be sold: equipment, tools, furniture, home, land. The dishes the two had left behind. Judith's chickens. George's John Deere tractor, with "Martha" painted in bold red on the side, a tribute to the hardworking mother who had raised him. I could see the picnic table where we had drunk lemonade on warm afternoons, now covered with paperwork for the auction. Judith's beloved garden was over-run with weeds, a single plastic milk jug left behind from her tomatoes. They never did finish painting the house.

I had to take a deep breath when I saw all of their things lined up in the front yard, each one tagged with a number. The auc-tioneer, a tall man in cowboy boots, had been hired from a nearby town, so he wouldn't be distracted by any unproductive emotion toward the family that was about to lose its farm. The yard was filled with nodding seed caps, blue jeans, and somber faces.

George stood off to one side with his lawyer, watching each new arrival, almost as if daring the farmers to meet his eyes. I felt his attention rest on us and then slide past. John's hand tightened on mine, and I knew that he had seen George, too. With only a moment's hesitation, he turned and walked across the yard toward his former friend. I followed him.

Two years earlier, George had decided he didn't want Mangenta corn grown on his land anymore and tried to break his lease with John. I remembered hearing John's loud voice from his office, the phone as it was slammed into its cradle. A minute later, John had come into the kitchen and sat down heavily across from me. His face was pale and bloated from too many beers the night before. "George said it's too much risk growing GMO corn so close to his own fields. He said he doesn't want that shit in his corn. If you ask me, I'd be doing him a favor." I listened without replying, not wanting his anger turned on me. Tommy had already headed upstairs with his homework, unwilling to face his father's volatile moods.

With help from Mangenta's lawyer, George was persuaded to allow John to finish out his season and mutually terminate the lease at year's end. George swore to everyone who would listen that he would grow only "real" heirloom corn from then on, using organic methods, a plan that left the other farmers shaking their heads.

Before that could happen, however, Mangenta had sued George for stealing their patented genes when his corn was cross-pollinated, acting on an anonymous tip to a hotline created specifically to prevent "seed piracy." George was outraged and chose to countersue. He said Mangenta had damaged the integrity of his seed stock. Of course, he faced an army of highly paid corporate lawyers; he never stood a chance. At his lawyer's urging, they attempted to settle out of court, and Mangenta agreed to dismiss the lawsuit if George would destroy his tainted corn and instead purchase seeds from Mangenta. He swore he would rather lose his farm. In the end, saddled with a mountain of unpaid legal bills, that's exactly the choice he was left with. It was never revealed who made the original phone call—if it had even been a real person at all.

As we walked slowly across the yard, George lowered his gaze, seeming not to notice John's approach. The two men stood for a long moment in silence. Finally, George said, "Come to claim my farm, have you? Take what's left of it. Ruin it, the way you have your own land."

"George, you know it's not like that."

"You planted that corn. Maybe you even made the phone call." He spat these words at John.

His fingers trembled as he lit a cigarette, a long-beaten habit resumed during the stress of the legal battle. George's skin was sallow, almost gray, his eyes puffy and red. I wanted to ask about Judith, but my words failed. She had not come to say goodbye when they moved. I could not picture her in the confined rooms of an apartment, with no garden, no animals, no birds to sing her awake. As if sensing my thoughts, George threw one quick glance at me and then turned away, his face strained with the effort of maintaining his composure.

There was nothing more to say. John and I joined the group in line to register for bidding numbers. Thin wisps of steam rose from tightly held foam cups of coffee. The auctioneer stepped up to the microphone, introduced himself, and explained the auction rules. The sheriff stood nearby, his thumbs hooked into his belt. His eyes roamed the crowd, as if he knew too well the potential for things to get out of hand. Feelings ran high when it came to your family farm, perhaps the only home you had ever known.

The bidding started with small items. Hands were raised in almost shamefaced embarrassment, folks feeling caught in the act of profiting by a neighbor's bad luck. Most of the people there knew George and Judith, knew their kids. The auction had the feeling of a funeral, of an unspoken loss that nonetheless had to be dealt with. Life on a farm was challenging, and not everyone made it.

I knew that John was planning to bid. After years of leasing one of George's fields, it would make good business sense for him to own the farm, especially if the price was right. I understood this, that it was logical. The thought still made me numb and cold.

After two hours of the yard gradually clearing, there was a stirring of interest as the crowd sensed they were nearing the sale of the land and its buildings. Even the auctioneer stepped down for a moment to take a quick break. When he returned, all eyes were focused on him. Conversation stopped. In the hush, I could hear the urgent call of geese flying overhead, their formation pointed south. The auctioneer cleared his throat. "And now," he said, "we'll entertain bids for the land and buildings . . ."

"I bid a dollar," called a familiar voice from across the yard. George was striding toward the table, his face flushed, waving a dollar in one hand. The sheriff turned in his direction. "You heard me, I bid one dollar," he repeated. "This is my goddamn land, where I farmed all my life, where my daddy and grand-daddy farmed. My folks are buried out back. Which one of you plans to take care of their graves? I thought as much.

"Don't you see what's happening here? Do you think that you all are safe from what's happened to me? You've let accoun-tants and lawyers tell you how to run your farms, how to treat your animals. Now we've got corn diseases we'd never heard of before. We've got chickens who can't walk without breaking a leg. We've got soil that can't grow anything without its daily dose of chemicals. And look what we've done to our river.

"I bid one dollar to keep what rightfully belongs to my fam-ily," George continued, his voice growing hoarse with emotion. "If you feel you've got more claim to it than me, then let me see you make the next bid."

A shocked silence followed his words. George stood breathing hard, searching the faces in front of him, unable to find eyes that would meet his. Finally, the sheriff took a step forward. "George . . ." he began, reaching out a hand to gently pat his shoulder.

"I know, I know," George said. He shrugged off the sheriff's hand and tossed his dollar onto the table. His anger had disappeared, leaving behind a sad, slump-shouldered old man. He wavered for a moment, almost as if he might fall, before grabbing hold of the table to steady himself. Then he turned and walked down the driveway, never once turning back to look at the home he was leaving behind.

The auctioneer, who had been frozen during George's speech, revived and announced a five-minute coffee break. From beside me, John said, "Let's go." I looked at him in surprise, but he was already moving through the crowd with blind determination. The farm would indeed be sold that day, but not to him.

For the next few days, John was unusually silent. When Thomas called one evening from college, John asked him point-blank if he had made the phone call about George's corn and listened, grim faced, to his son's answer.

"All I'm asking is—did you make the phone call?" he repeated. A longer pause followed.

"All right, then. I'll tell her." He hung up the phone and sighed. "He says he didn't make the call. But he thinks I made a mistake in not buying the land."

John turned to me then, with a question on his face. I could feel his concern about our son. Tommy had become John's right-hand man by the time he finished high school, always searching for ways to earn his father's approval. When we heard stories from other farmers about superweeds that had developed in response to the new seeds, it was Tommy who had reassured John that he'd made the right decision. Tommy was a true believer, and nothing, it seemed, would change his mind. He had grown up with computers and cell phones and chemicals; this was the future.

His question remained unsaid. To have asked it would have been too close to admitting failure, that after all his years teaching his son, he didn't know if Tommy shared his beliefs.

Instead, he laughed his doubt off. "That boy," he said, shaking his head. "He has plenty of ambition. Tommy is just young; he'll learn the hard way, like I did." He unfolded a newspaper and began to read, his way of telling me that life would go on as usual.

CHAPTER TWENTY-FIVE

Gaby Makespeace
2001

I was sitting on a stiff plastic chair at a dinky little airport in Nowhere, Iowa. On the television suspended above my head, a life-or-death discussion of Super Bowl teams led to mention of the Washington Redskins, and suddenly I was super annoyed to be the only brown person in the room. Oh well—I should have been used to it by then. I smoothed a wrinkle in my skirt, already on its second day of meetings, popped a diabetes pill with a sip of bad coffee from a foam cup, and tried to ignore the drone of the sports announcers.

For the previous three years, I'd been flying from one farm town to the next, all along the Mississippi River, talking to groups of mostly white people who would listen politely before telling me that our plan to clean up the river would cost too many of the taxpayers' precious dollars. My job was to then convince them otherwise, whether by appealing to their consciences, to their pocketbooks (in the long run, anyway), or even to old-fashioned white guilt. I'm very good at my job. After finishing law school, where I'd gotten tired of having to work twice as hard as the white students just to prove that I belonged there, I discovered my real talent was talking to people. Since I was already working for the Save Our Rivers task force, they promoted me to be their community outreach director. A nice title to make up for the small paycheck.

I must have been reading something when my phone rang—maybe a report on water quality, or a staff paper on congressional votes—because I remember the papers fluttering to the floor. The old gentleman sitting across the aisle watched me answer the call and must have seen my face change, because he bent down and picked up the papers for me. He set them in a neat pile on the empty seat next to me, but all I could do was give him a weak wave of my fingers.

It wasn't that the news was so bad, not considering what life is like these days for Indian kids—especially young men like Mathó, being raised mostly by his great-aunt Vera while I was in school and on the road and in meetings. My son and I had had a long talk a couple of years before about how important the river was, not just for Native people, but for everyone. He seemed to understand perfectly that I had to talk to citizen groups, to show up at the Capitol when the politicians were voting, and to go for dinner with a sleazy congressman—who, by the way, was the closest thing I'd had to a date in two years. Mathó knew that it was all part of cleaning up the river, so he never complained. I guess he was so used to Auntie taking care of him while I'd been in school that it didn't seem so different when I started all my traveling.

Auntie Vera called me from the police station so I could hear it from the Man that Mathó had been picked up with a couple of young men who were smoking dope. I gave a big sigh of relief that he wasn't lying dead on some street from a gang shooting or a scared cop with a gun. Smoking a little weed didn't seem so bad. I mean: Didn't we all, back in the day? As long as you didn't make the mistake of getting into the business, like Earl had. I didn't want Mathó going down the same road as his dad. The policeman told me Mathó was being released into the custody of my auntie on account of his clean record, but that he would still have to show up in court on this or that date.

After the call ended, Auntie phoned me again. She's not a woman who says much, generally, not like me. She just keeps working, cleaning, mending, beading, and watching every little thing. Now, however, she said to me, "It should be you picking your son up at the station. Maybe if you'd been around, this wouldn't have happened." She paused, but I knew better than to open my mouth when Auntie had something to say. "It's time for you to come home." And she hung up.

While I was still sitting there trying to take it all in, a tinny voice announced over the intercom that all flights were delayed or canceled due to the winter storm that was already burying the runways. Fucking perfect. I called the organizer at my next event, and he was not happy. Gave me an earful about the mayor coming, the congressman who was showing up for a whole twenty minutes, the vote that was scheduled in the House, how this event could really be a game changer. He told me to rent a car and drive slowly. I could still be there in six hours, a full two hours ahead of the event. My room was booked, I was scheduled for coffee with the local chapter in the morning, and then I'd be on to the next place.

"Let me call you back," I said, not waiting for his reply.

I shoved the papers into my briefcase, picked up my purse, and headed to the car rental counter, where there was already a long line of people who'd had the same thought about getting out. I needed a cigarette bad. One of the reasons they send me on these town hall visits is because I can think on my feet: I'm good with the snappy reply, and I can make quick decisions when something is about to go down. But here I was, all deer in the headlights, completely unable to make a call about my own fucking life. About my own son. I didn't even know he was smoking pot. I thought he had a job at Thriftway.

From a chubby boy in his grass dancer outfit, Mathó had grown into a big guy, his belly hanging over baggy jeans that hung so low I thought they'd fall off. He just laughed whenever Auntie offered to lend him one of her belts, still the good-natured kid beneath all his posturing. He was always the largest, quietest guy hanging out with the tough kids on the playground or in front of the Kwik Store. I thought he had enough sense to keep out of trouble. He had asked me once if I could get him a job at the casino, where he could learn to cook. He loved to eat and used to help me in the kitchen, back when I had time to make soup or fry bread. I couldn't remember if I'd ever made that call for him.

Shit. Maybe I was a lousy mother. I didn't have a fucking clue what I should do. It was so much easier to be carried along by the momentum of the work, to believe in the importance of what we were doing. Since the days when I had worked with Rosie, I had moved downstream, focusing on the Mississippi River as a corridor that carried farm chemicals from the Minnesota River all the way to the Gulf of Mexico. If Rosie only knew what had been done to the river. Thirty years of dumping garbage and toxic chemicals at the Pig's Eye wetland near Saint Paul, for example, where smoke billowed from burning tires and trash floated in the river. And that was just one place along the river's more than two-thousand-mile journey to the Gulf.

I had once stood at the headwaters—where she first flowed from Lake Itasca as a small, pristine river, surrounded by tall birch trees—a moment that felt like prayer to me. I had started crying, I was so grateful. Here was this life-giving gift, what the elders call the first medicine. It was the closest I've come to understanding what "sacred" means. That moment reminded me why, all those years earlier when I was a confused single mother, I had promised this river, my sister, that I would fight for her.

And then, being me, I had become even more pissed at the assholes who dumped their garbage and chemicals into this beautiful river until she was unfit for anything. I couldn't quit now, when we were starting to see real progress, a few groups beginning to work together to help pass new protective laws that would hold corporations accountable. We had hundreds of people turning out to clean up trash in the river and along the banks. For the first time in thirty years, after peregrine falcons had been nearly wiped out by DDT, they were back nesting in the cliffs upriver.

I thought about calling my brother, Anthony, but he still didn't have a cell phone. When he got out of prison in the early eighties, he seemed like a different guy from the one who had gone in. He had managed to get off the painkillers he took after his car accident, talked about moving up to the Cities to work with AIM. He gave them credit for helping him get sober in jail and reconnect with ceremony. I knew Anthony was trying to be a stand-up father to his son with his ex-girlfriend. But it seemed like he couldn't ever get ahead of his own bad luck. His car would break down and he'd miss his appointment with his PO, get his parole revoked, and find himself busted again for looking the wrong way at someone. Wasn't too long before he'd be back on weed, sometimes heroin, or even the new meth I'd been hearing about. All I could do was pray for him that each time he got sober, it would be the one that would stick.

What I really wanted was to call Rosie. I wanted to tell her everything, get her common sense, her careful opinion, knowing she would never overstep or tell me what to do. She would always ask, Have you thought about this? And usually, no, I hadn't. But I hadn't talked to Rosie in several years, not since her newspaper printed that blow job about Mangenta under her name. I was mad at first, but I knew she didn't write it. I was just so disappointed that she couldn't make a real story happen. And when I was offered this job, the days kept passing without my ever finding the time to call her back, like I was speedboating down a river and she was standing on the bank. Finally, I stopped worrying about it.

So what would I say to her now? I could apologize, say, I know it's been too long, my fault, let's start over. Rosie would see right through that. Or I could try being honest: Mathó's in trouble, and I don't have a fucking clue what I'm supposed to do. Now that would most likely appeal to the Rosie I knew.

I entered her number into my phone but hesitated before pressing the call button. What if she didn't want to hear from me? What if she said, Fuck you, Gaby, I'm living my own life now and I don't need you? At that moment, a young woman waved me up to the counter. She furrowed her brow while staring at the computer screen in front of her.

"It looks like all we have left is a pickup truck," she said, glancing at my wool suit, my manicured nails.

"No problem," I replied, slapping down my credit card. "Just give me the keys."

"What's your destination, miss?"

I sucked in a big lungful of air, let it out slow. What would Rosie do—no, what would Rosie ask me to think about? Ah, of course.

"Mankato. I'm going home."

CHAPTER TWENTY-SIX

Rosalie Iron Wing Meister
2001

And then one morning, everything changed. The life I had come to depend on began to unravel, and all I could do was watch it happen.

Just after sunrise in late September, I knelt between rows in the garden, my legs chilled and damp from the dew that clung to dry leaves. For the past week, a lone crow had joined me each morning, watching from the high branches of an elm tree. All too soon, only a handful of birds would be left, shrewd scavengers who knew how to endure the frigid winter that was coming.

I turned to see John standing at the end of the row, holding the truck keys in his hand. He looked tired and thin, a scarecrow dressed in middle-aged-farmer clothes: jeans that bagged in the seat, a plaid shirt, and his favorite John Deere cap, faded from too many years in the sun.

"Rosie, I need to run to Mankato," he said, looking past me, at his fields. Dry weather had allowed him to harvest his corn before any chance of frost damage. A good harvest meant money in the bank, enough to make our payments. "Doctor's appointment. I thought you might want to come." I took a minute to think about his suggestion before I stood up. Dr. Morris, in New Ulm, generally treated the families in our area. He'd even delivered Thomas, now in his last year at college. This was unusual.

John had also made an unannounced trip to Mankato the week before, driving away in the middle of the day. When he came home, he had allowed me to make ginger tea to soothe a stomachache, drinking it in a begrudging silence that told me how desperate he was for comfort. But he had not offered an explanation for the trip, nor would I ask. He would tell me what I needed to know in his own time.

Heading south, we passed rolling fields of corn and soybeans still waiting to be harvested. John's gaze followed a neighbor cutting a wide swath through his fields in a new air-conditioned, GPS-driven combine. He watched with the hunger of a man who believes that success comes with owning the right machine. "There, Rosie, that's the future," he said.

We slowed to observe how the neatly withered cornstalks were folded beneath a giant maw with rapidly spinning blades. After a minute, John gave a low whistle of appreciation and a quick wave to our neighbor before speeding up again. A gust of wind raised a swirl of soil behind us, blowing it across the field, to lay it down again on a neighbor's land, or on the highway, or even in the next county. Some fields out here were so barren that nothing grew in the spring until they were dosed with fertilizer.

In Mankato, we parked in front of a new office building four stories tall, with a long list of doctors' names on the sign by the road. John marched through the glass doors of the clinic and across the new carpet like the successful businessman he had become. After checking in with the receptionist, he chose a chair close to the door, and I sat next to him. He held his cap in his lap while we waited for his name to be called.

"Remind me to stop by the post office after," he said in a low voice. "This shouldn't take long. Just need some stomach medicine is all." When the nurse called his name, he gave her a friendly nod and disappeared down the hall.

I pulled a book from my pocket. An old woman walked into the clinic, leaning heavily on a cane, her hair pulled back in a thick gray braid, and sat down next to me. She dropped a canvas tote on the floor near her feet. Heaving a sigh, she settled into the cushion, smoothed a wrinkle from her long skirt, and folded her hands in her lap. She never once glanced my way, nor did she look at her companion, a young woman who slouched on the opposite side of the room as if they had been arguing.

A half hour passed in silence, broken only by the brisk phone voice of the front-desk receptionist. When John finally emerged, his mouth was pressed in a thin line. The receptionist offered to schedule another appointment, but John shook his head and held out his hand for the prescription he needed. She asked again, and he drummed his fingers on the counter, saying nothing.

Behind him, the nurse called out the next patient's name, stumbling over the unfamiliar sounds. When the young woman offered her hand to her grandmother, her lips trembled as if she was trying not to weep. Her grandmother stood up and turned toward me, dropping a small cloth bag into my lap. She nodded, pushed her lips toward the bag, and walked slowly to the waiting nurse. As they made their way down the hall, the young woman turned and looked back at me. Then they were gone.

John headed straight for the door, as if he could not wait to leave. I grabbed the bag without looking inside and followed. He did not like to be kept waiting. Outside, the wind was brisk, with heavy gray clouds covering the sky. I would not harvest any beans today.

John headed west, bypassing the post office and merging onto the highway toward home, driving with a white-knuckle grip on the steering wheel. He did not speak at all for the first ten minutes. Finally, he took a deep breath and slowly released it.

"What's that bag you're holding?" he asked. Not a detail ever escaped him, not even when he didn't seem to be paying attention, not even something as small as the cloth bag in my hands. That was part of what made him a good farmer.

I set the bag in my lap and looked it over. Clearly hand sewn from a piece of flowered cotton, like something I might have used to make a quilt. The stitches were tiny and evenly spaced, the mark of an experienced maker. A drawstring cinched the neck closed above its bulging contents. I loosened the string and pulled out a handful of dusty vegetables.

"Beets?" John asked, his curiosity getting the better of his mood. "They look a bit small for turnips."

"Prairie turnips," I said, pulling the name from a forgotten memory. The faint smell of dry soil rose from the small rough lumps in my hand. When I closed my eyes, I could hear my father telling me, "This is thípsiŋna. Their branches point the way to the next plant." He had once shown me how to dig the roots with a sharp stick, when we spent an afternoon filling a plastic sack from the grocery store. The memory faded as quickly as it had come. I had not thought of my childhood in a long time, had put away those years the same way I stored potatoes from my garden: well away from the light.

We made just one stop, at a drugstore, where John went in alone, carrying his slip of paper. The sun was well past midday by the time we turned down the driveway to the farm. Unlike the first time I had visited nearly twenty-two years earlier, the apple orchard was pruned and well tended. I remembered that when I had first seen the farm, I thought John must have been rich, owning all this land and a house with a porch swing and four bedrooms. That was long before I had learned about back taxes and bank loans.

John turned off the engine and sat for a moment, staring at the house. As the engine ticked quietly, he seemed to be searching for something to say. I glanced at him, at the tight clench in the muscles along his jaw. I felt numb, preparing for the worst, for my life to once again be emptied out and thrown away. John was not the same man who had left the farm a few hours earlier. He seemed hollowed out, a thin stalk that any stiff wind might carry away. His hands trembled and his voice shook when he finally spoke.

"You're to own the farm," he said, drawing in a ragged breath. "Our son will run it. You'll always have a home, just like I promised you."

He pulled the keys from the ignition and headed toward the barn. On the seat between us lay the sack from the drugstore, with a bottle of pain medication to be refilled as often as needed. Another chemical to remedy the chemicals that had run the farm.

I carried both bags inside, placed the turnips on a shelf in the pantry, and went back to my garden. I dug my hands into the soil. Breathed in the scent of moist earth as the shock of his words settled in. Until that moment, I had not realized how deeply I had come to care for him. I trusted him in a way I had never shared with anyone except my father.

After so many years, I felt the slow rise of a river that would carry me away from the life I knew.

CHAPTER TWENTY-SEVEN

Rosalie Iron Wing Meister

2002

I chose a rooster that was young and strong, his comb a deep lustrous red. Unlike the others, he refused to run. Instead he turned to look at me with a calm eye, almost as if he knew what I asked of him. I scattered a handful of chicken feed and waited until he had pecked every last seed from the frozen ground. I thanked him. Then I carried him behind the barn, slit his neck with my knife, and hung him from a hook until the blood had drained from his body.

When the rooster was gutted and plucked, I carried him to the kitchen, where my big soup kettle was waiting on the stove. I drew water from the well, ice-cold and sweet, to use for broth, and added dried onions and herbs from the summer's garden. When the meat had cooked long enough to leave its bones, I added late-harvest carrots and potatoes. Followed by the thípsiŋna from the woman at the doctor's office, dried and stored in my pantry the past three months. Scrapings from my last twigs of wild ginger. As I worked, I sang quietly, repeating the same phrase over and over again. *Wakháŋ Tháŋka, toka heya, cewakiye* . . . The few words I remembered from a song my father once taught me.

I turned the kettle down to simmer, allowing the soup to cook slow. When the kitchen was fragrant with thyme-scented steam, I carefully filled a bowl with clear broth and set it on a tray with a cup of warm cedar tea. I carried it upstairs and knocked once on John's half-open bedroom door. Only his eyes turned to greet me, returning from whatever it was he watched through the window. Today, perhaps nothing more than winter's frost on the glass. I had long since stopped see-ing his shrunken self, this bag of bones that could once ride a tractor for twelve hours or more through his fields. Now he lay broken like the ridge of corn stubble left after harvest.

After setting the tray on his table, I closed the shades to soften the glare of sun reflecting off new snow. I would need to shovel the sidewalk sometime soon. Our neighbor, Roger Peterson, had started plowing the driveway after John fell sick, not waiting to be asked and not expecting to be paid, either. I had sent over the last of my canned peaches as thanks. I knew John would hate to accept help when he couldn't repay the favor.

I smoothed the bedcovers, mostly from habit, as John had not moved much since the day before. Still, his eyes followed me as I sat down at his side. I raised a spoonful of broth to his dry lips. He sipped, more to please me than from hunger. When he'd had enough, he closed his eyes. I pressed a cloth napkin to the corners of his mouth. He refused the tea with a slight shake of his head. When I began to rise from the bed, his fingers found my wrist, their clawlike grip bidding me to stay. I felt his fear, felt the gathering chill beneath his skin. I picked up the book on his bedside table and began to read.

"The Widow Douglas she took me for her son, and allowed she would sivilize me; but it was rough living in the house all the time . . ."

John slept as I watched his bony chest barely raising the blanket. His hair was short bristles, his pale skin sank beneath the sharp ridge of his cheekbones. A stranger to us both. After a time, I heard the soft click of the front door opening. With a sigh, I rose, gathered the dishes onto the tray, and waited.

Whenever Tommy—or Thomas, as he liked to be called now—had called over the past few months, John had assured him that he was doing better every day; that he had caught hold of a bug he couldn't seem to shake, but that he fully intended to be back at work come spring. He and I both knew, of course, that this wasn't true. Even a month prior, when it had become clear that John didn't have much time left, still he had kept up the pretense with his son. One night, after he'd hung up the phone, I stood at the sink, washing our supper dishes in a pointed silence. After a moment, he spoke to the stiff curve of my back. "Leave it be. No need for him to miss school just yet."

John's pride in seeing Thomas become the first college student in his family had blinded him to the truth of his situation. It had been me who called Thomas a week ago, told him it was time for him to come home. He listened in silence, considering the contradiction between my words and those of his father. Finally, he agreed to come as soon as he could get away. As if to prove to himself that I was wrong.

But there was no arguing with the sight that greeted him when he walked into John's bedroom. His father's eyes were closed, his thin frame unmoving, the man entirely unaware of his son's presence. Even the air in the room smelled strangely sweet and metallic: the unnatural mix of chemicals and dying flesh. Thomas gazed down at his father, absorbing the details of his decay, of the slow unraveling of his life. For a moment, I saw John through my son's eyes, understood too late how poorly prepared he was for this awful truth. Then he turned without a word and strode back down the hall. I could hear his feet strike each stair; I felt his anger in the trembling of the wood. I waited for the front door to slam shut. Nothing.

Thomas hadn't always been this way. I remembered walking with him to the river, where he would play for hours in the water, and his joy when he was allowed to ride on the tractor with John. And now this once gentle boy was waiting for me downstairs, filled with rage that I was allowing his father to die.

I went to the kitchen. Thomas was sitting in his father's place at the table, fingers drumming, as I set the tray on the counter.

"Would you like some coffee?" I asked.

He gave a quick shake of his head, unwilling to be distracted or lulled by my words. I sat down at my end of the table and waited. Outside the window, a chickadee called from the feeder that John had hung for me years earlier. I made a note to refill it with seeds—one more chore that had been left untended over the past month.

"Why wasn't I told?" His voice shook as he spoke.

"Your father thought it was best."

He stood up and paced across the kitchen, leaning against the counter with his arms folded across his chest. I watched the chickadee as it scanned the ground for an overlooked seed among the husks that littered the snow. I could hear my son's breathing, his effort at control.

"Do you have any idea how it feels to be lied to about my own father?"

A cardinal landed on the empty tray, startling the chickadee into sudden flight, and stood still for two heartbeats, a shock of red against the dead white of our yard. Beyond the tall maple that held the feeder, I could see the spiky heads of the coneflowers and the withered vines of the wild grapes I picked for jam.

Thomas was still talking. Asking questions without waiting for answers. Why was John not in a hospital, where was his doctor, what treatment was he taking, there were new drugs all the time, why wasn't I helping? Was I just going to sit there while his father died, without doing anything but cooking up herbal medicine? His father's cup of undrunk tea smashed against the far kitchen wall. Water flew in every direction, and bits of broken ceramic seemed to float in the air, twirling and spinning like dust motes, suspended in the new silence that followed the shock of impact. Thomas stood breathing hard. Neither of us spoke. Finally, I walked to the closet where I kept the broom, giving him time to leave the room. When I turned back, dustpan in hand, he was gone. The front door slammed shut. I watched from the window as he walked past the deserted feeder, down the sidewalk to his car. Tires spun a spray of gravel as he raced back to the road.

Perhaps if I had known how to be a better mother to him, he would not have turned so hard against me when he grew up.

John was awake when I came back to his room, looking more alert than I had seen him in some time. I turned on the lamp near his bed, knowing he did not like to lie awake in the dark.

When John had stopped coming downstairs, I simply piled the mail onto his desk as if it would be waiting for him when he returned to work. How I clung to these small deceptions, believing in the comfort of routine as long as I could. I darned his socks and cleaned the mud off his boots, tightened all the buttons on his barn coat. I vacuumed, dusted, washed windows. Still there were so many hours in the day that needed filling.

"Thomas was here," I told him. "He said to tell you he'll be back later." When he has time to cool down, I thought to myself, to think things through, he *will* be back. The shock of seeing his father so ill had been too much to take in all at once. He was a good boy, a good son. John squeezed my hand to let me know he was listening.

We sat quietly for a while, as the wind whistled beneath the eaves of the house and rattled the windows. He startled me when he spoke, his voice so low I could hardly hear him.

"Did we do right by him?"

"By Thomas? What do you mean?"

"Did we—did I—make the right decisions about Thomas? I only wanted the best for him. More than I had."

I was silent. I had certainly asked myself the same question about Thomas. As parents, how do any of us answer it? Especially when we struggle with our own challenges, not realizing when we're young how much the past has shaped us, how we carry our parents' sorrow and that of the generations that came before them?

John's eyes closed, and I squeezed his hand back. We had surely tested each other over the years. Yet, after all the struggles, I felt as if I was losing an old friend, one that I had battled with and made love to, with whom I'd shared the raising of a child. His dying would leave an empty place in my heart.

⸻

That night I left the porch light turned on in case Thomas decided to come back. I was starting to lose hope, given how stubborn he could be. When I lay down in my own room for a few hours of rest, I couldn't sleep. My thoughts kept returning to Thomas, to his father waiting for him. I remembered long nights waiting for my own father to return from hunting, or from wherever he went when he disappeared for a day or two. How slowly the time had moved.

I heard the front door open and close. Soft footsteps on the stairs, carefully avoiding the creaky second step. John's door closing. And then quiet, soft and sweet, broken only by the low murmur of a son talking to his father.

Thomas left his father's room before sunrise, slipping away as quietly as he had come. John seemed further away when I checked on him, not really resting but preparing. His eyes were shut; his mouth hung slightly open. I moistened a sponge and ran it across his cracked lips.

As the shadows lengthened toward dusk, a new stillness settled around the house. The cold deepened until the wood cracked as the walls drew in. I turned on the lamp in John's room and left the rest of the house dark. I could hear the wind calling outside the window. I sat in my chair near John's bed with a pair of his socks that needed mending. My hands stayed idle. I couldn't seem to focus on anything. Once in a while I rocked a bit, but mostly I just sat, my thoughts far away. I was not interested in what would come next. I still had business with the past. I could feel the way it tugged at me, growing stronger as John's light dimmed. No matter what people said, when he finally left his body, this life of ours would go with him. There was so little left as it was. I was a burnt field, waiting for a new season to begin.

⚊

Every now and then I checked on John, adjusted his pillow. I could tell he didn't want any fussing. His entire being seemed to say, Leave me be. The sores of his body no longer mattered. I sat again. Listened.

I must have fallen asleep; I know I dreamed of my father. *It was deep in winter when he left home. Hours before daylight, when the walls of our cabin creaked from the cold, I woke to the smell of coffee and woodsmoke. The long needles of a pine tree scraped against my bedroom window with each gust of wind.*

I could hear his quiet movements in the next room. The rustle of heavy clothing; the whiplike sound of boots being laced. I knew his habits so well I could predict his next steps. He set his snowshoes outside the door, removed his rifle from the wall. I heard the thunk of logs as he stoked the fire, and the sigh of my door as he opened it. In a deep rumble, he told me he was going out to check his traps.

"Go back to sleep, mičhúŋkši. I'll be home to make you breakfast." His rough fingers smoothed the hair from my face.

I burrowed deep beneath the blankets and breathed the warm salt of my skin, aware of the silence that rose when the front door snapped shut. I drifted then, my eyes squeezed tight against the harsh light of the sun, until I felt a shock of cold air as my blankets were pulled back.

"She's here," a voice called out—too loud, I thought, too close, and not my father's voice at all. A stranger's hand gently pressed my shoulder. "Rosalie, wake up, something has happened to your father . . ."

I didn't wake up, not then, nor in the gray days that followed. I was stripped clean of my home, my father, my life. I heard my name repeated by people who spoke in whispers; I saw my future reflected in their sad eyes. When a woman brought me to a house surrounded by a metal fence, I tried to run. I wanted to go home. Eventually, worn down, I surrendered my past, my memories, turned them in for a new story of how I came to be.

All these years I had been living inside this dream.

John left on that cold winter night, passing from this world while I dozed in my chair. When I woke at dawn, with the sun just beginning to emerge behind a scatter of pink-tinted clouds, his face was still and calm. That gave me comfort, knowing he left with a peaceful heart. He, too, was traveling to the stars, to the place of spirits, where my father had gone. No longer would he carry the weight of what had happened between him and George, or his concern for his son. His mistakes were only lessons after all. I thought of him as he had been on that day we first met: his John Deere cap pushed high on his forehead, his eyes kind. He had kept his promise to me, that I would always have a home.

We scattered John's ashes beneath the oak tree where his family was buried. Thomas stood near me as Pastor Bob offered a prayer. While polite, Thomas had trouble meeting my eyes. Someone would have to bear the blame for the loss of the man whose love he had worked so hard to earn. He had never wanted to disappoint his dad, never wanted to appear weak in John's eyes, and so Thomas had no choice but to move forward as if he believed in his own strength. I would inherit the farm, but Thomas would manage the business. Whatever happened next, Thomas would need my signature.

After we saw Pastor Bob back to his car, it was difficult for us to walk back into the house, knowing that John would not be there. Unsure of what to do, Thomas and I sat together in the kitchen. I put the kettle on to make tea. Without the buffer of his father's presence, Thomas and I no longer knew how to talk to each other. I asked about school. He was taking a break. Neither of us could express what was in our hearts, an overwhelming sense of loss for the life we had known with this man, coupled with uncertainty about the future. There would be plenty of time in the weeks and months to come to talk about the farm.

But Thomas was too young to know this. He came out from his father's office carrying a stack of papers he had unearthed from the desk. I would have left the mail for another day, but Thomas was well trained by his father.

"We need to take care of this," he began, sifting through the papers until he found the one he needed. "Dad would have wanted us to get this signed right away. I can't believe it's been sitting here this long." On and on he droned, his voice tight with the loss he could not admit. He was willing to reach out to me if I would agree with him, with his father, about the way they had treated the land. "Sign these papers, please," he said. "It's the only way we can keep the farm."

Hadn't I heard those words before? Hadn't I signed, hadn't I agreed to whatever John had asked, even when I knew it was shortsighted and a risk to us all? And now John was dead, barely fifty years old. I said nothing, looked again to the window. Thomas left with a promise to return soon. I had no words to spare for him.

None of it mattered to me now. Not the farm, not the garden, perhaps not even my son.

One morning, I woke before dawn, just as I used to as a child. I thought I smelled coffee. I thought I heard a familiar voice. I left my bed and began to pack. I gathered everything I would need for a week. From the far corner of my dresser drawer, I drew out my father's hunting cap, now bare where the fur had fallen out. Inside it was $600 in twenties, the money I had earned detasseling corn so many years earlier. This was the only money I would take with me, wrapped inside my father's cap.

I wasn't sure about the gun. When I pulled it from the drawer, it felt heavy in my hand. I wondered if it carried John's longing, if his dying body had begged to be released from its pain. It seemed like a risk to take it. But I had listened for too long to warnings about the dangers of my old life, and I was no longer protected in the way that I once was. I packed the gun.

Before I left, I sat down at the kitchen table and tried to read the papers my son had left for me to sign. I could not shape the words in my mind, could not shake loose their meaning from the dense flood that spread across each page. Instead, I wrote a note and left it on the table as if I was going on a short trip. As if the silence in the house meant only that John was out in the fields.

I loaded John's truck with my few bags, turned the key in the kitchen door, and followed the long driveway back to the road I had first traveled twenty-two years earlier. I did not look back.

wačhékiye

the earth hears me

———(▪)———

CHAPTER TWENTY-EIGHT

Rosalie Iron Wing

2002

In time, the snow melted, puddled in soft mud that smelled like clay, like spring, like home. Shortly after the bloodroot bloomed, Ida returned. This time the front door was propped open for fresh air as I swept winter's dust from the floor, and so I saw them coming down the path, Digger loping along in front, his nose riding close to the ground. He glanced up, saw me watching from the doorway, and stuck close to his companion. Ida lifted her hand in greeting, a friendly smile on her face. I was glad to see her.

As I opened the door for Ida, Digger's ears suddenly pricked up. He took a deep sniff, then shot around the corner of the cabin. Ida looked at me, her raised eyebrows asking a question. I shrugged.

"I think he's about to meet Šazí," I said.

Before Ida could ask anything more, we heard a loud, blood-curdling howl come from behind the cabin, as an ancient battle was resumed with a furious scrabbling of claws on tree bark.

"Shazee? Digger's going to take that cat apart."

"I don't think so."

We sat at the kitchen table, and I gave Ida my one good cup, filled with coffee from the thermos. I told her we could take turns sipping, and she laughed. I laughed, too, mostly from the pleasure of her voice.

I handed her an old book, an encyclopedia of wild plants, that I had found on my father's shelf. Whether she knew it or not, Ida had helped me make it through the winter. I had so little to give her in return, but I knew how much she loved the woods. After looking through a few pages, she muttered her thanks in a voice rough with emotion. "So you survived the winter, then," she added quickly, covering her embarrassment.

"Thanks to you and your gifts," I replied. "Or maybe it was the little people who left all that good food on my step."

"More than likely it was them. I came once or twice just to be sure there was still smoke from your chimney. Seen plenty of wood out back." A silence fell between us. Comfortable, like that of old friends who don't fear the space between words. She continued, "Truth is, you seemed . . . poorly, that time I seen you in the woods. Don't take offense, but I thought maybe you were . . ."

"Crazy?"

"Not exactly. More like I didn't know if you were . . . well. You seemed kind of lost."

I was tempted then to tell her everything. To tell her how it felt to be woken one morning shortly after dawn, to learn that my father was lying in the back of her uncle's pickup truck, dead from a heart attack. I wanted to tell someone, finally, what it had been like to be taken from my home, never knowing if I would see it again. The strangeness of a new bed, a wool blanket that chafed my skin; how their eyes probed and stared, cold, like the fish that flopped in my father's canoe. How those eyes judged me because I had no family. How their food stuck in my throat until I gagged and was sent away from the table. Cruel words. Tall metal fences. Whispers, sideways glances. A throwaway child.

Our eyes met briefly, long enough for us both to realize we shared similar stories. We had much to tell each other. I stood up.

"I'll make us a fresh pot of coffee."

For the rest of that afternoon, we talked like two people who have been starved for the taste of words. Just as I remembered, Ida's family had left her behind after the trouble with her cousin.

"The sheriff come by the house twice, asking questions about where I was the day my cousin shot himself in the woods. Ma swore up and down that I was home with her, said she would swear on a stack of Bibles that it was God's truth, and that as she was a minister's wife, that ought to be good enough for him. She was something else when she was riled up, and he got her good and riled up.

"Thing was, all she knew for sure was that she seen me go into my bedroom and that the door stayed shut most of the day. I'd told her I had female trouble. When the sheriff came the second time, she warned him not to come back unless he could prove something. And then she did a funny thing. She came and sat with me at the table, put her hands in her lap. She didn't look me in the eye. She said, That morning when your cousin was shot, I knocked on your door. You didn't answer.

Your door was locked, so I called out your name, and you still didn't answer. Now. In my mind, I am settled that you were asleep and didn't hear me. If there is a different explanation, I don't want to know. I have arranged for you to go stay a spell with your aunt and uncle. At least until things quiet down. Your uncle was always partial to you, Lord knows why, so you'll be well taken care of. We can't stay any longer in a town where our good family name has been dragged through the mud.

"She must have seen something in my eye, because she put up her hand and said, Not another word, Ida. I've tried to raise you as a good Christian woman, but there is something in you that's not right. I have prayed and prayed, but I see now that you refuse to change. I've got the younger children to think about. Of course, we'll always care for you. I'll write you when we get settled.

"She kept her word. She wrote every month, long letters full of church news. They moved again, two years later. Then the letters came fewer and fewer. Now I hear from them once a year, at Christmas." Ida shrugged. For a moment, the strong lines of her face grew soft, and she looked like a child, missing her family. "In case you're wondering, I didn't kill my cousin. I didn't need to."

She handed me the coffee cup. My turn. I told Ida of my foster family, of my life as a farmwife, of Judith and George. Of my husband's slow death. Of the unsigned papers I left sitting on the kitchen table. Of my son.

Ida gave a low whistle and shook her head. "He doesn't even know where you are? Poor guy is worried sick about losing his dad's farm, and then his ma takes off. I'm not saying I wouldn't do exactly what you did, but maybe I'd leave a note."

"I did leave a note."

"Did you tell him where you were going?"

"No."

"That's what I'm saying."

I sighed, suddenly tired. Ida must have felt it, too, since she stood up and reached for her pack. Then she stopped with a quick laugh and tapped her forehead with her hand.

"Oh, I almost forgot. I thought you might be interested in this picture." She opened the pack and drew out a framed photograph carefully wrapped in a soft cloth. The photo was black-and-white, faded, with a sharp crease across one corner. She pointed to a young man who was standing with one hand on another man's shoulder.

"That's my uncle Clarence. There next to him is your dad, Ray. They were good friends, used to go hunting together. My uncle was the postmaster, so he knew everybody, knew their families, too. Next to Ray is your mom. Uncle Clarence said the photo was taken when your folks got married."

I took the photograph from her hands. I had no pictures of my mother, none at all. They had disappeared along with the stories of our life together. Agnes was tall, like me, her dark hair falling in thick waves to her shoulders. She wore a red suit, belted at the waist, and high heels. Her eyes gazed at the camera without smiling, as if to challenge the photographer. My father, dressed in his army uniform, was looking at her with an expression of pure adoration, his arm around her waist. Clearly pregnant, she was leaning slightly away from him. I wondered if the weight of his affection was too much for her.

I drank in this photograph like it was the one sip of water that would last me the rest of my life. There they all were: my family. My beautiful, unhappy mother. And my father, more content than I had ever seen him.

"Ida, who are these two women in the background?"

She leaned over my shoulder to look at the two older women sitting in chairs behind my parents. Ida pointed to the more heavyset one, who wore her coat buttoned up to her neck. She, too, gazed at the camera as if not really seeing it, her brown face impassive and closed.

"Uncle Clarence told me that's your grandmother Lorraine. She died of pneumonia when you and I were still kids. He said she was a hard one."

"What does that mean—'She was a hard one'?"

"I can't say for sure. He said that when she came back from boarding school, she was a fighter. She'd turned mean, just angry at the world. She used to hit her brothers."

"I have uncles?"

"Dead ones. They came home from school changed, too. Harry was killed in a car accident. Fred drank himself to death. Only Lorraine was strong enough to survive. The gossips said she used to make bad medicine on anyone who crossed her. They said she used to smack Agnes, too. Sorry." As if Ida were responsible for my family's mistakes.

"Who's the woman next to Lorraine?"

Ida bent close to peer at the blurred details of the woman's face. She was smiling at Agnes, her chin tilted up, her brunette hair pulled away from high cheekbones. She sat with crossed legs, a tailored skirt revealing several inches of her slender calf.

"They look kind of alike. Uncle Clarence mentioned a younger sister, Darlene, who was sent to live with relatives. They all came back around the same time."

"Is she still alive?"

"Dunno. Uncle Clarence passed on a year ago. I could ask Wilma Many Horses. She knows everything about everybody in this area. I bring her venison, so we get along pretty good. Why don't you come with me?" She asked this without looking at me, giving me room to decide whether I was ready to return to the world.

Yes. That's all I could say, as much determination as I could summon in the moment. I struggled against hope, against the possibility that I might have a relative, someone from my own family who had known my mother. There was something else, too, rising slow and burning at the back of my throat, that kept me from saying more. Grateful as I was for Ida's help, I didn't want to accept that she knew far more about my family's history than I did. I was a stranger to my home, my family, myself. As my understanding grew, the edges of my control slowly started to unravel.

Ida hefted her pack and turned to leave. Over her shoulder, she said, "I'll be back in the morning. You can keep the picture." Without waiting for my reply, she walked away, as the afternoon sun was beginning to sink behind the trees.

CHAPTER TWENTY-NINE

Rosalie Iron Wing
2002

The wind changed direction in the night, the way it does in early April—one day bringing rain, the next day heat, or even a late-season snowstorm. I woke well before dawn, worried that the weather might stop me from getting to town. But when the sun finally rose, it was in a clear sky, the blue so soft I wanted to stroke it, like the blanket Gaby had once given my infant son.

Ida walked through the door two hours later, coming straight in with just a single knock, red cheeked from the morning chill. She looked smaller, somehow, without Digger by her side. She refused a cup of coffee and began loading my truck while I searched for the keys, changed my pants for a less faded pair, rebraided my hair, and gulped my coffee without tasting it. When Ida whistled for me the way she usually did for Digger, I rushed out the door and promptly dropped my keys in the mud. Finally, however, we were in the truck, backing down the narrow road that had brought me here two months earlier.

Ida had offered to drive, perhaps sensing that I was far too nervous to pay attention to the road. To distract me, she began telling stories of each parcel of land that we passed, explaining who had owned it and for how long. Originally this had all been Dakhóta land, but after the 1862 war the reservation had been seized by the government and sold to white families like the Meisters.

"It's a darn checkerboard," Ida said. "But at least the casino helps provide jobs. If we have time, we can drive by the new clinic the tribe built. Wilma said they've started up new programs to help with addiction and suicide prevention. There's even a garden club and a Men's Group."

Growing up, I had often wished that we lived on the reservation, that we could become more a part of this community. My father carried a grudge against the tribal council for slights both real and imagined, which he extended to our neighbors in general. He had turned his back on the families here, just as he had turned away from teaching in public schools. His world kept shrinking until it was just the two of us. And then my decision to marry a white farmer had taken me to a different world entirely, a distance much greater than just miles. Coming to the occasional powwow as an adult had only reminded me how close-knit this community was, how they took care of one another. Then and now, I felt like a kid with my face pressed to the window—always on the outside looking in. After all these years, I couldn't think why anyone on the reservation would give me the time of day, much less help me find my family.

As Ida talked, I nodded as if I were listening, but in truth, I was picturing all the ways in which people could slam the door in my face. Couldn't say I would blame them. But right when I was about to say "Let's turn back," we drove into Milton, the same little town I had driven through in deep winter. This time, there were more cars on the road, children waiting at a bus stop. Two middle-aged Indian women were visiting in front of the post office. I asked Ida to stop while I mailed a letter to Thomas, telling him where I was staying. As I walked to the door, the women stopped talking to give me sideways glances, clearly wondering who I was. One of them raised her chin in greeting. Her small gesture gave me hope.

Three miles farther east, we parked in front of a two-story brick building with a handful of cars in the lot. Most of the window shades were up, like the people inside were already busy with their day. Maybe Wilma wasn't home. I followed Ida as she walked quickly up the clean, tidy sidewalk. On the front door, a handwritten sign read "Elders' Lodge, No Smoking!"

"This time of day, Wilma is probably having a cup of coffee downstairs. There's a bunch of them like to play Uno," Ida said.

I had no choice but to keep following Ida as she pushed through the unlocked door and turned toward the stairs. I took a deep breath of cooking grease, coffee, and the sweet smell of burning sage. I remembered my father standing in front of the cabin, holding a half shell, while he fanned a wisp of smoke through his hair, around his body, across his heart. His low voice as he prayed using the few words of Dakhóta that he knew. The smudge helped steady me. I kept my hands in my pockets so Ida would not see how my fingers trembled.

We entered a large white room with leftover shamrocks decorating one wall. A dozen tables were scattered around the space. On the couch near the television, two old men wearing beaded baseball caps were watching a cooking show with the sound turned off. They turned to look at me and Ida as we walked in. Nodding at the men, Ida strode toward the table at the back of the room, where four gray-haired women were playing cards. They did not look up as we approached. Ida gestured at me to sit with her at the next table.

Each player had a coffee cup and a small stack of quarters. A metal walker stood nearby, tennis balls covering the bottoms of the back legs. The women might have been sisters, so closely did they resemble each other; each wore a loose cotton shirt and tennis shoes, with glasses perched on the end of each nose. Their large purses were tucked under the table. The woman facing us wore her long silver hair pulled back in a loose clip. A crumpled Kleenex was tucked in her rolled-up sleeve.

The women were completely focused on their game, the silence broken only by the players' terse verbal commands: spades, hearts. Finally, Uno. As if a spell had been broken, they relaxed, chatted, sipped from their cups. The woman across from us, the winner of that round, glanced in my direction before looking back to Ida. She shuffled the cards for a moment.

"Ida, who is your friend?"

Ida stood up and walked around the table to shake the woman's hand. I followed behind. "Wilma, this is Rosalie Iron Wing. She's the daughter of Ray Iron Wing and Agnes Kills Deer."

Wilma stopped shuffling. She looked up at me with her full attention. I offered my hand, which she held between both of hers. Wilma studied me for a moment before she spoke. "Welcome home, child. We didn't know if we would ever see you again."

My heart caught in her words. I had to struggle for control. Wilma let go of my hand, gave me a moment to compose

myself. Then she stood, slow, and pushed her lips toward the
coffeepot at the back of the room.

"We'll take a break. I need to visit with thakóža."

When we were sitting again, Wilma said to me, "Are you
back home to stay?"

I shook my head. "I don't know. I have a son. And a farm. I
don't know. I'm hoping to learn more about my family."

Wilma smiled and nodded as if she understood. "I knew
Ray, of course. In fact, we're related—through your father's
people, the Iron Wings. Your grandmother's cousin was my
aunt. That makes us kin and you related to at least a dozen
families on the reservation. I used to see you riding in your
dad's big pickup truck, barely tall enough to see out the window. You were a good girl, he raised you well. That's not easy
for a man to do alone." She looked away.

One of the old men walked slowly to the table and shook
hands with Ida. Wilma said, "Carlos, you need to meet this
young lady, she's finally come home to us. You knew her father,
Ray Iron Wing. Carlos is my adopted brother, moved here
from the southwest when his family was looking for work."

While she spoke, Carlos took my hand in both of his, just
as Wilma had, and shook his head. "Shame what happened to
your family. He was a good man, your dad. He'd give away the
last dollar in his pocket if someone needed it."

"Rosalie has a farm now. And a son."

"I used to work on farms," Carlos said. "Grew up picking fruit, then we kept our own truck farm until I left for the
army. Still miss it. I wake up in spring thinking I need to get to
the fields to plant. Then I try to move this old body."

He gave me a wink and smiled. "You remember when

your dad used to stop at Victor's on his way home? I knew you when you were just a kid." Giving us a quick salute with a knobby finger, Carlos hobbled back to the couch, where his friend had fallen asleep, snoring with his mouth open.

I turned back to Wilma. "Did you know anyone else in my family?"

"Yes. I grew up not far from your grandmother. Although Lorraine was a few years older than me, so I was better friends with her sister, Darlene."

"Do you know where I can find her?" I asked, steeling myself for the possibility that she, too, had already passed.

"No."

I exhaled, not realizing I had been holding my breath. Then Wilma continued, "But I heard she might be in the area. Check at the tribal office and maybe they can help you out."

It was that easy. After saying goodbye to Wilma, with a promise to return for a longer visit, we went back up the road to the agency. The young woman who handled tribal enrollment wore a powwow T-shirt and beaded earrings, snapping her gum as she listened carefully to my request for information about my great-aunt.

"I'm not supposed to give out personal details," she said, while flipping through files in her drawer. "But I'm damned tired of hearing how social services broke up families like yours. You were placed a few years before you would have been covered by ICWA."

"What do you mean?"

"Indian Child Welfare Act, passed in 1978. Indian children have to be placed first with their own family, or with someone in the tribe, before they're sent to foster care. Before ICWA, children could be removed by social workers, and ninety percent were placed in non-Native homes. Even Congress finally admitted that separating so many Indian children from their families was one of the biggest tragedies affecting our communities today."

"I was told I didn't have any family."

"Well, you were told wrong. It looks like your great-aunt is still alive. Here's the last phone number I have for her. She can decide if she wants to give you her address." She handed me a slip of paper: Darlene Kills Deer, and a phone number with the same area code as my foster family's in Mankato. All those years I had waited for family to come for me, Darlene was living in the same city.

We drove to the gas station and pulled up next to the public pay phone. Ida said she needed a few things inside. I got out and leaned against the wall, hesitating, my fingers closed tight around a handful of quarters. What if Darlene had known where to find me—what if she didn't care? With trembling fingers, I dialed her phone number.

The phone rang and rang and rang. I was about to hang up when I heard a click, the sound of fumbling, and a voice with a slight tremor saying hello. When I could speak, I explained who I was. Followed by a few minutes of silence on the other end.

"We didn't know where to find you," Darlene said, finally. "I have your picture on my shelf, taken when you were four years old. They wouldn't tell me—nobody would tell me—how to find you." She had searched for me, and in the end she'd had to wait for me to find her.

I don't know what we said next. Maybe we laughed; maybe we cried, especially when I told her where I had been living with my foster family. "Oh" was all she could say, over and over. "Oh, oh, oh."

We agreed that I would come to visit in four days. Darlene had a doctor's appointment and would need to rest up for my visit. "I'm ninety," she said, "and everything takes a little more time."

When Ida came back to the truck, she gave me a quick glance. I reached for her hand and held it tight, squeezing all of my relief, anxiety, gratitude, and sheer joy into the pressure of my fingers. She knew not to ask, merely squeezing my hand in return before she turned the truck toward home. I felt my life shaping itself into a new story. Without family, I had drifted like a dried leaf in autumn, blowing in a new direction with each gust of wind. Family gave me a place, history, connection, identity. Even in the midst of terrible pain and heartbreak, family held the possibility of love.

CHAPTER THIRTY

Rosalie Iron Wing

2002

I don't know what I expected to happen when I wrote to my son. I thought he would relax a bit, knowing I was only two hours away. But then I had never understood just how deeply he cared about the farm, about continuing the legacy his father had left him.

Early on the day I was to visit Darlene, I spent some time in the woods gathering spring plants for her as a gift. Even if she didn't use them, I hoped she would recognize the gesture of respect that they carried. It was also a way to calm my unsettled nerves. Walking through the woods just after dawn, when the shadows had yet to retreat beneath the tall trees, I felt at peace. This was my sanctuary, the place my spirit called home.

As I made my slow way back to the cabin, the hem of my pants soaked with dew and my hands muddy from the plants I carried, I looked up to see Thomas sitting on the front step. For a moment, I thought it was my father as a young man. But then he heard my step and turned toward me, revealing a face that was closed and angry, the face of my son. He wore a neatly ironed cotton shirt and khaki pants that were too short for him, revealing his white socks. He appeared uncomfortably out of place. Nonetheless, I was happy to see him. Time had eased the memory of our last words to each other.

"Mother," Thomas said, standing to embrace me awkwardly. "You look well," he added, seeming to see me clearly before the shadow returned to his face. "You have no idea how worried I've been. Not knowing where you were. Leaving me to handle everything." His cheeks clenched as he struggled to control his anger.

"Come in" was all I said. We walked inside and sat at the table. I offered him coffee in my one cup, but he left it untouched. Instead, he looked carefully around the room, unable to disguise his curiosity.

"So this is where you've been living for the past two months? With just this stove for heat? And no bathroom?"

I looked around the room, trying to see it with his eyes. It was rough, worn, and faded. The couch sagged in the middle, the table was pocked with knife marks, the Coleman lamp spoke to the utter lack of amenities. What he couldn't see was that his chair was where my father used to sit, that the faded quilt at the end of my bed was made by my mother's hands. His grandparents. The woods around me. These were the things that mattered.

"Yes. This is where I grew up. Your great-great-grandparents built this cabin." I handed him the photograph that Ida had brought me. I pointed to his grandparents, to his great-grandmother and great-aunt. Waited to hear what he would say.

"I always knew we were Dakhóta, but you never talked about your family. I didn't know what to think. The kids at school used to tease me, call me Chief. One kid said, Your mother is a dirty squaw, and I busted his nose." I remembered the day I'd had to pick him up from school for fighting. He got in the car and stared out the window while I drove. He never said a word about what had happened.

"This is where you're from," I said, simply. I didn't know what those words would mean to him, if he could even see past the rugged form of this place to the legacy that was equally his, that came not from things but from within.

He shrugged. Opened his backpack, drew out the papers that I had left behind on the kitchen table at the farm. Arranged them in a careful stack, edges straight, just as his father would have done. Cleared his throat.

"I would really like to hear more," he said, speaking slowly, as if that would help me understand. "But I need to get these papers to the bank. If I don't have a signed contract, the bank will not lend us the money we need to plant. We also need to renew our contract on the acreage that Dad used to lease.

"Now, I know that you had a tough time taking care of Dad through his illness. I'm sorry that I wasn't much help. I understand that you might have needed some time away." Here he paused, clearly struggling to stay with his prepared speech. "But we have to sign these papers. Dad would have wanted it."

Taking my silence for assent, he pointed to the first document. "This one is a contract to purchase seeds from Mangenta, agreeing not to save them and to grow only the GMO corn that they provide. By the way, Mangenta has offered me an internship as a marketing associate, starting this summer. I know Dad hoped I would take over the farm, but

I think he would be pleased. We can always hire someone to run the equipment."

I was not surprised. Thomas had always seemed more interested in the business of farming than in the actual work. Still, I wished he had not chosen Mangenta. Even though Thomas refused to see it, I believed that Mangenta had cost John his life. But as John had said, he was young, and he would learn in his own way.

"Congratulations."

"Thank you." He shuffled to the next document. "This one is the lease that keeps four hundred forty acres available to us for cultivation, including two hundred ten acres belonging to the Petersons and the rest from the Engbretsons' place, up the road."

Engbretson? The farmer who'd bought George and Judith's farm for half of what it was worth? John might not have bought their farm at auction, but evidently he did not mind leasing the land later on from the new owner. Thomas's revelation was the last thing I heard—from that point on, it was just his voice, drained of anything but bushels and dollars. I had rarely felt so defeated. Finally, I realized that he had stopped talking and seemed to be waiting for me to say something.

"My trees are gone," I said, looking directly into his eyes. "Do you hear that?"

"What? I don't hear anything."

"Exactly. The warblers and the owls and the wood thrushes: who thought of them before coming to take my trees? Who apologized to the birds?" Thomas said nothing, watching me as if I was not quite in my right mind. "If you want me to sign these papers, there is something I want you to do for me."

"Sure, of course. Anything within reason." Always the careful negotiator.

"I want you to come with me this morning to visit my great-aunt Darlene. Come with me now, and I'll sign these papers when we get back."

He hesitated only a moment before agreeing. I doubted whether he saw any value in spending the day with his mother and an old relative. I could tell he was weighing the pros against the cons, calculating the hours of driving, the time spent visiting and signing papers, whether he could be back home by nightfall. But he could meet with the bank in the morning. He would have the signatures, and it would be worth it.

While I cleaned up, he went back outside to the front step. First, he tried making a call on his cell phone, then returned it to his pocket. As I grabbed my jacket, I could see him watching a deer that had stopped to taste the buds of the dogwood shrub. His shoulders seemed to relax, to unbend ever so slightly. It was good that he came, I thought, no matter what happens next.

CHAPTER THIRTY-ONE

Rosalie Iron Wing
2002

Darlene Kills Deer had just finished lunch when her nurse invited us into the apartment. Darlene's voice had sounded so frail on the phone that I was not sure what to expect. My throat was tight, and my eyes burned with fatigue. I felt oddly numb. I couldn't wait to get this over with. Already I regretted bringing Thomas with me.

As I waited for the nurse to hang up our coats, I looked around at the faded carpet, the scuff marks on dingy white walls. Darlene's third-floor window looked out at an elementary school. The apartment was less than ten miles from where I had once lived, on the other side of town.

The living room was small, with a television in one corner and two mismatched chairs for guests. A few steps into the room, I stopped abruptly, stunned by the sight of tall cornstalks growing in buckets and cans set on yellowed newspapers, their edges curled and stained with mud. The floor was littered with brown leaves. From the curtain rod hung a dozen ears of blue and rose speckled corn, neatly braided. On the ledge outside the window, I could see bits of bread and apple. I began to wonder if Darlene might be senile.

As the nurse quietly stacked a tray with dishes, she nodded toward the two chairs. I moved a pile of folded laundry to the floor and sat down, Thomas next to me.

Darlene was leaning back in a recliner with her eyes closed. An oxygen tank stood on the floor near her chair. A thin cloud of dark hair, streaked heavily with gray, fell around her shoulders, framing her thin face, her skin a translucent yellow. I knew her high cheekbones, the sharp ridge of her nose. Bony hands rested on the blanket that covered her lap, the two thin mounds of her legs.

I set the damp package of nettles that I had gathered that morning on the table near Darlene's chair. As we waited for Darlene to open her eyes, we listened to the low murmur from the television as Bob Barker announced a new winner on *The Price Is Right*. Thomas straightened the collar of his shirt and sat jiggling one foot, unable to keep still. A plaque on the shelf above the television named Darlene Kills Deer as Miss Indian Princess for 1939. A birch-bark basket held a long braid of sweetgrass. Inside a dusty frame was a photo of a child standing next to a much younger Darlene. They were posing in front of the cabin. The child was me.

When I turned back, Darlene was awake. We studied each other. "It is you," she said. "You have your mother's eyes."

When I introduced Thomas, he stood and extended his hand to her. She looked up at him and frowned. Turning to me, she said, "Rosalie, why is your son in such a hurry?" An awkward silence fell in the room. Then I felt a soft touch on my arm. Darlene leaned forward and patted my hand.

"You did the best you could," she said. "You had no mother to learn from. Your father passed too soon. And they took you before any of us knew what had happened. That's how it was back then. They could just come and take your children. That's why, that's why . . ." Darlene began to cough, raising a white handkerchief to her lips. The nurse came in with a glass of water and a pill. We waited while Darlene took her medicine.

"That's why I had to plant this corn," she continued with a weak smile. "That's how I found you. Plants have their own way of talking. It's not the same here as in the garden, but it was something I could do. I could ask the plants for their help. I could ask the crow for his help. I could talk to the oak trees on the boulevard outside my apartment and ask them to watch for you.

"You must have been twelve when they took you. I pounded on desks and filled out paperwork and walked and walked just hoping I would catch sight of you somewhere. Every time I walked past a school, I would stop and look at all the little girls running on the playground. Every time I climbed on a bus, I looked in the face of each child. I dreamed you at night, living somewhere behind a metal fence, your face always turned toward the door.

"Year after year, we've kept this vigil. I promised to wait for you until my last breath. And now you're here." She stopped, wheezing slightly. "Tell me this. Does your son have his name?"

Thomas started to speak, but I held up my hand to stop him. "Wakpá," I said. "I gave it to him when he was born." I felt Thomas grow still. I had not used his name since he was a young boy.

"Wakpá," Darlene repeated. "River. We've always relied on rivers for fishing and traveling between camps. You're named for water. Your mother must love you a great deal." She smiled at Thomas. I could feel his eyes staring at me.

"I'm tired today," Darlene said, the tremor returning to her voice. "Come in the morning, and I'll have something for you." She looked directly at Thomas. "You, too, Wakpá. You come back with your mother. I have something for you." She closed her eyes and leaned her head back against the cushion.

⸻

We sat in the front seat of Thomas's car, unsure of what to do next. Thomas seemed unusually quiet, his bravado replaced with a thoughtful silence. For once he sat without tapping his fingers or his foot. I waited to hear his plans.

He sighed deeply and started the engine. "We can spend the night at the farm," he said. "And go back to see Darlene in the morning. God knows why, but I feel like I can't refuse her request. Even if she didn't seem to like me very much." His mouth was set in a firm line, the look of a man used to disappointment. He said nothing about his name.

Ah, I knew I would eventually have to go back to the farm, but I thought I would choose my time, when I felt more . . . whole. Better prepared to resist the pull of those old ways, the habits of thought, the invisible place I'd held in that world for so many years. And yet I said nothing. I agreed to go by not resisting.

When we turned in the driveway, I felt numb. Less than three months had passed, but the apple orchard was in full bloom. The rain had carved deep grooves in the gravel. When we pulled up near the house, it was strangely silent. No dog came to greet us, no chickens pecked and strutted around the yard. The shades were drawn on the windows. A house in mourning.

Thomas used his key to let us in. I stood in the doorway, listening, while he carried his backpack to the office. The house creaked as he walked, the echo of our long absence. To my left was the kitchen, to my right the stairs that led up to the spare room where John had spent his last months, and to the bedroom where I had slept for twenty-two years, where I had woken one morning as a widow. I had no bag or toothbrush, but it didn't matter. Everything I needed was already there: clothes, toiletries, a washing machine. Real plumbing. Cotton sheets. My garden. How easy it would be to pick up the thread of this place, to continue a rhythm that still haunted my bones. With my son in the house, could I walk away again? I didn't know.

I turned to the kitchen, my most familiar room. I made tea, sat again in my old chair, looked out at the empty bird feeder. I would have to check whether we had any seed left. I took out a tub of frozen soup and set it in a pan to reheat. Rummaged in the pantry until I found a jar of pickled beets. My pressure cooker and boxes of glass jars stood in neat rows on the floor, waiting for the next harvest. The farmwives I knew took great pride in their skill, entered prize jars into the county fair, kept gardening and canning until they quite literally dropped in their tracks. Like Judith, they hid their sorrows beneath a lifetime of endless work.

More than anything, it was the box of seeds, sitting on a shelf, that called to me. Many years of planting and saving these seeds had formed a deep bond between us. They belonged to this land, just as I did. If I didn't stay, who would care for them?

I set bowls on the table and called to Thomas when the soup was warm. We ate together in silence but without hostility. He seemed distracted, not even raising the issue of the papers that needed to be signed. After thanking me politely for the meal, he returned to the office, and I washed the dishes. Again, I waited for him to bring forward his papers. I could see the light beneath the office door, but he never came back out.

At dusk, I stood outside, breathing the sweet fragrance of lilac and honeysuckle, the scent of newly mowed grass. I could see the dark silhouette of the windbreak at the edge of the tilled fields. A nighthawk flashed by; something rustled in the tall weeds behind the house. A raccoon, perhaps, or a possum. Foraging for a lost carrot in my untended garden, the place where I had spent my best hours on this land. A place that would soon grow a new green skin if left unplanted.

Upstairs, I lay down on the bed where I had first slept as a wife and mother so many years earlier. On the window hung lace curtains that I had mended more than once. There was so much to be done. John's clothes to be given away, my sweaters replaced with summer cottons. Tomato seeds, which should have been started a month back. Mail to be sorted. Windows to be washed.

I fell into a deep, dreamless sleep. Sometime near four in the morning, I woke to the sound of a barn owl calling from a nearby field. From habit, I reached out to John's side of the bed, my hand finding only his absence. I could not lie there any longer. I wrapped up in my warm robe and crept downstairs, avoiding the known squeaks. The light was still on beneath the office door. I paused, wondering if I should check on Thomas. Then I heard it, ever so soft: the sound of a man who does not want to be caught crying. It took me by surprise; I had not heard him cry since he was a baby. His father had always encouraged him to be strong, and Thomas had done his best to please him. I wondered what wounds he carried that I knew nothing about, what wounds I might have inflicted. I went back upstairs and spent the rest of the night in my chair, rocking.

In the morning, Thomas seemed to be himself again, brisk and all business. He made a show of placing the papers in his backpack, as if reminding me that a deal was a deal. He wore the same shirt and pants as he had the day before, plus a denim jacket that once belonged to John. As he locked the door behind us, he noticed that I was holding my favorite coffee cup in my hand. He stopped, looked at my face. "You're not coming back here, are you?"

I shook my head. Neither of us spoke as we drove the twenty miles to Darlene's apartment. When we entered, Darlene was sitting at the table, dressed in tan pants and a warm sweater. She smiled and gestured at the chairs.

"Good morning," she said as we sat down. "Thank you for coming back. Yesterday was not one of my good days. I do not have a lot of time left. I have no children, so you two are my closest family. And yet we met only yesterday. How can this be, that families have been pulled so far apart? I prayed about it last night.

"I have a story to tell you. I ask that you listen with an open heart."

CHAPTER THIRTY-TWO

Darlene Kills Deer
2002

Rosalie, when you finally came here yesterday, I felt your hunger to fill the empty space left when your mother, Agnes, disappeared. All these years, and never once have I told this story. Last night, I heard my sister Lorraine's voice telling me to get on with it. Even now, so many years after she passed, I am no match for her.

We grew up in the same cabin where you're living now. It was built by my grandfather Oliver Bordeaux, who died before I was born. Lorraine was the eldest of my siblings, born in 1910. I came two years later, followed by Frederick and Harry. It was a tight fit in that cabin, but my grandmother, Khúŋši Marie, said it was no different from living in a thípi. The boys shared one of the beds in the main room, and Marie had a little cot by the wall.

Marie taught Lorraine and me how to sew by stitching quilts from the secondhand clothes that had been donated by the church. My mother, Susanne, taught us how to cook, bead, and make baskets, and she gave us each a doll she'd made from cornstalks. Back then, women needed to learn all these things to be a good wife. My father, Clayton Kills Deer, did anything he could to earn his living. Mostly he liked to fish and hunt, and some said he was known to bootleg to make a few bucks. Hard to say whether that's true or not.

Most important, we had to know how to gather and grow food for our family. This was before they started handing out commodity foods. Every morning in the summer, we would head to the garden. We'd put on a big pot of coffee, the kind you make with the grounds on the bottom of the pot. Then I'd do whatever I was told. Not like today, when kids sass back and watch television all day. We knew that if we wanted to eat, we had to work.

Lorraine had a gift for gardening. My mother was always saying, Lorraine, water the beans, or Lorraine, check the squash for bugs. She had a way with plants, almost like they listened to her. We all knew that one day she would inherit the seeds that my mother and Marie stored in a willow basket. When I asked why the seeds were kept there, Marie said, In case we have to leave suddenly, so we can take those seeds with us.

In the winter, when there was snow on the ground, sometimes Marie would tell us stories if she wasn't too tired. We'd all sit by the fire with our blankets and listen. She told us about the corn boys, how they had traveled to the underworld to rescue their father. Her stories would make us laugh and cry and forget all about the holes in our socks and the cardboard we used to patch our shoes.

But I was just a child back then and learned the hard way what those seeds meant to my family. I remember it clearly because it was the same day the agent came. Fred threw dirt at me, and I returned his teasing by hurling what was in my hand, an ear of corn. My mother grabbed my arm, she was so angry. I think she was almost as shocked by her anger as I was. But, you see, I never forgot that lesson. Those seeds were sacred, and I was disrespectful to them.

Maybe that's why she used to send me and Khúŋši Marie to the woods when she needed something like kindling or berries or wild bergamot. We liked to wander together and visit with plants. So when the agent came, we weren't even there. We were out in the woods, picking hazelnuts and dawdling, like usual. I know the sun was low in the afternoon sky when we got back home. I was worried that I would be in trouble.

I'll never forget the look on my mother's face, like she had grown old since I'd left her that morning. Her eyes were red. She said to me, The agent came and took your sister and brothers away to school. He must have surprised them: we all knew not to answer the door if a stranger came. If a white man stopped his car, we were supposed to run as fast as we could into the woods.

I don't think any of us slept well that night. There I was, alone in our big bed for the first time, and all I could think of was how much I missed my sister. Khúŋši Marie lay down with me to keep me company. It was still dark a few hours later when my mother came in and told me I was going to live with her cousin Pauline in Mankato.

When I was packed, my mother pushed me through the open door and closed it quickly behind me. I thought then that she did not love me. That maybe she wished it was me who had been taken and not Lorraine. Now I know better. I know how much it hurt her to lose her children.

Before the door closed, I turned to look at my grandmother

Marie, standing near her cot. She was fully dressed, wearing her moccasins as if she was ready to leave. She never said goodbye. Even now, I don't like to think about that day.

Of course I was homesick. But Pauline and her husband were nice people, and I liked their baby. He had a job at the cannery and she was a seamstress. I had my own bed in the baby's room. They bought me new clothes, sent me to school. I used to wonder about Lorraine and my brothers, if they were homesick, too. Every now and then I'd get a letter from my mother. She'd tell me about the garden, about my dad's health and Marie's passing. Then she'd say at the end, like she'd just thought of it, "No word yet from Lorraine and your brothers." I don't think she even knew what school they got sent to.

Then the cannery laid off Pauline's husband, and he was out of work for a long time. My mother wrote a letter saying that I should come home. Pauline couldn't afford to keep me any longer. My dad was sick, too. By then I was sixteen and thinking about other things than going back home. But I did. I took a bus most of the way, and my dad met me at the station. He had bought an old car that he was proud to show me. I couldn't get over how thin he was.

We drove down the back roads, same as always, and when we got to the cabin, I wondered why Mother didn't come out to greet me. I was so proud of my new dress and wanted to show it off. I ran in, expecting to see her at the stove. But the kitchen was empty, just as it had been on that last day. Turned out she was in bed. Tuberculosis, the doctor said. They were both sick. Lorraine and the boys were expected the next day. My parents had finally found out where they were and had written asking for them to be sent home.

I did what I could for my parents. Cleaned up the kitchen, washed a big pile of laundry. Asked Dad to drive me into town to buy some groceries with my savings. I wanted to put on a nice meal for my siblings' homecoming. I bought flour to make gabúbu bread, a big piece of beef to make a hearty soup. It was all ready—even my mother had gotten dressed and was sitting at the table—when we heard Dad's car come back from the bus station.

They all got out and stood there like they had forgotten the way to the front door. Lorraine was tall and lean, and her hair was cut at chin length. She wore a long jumper and pointed shoes with lots of buttons. But it was her face that had changed the most. There was something hard about her, like stone. Frederick and Harry moved like ghosts. They hardly made a sound, almost as if they wished no one could see them. It was a very strange meal we shared that first night.

After dinner, the three of them stood up without a word and went outside. I cleaned the dishes, helped my mother get back in bed. When I went out looking for them, they were standing by the old oak where we used to play as kids. They were smoking and passing a small flask between them. Fred held it out to me, but when I said no, Lorraine laughed. I think she held it against me that I didn't end up at the school with them. Not that she wanted me to go. She wanted what I'd had, a good home where people were nice to me. She never talked about the school, none of them did. The boys were afraid of her. I was afraid of her.

Our family didn't last long after that. My parents died within six months of each other. I went back to the city, where I found work as a nurse's aide and eventually put myself through nursing school. Lorraine and the boys lived in the cabin for a long time. I used to hear things from old friends who would come to visit. They said Fred did nothing but drink all day. Harry refused to talk; he just disappeared into the woods if anyone came by.

When Lorraine gave birth to Agnes, no one had any idea who the father might be. But she started gardening again. The plants grew, although not in the way they used to, not like they do when they feel surrounded by love. They could tell the difference: Lorraine was anything but loving in those days. She used her fists on anyone who crossed her, including her brothers and her daughter. She was always careful not to leave marks where people could see.

That's when she asked me what had happened to the basket of seeds, said it was rightfully hers. I said I had no idea where it was. She accused me of stealing it. She held that grudge against me till she died.

We were distant for a while, but I thought it best to mend our relationship, for the sake of my niece. I started visiting again, and slowly, over the years, Lorraine began to seem more like her old self. By then, however, the damage had already been done. Harry rolled his car into a lake. Fred was dying from kidney failure. And Agnes broke my heart. She was like Lorraine, strong willed, but growing up without my mother's firm guidance. The first time I met her, she stared at me like a wild thing, her face dirty and her hair all matted. I used to give her candy so she would take a bath. Such a beautiful child. But no one could tell her anything. She began running away when she was sixteen. Sooner or later she would come back home, although she stayed away a little longer each time. Eventually we stopped hearing from her.

Then, one morning, the phone rang. It was Agnes, telling me she was getting married and wanted me to come. And bring Lorraine, she said, using her mother's first name. I drove to Lorraine's apartment to pick her up, even brought her a dress to wear. She put on her big old coat, buttoned up to the neck, and asked, Why should I go to any trouble for her? We met them at the courthouse, Agnes and Ray. I could tell he was head over heels in love. He couldn't take his eyes off her. She was about six months pregnant with you. Afterward, she took me aside and asked if I could spare some money. I gave her twenty dollars and asked if she was okay. She said, I know what I'm doing. I'm not going to make the same mistakes as my mother.

For a while, it seemed Agnes had really changed. They both stopped drinking. They moved into the cabin and worked hard to fix the place up while Ray finished school. He adored you, even more than he loved your mother. Over time, her dark moods began to wear on him. He suspected that she was drinking again. She made trips into town, came home late, found excuses to spend the night at a girlfriend's house. But she never, ever struck you, Rosie. In her way, she loved you. She was gifted at sewing—I remember she said she tried to teach you, but you wouldn't learn. I think she just didn't know how to be around a young child, had forgotten what it was like to be part of a family. Just like Lorraine after she came home from boarding school. Sometimes too much harm has been done.

One night, when I was babysitting you, she came to pick you up at my apartment. Her lipstick was smeared, and her eyes were just wrong. I tell you, it was like something else had moved into her body that night and stolen away her spirit. I offered to keep you overnight or to have her sleep on my couch. She said,

No, it's better this way. What do you mean? I asked. It's better this way, was all she kept saying. When she picked you up, you were crying, you didn't want to leave. Still—and this is the part I regret—I let you both go. But I couldn't stop worrying. I threw on my coat and followed your mother toward her car.

She kept walking right past it. I could see your head on her shoulder, that you had fallen asleep. She was singing very softly as she walked. In those days, I lived a block from the big bridge. Agnes kept walking and singing; it was all very peaceful. I stayed well behind so she wouldn't get mad. I wasn't worried, not really; I just wanted to be sure that you were okay.

It was a beautiful evening, a soft night in April. All the snow had melted, and the river was roaring with the usual spring flood. Then she stopped in the middle of the bridge and took off her shoes. That's when I started to run. I got to her just as she was swinging your little legs over the railing. Agnes, I called, Agnes, wait. She froze, and for a moment I thought I had spooked her. I said, Wait a minute, Agnes, I have some candy for you. I always carried a few pieces in my pocket in case you started fussing. She turned to me with the same empty smile she'd worn in the apartment. I said, I'll hold Rosie while you eat this candy. She gave you to me without a word. I tell you, I never held on to a child so tight as I held you then. I said to Agnes, Let's go home. She nodded and bent to pick up her shoes. I turned away, Rosie, I turned toward home. And that's when she jumped. I looked back over my shoulder just in time to see her fall. I'll never forget it. At least when I die, I can finally let go of that moment.

You were only four years old. You didn't wake up, not when I screamed, not even when the sirens came. Only when your dad showed up, breathless, his face split with grief and anger and relief, only then did you wake. When we were finally done talking to the police, you both spent the night at my apartment. In the morning, they began to drag the river for your mother's body. She was never found. When I told Ray what she had tried to do, he didn't say a word, but his eyes changed; his face looked like a mask. He never again said her name. He refused to have anything to do with me or with anyone in her family. He never told you because he didn't want you to carry that story. But I can see that you need to know.

Your mother was not well. Whatever it was that had come home from the boarding school with your grandmother, it lived on in Agnes. She never found a way through it. It lives on until somebody finds a way to stop it.

CHAPTER THIRTY-THREE

Rosalie Iron Wing

2002

Darlene's voice faded until it was little more than a whisper. The loud tick of the clock on the kitchen wall was the only sound in the room. My eyes were closed, and when I opened them, I saw Thomas holding his head in his hands. Darlene's face was drawn and tired, her thin shoulders slumped forward. The nurse appeared and said, "Miss Darlene, you've worn yourself right out."

Taking my great-aunt's elbow, she helped Darlene stand up on shaky legs and make her slow way from the dining room table back to the recliner in the living room. Thomas and I followed. The nurse placed the oxygen tube beneath Darlene's nose, hooked the plastic behind her ears, and held out a white pill. Darlene took several deep breaths. Then she sat up, pushed the pill away, and pulled the tube from her face.

"I'm not done yet," Darlene said. "There's one more story she needs to know."

"You really need to take this . . ."

"I don't have time." With a sigh, she looked first at Thomas and then at me. "We're a mess," she said. "A broken-down mess. And we're all that's left. Don't go wasting time feeling sorry for yourself. Plenty of people have had a rough life. You just make the best of it—that's all anyone can do. The two of you still have time to do better. It's up to you."

Pointing to the scrawny corn growing in buckets of hard-packed soil, she said, "That's the best I could do. Hauled those buckets myself, with no help from anybody. All the old people downstairs said, You can't do it. I said, You have no idea.

"Rosalie, I didn't expect to see you again. I didn't think anyone but me would ever care about these seeds. I thought they'd die with me. But there you sit, my great-niece, my last relative. You have the truth, and more, to take home with you. Nurse, I need my basket. Please. I need my basket."

We waited in silence for the nurse to return and lay a large handwoven basket on Darlene's lap. She smiled as her arthritic fingers ran slowly across the rough willow exterior. Reaching inside, she carefully pulled out a piece of deer antler and several small sacks, each one tied closed with a red string. Opening one bag, she shook a few corn kernels into her palm and handed them to me. Tiny jewels of lavender blue, rose, and cream.

"That's Dakhóta corn, wamnáheza, a gift from my great-grandmother Maȟpíyamaza to Marie, and then to my mother, Susanne. I don't think it's been grown since the summer Lorraine was taken away to boarding school. Every fall we dried most of the corn in braids that hung in a dark corner of the cabin, not too near the fire. We kept baskets filled with beans, another with strips of dried squash.

"The willow basket was supposed to go to Lorraine, and she knew I was lying when I said it was lost. She hated me for keeping these seeds from her. They were her birthright, the only thing left from her old life. But when she came back, everything she touched withered and died. My brothers, her daughter. I couldn't let her have the seeds. Deep down, I think she knew it, too. To this day, I don't know if I did right. Maybe they would have helped her find her way back. I couldn't risk it.

"The old ones told Susanne that a time was coming when the seeds would go into hiding. They said that people would no longer respect them or the land or the water. That the seeds would leave—some returning to the soil, others simply waiting in darkness. They told her to be ready. Just before she died, my mother gave me the basket. She knew that Lorraine was not coming back, not the girl we had known and loved. The spirit of the schools was too strong, she said, too hungry, and it would not ever let them go.

"Rosalie, I am giving you this basket. Find a safe place to grow the seeds. I don't know what else to tell you. Love them like your children, the way you love your son." Darlene turned to Thomas. "Come closer, thakóža. Let me look at you. You have your grandfather's face. I'm going to give you this."

From the basket, she withdrew a small object and carefully unwrapped it, revealing a perfectly preserved cob of corn that had faded to a dull, lifeless red. She placed the cob in Thomas's hand and closed his fingers gently around it.

"This corn has been in our family for many, many generations. It came with the antler so that we would always remember. Take it, thakóža. Maybe it will help you remember."

⹀

We were quiet on the ride from Darlene's. Before getting in the car, Thomas took off his jacket and laid it carefully in the back seat. With sunglasses hiding his eyes, his face was closed to me. Just as well. I leaned my head back and dozed in the warm sun. I woke as Thomas pulled in to the nearly deserted parking lot of Emma Lou's Café.

"We'll get something to eat," he said. "And then I'll take you . . . back."

At the table, he opened his backpack and stacked his papers neatly in front of him. Neither of us spoke. I still could not find his eyes. When the waitress left with our order, he said, "We had a deal. I went with you to meet this long-lost relative, and now it's your turn. Do you need me to explain again what these papers are for?"

"No."

"Since you're . . . not coming back to the farm, I'll stay there until I can hire someone to manage it. Running a tractor was never my strength," he said, as his mouth tightened in a humorless smile. "Dad would have been the first to tell me. So. I've run the numbers a dozen ways, and this is what makes the best sense. Without this lease, we just don't produce enough to break even, much less make a profit. Are you even listening to me?"

"No."

"Well, someone has to take care of things. What do you expect when you drag me along to hear that your family is just a bunch of . . . of . . . broken-down drunks? Your own mother tried to kill you, for God's sake. And you want to go back to that? Not me, not ever. Life goes on, Mother, and living in the past won't change anything." Breathing hard, Thomas slapped a pen onto the table. "Sign it."

Without a word, I signed each page. When the food came, we ate in silence. By the time we turned down the dirt road to the cabin, we were thoroughly tired of each other's company. I was well aware that I might not see him again, at least not until the next batch of papers needed to be signed. And yet he was my son. He was more lost than any of us. But it would do no good to tell him.

When Thomas parked in front of the cabin, he did not turn off the engine. We sat in silence for a moment while I searched for something to say that would make his departure feel less abrupt, less final. My ramshackle house stood in deep shadow below the trees, its windows dark. Not a home, not even a place where someone would want to live. Yet here I was, and here I would stay. Thomas spoke first, his voice strained and tired.

"I just want to say that I wish you well. I don't pretend to understand why you're here or what you're looking for. But I will make sure that the farm is taken care of the way Dad would have wanted it."

I nodded, hearing the gift of his words. When I laid my hand on his arm, he jumped slightly but did not draw away. "I know you will. You might think about taking care of the farm the way that *you* want it done. Your dad did the best he could. You can learn from his ways. And then you do the best that you can. In your own way."

As I spoke, he turned toward me. I had his attention. Because he was young and grieving for a father whose respect he had worked hard to earn all of his life, he had not yet considered that the farm was now his to run and even to change. I patted his arm.

"In a few weeks, the wild strawberries will be ripe," I said. "It will be time to plant the corn that Darlene gave us. I would be glad of your help. You may not have been the best tractor driver, but you used to like to help me plant the garden. Think about it."

I climbed out of the car and stood watching him as he drove away, back to the city, to a life that I knew so little about. I wondered when I would see him again. Despite his bitter words at the café, the little corncob was still riding in his pocket.

CHAPTER THIRTY-FOUR

Rosalie Iron Wing
2002

I dreamed a river rose from its banks and reached out to me with long arms, like a mother reaching to her child, and I knew then that the story was true. When I used to play along the banks, trailing my sticks in shallow water, my mother was there, in the ripple of waves over hidden stones. My father would not fish this river. When asked, he turned his head away with a silent shake, grim, his mouth set firmly. This is what he would not tell me: that she had never left, would never leave. She was there now; I could hear her voice in the roar of the current, calling to me.

I woke, my heart pounding. The fire had burned down to coals. In the quiet, I could hear my own shallow breath. I had not yet decided whether it was better to know the truth of my family. Perhaps I would become like Darlene—longing for the end, so I could let go of the knowledge that my own mother had tried to kill me—but deep down, I knew Agnes's motives had been more complicated. She had tried to kill herself, to end her own suffering in the only way she could. She had meant to take me with her, to keep us together. Knowing this brought small comfort.

Later that morning, sitting on the front porch with a cup of coffee, I watched bees burrow into the long throats of wild columbine. The white blooms of spring trillium brightened the edges of the clearing. From a high branch of the oak tree behind the cabin came the flutelike song of a wood thrush. Šazí must have been out hunting. All my neighbors were busy mating, nest building, and food gathering, and after a while, I began to feel guilty for simply enjoying the morning. I could sit there drinking coffee, or I could follow Darlene's advice that there was still time to do better.

I carried the seed basket to the truck and carefully strapped it into the passenger side with a seat belt. No accidents on my watch. Then I drove to the Elders' Lodge in search of Carlos and Wilma. When I got there, feeling uncertain about not calling first, they were sitting together in the community room. Wilma immediately waved me over to join them. Carlos smiled and offered his hand to shake.

"Grab yourself a cup of coffee," Wilma said. "We were just talking about you."

I filled a foam cup, added a packet of sugar and powdered cream to cut the overcooked bitterness, and joined them at the table. I tucked the basket beneath my chair until the time seemed right to introduce the seeds. After the three of us exchanged pleasantries about the weather, the arthritis in Wilma's knees, and what time the shopping van was leaving in the afternoon, I told them about my visit to Darlene. The words came tumbling from my mouth like a rain-swollen waterfall, so badly did I need to share the story with people who would understand.

As I talked, Wilma kept her eyes on her cup and Carlos stared at the far wall, where the shamrocks had come loose. When my voice finally trailed off into an exhausted silence, I realized I had crushed my cup and my cheeks were damp. No one spoke for a few long moments. Then Wilma sighed and shook her head.

"The schools harmed a lot of families. Some are still trying to find their children. Or to bring their bodies back home."

Carlos brought the coffeepot to the table, along with a new cup for me. As he poured, Wilma leaned over and said, "I spent eight years at a school west of here. I still have the scars. But others had it much worse. What priests did to your uncles, most likely to Lorraine, they're the reason why that abuse is still happening to children today. Those schools are partly to blame for the mess we're facing in our communities."

I hesitated before asking my next question. I was afraid to hear what she would say. "Do you think if my family hadn't been taken, that they might have turned out different?"

Wilma snorted in disgust. "Oh, hell yes. Strong, loving families were the backbone of Dakhóta communities. Our tiospaye included our aunties and uncles and elders who made sure that each child grew up knowing they were loved. All the addiction and abuse you see today, that came over with the Europeans."

Wilma picked up a deck of cards lying on the table and began laying out a hand of solitaire, her face unreadable. No one spoke for several minutes.

"Khúŋši," I began and then stopped. I was unsure how to form the words I wanted to say. Wilma waited for me to continue, her fingers moving cards with a deft sureness. "How have you ..."

"How have I dealt with it?"

"Yeah. How do you get past something like that?"

"What makes you think I have?" Wilma snapped. She swept the cards back into a pile, tapped them until the edges were perfectly straight, and left the room without looking at me. I was mortified.

Carlos patted my hand. "Don't worry, kid. She's not mad at you. She just can't stand thinking about the schools. She'll go upstairs and scrub something until she calms down. I'll check on her later. Maybe we'll take in a twelve-step meeting tonight."

He pulled out a toothpick and chewed on it. "There's something else I've been thinking about lately. Have you ever noticed how much of our history has something to do with food? The 1862 war began because people were starving, with their food locked away in a warehouse. Kids were poorly fed at the boarding schools. When they put us on reservations, they gave us commodities that were a slow way of killing us off with diabetes. All because they wanted our land. They said they wanted us to be farmers, like them. Wouldn't you think they'd be falling over themselves to learn how Indians teamed up with a wild grass like teosintes to make corn? I wonder about that sometimes."

Grateful for the distraction Carlos provided, I thought about John's struggle to decide which crops to plant on his farm. He thought mostly about the cost, the quantity each variety would produce, the amount of chemicals they would require, and the specific demands of his contract with the ethanol plant. He had never been taught to think about his seeds as relatives, as living beings deserving of loving care. While not intending harm, he had been raised to believe that it was man's God-given right to "fill the earth and subdue it; to rule over the fish in the sea and the birds in the sky."

I also thought of my son. I didn't know what he believed in. I was afraid he would follow his father's teachings, that I had not done enough for him.

"People don't understand how hard it is to be Indian," Carlos said. "I'm not talking about all the sad history. I'm talking about a way of life that demands your best every single day. Being Dakhóta means every step you take is a prayer."

I had never thought about my family's story in that way. The seeds Darlene had given me were saved by generations of women who believed their work was essential to their families' survival. Not just as food, but as an expression of who they were.

I lifted the basket onto the table and told Carlos about Darlene's gift. As a farmer himself, he held each bag of seeds like it was a tender infant. He told me that Indian people had used old trade routes for bartering food, tools, cloth, beads— and seeds. Meaning that this corn, for example, might have been grown by both the Hidatsa and the Dakhóta, changing over time as women selected seeds for certain traits, like color or size or ability to survive a drought.

"Just think of the stories these seeds are carrying," Carlos said, his voice rough. He cleared his throat. "Well, what are you sitting around here for? You need to plant a garden. From what I hear, you're quite a gardener already."

"I've never planted seeds this old," I said. "There's so few left. What if I make a mistake and lose them? I'd never forgive myself."

"Phhh. Just choose a good spot with plenty of sun. The old ones used to say that the soil is good wherever you find wild artichokes. I'd be happy to help you, but tomorrow I'm heading back home for a few weeks. Tell you what—you get it planted, and I'll come out later this summer."

"About the time the green corn is ready to eat, I'll bet," Wilma said, again taking her seat at the table. She gave me a quick glance, enough for me to see the red rimming her eyes.

"I can already taste it," Carlos said. "Roasted over a fire, with a bowl of venison stew on the side. Maybe you'll even grow enough so we can make hominy this fall. Wouldn't that be something?" He pulled his cap from his back pocket and nodded to us before heading upstairs.

Wilma laid her hand gently on my forearm. "I'm sorry, thakóža. What the schools did to us is something we have to carry all our lives. Every time I think I've gotten the best of it, something comes up to remind me."

"I'm sorry, Khúŋši, I didn't know."

"Not your fault. I've learned to just let it pass through me, like a bad stomachache."

While she spoke, I carefully replaced the seed bags in my basket. Near the bottom, my fingers brushed against something that felt different. I pulled it out slowly, curious but also cautious of what I might find, and saw that it was a small rolled-up deerskin, tied with a piece of cracked sinew. Wilma watched as I unrolled it to reveal a piece of fragile yellowed paper. The ink was faded, barely legible, the words written in Dakhóta. I set it down between us. Neither of us could take a full breath. It was like an unknown voice was speaking from a long-ago time.

"Can you read it?" I asked.

."Just a few words here and there. It begins with 'my relative' and 'in prison.' I wonder what Darlene knows about it." Wilma wiped her eyes with her handkerchief as I rolled the letter back inside the deerskin.

"One more thing before you go," she said. "Sometimes women, and men, can lose their minds when they've been traumatized. Especially when they were not able to keep their children safe. That loss can be too painful to carry. Remember that about your family."

=

Before leaving the reservation, I stopped at the gas station's pay phone and called Darlene. When I told her about the letter, she didn't seem surprised.

"You know, I'd forgotten all about that," she said. "I remember Khúŋši Marie wouldn't talk about it, wouldn't let any of us touch it. After she passed, I took it over to an elder and asked her to translate it. She wrote the English down for me, keeping it close to the original Dakhóta meaning. I put a copy inside my Bible. You want me to find it?"

"If it's not too much trouble."

Darlene set the phone down with a clunk and called to her nurse to bring the Bible from her bedside table. I heard the rustling of thin paper, Darlene's labored breathing. "Here it is," she said.

My relative, I write this letter to you. They say the Holy Spirit alone is most great. I suppose, for that reason, now we men are now in prison. Several said it is terrible. A lot of the young men who learned to write are always dying. I am saddened, my relative—it is so. Since we have come here, forty-five and more have died, and a lot will die. Now they have brought lots of letters from the Missouri River, but I think we will hear bad news, we are imprisoned, the women are pitiful and frightened, and some have not eaten, they flee. I am always sad, every day. My dear wife, because of you, I am sad every day. Right now, they said nobody is taking care of you. Write to me in the Long Knives language. I shake your hand—it is so.

Mázakhoyaginape

My great-great-great-grandfather's words came alive across generations as they were spoken out loud, carried on the wind through Darlene's open window, whispered from treetops to passing birds to a community who needed them more than ever. I felt the world around me shift and change because his voice was still here, because we witnessed his sorrow, we recognized and shared his grief.

"Are you still there? That was Mázakhoyaginape, who died at the Davenport prison. I never knew what to do with the letter. It should have been buried with his wife, Maȟpíyamaza, who suffered so terribly after the war. She's at Santee. I always thought maybe I could get back there to visit her grave. Khúŋši Marie used to talk about burying her mother's hair by a cottonwood tree, but I have no idea where."

"I'll find it," I said, when I could control my voice. "Thank you for everything."

The next morning, before the sun cleared the horizon, I walked down to the river, where I knew I would find several cottonwoods that were at least one hundred years old. I chose the tallest one, with a massive trunk. After I sang to the east, to the rising sun, I thanked my relatives for their sacrifice, for their suffering, for their endurance. And then I buried my grandfather's letter with a pinch of čhaŋšáša, knowing that the web of life that connects everything would reunite his words with my grandmother. It was the best I could do.

When I stood up and looked at the sky, I was content. I turned and walked back uphill with a brisk stride. I had a garden to plant.

CHAPTER THIRTY-FIVE

Rosalie Iron Wing
2002

If I listened closely enough, I could almost hear the sap rising in the trees outside my window, feel their roots burrowing deeper underground, as their branches reached for the light. The air was sweet with honeysuckle, scented by long grasses warmed in the sun. Newborn leaves tested the wind, accompanied by the steady drone of bees at work. Today was planting day.

The sky was perfectly clear, giving us the dry weather we needed to plant the newly turned soil in the garden. After much discussion, we had decided to plant the garden in the clearing where the cedar trees used to grow. Ida had borrowed a rototiller from a neighboring farm and taken on the job of breaking down the surface layer of hard-packed soil and weeds. We had already removed a grueling number of small shrubs and stones, leaving a long rectangle with plenty of room to expand later. If the next few months went well, we could add a few rows at the end of the season.

I knew exactly what I wanted to grow. The first seeds I planted would be wamnáheza, Dakhóta corn, used to make a traditional soup after being dried and boiled with wood ash. This corn had been grown by our family even before they were removed from Minnesota in 1863. Except for herself, and the half dozen stalks lined up in her buckets, Darlene didn't know anyone who was still growing it.

On one side of the garden, we planned to grow potatoes, greens, tomatoes, squash, carrots, onions, and beans for drying. On the other side, we would plant five rows of the wamnáheza, enough to save for next season and to share with Ida and the elders. That is, if it grew. The seeds had been dormant for many years; they might not have survived. It was too late in spring to test them in pots. We would have to plant directly into the garden and hope for the best. I was also worried that planting a garden of this size would use much of the corn in the bag. My hope was that with good soil and decent weather we would have plenty more by summer's end.

Working together, Ida and I carefully measured off each row, placing a stake at both ends and joining them with a long piece of twine. We planted the corn kernels ten inches apart, with three feet between the rows. By late morning, my back ached and Ida's shirt was damp, but we'd made real progress. We stood for a moment and admired the results of our efforts. Five neat rows of corn were planted in nearly virgin soil that smelled of new life. A gardener's dream. We would plant green beans and carrots and tomato seedlings the next day.

A steady rain fell that night and continued into the morning, another blessing for the garden. Knowing it would be too wet to plant, I worked around the cabin, chopping wood and clearing a space for wildflowers. Šazí still appeared every few days, watching me work from his perch on the old truck. His belly was round and full, his patchy orange fur regrown so that he was, if not handsome, at least healthy.

I hummed as I worked, filled with contentment. For the first time in my life, I felt the sweet gift of purpose that went beyond taking care of a family. The seeds reconnected me with my grandmothers, and even my mother. I could imagine these women planting their gardens, singing to the plants as if they were children, harvesting the ripe corn, and choosing the best seeds for the next season. Here, in these lonely woods, I felt as if I belonged once again to my family, to my people.

When I returned to the garden the following day, several rows of corn had been plundered for the bare seed. I felt a shock through my body, as if someone had attacked my family, and began to realize what a long, difficult road lay ahead. These seeds were so few in number and vulnerable to hungry rodents. Even if they did survive, what about deer and rabbits, later in the season? How could I possibly keep them safe without a fence? I stared at the damage, thinking, while Ida stood shaking her head. "Damn squirrels. Do we replant?"

Replanting would use up almost all of the remaining seeds. A risk, should something happen to the entire crop. But if I didn't do it, we would harvest far less than we had hoped. I needed enough to share with Darlene, as well as Wilma and Carlos. They were the most important reason for growing the corn this year. And from my own garden, I knew that we needed to grow enough plants to exchange pollen, to keep them strong and healthy. I was beginning to understand the tough decisions that seed keepers had to make, weighing the risk of losing the seeds against the pain of going hungry in the winter. I decided to replant using all but a dozen kernels of corn.

Ten days later, we witnessed the miracle of tiny green leaves breaking through the earth. Encouraged by the warm sun and fertile soil, the fragile seedlings grew quickly. In the early mornings, before the sun grew too strong, I pulled weeds so the seedlings would not have to compete for water. As I dug into the cool soil, I thought about teosintes, the plant Carlos had mentioned, and how that grass had collaborated with human beings to become maize, a sacred food for so many tribes.

Sometimes, when I was working in the garden, a wordless prayer opened between me and the earth, as if we shared a common language that I understood best when I was silent. Only by paying attention with all of my senses could I appreciate the cry of the hawk circling overhead, or see sunflowers turning toward the sun, or hear the hum of carpenter bees burrowing into rotted logs. Just as birds make their nests in a circle, this clearing encircled us, creating a safe place to grow and to live. History might have cost me my family and my language, but I was reclaiming a relationship with the earth, water, stars, and seeds that was thousands of years old.

Every day we came to the garden just after sunrise, Ida arriving from the west with Digger at her heels, and me from the east, carrying a thermos of coffee and a hunk of bread. First, we built a fire and decided what needed to be done that day. Ida was willing to do whatever was asked of her, but she was more of a hunter by nature. She would gladly weed or water for an hour or two before beginning to glance at the woods. By midmorning she was making short trips to check on things. By noon she would be gone. Some days, after she left, I would sit in the shade and simply watch the plants. Other days, I'd sing whatever I could remember, starting with the morning song I had learned from my father.

By the end of June, the corn was near a foot and a half tall. We had eaten all the early greens, planted another batch that would be ready in late summer, and mulched between rows against the heat we knew was coming. Aside from early-morning weeding and watering, the garden was now finding its own way, growing and thriving with little help from us.

Thomas had not returned to help me plant, or to simply visit. I hoped that he had found some measure of peace with the memory of his father, out at the farm. Living at the cabin felt as if my own childhood memories had been returned to me. Some days I could almost hear my father whistling just ahead of me on the path to the garden.

In July, Ida persuaded me to spend a morning gathering blackberries on her land, about a half-hour walk downriver. We met at the garden first, so I could check on the plants. Everything seemed to be thriving. There were new blossoms on the squash, and the corn was already three feet tall. It was one of the most productive seasons I'd ever had. Satisfied, we headed out, Digger in the lead and Ida following closely behind, with the sure step of a woman who has spent her life in the woods.

"Don't take this the wrong way," she said, whacking a low branch out of her path. "But I'm more than glad to not be on my knees chasing bitty bugs on potatoes. There's something so tedious about the work, although I'm happy as can be to enjoy the harvest. I just never knew about it before, is all. All the weeding. And the weeding. And then more weeding. At least out here, you can find plants that don't need all that tending."

As we walked slowly through dense underbrush, a layer of clouds moved across the sky, bringing relief from an increasingly hot sun. The air was heavy with humidity, the trees unmoving, the stillness broken only by the hum of mosquitoes. Even the birds were silent. My face was moist with sweat and my T-shirt clung to my back.

Finally, Ida declared with a triumphant "Ha!" that we had arrived. We found a thick cluster of wild blackberries and spread out with our baskets. We picked for a couple of hours, enjoying quiet conversation and peaceful silence. After a leisurely lunch of bread and coffee, Ida leaned back to study the clouds, which had continued to gather all morning. I had enjoyed the berry picking so much that I had neglected to watch the sky.

"Looks like there's weather heading our way," Ida said. "If we leave now, we might make it back before the rain finds us." Her casual tone suggested that getting caught in the rain would not be an issue. I wished I felt just as comfortable in these woods, the way I had as a child. But with the first rumble of distant thunder, I was up and brushing crumbs from my lap. I couldn't help but remember the storm that had greeted me on my first night at the cabin.

As we walked quickly back toward the garden, the wind began to pick up and the temperature fell to a sudden coolness. We were halfway there when the first scattered drops of rain began to fall. Ida turned to me and smiled, both of us nodding our relief that the garden would be watered. Within minutes, the rain came fast and hard. The wind whipped the branches on the trees in a mad dance. Digger continued to lope forward, his ears pressed flat against his head, occasionally turning a wild eye to look at Ida, but trusting her judgment.

We followed blindly as Ida veered off the path and ducked

beneath a cluster of red cedars near a rock cleft in the hill, just as a torrential rain began to pummel the earth. We huddled together, dripping and shivering, while the wind blew straight sheets of water that bent young trees nearly in half. Then the frenetic drumbeat of the rain grew louder. Even beneath the shelter of the trees, we were hit by a stinging shower of ice pellets. Hail! I jumped to my feet to run back to the garden, to do whatever I could to protect my babies, my tender plants.

"No!" Ida shouted, grabbing my arm and dragging me back beneath the tree. "There's nothing you can do."

We huddled in our makeshift shelter, backs pressed against the rock, Ida's arm wrapped around Digger. Not far from us, a white pine blew over, its shallow roots no match for the wind. After several minutes of raging intensity, the hail turned back to rain and slowly subsided to a steady downpour. Pulling on Ida's arm, I said, Let's go. Rain poured from my hair into my eyes, drenching my clothes so they moved like a heavy wet skin. We walked as rapidly as we could down a path now strewn with torn leaves and broken branches. I was dreading the moment of discovery, yet hoping—praying—that somehow the corn had been spared. The wind died as suddenly as it had come up. Weak sunlight began to filter through the trees as the dying rain dripped onto the leaves below.

At the edge of the clearing, we stood in shocked silence. Every plant in the garden had been broken, shredded, and beaten into the wet soil. The rain had formed large puddles when it fell too fast to soak in. We would have nothing to harvest in the fall. The corn was completely destroyed. All the wamnáheza was gone, except for the dozen seeds left in my bag.

"Damn," Ida breathed, not looking at me. She bent to pick up a snapped leaf from a squash plant that had just set its fruit that week. "Maybe there's still time . . ."

I ripped the leaf from her hand. Turned on her as if she had allowed this to happen. My fingers twitched, wanting so badly to hit her, to wound her, to move this pain anywhere outside my own body.

"Shut up!" I yelled, not recognizing my own voice. "I am so tired of hearing how you can fix everything. How you know what's best. So what if you knew my family? You have no right to be here." I turned away, shaking from the emotion that rolled through my body in waves, blood pounding in my temples. Without a word, Ida and Digger disappeared.

I fell to my knees in the mud, surrounded by the broken stalks of corn, their slender bodies laid down by the wind and torn apart by hail. I picked up a leaf and a bit of stalk, and I crushed them in my fist. I threw the clump at the sky, then filled both hands with more debris and mud, scraping my knuckles against the pebbles in the soil, and screamed until my throat was raw. I shrieked my rage, my hate, and cursed my lonely, unloved, wasted life. I was no better than my mother, no better than Lorraine. Their anger filled my unwanted body and withered everything that came too close. We were a cursed family, and I had just been shown how worthless I was. I had destroyed the seeds that were given to me to protect, to keep safe. If only I had kept that gun.

CHAPTER THIRTY-SIX

Rosalie Iron Wing

2002

She whispered, Thakóža. Her voice was like rain, like wings migrating home. Thakóža, walk with me. At the bottom of a hill, a garden overflowing with the tallest, plumpest corn I had ever seen, the meatiest pumpkins, the longest beans. Thakóža, she said, seeds share a memory that is a vast ribbon of time, flowing back through each season of rain, and the seasons of not enough rain, and the years when the wind blew and made the plants stronger. The seeds you planted carried the imprint of your grandmother's mouth and of her grandmother's. The seeds knew the touch of their hands, when they gave the seeds to the earth with a song. Your garden has kept our agreement with the seeds and helped me fulfill a promise I made. I am at peace.

In this world there is no death. There is only the eternal cycle of birth and rebirth moving from one body to another. Our flesh lives in the belly of a deer, in the wing of a butterfly, in every seed you plant. Our bodies nourish the roots and leaves that keep us alive. When you care for the seeds, you care for all of our ancestors. Nothing is lost. Nothing is lost.

When I woke, the room was dark. Shadows flickered from
the light of flames still burning in the woodstove. So many
mornings I had woken before dawn in this room, finding only
the emptiness of loss, of absence. The quiet that falls when no
voice has spoken for too long.

I could feel a presence in the room. A breathy sigh, a rustle, even a snore. I was not alone. My open suitcase was on
the floor near the table, half-full of the clothes I had begun
to pack. A fresh pile of wood was neatly stacked by the stove.
On the floor nearby, Ida slept with her mouth open, snoring
softly with each inhale. Wilma Many Horses was asleep in the
rocking chair, covered with the wool blanket from the couch.
Her face was turned away from the light of the fire.

Slowly, memory began to return. Waking once to drink a
foul-smelling tea from a cup that Wilma held, her eyes hidden
in shadow. A cool hand smoothing the hair from my forehead.
Each time I opened my eyes, my body burning from the fire
in my lungs, each time I remembered the broken field, Wilma
was rocking in her chair. She never spoke, never left my side. I
had only ever dreamed of such care, imagined it on the nights
I slept in strangers' homes. If my mother had been born to
another life, maybe, in another time. If my father had lived. If
Darlene had found me sooner.

Later, I woke again to the smell of coffee brewing, to the
thump of logs added to the fire. The sounds of life, of a family.
My suitcase had been returned to the bedroom. Bacon sizzled
as an egg was cracked against the side of a frying pan. I was

struggling to sit up when the door flew open, bumped by Ida's hip as she grunted behind an armload of wood. Kicking the door shut with her boot, she managed to drop to one knee and unload her burden with a loud clatter. Then she stacked the wood in a pile, after throwing a half-guilty grin at me.

"Hope I didn't wake you," she said cheerfully, wiping bits of bark from her pants. "Wilma said we needed to keep this place warm at night. Glad to see you're doing better."

"Ida," I said, and then stopped. What could I even say?

She waved a hand, brushing away my words. "Never mind. I get it. I know how hard you worked on that garden."

"No, Ida, you deserve better," I said. "You've been a good friend to me. I wouldn't have found my family without you. I shouldn't have said what I did. I'm sorry." Smiling, Ida walked over and gave me a warm hug.

"Breakfast!" Wilma called out, carrying in three plates of eggs and bacon from the kitchen. Coffee was already steaming from cups set on the table.

"I'm not sure . . ." I started to say.

"It's not for you," Wilma replied, handing me a cup of hot broth. "Carlos," she said in a loud voice. "Breakfast is ready."

My father's bedroom door opened and in walked Carlos, his white hair rumpled from sleep. He was pulling a pair of red suspenders over a faded T-shirt that he had tucked into old-man blue jeans, the waist riding high on his belly. A long yellowed nail on his big toe poked through a hole in his sock. He gave a quick nod in my direction and sat at the table. As he ate, shoveling eggs onto his toast, I heard him tell Wilma, "I couldn't hardly sleep last night. I swear a cat was staring in the window."

After breakfast, Carlos and Ida headed outside. Carlos grabbed my father's summer cap from a hook by the door. "By the way," he said. "I buried that other cap, the one with the bald patches. Put it out of its misery." He pushed open the door as Ida whistled for Digger. Dishes clattered in the kitchen.

When she was done cleaning up, Wilma handed me a cup of tea and eased her old bones into the rocker. We sat quietly for a few minutes, listening to the sound of an ax hitting wood. Wilma set her cup down.

"You know that your great-grandmother Susanne was a gardener. When Iná Maka, Mother Earth, blessed us with the gift of Corn, we held ceremonies to thank her for our abundant harvest. Susanne was a seed keeper, and not only her family, but our tribe, relied on women like her. They were the ones who took care of Corn's gift.

"After moving back here, she spent every morning in her garden hoeing, planting her precious seeds, weeding. Feeding her family was hard work. Some years, there was too much rain early on; other years, she carried endless buckets of water because of drought. She battled mold, worms, deer, raccoons, and birds. She was a warrior, that one. Every year, by summer's end, she had enough food to feed her family for the winter."

Wilma must have seen the way I stared into my lap, how my head hung lower and lower in shame. Her voice softened.

"Susanne had good teachers, the best—including her own mother, who knew the prayers and the planting songs, kept the ceremonies, and protected those seeds no matter what happened. Marie grew up in a time before the schools, before they started taking children. Her family suffered, as we all did, but they held on to their knowledge longer than most.

"Thakóža, you've had no one to teach you, not even how to be part of a family or a community. You know what the grandmothers went through to save the seeds. That's how tough you have to be as an Indian woman. And as a seed keeper.

"I want you to remember what I'm about to tell you. You have to forgive your mother. And yourself. The next time you're in Mankato, stop by Reconciliation Park and read Amos Owen's prayer there. Even a city like Mankato has to find ways to ask for forgiveness. It's challenging work, but we all have to do it. It doesn't mean forgetting, either. You have to heal yourself first before you can go out and change the world.

"Now, Carlos is out there helping Ida clean up the garden. Or, more likely, telling Ida how to do it. He'll help you replant what you can this year. Next year, you take your twelve seeds, plus whatever that crazy Darlene has grown in those buckets of hers, and you save half. You plant half of the rest right here, and half in another garden, somewhere far enough away that one hailstorm won't wipe out both gardens. And next time, remember that you have a family, and a community, that are here to help you. Carlos will help you learn what you need to know." She grimaced. "He also said to tell you that he has a son who is almost as good-looking as he is. Humph."

Wilma patted my hand and stood up as we heard a car pull in to the yard. "There's my niece," she said. "Only a day late." She walked to the door and opened it, smiling, reaching up to hug her niece as she walked in apologizing, saying, Sorry, Auntie, I couldn't leave . . .

And then Gaby Makespeace turned toward me, wearing a sweatshirt and jeans, her long hair loose around her shoulders. She walked over to the couch, where I was trying to look as if I hadn't been lying there for days, hurriedly smoothing the blanket and pushing the hair from my face.

"No, no, don't move," she said. "I know you've been sick. And I'm sorry that I can't stay long, but I promise I'll come back soon. I brought you these." She handed me a bowl of fresh-picked blackberries. Smiled like the old days. "My auntie told me what happened. Can't imagine how that would feel for a gardener." She squeezed my hand. "She says you've come home to stay."

I glanced quickly at Wilma, who shrugged and gave me an innocent smile.

"Maybe," I said. "So much has changed that I need time to figure out what's next." I took a deep breath. "I'm sorry about the newspaper, all those years ago. I tried to reach you so I could explain what happened."

"I know, I know, I'm sorry I never called you back," Gaby said. "I knew it was that asshole editor. I was just so mad at the world for not caring, and my anger spilled out on you. And everyone else around me. But things are different now, for me, too."

I looked more closely at Gaby. There did seem to be a calmness, a stillness in her I'd never seen before. "How so?"

"I quit the task force," Gaby explained. "I'm trying to rebuild my relationship with Mathó. It's slow going, since he's not used to me being around. But he just started a new job as a cook at the casino. He's hoping to open his own restaurant someday—and he wants to talk to Wakpá about raising bison for the tribe, growing meat they can use at the casino." She put a finger to her lips, as if thinking. "They're buying back land, so the Dakhóta will always have a place here. Might make it easier to keep the river clean. Wilma says you have a farm you might be willing to sell back to the tribe?"

I choked on my tea as Wilma laughed. "What will you do next?" I asked, thinking of Gaby's high energy, the way she always needed to keep moving.

"Don't know yet," she said, with a sigh. "I'm working at the community center, helping wherever I'm needed. It's enough for now." She smiled. "I'm glad you're back. Maybe you can teach me how to garden."

"Do you realize there's dirt involved?" I asked. I couldn't imagine Gaby getting her hands muddy.

"I was thinking more of a management role." We both laughed. She picked up Wilma's overnight bag and set it by the door. Turning back, she said, "You know this makes us cousins, right?" She walked out without waiting for an answer. Always the last word.

As they left, the screen door slapped shut behind them, bouncing a bit as it used to whenever my father would walk outside. That tiny bounce of wood on wood, the sound of summer, of his light footstep in the long grass, the whisk of his knife carving wood. Šúŋka's happy bark when she chased a rabbit into the heavy brush. The rustle and snap of a living, breathing forest around them.

It was easier to think about a future now that Gaby was back in my life. Our friendship had had its ups and downs over the years, but we still fit together, the mouth and the ears, needing each other. With Ida living nearby, and Wilma and Carlos just a short drive away, I felt the comfort that comes with belonging to a circle, to a community.

Two days later, I forced myself to visit the garden. Carlos was sitting in the shade on an old log, rolling a cigarette by hand. He beckoned me to sit by him. After sealing his cigarette with a quick swipe of his tongue, he took a deep inhale, releasing the smoke with a long, satisfied sigh.

"Poor man's pipe," he said, offering the cigarette to me. I shook my head.

As Carlos smoked, I looked at the garden. All of the torn leaves and shredded plants had been raked into a compost pile. The stakes and twine were gone. The corn rows were now covered with small mounds of soil, as if a gopher had gone mad and dug up half the garden.

"Your son stopped by yesterday," he said. "You were asleep, so he didn't want to bother you. Dropped off some of your things. He's an interesting young man. Didn't want to stay. He looked downright uncomfortable. So I asked him to help an old man carry his tools to the garden." I looked at the wiry muscles on Carlos's arms, his erect posture even sitting on a log, and smiled at his obvious ruse. Evidently it had worked, however, because Thomas had spent the next two hours helping Carlos build the mounds in the garden.

"Most likely you won't get anything out of those mounds this year," Carlos said. "But you can see how it's done, and next year you can do it yourself. No telling where I'll be." He spat a bit of tobacco to the ground. "Here's what you want to do. First, quit reading all them damn books. Everything you need to learn is right here in the garden. If you need help, just put out your tobacco and ask. In mid-May, when the Seven Little Girls drop below the horizon, you plant your corn. When the Girls return in the western sky, then you plant your beans and squash. The corn gives the beans a place to climb, the squash shades the roots, and the beans fix nitrogen in the soil. Your son called it 'perm-ee-culture.'"

"I think you mean 'permaculture.'"

"I never heard of it. We just called them the Three Sisters," Carlos added. "Your son was sorry to hear what happened to your garden. Especially those seeds. He asked if you were okay. I said you'd pull through. Lots of people around to make sure that you do. Then he told me about your aunt Darlene's corn, the one she gave to him. He seemed troubled about it."

I could well imagine Thomas's struggle. I had so wanted to tell him not to do anything that would jeopardize those seeds. Darlene had given him the corn without knowing that he was considering an internship at Mangenta, where it would be his job to encourage farmers to grow the mutant crops. I could only hope that maybe Darlene *had* known, in her own way.

"After we hoed awhile, we took a break," Carlos continued. "We sat here and smoked a cigarette together. And then he told me what was on his mind.

"He had a big idea about that corn. Talked to one of the scientists at Mangenta about making a gene map. Said they take a little piece out and call it a patent. They could even use it to make a whole new kind of corn. Anybody who wants to grow that corn has to pay him. He said there's a lot of money to be made from those patents. He seemed kind of excited about it. The scientist he talked to was even more excited.

They scheduled a big meeting so he could show the corn to the boss over there.

"He had trouble sleeping that night. Couldn't get past the thought of your aunt Darlene growing her corn in those buckets. Damn nuts, if you ask me. But she'd hauled all that dirt on the bus, up the elevators, past all those busybody eyes. Held on to our old ways, even when those buckets were all she had. Then she told him, 'Maybe the corn will help you remember.' 'Remember what?' he asks me. 'How can I remember something I don't know?'

"The day before his big meeting, he drives all the way here to bring you those boxes. You're asleep, so he talks to me instead. He says, 'I don't think I'm the right person to be responsible for that corn.' I ask him why not.

"'All my life,' he says, 'I believed that farming was about how many bushels we could grow per acre. My dad taught me that farmers have to change with the times. My grandfather refused to adapt, so he was just left behind. And there's what happened to our neighbor George. So I'm not a good farmer. And I'm not who Darlene thinks I am. I'm tired of people telling me what to think.'

"We sat there for a while, not talking," Carlos said, "while he pulled himself together. I thought about what he said and what he didn't say. I thought about those seeds, too. And Darlene. Finally, I said to him, 'As long as you remember that no one owns the seeds, seems like that corn is just fine where it is.' Then I asked him if he planned to sit there all day. We still had tomatoes to plant."

We both laughed. A warm breeze fluttered the few leaves that had been spared by the storm. The trees would grow new leaves, but it would be another season before they regained their full, vigorous canopy. The trees farther away, which had suffered less damage, would share what they had through the miles-long web of roots and fungi that connected this forest as a community.

"Rosie," Carlos continued, sounding more serious. "Whether your boy knows it or not, those seeds are bringing him home, too. You have to be patient."

Ida emerged from the woods and strode through the long grass that surrounded the garden. Digger was right at her side, his attention focused on something in her hand that she held carefully away from him. She gave a quick wave when she saw us. A kerchief was tied around her damp forehead, and her arms were covered with thin red scratches from whatever berry patch she had been in. "Whew," she said. "It's hotter than blazes. Take a look at this. Digger found it."

She handed a broad, flat bone to Carlos as Digger's eyes followed it closely. Carlos turned it over in his hands, studying it from every angle.

"Well, I'll be damned," he said. "Where did you find it?"

"Back there a ways," Ida said, gesturing over her shoulder.

"Show me."

The three of us walked in silence for several minutes, slapping mosquitoes and brushing away the black flies that swarmed in the heat. A cicada buzzed its loud, long call overhead. Ida stopped and pointed at a recently dug hole. A stone with a flat top and bands of dark and light gray had been pushed aside. Carlos knelt by the side of the hole, set the bone on the ground, and dug through the loose soil with his hands.

He pulled out small pieces of rotted wood before striking something solid. He nodded and stood up.

After wiping his hands on his jeans, Carlos picked up the bone and handed it to me. Yellowed with age, the bone was wide at the bottom, with an edge that appeared to have been sharpened, and tapered at the other end, almost like the neck of a broom or a rake.

"It's the shoulder bone from a buffalo," Carlos said. "They used to cut a handle from a cottonwood tree and attach it to the neck with a piece of rawhide to make an old-time hoe. They also used it to dig cache pits for dried squash and corn. Seeds for the next season. Like an underground root cellar. And what I just felt, in that hole, is the wood that is usually laid on top of a cache pit." He squinted at me. "This was your family's land back when they used to build those. Your relative must have been in a hurry, to leave this hoe behind."

"That would have been Marie's mother, Maȟpíyamaza," I replied. "I think she was afraid. Afraid of what was coming."

Carlos nodded. "She saved what she thought would be needed one day, what might help her grandchildren survive."

"Should I run and get some shovels?" Ida asked.

"No."

"Carlos," I said. "Is it right for us to open it? We don't know what she was thinking. What should we do?"

Carlos pulled a pouch of tobacco from his pocket.

"We pray."

As they prayed, we heard the song the old ones used
to sing at dawn.
Their voices blended with the wind that swayed
the star-filled branches of the cottonwood tree.
We heard a song that was our own,
sung by humans who were born of the prairie.
Love the seeds as you love your children,
and the people will survive.
Wačhékiye

AUTHOR'S NOTE

The Seed Keeper was inspired by a story I heard years ago, while participating in the Dakhóta Commemorative March, a 150-mile walk to honor the Dakhóta people who were forcibly removed from Minnesota in 1863, in the aftermath of the US-Dakhóta War. Walking fifteen to twenty miles each day, we prayed for the seventeen hundred women, children, and elders who were marched at gunpoint from the Lower Sioux Agency to a concentration camp at Fort Snelling. By following their same route, we honored the suffering and sacrifices of our ancestors.

On one especially long, cold day, one of the walkers shared a story about the women on the original march. He said they had little time to prepare for their removal, yet they would need to feed their families in whatever place they were being sent. These women sewed seeds into the hems of their skirts and hid more in their pockets, so they would be able to plant in the coming season. During the long winter at Fort Snelling, hundreds died from disease and starvation. In the spring of 1863, when they were loaded onto flatboats for the long ride to the Crow Creek reservation in South Dakota, people continued to die from the meager, rancid food. Through it all, the women knew they had to protect the seeds, to ensure food for the future, for the next seven generations. The strength these women demonstrated, the profound love they showed for their children, and their willingness to make sacrifices so the people would survive became the heart of this book. I have no words to express the gratitude in my heart. These women are the reason why we have Dakhóta corn today.

A new generation of seed keepers has risen up to carry this work forward: Rowen White, Terry Lynn Brant, Jessika Greendeer, and Deborah Echohawk, to name a few. More and more women, as well as men, are relearning how to grow, protect, and save our ancestral seeds.

While today's risks and challenges differ from those faced by our ancestors, they are just as threatening to the future of our indigenous seeds. Genetic engineering, industrial agriculture, and patents have centralized control of the world's seeds with a handful of international corporations: Monsanto and Bayer; Syngenta and ChemChina; Dow and DuPont. According to the documentary *Seed: The Untold Story*, 94 percent of our global seed varieties have already disappeared. Scientists warn that a million species of plants and animals are at risk of extinction. The loss of these relatives and our seed varieties is devastating for the genetic diversity of the earth, and for our survival as human beings. We have forgotten our original Agreement with the many beings who share this planet with us. As activist and scholar Harley Eagle once said, "We need to fall back in love with the earth."

In the face of such overwhelming loss, what can we, as individuals, even do? The answer is as close as the nearest garden. We keep our seeds safe by growing them, cooking with them, and sharing them with friends, family, and community. When we reestablish a relationship based in reciprocity, when we nurture the soil and protect the water that, in turn, grows healthy seeds, we are reclaiming an indigenous connection to the earth. These seeds carry our stories; they are witnesses to their own long history on this land. Seeds and our indigenous foods are central to our cultures, reminding us of our ancient relationship with the natural world around us. Mitakuye Owasin, we are all related.

I invite you to join in the joyful, life-affirming work of protecting our seeds. I've listed a few resources below for more information, including two nonprofit organizations that support this work and a source for heirloom and indigenous seeds. There are many other indigenous garden projects occurring in tribal communities throughout the country.

Dream of Wild Health: A Minnesota nonprofit farm that specializes in growing and protecting a collection of indigenous seeds, and passing on this knowledge to Native youth. For more information: www.dreamofwildhealth.org

Native American Food Sovereignty Alliance (Indigenous Seed Keepers Network): A national nonprofit working to support Native communities in reclaiming their indigenous food systems. For more information: www.nativefoodalliance.org

Seed Savers Exchange: Since 1975, this nonprofit has shared heirloom and indigenous seeds with gardeners. Located in Iowa, this organization is home to more than twenty thousand rare heirloom seed varieties. For more information: www.seedsavers.org

To share the story of the seeds within the context of actual Dakhóta history, this book was crafted as a blend of fiction and history, with imagined characters, incidents, and dialogue superimposed on a layer of real-life events. Given the power of story to persuade and inform, as the author I feel a responsibility to share what has been imagined as well as the history that continues to impact Native communities today:

The Dakhóta reservation is an imagined place, inspired by but not reflecting the actual Dakhóta communities in Minnesota. Mankato and New Ulm are real cities, but the locations and street names are not. The memorial in New Ulm exists, and the inscription quoted in the book is nearly identical to that of the actual monument. Mangenta is not a real corporation, although it bears resemblance to international chemical companies that control the majority of our seeds today. The rebranding of wartime chemicals for agricultural use and the development of genetically modified seeds resistant to those chemicals is accurate.

A thread of true history runs through the book, in its reference to the 1862 US-Dakhóta War and the memorial run that takes place every year in December. Amos Owen was an elder and spiritual leader from Prairie Island Mdewakanton community, who played a pivotal role in supporting reconciliation efforts. His prayer—inscribed on a boulder at Reconciliation Park in Mankato—includes the statement "I pray to the Mother Earth to help us in this time of reconciliation." The experience of the fictional character Marie Blackbird follows the actual events and removal of Dakhóta people to reservations in South Dakota. I have used the names of my own ancestors as often as possible, in an effort to avoid referencing other known family names. Any resemblance to existing Dakhóta family names is unintended.

The Dakhóta language throughout the book uses orthography developed by the Dakhóta Iápi Okhadódakičhiye in their *Dakota Language Textbook* as well as the *Dakota-English Dictionary* by Stephen R. Riggs. I am especially grateful to Kachina Yeager, Milkweed Fellow, for her generous support and review of the manuscript, as well as Monica McKay, who shared her expertise. While I have made every effort to use the language in an accurate and respectful manner, any mistakes are entirely my responsibility.

Finally, woven throughout this book are references from the work of scholars and artists that have enriched its story. This is an acknowledgment of their work, with deep gratitude:

For the star knowledge used throughout, I am indebted to two books: *D(L)akota Star Map Constellation Guide* by Annette S. Lee, Jim Rock, and Charlene O'Rourke; and *Lakota Star Knowledge* by Ronald Goodman.

I am especially grateful to the book *Buffalo Bird Woman's Garden*, by Gilbert L. Wilson, for its descriptions of traditional planting methods and building a cache pit.

My framework for understanding an indigenous perspective of science comes from *Native Science: Natural Laws of Interdependence* by Gregory Cajete. His book introduced and explained the phrase "that place that Indian people talk about," paraphrased by Ray Iron Wing as "the place that Indians talk about."

The reference to the "bluest eye" is a nod to Toni Morrison's first novel, *The Bluest Eye*, which addresses racism in the United States.

The poem fragment "And the Corn said / know me" is a quotation from *Inventos Míos*, a collection of poems by Rubi Orozco Santos.

The courageous water protectors at Standing Rock helped me, and Rosalie, understand the complexities of choosing between protesting what is wrong and protecting what you love.

Rosalie's reference to the Apology to the Birds—"The warblers and the owls and the wood thrushes: who thought of them before coming to take my trees? Who apologized to the birds?"—was inspired by *Waterlily*, by Ella Cara Deloria. I also relied on two of Deloria's other books for cultural references: *The Dakota Way of Life* and *Speaking of Indians*.

Mni Sota Makoce: The Land of the Dakota, by Gwen Westerman and Bruce White, is an exceptional resource on Dakhóta culture and history. The foreword was written by Wambdi Wapaha Glenn Wasicuna, who quoted his father, Heȟaka Cuwi Maza, as saying, "It's hard to be an Indian," and explained that "being Dakota means every step you take is a prayer." This phrase and its meaning were quoted by Carlos.

The Dakhóta prisoner letter is an adaptation of an actual letter from *The Dakota Prisoner of War Letters* by Clifford Canku and Michael Simon. Clifford gave his permission to adapt the letter that was written by Mázakhoyaginape. I am indebted to Clifford for the wisdom he has shared over the years.

One of the best contemporary books for understanding an indigenous relationship with plants is *Braiding Sweetgrass* by Robin Wall Kimmerer. My research for this novel included many additional books and articles about the traditional use of plants, contemporary farm practices (including the use of genetically modified seeds), nitrogen pollution in the Minnesota River, native prairie, and much more, and I extend my gratitude to all of these writers as well.

Although *The Seed Keeper* focuses on the role of Dakhóta women in caring for the seeds, I would like to also acknowledge the courage of Dakhóta men, who suffered greatly when they were unable to keep their families safe. This novel is in honor of all the men who try their best to protect their children, including my father.

ACKNOWLEDGMENTS

Wóphida tháŋka ečhíčiyapi ye!

My greatest thanks belong to the seeds themselves, for generously sharing their lives so that human beings could survive and thrive. The seeds are my teachers; they show me the way to reconnect with my ancestors and my own cultural identity through gardening.

Sharing this story is also a way to honor Dream of Wild Health, a Native nonprofit where I spent nearly twenty years, first as a volunteer and then as its director. This story slowly took shape in my imagination as I learned from elders Ernie Whiteman, Hope Flanagan, Sally Auger, Donna LaChapelle, Ida Downwind, Jewell Arcoren, Yako Tanaga, Kathleen Westcott, and many others about the spiritual nature of this work. The Garden Warriors and Youth Leaders helped me understand the importance of passing this knowledge on to the next generation. Sharing this story is a way to honor Ernie's wish that we "carry the work forward."

For every book, there are people who believe in it from inception through the yearslong road to publication. For *The Seed Keeper*, those people are my brother Dave; my writing buddy Carolyn Holbrook; the Women from the Center, an awesome circle of badass women writers; my husband, Jim

Denomie, who is my hero in all the ways that matter most; and my daughter, Jodi, and sister, Sue.

I am beyond grateful to the readers and historians who shared their wisdom with me on Dakhóta language, culture, and history: Teresa Peterson (and her husband, Jay); Gabrielle Tateyuskanskan; Marcie Rendon; Nora Murphy; Colette Hyman; John Campbell; Anitra Budd; and Franky Jackson.

Of course, as writers we depend heavily on the editors who nurture, nudge, and help shape the vision for the final book. I was blessed to work with Joey McGarvey, who confessed her own passion for seeds in our first conversation. She was invaluable in helping me see and develop the full scope of the book, and suggesting the cover art. Pidamayaya to Holly Young for honoring this book with her beautiful beadwork.

The long nurturing of this work was supported through the generosity of several foundations. A 2013 Bush Foundation Fellowship allowed me to focus on writing and indigenous seeds; it also supported a residency awarded by the Camargo Foundation in Cassis, France. The research and writing was supported by a 2017 grant from the Minnesota State Arts Board, thanks to a legislative appropriation from the arts and cultural heritage fund. I am also indebted to the Hedgebrook Residency Program, where I met a circle of brilliant women writers in 2009, who first suggested that I should write a novel about seeds. Finally, I would like to thank *Yellow Medicine Review* and the *Massachusetts Review* for previously publishing excerpts of this work.

My closing thanks go to Milkweed Editions, for supporting the vision for this work, and to the talented staff who have helped make it real.

Sarah Whiting

DIANE WILSON (Dakhóta) is the author of a memoir, *Spirit Car: Journey to a Dakota Past*, which won a Minnesota Book Award and was selected for the One Minneapolis One Read program, as well as a nonfiction book, *Beloved Child: A Dakota Way of Life*, which was awarded the Barbara Sudler Award from History Colorado. Her most recent essay, "Seeds for Seven Generations," was featured in the anthology *A Good Time for the Truth: Race in Minnesota*. Wilson has received a Bush Foundation Fellowship as well as awards from the Minnesota State Arts Board, the Jerome Foundation, and the East Central Regional Arts Council. In 2018, she was awarded a 50 Over 50 Award from Pollen/Midwest. Wilson has served as the executive director for Dream of Wild Health and the Native American Food Sovereignty Alliance, working to help rebuild sovereign food systems for Native people. She is a Mdewakanton descendent, enrolled on the Rosebud Reservation, and lives in Shafer, Minnesota.

milkweed
EDITIONS

Founded as a nonprofit organization in 1980,
Milkweed Editions is an independent publisher. Our mission
is to identify, nurture and publish transformative literature,
and build an engaged community around it.

Milkweed Editions is based in Bdé Óta Othúŋwe
(Minneapolis) within Mní Sota Makhóčhe, the traditional
homeland of the Dakhóta people. Residing here since time
immemorial, Dakhóta people still call Mní Sota Makhóčhe
home, with four federally recognized Dakhóta nations and
many more Dakhóta people residing in what is now the state
of Minnesota. Due to continued legacies of colonization,
genocide, and forced removal, generations of Dakhóta people
remain disenfranchised from their traditional homeland.
Presently, Mní Sota Makhóčhe has become a refuge and home
for many Indigenous nations and peoples, including seven
federally recognized Ojibwe nations. We humbly encourage
readers to reflect upon the historical legacies held in the
lands they occupy.

milkweed.org

Interior design by Mary Austin Speaker
Typeset in Adobe Jenson

Adobe Jenson was designed by Robert Slimbach for Adobe
and released in 1996. Slimbach based Jenson's roman styles
on a text face cut by fifteenth-century type designer Nicolas
Jenson, and its italics are based on type created by Ludovico
Vicentino degli Arrighi, a late fifteenth-century
papal scribe and type designer.